Pieces of Us

NEW YORK TIMES BESTSELLING AUTHOR

A.L. JACKSON

First Edition

A.L. Jackson
www.aljacksonauthor.com
Cover Design by RBA Designs
Editing by AW Editing and Susan Staudinger
Formatting by Mesquite Business Services

Print ISBN: 978-1-946420-74-9
eBook ISBN: 978-1-946420-29-9

Pieces of Us

More from A.L. Jackson

Redemption Hills
Give Me a Reason
Say It's Forever
Never Look Back
Promise Me Always

The Falling Stars Series
Kiss the Stars
Catch Me When I Fall
Falling into You
Beneath the Stars

Confessions of the Heart
More of You
All of Me
Pieces of Us

Fight for Me
Show Me the Way
Follow Me Back
Lead Me Home
Hold on to Hope

Bleeding Stars
A Stone in the Sea
Drowning to Breathe
Where Lightning Strikes
Wait
Stay
Stand

The Regret Series

Lost to You

Take This Regret

If Forever Comes

The Closer to You Series

Come to Me Quietly

Come to Me Softly

Come to Me Recklessly

Stand-Alone Novels

Pulled

When We Collide

Hollywood Chronicles, a collaboration with USA Today Bestselling Author, Rebecca Shea

One Wild Night

One Wild Ride

one

MACK

Do you ever wonder if you're being framed? Set up for disaster? Jumping on a freeway that you can never exit from?

You don't even realize you're barreling down the wrong direction until it's too late.

A collision waiting to annihilate you up ahead.

Invisible to the naked eye. A trap.

Or maybe, it was just the direction I was supposed to be traveling all along.

Standing there, I had no idea what I was heading toward.

I reached up and grabbed the oversized box.

"Got it. One size small box of diapers, my friend. Mission accomplished. And you said I was good for nothing." It was all a rough tease into the phone that I had pressed between my ear and shoulder.

Nothing more badass than going on a diaper run. But it was man up time. Be there for your crew when they needed you most.

And when my best friend, Ian, had sent out an SOS call, I'd dropped everything and come running.

Of course, I did. Would anyone have expected less of me?

I'd had Ian's back so many times I'd long since lost count. Maybe as many as he'd had mine.

We didn't keep score.

We just did whatever the hell the other needed, and did it without questions.

Of course, this commission was a whole ton cleaner than some of the filthy shit the two of us had been involved in back in the day.

Something that wouldn't get my hands dirty because I'd given up dishonest deeds a long time ago.

Ian blew out a relieved breath around the cries of his newborn son. "Thank you, man. Take it all back. Pretty sure I'm going to regret saying this, but you're basically my favorite person right now. You need to get here and get here fast. Grace will be back from her writing workshop in like . . ."

I could sense him checking the clock.

"Shit," he whispered. "Less than an hour. I can't mess this up . . . and dude, I am seriously messing this up. It's a fucking disaster over here."

His voice dropped on the last, keeping it low from the kids.

He might not think so, but I was convinced the asshole deserved a *father-of-the-year* award. And that wasn't me being sarcastic.

It was mad crazy at their house. Straight mayhem. The good kind you'd do anything to protect, commit your whole life to, but it would still have you laid flat out on your ass at the end of the day.

The guy had become daddy to four in the period of a year. That took some serious man balls, and I was honestly proud of him.

Didn't mean I wasn't gonna give him shit.

"Sorry to break it to you, brother, but in case you've forgotten, you've been messing things up with that amazing girl since the day you met her, and somehow, your ugly ass got lucky enough that she still wants to crawl into bed with you every night. Think you'll be just fine."

A huge crash of shattering glass and splintering wood reverberated through the line. The magnitude of it had me wincing for the poor sucker, the disaster he'd just been talking about clearly coming to fruition.

"Oh, shit," he muttered in abject horror before his voice twisted in defeat. "Sophie Marie, sweetheart. What did you do?"

"I *bwoke* it, Daddy." Sophie Marie was clearly working up to a meltdown, the way she did best, hiccupping through the words and sucking for air. Two seconds later, a loud, mortified cry came wailing out of her little body.

At three, she was nothing but a tiny ball of energy, all white, wild hair.

A demolisher with an angel face.

Couldn't ever get frustrated at her since she was the sweetest little thing, all crazy smiles and wide blue eyes.

Oh, but the kid could belt it out. Her cries coming through the phone were so loud, I was pretty sure the entire store was being subjected to it from across the distance.

It only made Baby Collin cry louder, and if it were possible, Sophie started to do the same.

A terrible case of sibling rivalry.

A battle to see who could bring the walls down first.

"You did, didn't you?" Ian mumbled his encouragement through the disorder. "You really, really did. It's okay. It's okay. Come here, sweetheart. You're not in trouble. It's okay."

I could almost see him trying to wrangle the weeping toddler into one arm while he balanced his screaming infant in the other.

No doubt, Collin was flailing his little fists all over the place.

Like I said, father-of-the-year.

Don't tell his brother Jace I said that, either. I wasn't picking favorites. It was four to two. A simple mathematical equation, and not that shit they tried to teach in school these days.

Cringing for my best friend, I booked it up to the registers, picking up the pace.

Because let's be real. Dude was totally messing it up.

But his heart was in the right place. I knew Grace well enough to know that was all that mattered. Still, my boy was about to have his own meltdown. I needed to get my ass over there and do it quick.

"Hurrying as fast as I can. Be there in like ten."

"Ten? Come on, asshole. This calls for sirens and lights. Straight-up emergency." I could almost see the wry grin pulling to his smug face.

A light chuckle rippled out. "Pretty sure you can handle it. Take a deep breath and count to ten." I was only half teasing when I said it. "What happened to that tough-as-nails attorney I used to know?"

Soggy cries were still coming from his kids, though somehow the volume had decreased by a decibel, the guy no doubt managing to soothe them.

"Uh . . . that asshole got disbarred and then went and got married and inherited a brood of kids. He's been unmanned." His words left him on a self-deprecating chuckle.

"And you need me to rescue you? Whisk you away to safety?"

Or more likely, hit up Monty's, our favorite bar in Charleston. Of course, now that he'd moved back to Broadshire Rim, those nights spent bellied up to the bar came fewer and farther in between.

More laughter, softer this time as the hiccupped cries of his children faded. "Nah, man, wouldn't trade it for the world."

There was nothing but tenderness in his voice.

Couldn't help the way gratitude stretched across my chest.

Ian used to spend his nights living the fast life.

Now he was living the good life.

That was the thing though . . .

Sometimes it was the hardest fall that cracked the mold and opened us up to something greater than we ever imagined. And Ian had slipped, shattered, and broken at Grace's feet.

She had been exactly what he'd needed, what he'd had no clue he'd been looking for. She was the one who'd been there to make sure when he'd healed, he healed with a whole heart.

It was one of the things I'd wanted most in this life—to see Ian and his older brother Jace find joy outside the unfair brutality that had been our childhood.

It'd been so fucked up, it was a damned wonder that any one of us were still standing today.

Maybe it was the fact I was thinking about us in high school, or maybe it was the simple fact my ass was in Broadshire Rim on a diaper run, but the second I even cracked my mind open to that time, a flood of memories came rushing up through the fissures.

It was a wave of that old bullshit I never allowed myself to agonize or fret or fucking brood over.

What was done was done.

I'd made my own choices. Followed the path that was set.

Even if it wasn't the one I'd wanted to take, I was committed to it. Knew it was what I was meant for. Proof of that was the badge in my pocket and the gun strapped to my side.

I shook off that bullshit and pasted on a smile. "Hold tight, brother. I'll be there as fast as I can."

Ending the call, I shoved my phone into my front pocket and went for my wallet.

There was only one woman ahead of me who was unloading a few things she had from a small, hand-held basket.

I wasn't really paying all that much attention, but there was something about her that had me doing a double take.

Gaze getting tossed from my wallet to the shape in front of me.

My heart rate kicked, a smack of uneasiness slamming into my senses.

But that was the thing about the past. It liked to haunt you. Just like it'd been doing not twenty seconds before. That's what happened when you let the shit you couldn't control get to you. When you let the past remind you of what you'd lost and what you'd never fucking have.

She loaded her things onto the conveyor belt, a couple boxes of cereal, apples, oranges, and bananas. She seemed to waver before she tossed a lipstick onto the pile, like she wasn't quite sure if she should buy it or not.

Maybe it was the price or the color or the necessity. Or maybe she was just throwing off the vibe that she was questioning everything.

Just. Like. Me.

Because my mouth felt sticky, and my head felt light. That crazed feeling of being willing to do anything to protect a girl welled so fast I felt it like the surge of a storm.

With her back to me, I took her in from head to toe, trying to slough the familiarity from my bones. To remind myself that it just wasn't possible.

Still, my eyes were held, taking her in.

Lush locks tumbled in loose waves down her back. This crazy, wild mix of blondes and browns that shimmered like bronze beneath the light.

She was short, but wearing black high heels, a black skirt, and a white blouse. Dressed up, but somehow, she still appeared a little disheveled.

Like maybe she was wearing an extra layer of anxiety.

Too thin and too frail and too vulnerable.

A spike of energy pulsed at my veins, and a goddamned stone ridged itself in my throat.

I tried to swallow it down. Exactly like I was trying to do with the moment's idiocy. There was no chance . . . no way—

She shifted to the side, and her profile came into view, and my heart that was beating double time completely stalled out, faltering at the sight in front of me.

My skin went clammy at the same second I was belted with a punch of lust.

Overwhelming.

The same fucking way it'd always been.

And there I was, out of control as I raced down that freeway, a collision coming into a quick, sharp view.

Izzy Lane was standing three feet away.

The girl had been a hazard for me. I'd never once been able to look at her without getting greedy. Wanting to take it all.

The most striking, unforgettable girl a man could ever hope or dread to stumble upon.

Sexy as fuck.

The kind of sexy that had gotten under my skin and wedged itself deep. Kind that had kept me awake at night, dreaming of things I couldn't have.

I'd learned that the hard way.

Still, I just stood there gaping while every cell in my body screamed, stretching that way, like it was remembering its home.

No doubt feeling the weight of my stare, she glanced my way.

That was all it took for time and space to freeze.

All except for the widening of those hazel eyes, mostly brown except for the tiny rim of green at the edges, this smoky topaz that held the power to suck me right into oblivion.

She had always reminded me of some sort of wild fairy. A piece of a fantasy while she'd been creating her own. Her mind so big and vast that she'd opened mine.

Waif-like with her high cheeks, angled chin, and pale skin, that starkness getting confused with the pinked flesh of her plump, bowed lips.

She was the kind of beauty that you couldn't look away from. The kind that you got stuck on, wondering if you stared long enough, you could figure out if it was real.

She stumbled, reaching out to catch herself on the counter, like she was two seconds from being knocked to her ass.

I was already there.

Floored and somehow still standing.

What the hell was she doing here?

Regret and greed bubbled in my blood, and everything only got fuzzier when I inhaled. Swore, I could taste her on my tongue when I sucked down the gush of surprise that tore from her lungs and became one with the air.

Attraction and hate, all wrapped up in a bough of yellow jasmine.

Sweet and intoxicating.

"Maxon." My name wheezed from her mouth, like it was pulling free before she gave it permission to.

I blinked hard, hoping to hell it might break me out of the stupor I'd fallen under. But the soft timber of her voice only made it worse, clouding everything.

That sultry sound kicked me straight back to a time I'd done my best to forget.

Maxon.

No one had called me that in years. Thirteen years.

I scrubbed a hand over my face, still wondering if I was hallucinating. "Izzy?"

When I said her name, it snapped her out of the trance, and that chin trembled, a broken smile pulling to her mouth.

I was pretty sure if I could read it, it was saying regret.

"Hi." She was wincing a little, on edge, and she turned back to watch the cashier ring her things.

Like that was it.

But what did I expect?

I roughed an agitated hand over my face, mind racing with what to do, while my body was taking another step forward, drawn, completely at a loss to stop myself.

"You're back?" My voice was rough with the question. A loaded one.

Was kind of surprised she'd never come back once in all this time. Had expected for her to. Even prepared myself for it.

But hell, I was a fool because there wasn't a thing in the world I could have done to prepare myself for this.

She slowly turned back my way.

I got blasted with a shockwave of heat that hit the air, the intensity of it so fierce it had me sucking in a staggered breath.

Two of us magnets.

The only sound was her items beeping and the roar of blood pounding through my veins, hammering so hard through my body I was wondering if she could see it jerking my limbs.

"Not sure how long, but for now," she quietly admitted.

Sadness had chased off the surprise, the girl standing there looking like the sight of me might make her cry, those big eyes watery and lips doing this trembling, distracting thing.

And fuck. I wanted to reach out. Stroke the lines of misery that marred her gorgeous face. Tell her I was fucking sorry. If I could take back every horrible thing I'd done, I would.

Wouldn't change anything though, would it?

I would always be the same man underneath.

She glanced down and then jerked her attention right back up, another spear of shock seizing her expression. Though this time it was softer. A little hurt and a lot wistful. "You have a baby."

"What?" My brow pinched in confusion, my mind struggling to catch up. Took me about two seconds to realize what she'd focused on—the box of diapers I'd grabbed for Ian. I had the urge to hide them behind my back or some stupid shit like that. Like worrying about her thinking I had a kid should even register as important.

But there I was, rushing to clarify, "No . . . No . . . I mean . . . these aren't for me."

Stammering.

Tongue tied.

Big, bad detective reduced to putty by a pretty face. But it was the only face that had ever mattered.

She shook her head a little bit, fighting for a smile to rise over the heartbreak muting that light that had always glowed from her. "You don't need to explain. It's none of my business."

I swallowed around my unease, explaining anyway, needing a reason to keep her longer. To make her stay while I figured out what the hell I was supposed to do. "I mean, they're . . . they're not for my kid. They are for Ian's baby boy."

She pinned another one of those feigned smiles onto her mouth, one-hundred percent forced, pretending like everything was just fine when it was clear that it was not.

"What you do with your life is none of my business. I'm sorry I asked . . . I just . . ." Her brow pinched in regret, the girl tripping over her thoughts, and she squeezed her eyes closed and gave a fierce shake of her head. "It's just been a long time and seeing you here caught me off guard. That's all."

I edged closer, not even able to stop myself. Not sure that I wanted to. "Maybe that's exactly what you should do. Ask."

What answer I'd give her, I wasn't sure.

Her face pinched in more of that honesty. "I'm not sure that's a good idea."

"Excuse me." We both jumped when the cashier lifted his voice, all kinds of irritated considering the two of us were completely oblivious to anything else but standing there staring into the past.

"Oh, I'm sorry," she mumbled.

Tearing herself from that tether I could feel stretching between us, she balanced her small bag next to the card reader.

"Twenty-seven, thirty-two."

Hand shaking, she fumbled to get a card out of her wallet. She swiped it and fidgeted like she was counting the seconds until she could make a break for it, while I stood there trying to figure out a way to get her alone.

Just for a few minutes.

I wanted to know how she was.

Who she was.

If she was happy.

"It says your card is declined." I tore my attention from the spiral of thoughts going down in my mind and whipped it to the prick who was looking at Izzy like she'd committed some sort of felony.

Just as fast, I darted my gaze to her, catching her in the moment she was slamming those eyes closed.

Like she was expecting this result but had still been praying for a different outcome.

"Oh, I-I guess I brought the wrong card," she stammered. She dug into the paper sack and pulled out the lipstick. "Can you take this off, please?"

Her voice lowered, embarrassment rolling off her like a disease. For the barest beat, she glanced over at me.

Hoping I hadn't noticed the exchange.

Highly unlikely.

The cashier rolled his eyes.

Little fucker.

I had the urge to reach out and grab him by the collar. Like he was raking in the dough? I forced myself to hold back, not to say anything.

Still, that thunder in my chest was growing louder by the second.

I could feel it collecting speed, something severe gathering at the horizon of my mind.

He re-rang it. "Twenty-two, ninety."

He ran the card again, and she was already wincing before the punk had the chance to make her feel any worse, her card clearly being rejected again.

Defeat dropped her shoulders, and there was no missing the dejection that fully took her over. Looked like she wanted to crawl under a table and disappear.

Leaning around her, I handed the cashier my card. "Put the lipstick back on."

She whirled on me. "I don't need any handouts."

Pain and defiance reverberated with the words.

I shook my head, not sure what situation she'd gotten into, but whatever it was, I didn't like it a bit.

Didn't like any of this.

"Not a goddamned handout if I'm helping out a friend."

A friend.

That was probably an insult, but anything else would no doubt send her raging.

"You forgot your card, remember?" I cocked my head, giving her an out.

"Maxon, please, just don't—"

I set my hand on hers to let her know it was no big deal.

The least I could do.

But that was a mistake, too, because at the contact, a fire consumed me whole.

Fucking flames and heat and need.

Everything coming alive in an instant.

I jerked my hand away, feeling like I'd been sucked into a vortex. Tossed thirteen years back in time.

Izzy froze beneath it, drawing in a shattered breath, and the cashier had swiped my card and handed it back to me before she'd regrouped and had the chance to argue.

The girl was clearly as shaken as me.

He handed her the receipt. She grabbed it and the bag.

She barely slowed to toss a whispered, "Thank you," over her shoulder before she was bee-lining for the double-sliding doors.

I wanted to shout out for her, beg her to wait. To give me five freaking minutes.

But Ian was relying on me. Couldn't bail on that.

As hard as it was, I forced myself to stand there and pay for the diapers, my attention flying toward the door about fifteen times during the transaction, and I let loose just as many silent curses when she disappeared out of it.

As soon as the little prick handed me the receipt, I grabbed the box and darted after her, jumping between two old ladies pushing carts, leisurely doing their shopping in the early afternoon, dodged a few stockers hauling in boxes, and basically took the store like it was my own personal obstacle course.

I almost laughed.

My entire life had been nothing but a long string of hurdles. No finish line in sight.

Except for Izzy.

She'd been my beginning. The girl had breathed her beauty and grace and goodness into my being. Made me think I could be something better. Saw me in a way I'd never seen myself.

In the same way, she'd been my ending.

My collision.

The breaking point of who I'd been and who I'd come to be.

By the time I made it out the door, eyes hunting the parking lot, an old, beater of a car rumbled to life toward the far end of the lot. It jerked out of the spot, engine sputtering and a cloud of exhaust billowing into the air as it lurched into drive.

I struggled to peer into the distance.

To get a read on the license.

But she was gone before I could make sense of her return.

Disappearing in a haze of smoke and dust.

Just like she had then.

two

IZZY

If you could be anything when you grow up, what would you want to be?

It was a question I would venture to say most every parent had asked their children, at least I knew it was a topic my parents had loved to visit.

Maybe they'd just always been hoping for a different answer.

Most kids typically responded with things like a doctor or a teacher or maybe even a rock star.

That answer had always come so easily to me.

I'd wanted to be Maxon Chamber's wife.

Pathetic, right?

But that's what happened when a four-year-old girl fell in love with the troubled boy-next-door. The boy who made her heart swell and hurt at the same time.

She became infatuated. She believed they were destined. That together, they made each other better. That they could overcome anything if they stayed by the other's side.

It's what I'd done.

I'd followed him around for years, nothing but a pest, nipping at his heels like a puppy, praying one day that boy would notice. I'd made up whimsical stories about him, somehow tricked him into a fake wedding in the meadow under the trees, and I couldn't imagine a different outcome than that one I'd believed in as if it'd been prewritten.

Maybe it hurt all the more when I realized believing those things only made me a fool. Chasing after something that was never really there. When I realized that destiny was nothing but a fake, half-witted dream.

Only thing certain?

I'd never forgotten his face or those eyes or the heart I'd prayed would find something better, even when I'd come to accept that heart could never belong to me.

On top of that?

I'd never imagined in a million years that at thirty, I'd be standing in a dentist's office, getting ready to beg for a job.

Praying no one would notice the tears that had been streaking down my cheeks. Praying even harder that the world might actually right itself, considering I'd never in all my life felt so off-kilter.

I had to pull this off.

I needed this job.

God, I needed this job.

That declined credit card was proof of that.

Panic still thunderin' so hard I could feel it in my veins, I approached the reception desk. "Hi, I'm Isabel Lane. I have an appointment for an interview at 1:30."

When I introduced myself, I pasted on the prettiest smile I could find, one that had never felt so brittle or fake.

Especially when my lips were coated in the same rose-petal pink lipstick that Maxon had just paid for, swooping in like some kind of devil or deliverer, I couldn't be sure.

Something about it felt ironic.

The man being there to buy me a stupid tube of lipstick and not when I'd needed him most.

"Oh, hello, Isabel. You can go right in, down the hall, second door on the right. She's waiting for you."

"Thank you," I murmured, pulling in a deep breath and hoping it would pull in a load of confidence with it.

"Good luck."

"I'm gonna need it," I said.

On wobbly legs, I moved down the hall, trying to refrain from reaching out and letting the wall help me along, my heartbeat still a clatter, running wild from the mere sight of him.

Didn't even want to admit the way I'd been struck by his touch.

The overwhelming rush of lust that had slammed me from out of nowhere.

So gorgeous I'd momentarily lost function when I'd found him standing there, like a vapor in the recesses of my mind that had suddenly materialized.

Foreboding and arrogant and imposing.

That was all mixed up with that charm and the stupid adorable dimple in his cheek, those two things far more dangerous than the others.

When I made it to the second door, I drew in a steeling breath.

I could do this. I'd have time to fall apart later, but right then, I needed to focus on what was important.

I peered inside to find a woman sitting behind the desk, dark, frizzy hair and readers perched on her nose.

I lightly tapped my knuckles on the jamb.

Her head popped up.

"Hello, I'm Isabel Lane. I believe I'm up next."

I wondered if my smile was wobbling as badly as my knees.

"Come right in, Isabel." She stood and extended her hand over the desk. I tried to remain steady when I edged inside. "I'm Helen Montoya, the office manager and head of HR."

"It's so nice to meet you," I told her, voice wispy and thin. I was searching all over for confidence as I returned her handshake.

She almost laughed, her attention dropping to where our hands were connected. "You don't have to be nervous."

"Oh." I jerked my hand away, realizing it was sweaty, and wiped it on my skirt.

Wow, was I ever making a great impression.

Light laughter tinkled from her. "Or maybe it might be this humid weather. It's so thick, I thought I was going to have to swim to work," she said, sitting down and gesturing to the seat across from her.

Fumbling, I sat down, adjusting my skirt and clasping my hands tight on my lap. "Oh, yes, that might be the humidity. I'm also a little nervous," I added, peeking over at her.

She smiled a soft smile. "No problem at all." She glanced at my resume on her desk. "So, I see you previously worked in a dental office in Idaho?"

"Yes," I said, probably sounding a little too eager.

"And what were your responsibilities there?"

I shifted forward, my knees angled to the side. "I did scheduling and appointment confirmations, checking in patients, answering phones, all the typical things in the office."

"Good, good," she said, glancing at my resume.

I sat forward a little farther, nerves rattling through my senses. "On top of that, I handled the office's marketing . . . managed the website and some of the promotional flyers and graphics. Illustrations and that sort of thing."

"That's wonderful."

"Thank you. I enjoy the hustle of the office, but I have to admit, I was really proud of that part of the job."

She lowered the sheet of paper, one side of her mouth lifting at the side. "You're an artist." It wasn't much of a question, and my thundering heart decided it would be a good time to give a little kick.

"I . . . well . . .I . . ." I stuttered.

Goodness, I sounded like a blabbering fool. I clenched my hands tighter like my own personal reprimand. *Do not mess this up.*

"I guess I would have liked to have been," I murmured.

God, that was probably stupid, too. The last thing you were

supposed to do in an interview was admit that you'd prefer to be doing something else.

"But you don't have to worry about me doing a good job here. If I'm doing a job, I'm committed to it. One-hundred percent."

I was inching forward again. At this rate, I was gonna fall off my seat.

She chuckled again and took off her glasses. "It's okay, Ms. Lane. I totally understand. I think it's safe to bet most of us might have different dreams or goals that we missed."

A somber, appreciative smile pulled at my mouth, my chest squeezing and pulling, all the emotions I battled to keep down trying to break their way free. "Thank you. But I really do enjoy working in an office."

"I like you," she said.

I could feel the redness creeping up my cheeks. Great, now I was blushin', too. "Well, I always hope to fit in. Help my co-workers. Make patients feel comfortable if they're nervous for their procedures."

"You mean, you're nice?" She lifted her brows a bit playfully.

A tiny bark of laughter escaped. "I try to be."

She blew out a strained sigh, and I almost jumped out of the chair, or just slid to my knees to do some begging because I could almost see the regret at having to tell me, in spite of all of those things, I wasn't a good fit.

"Can you start on Monday?" she asked instead. "I know that's only a handful of days from now, but we're in a bit of a bind, and we could really use you around here."

I shot to my feet. "Oh, yes, of course."

Why was I standing?

Oh my gosh.

Think quick, Izzy.

I moved for the desk and put out my hand. She shook it, chuckling.

"Thank you so much, you won't regret this."

"I think you're right."

I pulled my hand away. In all my excitement and relief, it flailed a little too far to my right. My eyes went round in horror when I realized it'd struck something—a glass vase filled with a bouquet of roses and lilies that was tipping to the side.

"Oh my gosh," I all but shouted, scrambling to catch it, grabbing it right before the glass smacked the desk. Water splashed out, a river of it heading straight for her pile of patient folders. I righted the vase and then rushed to gather the stack before they got wet.

"I'm so sorry. Oh my gosh, I'm so sorry."

She was laughing more. "It's fine. It's fine." She grabbed a couple paper towels from a cabinet behind her, and I was laughing, too, as we sopped it up.

"You can put cleaning up the messes I make on the list of my qualifications."

She glanced up, smiling wide. "Good. Considering I spilled my tumbler of coffee I brought in this morning, I'd say we're going to make a good team."

God, was I really getting cut this break? With my performance, she should have sent me packing. Instead, she was looking at me like I was the one who was saving her.

"I really am grateful for this job."

"I'm excited to work with you. Now go on, take a little breather. I'll see you at eight a.m. on Monday, if you can come in a little early to fill out the paperwork?"

"That would be great," I said, shaking her hand once more, though this time giving it a squeeze with the other hand. I started backing away, then gasped out and whirled around when I ran into something hard.

A man.

A man wearing light blue scrubs and a bright white smile.

"Whoa there," he said, hands darting to the outside of my shoulders to steady me.

I just stood there, gaping.

He smiled wider, and my heart was thumping, racing out of control.

"You okay?"

I barely could nod, totally mortified by the fact I was a mess. Only Maxon Chambers could send me into a tailspin like this.

"I'm Dr. Nelson, but everyone calls me Trevor. Did I just overhear we finally have someone to take over the front office?"

Oh awesome.

I'd just knocked into my new boss.

"Yes, we do," Helen said from behind. "This is Isabel Lane."

He kept his hands on me, holding me up, but stepping back a little as he angled his head to the side.

That was right when I was noticing just how attractive that he was. I mean, not quite like Maxon Chambers. That man was a brand all his own. But attractive in that clean-cut way, light brown hair and dark brown eyes.

"Well, I have to say it's great to meet you. I was hoping we'd find someone to fill Sandy's spot."

I stepped back and stuck out my hand. "It's nice to meet you. I just hope I can fill her shoes."

His eyes glinted when he returned the shake. "I'm sure you'll do perfectly fine."

I glanced between them, flustered, not even sure where it was coming from anymore. "Well, I'll get out of your way. I'll see you Monday morning."

I ducked out, glancing over my shoulder, redness hitting me again when I saw that Dr. Nelson was watching me go.

My old car bounced down the narrow, dirt lane that led to the house where I'd grown up.

Our home was secluded in a dense thicket on the far east side of Broadshire Rim, the forest surrounding it lush and alive, fed by the river that twisted through our property.

I wound along the mile-long lane that was hugged by towering trees, their huge trunks covered in moss, massive arms winding and curling as they fought their way toward the sky. The branches were covered in green leaves that protected the earth from the scorch of the blistering South Carolina summer.

Glittering streaks of sunlight broke through, and I leaned forward to see them dancing across my windshield, sprinkling like stardust where they played on the ground.

The sheer beauty of this place struck me with awe.

I'd missed it.

I'd missed it so much, just another piece of myself that had been ripped away when I'd left.

My parents.

My home.

Maxon.

All those stupid, childish dreams that he'd crushed in one sweeping blow.

I looked out to the right to see the meadow peeking out from the copse of dense trees. The tiny house where he'd lived was barely visible in the distance.

A lance of pain tried to cut through the joy I felt at getting the job. I forced it down. I wasn't going there right then.

I kept driving, winding around one curve and then another until the estate came into view. It had once been a bit lavish, if not pretentious, though there were far more grandiose mansions in the area.

The years had taken its toll on it, though.

The white, two story home fronted by pillars and a sweeping porch had deteriorated, the paint peeling and wood splintering. The once perfectly maintained lawn was shabby in spots, and the wild jasmine was living up to its name, growing completely out of control.

The money had run as dry as the gargoyle fountain that stood not so proud out front.

But still, it was breathtaking. Welcoming. My home.

I pulled to a stop in front of the garage on the left side of the house and climbed out, my heels clicking on the red-brick pathway as I made my way to the porch steps. I climbed them, the wood creaking with my weight, and I wiggled my key into the lock.

Turning the knob, I pushed open one side of the double doors. "I'm home," I called, just because saying it felt so good when I'd been gone for so long.

A trample of footsteps pounded down the stairs. "Did you get it? Did you get it?"

"Yes, baby, I got it," I breathed out, my own relief and excitement uncontained.

"Yes!" Dillon threw his fist into the air before he was throwing his little body across the room. I picked him up, swinging him around, even though he wasn't much of a baby anymore, already five years old and larger than life.

He pulled back and looked at me seriously. "I'm really proud of you, Mom. I knew you could do it. Didn't I tell you that you could? You had nothin' to worry about. Just like you're always tellin' us we can be whatever we want to be."

If you could be anything when you grow up, what would you want to be?

So yeah, I was guilty of that question, too, and didn't feel bad about it at all. I was just glad he wanted to be a jet fighter when he grew up rather than to marry Brigid, the poor little girl next door who'd bawled her eyes out when she'd found out we were moving and her favorite playmate was leaving her behind.

I poked at his chubby belly, giving him a tease. "Does that mean you've been listening to me?"

"What do you think? Listenin' is part of the rules, isn't it? And you're the one who said I had to follow all the rules, and I was listenin' then, too. See?" he rambled out so fast it was a wonder I could process through the words.

"Just makin' sure," I said with a playful grin.

He was my life.

My soul.

My soul that was completed when I carried Dillon across the room and through the swinging doors that led into the kitchen. It was where I was sure I'd find Benjamin at the bay window that had been converted into a big reading nook at the far corner of the expansive room.

The second he'd seen it, he'd claimed it as his own, and if I was looking for him, I could bet that's where I would find him.

I ruffled a hand through Dillon's hair and smacked a kiss to his temple before I set him on his feet and headed for my oldest son.

"Hey there, handsome man." My heart leapt as I took him in

where he sat in the swath of light that blazed in through the window behind him. He had a book on his lap, five others spread out on the cushions around him—those words Benjamin's own escape.

My eyes moved over him, taking in his super skinny legs and arms, the joints of the right side of his body set at an odd angle from the contractures he'd dealt with his entire life, his knees and shoulders knobby and his mouth permanently twisted on that right side.

He looked so frail sitting there. Fragile. But I'd never met anyone quite as strong.

He struggled to push himself up higher against the pillow rested against the wall.

I knelt down in front of him and nudged his chin with my knuckle.

Redness climbed to his cheeks. "Mmmmom, I'm nnnot a baby," he said, though he was grinning and trying to hide his angel-smile that was brighter than the sun that shined like a halo on his head. "Sttop it."

His speech was slurred, elongated and lurching as his tongue grappled to form the words.

Sometimes it was difficult to understand him, but to me, they were the most beautiful sounds on the earth considering I'd been told he would probably never talk.

"Never," I told him, pinching his chin instead.

"You're embarrrrassing." Only he was grinning and playfully swatting at me.

"What are you talking about? Being embarrassing is my job. I'm your mom, remember?" I drew out.

"How could I forrrget?" he slurred, a glint in his eyes.

"Punk," I teased him.

He gestured at himself. "Total troublemaker."

"Hey, what have I told you? You can be anything you want to be, you just have to set your mind to it. Work hard enough for it, and it's yours." I tried to keep a straight face when I said it.

He laughed from his belly, his head flopping back a little bit. "I donnn't think that's what you meant."

Dillon leaned on the window seat, poking that adorable, inquisitive face in between us. "Hey, I thought troublemaking was bad? I think you're givin' bad, bad advice, Mom. You better think twice."

Light laughter danced on my tongue, and I hooked my arm around his waist and drew him closer. "You're right. Troublemaking is bad. I take it all back. A troublemaker is something you can't be, no matter how hard you work for it."

Bad boys were just . . . well . . . bad. They were a terrible idea for everyone involved.

Dillon giggled, holding his shaking belly. "But what if that's what I really wanna be?"

"No way."

Benjamin was grinning, watching our interaction, my sweet little man turning serious, his eyes lighting with pride.

"And you gggot the job?" he asked.

"I did. Pretty amazing, right? I told you everything was going to come together exactly like we needed it to." I tapped his chin in emphasis.

He'd been worried over our reason for returning to the place he'd only heard about in stories.

His disability had been a good excuse not to visit, my parents always coming out to see us since traveling truly was a bit of a trial.

But he knew.

It was crazy how insightful that he was, the boy so smart, his intelligence extending into the realm of *knowing*. I wondered if it was because he had to spend so much time on the outside looking in, an observer, excluded from conversations because people often assumed that he wasn't smart.

Immediately, he'd picked up on the fact we were making this move because of him.

For him.

Not only had I been told Benjamin might not talk, I'd also been told that he might not walk, either.

Diagnosed with cerebral palsy, my son had endured seven different surgeries and a series of castings for years to help with his contractures.

He'd suffered through intense pain, but he'd worked so hard and made incredible strides.

The day he'd taken his first step with his walker, I'd fallen to my knees, unable to stand beneath the swelling of gratitude that had hit me like a landslide.

It was what he'd wanted most.

To run and play with other children, to be normal like the other boys who he hoped one day would call him friend, even though I spent every day of his life trying to instill in him that he was normal in his own, beautiful way.

Or that maybe none of us were normal. We were all different. Special.

But I understood the need to run free. Wild and alive. Who didn't want the best life for their child?

He'd progressed so far that he no longer had the walker and now used forearm crutches.

So, when his therapist in Idaho had mentioned a new two-year study in Charleston, I'd made the decision to betray the promise I'd made to myself that I would never come back here.

Hatchett's specialized in experimental treatments that had shown major strides in treating children with cerebral palsy.

Considering we were basically broke, and I could never afford the type of care they were offering, I had to take the chance.

My parents weren't really in all that better of a situation than I was financially. My father had made some bad investments through the years that had eaten through our family's wealth. But at least they still had the house and had offered us a home, and I figured I could do my part with fixing up around the place.

It was a win-win-win.

Especially for Benjamin.

When we found out he had been accepted, we packed up our things and left.

I glanced back at my mother who was on the other side of the room, across the huge butcher's block island that separated the cooking area from the dining space and den, watching us softly as she dried the dishes she was doing at the sink.

She sent me a gentle smile.

I turned back to my boys, soft affection riding through my expression.

"Tell me you two weren't too much trouble for Nana and Grand-Pop?"

Dillon looked at me, a tease in his dark eyes. "What are you talkin' about? Boys are supposed to be noisy and rambunctious and like to get into trouble. I mean, we are *troublemakers*, after all."

Dillon's gaze slid to his brother. Two of them thick as thieves.

Benjamin cracked up, a laugh so big and genuine that it stole my breath. "Yuuuup. Told you, Mmmom, total troubbblemaker." He gestured to himself with that crooked grin.

"Fine, you're right. Boys are noisy and rambunctious and totally like to get into trouble. What am I supposed to do with you two *troublemakers*?"

"Love us?" Dillon grinned up at me, sarcasm thick.

"Hmm . . . no problem there," I said, pushing to my feet, "but that doesn't mean I won't gladly send you to time-out, too."

"Ah, man. Mom's nothin' but a funsucker."

I bit back a smile. "Watch it, little man."

He held up his hands in surrender. "Fine, fine, I won't be a troublemaker. Crush my dreams, why don't you?"

This kid.

I laughed, kissing Benjamin on the top of the head and running my fingers over the top of Dillon's before I turned around and headed toward my mama. She was plump and as pretty as ever, lines starting to deepen on her face, like maybe she'd aged right along with the house.

"How did it go?" I asked, edging up to her side so I could help her dry the dishes. "Did they wear you out? I hate to be any trouble."

I added a little extra emphasis for the sake of my two troublemakers.

She knocked into my hip. "Oh, stop it. They were just fine, exactly like I told you they would be. You worry too much."

I let a light chuckle ripple free. "Of course, I worry too much. I'm a mother."

She angled her head. "Who finally has a little help. You need to take a breather and relax. Rely on us a little. We want you here. We want your boys here. It's what we've always wanted. So, stop walking around like this isn't your home when that's exactly what it's always been."

I blew out a strained sigh, taking a dishtowel to a plate. "I know. It's just . . . strange being back. Especially with the boys. It's like my old life here and the one in Idaho were completely separate. It's hard to see how to mesh them together."

She set down her towel and turned to take me by the chin, studying my face. "You do it just like you're doing now. A day at a time. You've always been the bravest, strongest person I know. You have more power than you're givin' yourself credit for."

Old grief lapped, and I tried to swallow down the emotion that gathered at the base of my throat, quick to sting my eyes. "I saw him today."

Worry traipsed across her face, brow twisting in a frown. "Well, we knew that would be comin', didn't we? I've seen him around over the years. There was no avoiding it."

"I'd just . . ." I fidgeted, warring with what to say. With what I felt. "I'd hoped to have a little more time to prepare myself, I guess."

I glanced around, as if I could picture the thousand times that he'd been in this room, then darkness came speeding in when I thought of the last time he'd come through this door. The day that had changed everything.

She brushed her thumb along my cheek where a single tear got loose. "I hate him for chasing my baby away. I won't let him do it again."

Sniffling, I lowered my voice, "I'm scared, Mama, of having to face him. Of the way he still made me feel."

It was just like those two segmented lives. Once I'd jumped back into the old one, it felt like a day hadn't past.

The wounds just as raw. The connection just as real.

"He hurt you somethin' terrible. But the one thing I am certain of when I see him is the guilt he carries."

I winced. "He left me, Mama. Left me and turned his back as if what we'd shared for our whole lives didn't matter at all. He can feel guilty all he wants, but it doesn't change what he did."

I swallowed around a tremble of sorrow. "He hurt me in a way no one has ever hurt me before. In a way that no one else ever could."

"And still, he inspired you through it. Made you feel all that time. And you continued to hope for the goodness to shine."

She brushed her knuckles down my cheek.

"Who knows what love is if he hasn't experienced grief?" She almost sang the words, the quote hitting me square in the chest, and I sucked in a staggered breath.

"How could I ever forget what he went through? How could I ever stop hoping that he would escape that life?"

Her smile was close to sympathetic. "I think that says more about you than anyone else."

three

MACK

I drove up the short gravel lane to Ian's house, the sun a blister in the sky, my hands and my legs still shaking like a bitch. Squinting against the glare, I came to a stop in front of the house.

It was painted a light blue, the trimmings and porch white.

Quaint and sweet and homey.

Such a mindfuck that Ian was really living this life.

I shut off the ignition to my unmarked patrol car. The white Suburban with super tinted windows was supposed to come off as incognito. Still, it stuck out like a car coming at you in the dead of night with high-beam lights.

Pushing out a sigh, I just sat in it for a second, trying to get myself together before I went inside. But I couldn't shake the girl from my skin, the surprise at seeing her.

The devastation that still remained clear.

Hurt flashing like a beast, toiling in the air between us.

Did I think she'd feel any different? Did I think that enough time had passed that she'd give me a quick, careless hug and offhandedly ask how I was?

Like she hadn't thought about me in years?

But I guessed maybe that's exactly what I'd hoped she'd done. Moved on. Found something bigger and better away from this dead-end town. God knew, I couldn't give her the kind of life that she deserved.

Hoped she'd realized it'd been for the best.

Maybe even thank me for it.

Which was damned stupid because she didn't even slow down long enough to *thank me* for buying her things, hightailing it out of there so fast I was left wondering if I'd hallucinated seeing her in the first place.

Hardest part was that *feeling* was still there, this sensation of coming alive when I was in her space speeding beneath my skin, seeping all the way down to my bones.

Need and lust? Yeah. They were there. No question.

But it was bigger than that.

Something unfound.

Special.

I guessed maybe that's what it'd always come down to.

Izzy Lane was special.

I huffed off the confusion trying to drag me under and grabbed the box of diapers from the passenger seat, hopped out, and started up the sidewalk just as the front screen door was flying open and banging against the wall.

Mallory Paloma came bounding out at full speed.

If I said Sophie Marie was a ball of energy, Mallory was a tornado getting ready to touch down, though her velocity hit you in an entirely different way.

"Uncle Mack Attack! You're here! You're here!"

She clamored down the steps. Well, calling it that was actually a disservice, considering she basically soared off the porch, propelling herself into the air with a leap and a spin, landing in some kind of awkward backward plié. It almost had me dropping the diapers to sprint for her to keep her from falling and cracking her head.

The fumble didn't even slow her down.

She booked it down the walk and threw herself at me, not even giving me time to adjust the diapers.

I caught her with an oomph, swinging her up into one arm while I tucked the box under the other.

"Hey," she grinned with all her teeth, arms wrapping around my neck tightly as she leaned the rest of her body back, her pin straight white hair and bangs framing her cherub face.

Yup, another angel, this one with wings.

"Hay is for horses," I told her, giving her a little tease.

"That's the oldest joke in all of ever, Uncle Mackity-Yak," she said, hiking a sassy shoulder.

"Oh, really?"

"How old are you, anyway?" she asked, her blue eyes narrowing in a combination of disgust and sympathy.

"Old enough to know better, apparently," I mumbled under my breath. "Don't worry, I'll try to be cooler the next time I see you."

"You can try, I guess." Another shrug. "Not sure how that's gonna work out."

Awesome.

I was getting skewered by a 6-year-old.

I just was winning at life, wasn't I?

"Breaking my heart here, Mal Pal. Breaking my heart," I grumbled, starting up the walk.

She broke out in a howl of laughter. "I'm playing with you, Uncle! Don't you know a joke when you hear one? You're the coolest of all the coolest. At least that's what my daddy says. Coolest guy around. That's what he told Mommy." Her head pitched to the side in consideration. "But that you're gonna die alone because you won't pull your head out of your ass. I don't want you to die so you should definitely pull it out."

My eyes about bugged out of my skull, and I stumbled to a

stop, reminding myself to kick Ian's *ass* once inside.

Glad to know I was such an interesting topic of conversation.

Her mouth puckered in an 'o'. "Oops. I'm not supposed to say that, am I?"

"Definitely not."

Not the word or that she'd let on that her dad was throwing me under the bus.

"Daddy says bad words sometimes, even the really, really bad ones, usually when he thinks we're not listening or when he gets stressed out. Like he is right now. It's a good thing you got here when you did," she rambled, all matter of fact, that speeding train so easily jumping tracks. "Things are gettin' crazy in there. Looks like a tornado hit."

She was totally spot on. I was holding it in my arms.

I feigned a worried frown. "Is that so?" I asked as I mounted the steps.

She gave an emphatic nod. "Yup, that is so. Soph is being a handful again, and Collin is screaming like a banshee, and Daddy-the-Great looks like he might be at his wit's end. Grams said she is always at her wit's end, and I don't think we need to be driving Daddy there, too. It seems like a dangerous place to be. We might need an intervention."

There she went, round and round and round. Spinning her little disorder.

"An intervention, huh? And what kind of intervention would that be?"

"The kind where everyone listens and does what they're told to do. You're a cop. Make it happen, Capin'."

Amusement had me chewing at the inside of my lip.

"And am I to assume you're already doing everything right? Following all the rules? No issues there?"

"Hello? Who do you think I am? I do all the things." Her voice lowered conspiratorially. "And if I wasn't, I sure wouldn't be tellin' a cop."

Wow. I was gettin' concerned this was how criminals were born.

"And what if I had to do a lie detector test on you?" I razzed.

She inhaled a sharp gasp. Clearly what I was offering up was cruel and unusual punishment. "Now that's just not playin' fair."

"Who said life was fair?" I asked with my brows knitted up, trying to keep it light, but feeling the way my spirit wanted to trip into turmoil at the thought.

My own personal regrets and fuck ups on top of the bullshit that I couldn't control.

Life wasn't fair.

I saw the truth of it, day in and day out.

And fuck if I wasn't feeling the weight of it right then.

The kid looked at me with a completely straight face. "Life is not *fair*. Mom already told us that life can be hard." Her brow stitched up, clearly struck with an important thought. "But we already got our hero, so it's not really hard anymore."

She frowned in worry. "Well, except our hero is about to crack. Our hero needs a hero. You feel like bein' a hero today?" she asked.

Emotion fisted my heart. Those steel bindings cinching tighter and tighter. Forever holding me prisoner. Didn't matter that I'd dedicated my life to wiping some of the scum from the city. I'd already committed too many wrongs to earn that title.

I set the little girl onto her feet, and she grinned up at me, so damned sweet and innocent. I could feel the magnitude of it twisting through my spirit, this feeling that shouted out that there was something inside of me that would always feel off.

Something missing.

A piece I couldn't regain.

I gave a little tug to a lock of her hair.

"Not sure I can reach hero status," I told her, straight-up honest, "but I definitely think we can help out your dad."

I stepped through the door into the cozy house. Inside, it was quiet. A distinct contradiction to the mayhem that had been going down in the background during our phone call that made it almost eerie.

My attention darted around as I crossed the living room. Guessed it was the detective in me that had jumped into action, taking note that the place was completely trashed, a fucking mountain of toys strewn everywhere, pillows and cushions tossed from the couch, trails of crumbs leading from one room to the other.

We definitely needed to sneak in a quick clean up before Grace made it home from her writing group.

First things first.

Hitting the swinging kitchen door, I pushed it open, making sure I had a smile pinned to my face. Last thing I needed was to go blurting out what was on my mind, the words a bitter burn on my tongue, vying for release.

But it made no sense to go spouting things I couldn't change.

For a second, I froze at the archway, feeling a crack go breaking through the middle of me.

Guessed it was witnessing the sight of things turning out the way they should have always been. Something good for a guy who'd been dealt such an unfair life.

Ian was standing in the middle of the kitchen, a sleeping kid nestled in the crook of each arm. From the side, I watched as he gazed down at them, the guy appearing haggard and worn and lacking about a thousand hours' sleep, and still, he looked the fucking happiest I'd ever seen him.

Inhaling deeply, I pushed the rest of the way through.

When he heard me, he shifted all the way around, lips pursing in a silent, "Shh."

Mallory instantly followed suit, pushing a finger to her lips that had been flapping since the second I'd pulled up.

"Shh," she repeated before she edged right back out.

I was pretty sure the silence scared her.

I lifted my chin in acknowledgement, quieting my steps as I crossed the kitchen so I could set the box of diapers on the island, stifling a chuckle when I looked at Ian's infant who was wearing nothing but a towel duct taped around his waist.

"Clever," I whispered.

"Desperate times, dude. Desperate times. Told you I needed you. Did you think I was joking?"

"You need me to take one of those?" I asked, gesturing for the conked-out kids.

"Please." Carefully, he transferred Sophie into my arms, that ball of energy completely spent. "If you can get her into her bed for a nap without waking her up, I'll give you a thousand dollars. Strike that, I'll give you my car. Hell, you can keep her," he uttered barely over his breath, shooting me a wink.

Carefully, I cradled her, the sweet thing weighing next to nothing, her little hand coming up to fist in my shirt.

I kissed the top of her head before I whispered over the top of it. "Uh, like your kids and all, but I think I'll opt for the Mercedes."

He shook his head at me with a muted laugh. "Asshole."

I shot him a smirk right as I was turning away, quick to climb to the second floor on the narrow set of stairs that led from the kitchen. At the landing, I headed straight for Sophie Marie's room. All four walls were painted in pinks and princesses and unicorn magic, a mural depiction from one of the scenes in the children's book Grace had written.

Pretty fucking awesome, if you asked me, the fact Grace had taken this book she'd used as an escape for her and her kids when they'd been going through the biggest challenge of their lives and turned it into something amazing and successful. You could find it on the shelves of just about every bookstore from here to L.A.

I edged farther inside, trying not to laugh out loud when I heard that tornado touching down again in the next room. Mallory was belting out a terrible pop song at the top of her lungs.

Thank God the walls were thick.

Or maybe Ian and Grace had put a little extra insulation on Mal-Pal's. Seemed about right.

In some kind of miracle, Sophie only made a few grunting noises when I laid her on her toddler bed before she flopped over and sprawled out facedown.

Down for the count.

I quickly slipped out, leaving the door open a crack, and bounded back downstairs toward the kitchen.

Blinking as I went.

Fighting back the storm I felt gathering at the horizon of my mind.

Didn't matter.

It grew thicker.

Darker.

More desperate.

Was taking everything I had not to bypass the kitchen and go bolting out the front door.

Drive the ten miles to her parents' place, sure that was where I would find her.

Just as sure as her dad would be waiting to chase me off with a shotgun.

Didn't matter that I was a cop, dude was likely to take me down, anyway.

I didn't blame him for a second. I deserved his distrust.

I'd risk all of that to get one more look at her. Figure out if she was actually as worn down as it'd appeared.

Fix it, if I could. Wondering if she would let me. Knowing I didn't deserve the chance.

I scrubbed both palms over my face, hoping it would break me out of the muddle of mayhem staging an assault in my mind.

Stepping into the kitchen, I found Ian trying to rip into the box without setting Collin down.

"Need a hand?" I offered, crossing to the island.

"Need about ten of them, apparently."

"Poor bastard," I mumbled, eyeing him with a glint in my eye. "Guess that's what you get for telling your kid I was gonna die alone."

He just laughed. "Don't act like that's not exactly where you're headed. Don't worry, man, I'd have been happy to die alone right along with you until I met Grace."

Funny how my life was filled with all these amazing people and still was utterly lonely. My house was so vacant that sometimes I thought it might swallow me up.

Sometimes I thought Ian could see right into my mind because he frowned. "You know the house next door is for sale. You should think about moving back to Broadshire Rim. Would be awesome to have you nearby."

"What, you need me close for all the spur-of-the moment diaper runs?"

"Hell, yeah. Like I told you earlier, you're basically my favorite person." He pointed at me. "Repeat that, and I will kill you."

I laughed, brushed my fingers through my hair, and shifted around to lean my hip on the island. Changing the subject, I gestured my chin at him. "Mallory said you were about to crack. Something about being at your wit's end. You good, man?"

"Almost got there when this little guy crapped again, and I realized there wasn't a single diaper left in the house. Seriously, how many times can a kid this size poop a day? That shit's just not normal." He rocked him protectively against his chest, this little peanut wrapped up in his arms, wearing nothing but that towel.

"Pretty sure all that *shit* is normal."

He chuckled again, the sound fading out as he gazed down at his little guy.

Everything inside me softened. Couldn't help it. Was fucking happy for him. "Looks to me like you had it under control."

He leaned against the counter, holding Collin closer, not even making a move for the diapers.

Guessed he was riding out the calm. The storm passed. Surprised that they'd all made it unscathed to the other side.

His voice quieted with something close to reverie. "Trying hard, man. Most of the time, I don't have the first clue what I'm doing. So out of my element. I mean, a year and a half ago, would you have ever imagined this would be my life? And then Grace goes and trusts me to take care of all four kids . . . that kind of responsibility still sometimes scares the shit out of me."

He blinked a bunch of times. "It's like, sometimes I pause for one second, and that's all it takes for every mistake I've made, every crime I've committed, to catch up to me. Then I'm standing there, wondering how this is my life. How it's possible I could deserve it. Questioning if I really do. Terrified I'm going to fuck it up." He looked up at me, his throat bobbing heavily when he swallowed. "And I can't fuck it up, Mack. I can't lose them."

My chest tightened. The bullshit the two of us had endured should have been insurmountable. I'd gone one direction. Ian had gone the other.

He'd paid for his crimes, and he'd come out better on the other side. The guy I'd always believed he could be. The one I wouldn't second guess to call on for anything.

"Pretty sure she trusts you because she knows you can be trusted, Ian. You're not gonna fuck it up," I told him, sincerity bleeding free. "Not when you're doing it with the right heart. Mistakes don't mean we're ruining something. It just means we're learning. Getting better every day."

He gazed down at his son. "Just want to do it right."

We both looked up when his oldest son, Thomas, came shuffling into the kitchen.

Ian had adopted all three of Grace's kids.

Thomas.

Mallory.

Sophie.

He was right.

He'd been given the greatest gift of all, not to mention that little bonus point of Collin who he cradled tenderly in his arms.

Thomas's socked feet slid across the wood floor, all of his attention wrapped up in his iPad. He barely glanced up, totally absorbed in whatever was on the screen. "Hey, Dad," he muttered.

When the kid said it, Ian lit up like a lightbulb.

Kind of had one light up in the middle of me, too.

"Did you see that interest rates are expected to go up? Wall Street Journal is reporting it. I think you and Uncle Jace should go for it if you're thinking about getting something new and you plan on financing. It's a good time to buy."

Ian and I shared a glance. The kid was too much. As brainy as they came, always reading all these advanced articles and journals that I wouldn't have dreamed of reading at that age. Hell, I still didn't get half the shit he was talking about.

"Oh, hey, Uncle Mack," he said off-handedly, just then noticing that I was there.

I refrained from using the *hay* joke on him.

"What's up, Thomas, my man? I see you're keeping your dad in line."

Way cooler, right?

Yeah. I was with Ian. Totally out of my element.

Because I was pretty sure the one I knew about two hookers and a fisherman would be way out of line.

Thomas shrugged a shoulder. "Trying."

"Come here," Ian coaxed him softly, and he looked over the kid's shoulder, reading whatever report it was that Thomas had pulled up. "Whoa, good job finding that. I didn't hear. Uncle Jace and I need you looking out for us like this."

Ian dropped a tender kiss to the top of Thomas' head, lingering a bit, like he didn't want to let go.

Thomas tipped his head up backward, beaming at him, before he fumbled right back out.

Easy, but the interaction seemed wholly profound.

I met Ian's eye. "Pretty sure you're doing it right." Was doing my best to try to keep my voice from going rough.

That unsettled, sticky feeling hitting me in waves.

"Looks to me like you and Jace might have yourselves a new partner."

Ian watched as the door stopped its slow swing and fell completely still. "Kid blows my mind. Did we think about stuff like that when we were his age?" he asked as he angled his attention back to me.

A snort blew through my nose. "Hell, no. Pretty sure the only thing either of us were thinking about at that age was the next thing we might be able to swipe without someone noticing or what girl would be game to let us touch their tits."

"If I was my kid, I'd kick my own ass." He laughed out a subdued sound, wonder filling his tone. "It was different back then, yeah?"

I shrugged, hating the heaviness that came rushing in, the weight of the reality of this world that could never be outrun. "It's different for them, Ian. Different because you and Grace work hard to give them a good life. Because you love them more than anything else. Put them first. Not everyone gets that. These kids are damned lucky to have you. To have both of you."

Pain leached into my chest.

Ian, Jace, and I had been bred into that kind of life. Their mom an addict. My dad a low-life thief. At least Megan Jacobs had good inside of her. The willingness to sacrifice.

If only my father would have possessed a sliver of those qualities.

Shouldn't even have let that asshole get into my head because the second I did, all I could see was the heartbreak written all over Izzy the last time I'd seen her before she'd left town.

That striking, unforgettable face flashed through my mind, moving through me like a reel of time.

Progressing.

Now and then.

The girl so pretty I felt her like a punch to the gut. Her face and that smile and that body.

There was no forgetting her belief in me that I could be something better than my circumstances. She'd never given up on me no matter how hard I'd tried to keep her at a distance. Arm's length.

It was when I'd started taking her into my arms that everything had gone to shit.

A pang of agony rattled my ribs, this choked sensation that was suddenly constricting the flow of air. Because all of it suddenly felt like too much.

The grief and the worry and the pain.

The regret.

The fear that I would never outrun myself. That I'd get sucked into that black, vapid hole, become the man I'd been bred to be.

Ian caught it.

But what did I expect? The guy knew me better than anyone else.

"What was that?" he asked, speculation written all over him.

Needing support, my hands curled around the counter. "No clue what you're talking about."

"Don't bullshit me, man. You think I didn't just see that . . . that thing go down in your head?"

He kept Collin nestled in the crook of one arm, the other coming to his head where he made a little exploding motion, replete with sound effects. "Looked like a bomb just detonated in that tiny brain of yours. Now you're as white as a ghost. You working on something shady that has you on edge?"

"I'm always working on something shady."

It was the truth.

"True," he said. "Then why don't you tell me what the hell that was."

"It wasn't—"

"Don't even say it was nothing. You think I can't read you?"

Heaving out the breath I'd been holding, I scrubbed both palms over my face. Thinking it might perk me up. Get the blood flowing.

Problem was, the blood was flowing too hard. Sloshing and sliding and thumping.

Groaning, I dropped my hands. Might as well fess it up because the asshole wouldn't stop until he pried it out of me, anyway. Not sure I could keep this from him.

"Might have seen a ghost," I admitted, attention dropping to my boots. "At the grocery store."

Could sense his brows knitting up, the confusion riding free as he cocked his head to the side.

Slowly, I lifted my eyes.

One look at me, and his expression paled in realization.

No doubt, my face was a mask of fury and guilt and regret.

"Izzy?" he chanced.

Izzy.

Isabel.

"Yeah." I shrugged like it was nothing when it was everything.

"How is she?" he asked, tone wary, like he was wondering at which point it was going to push me over the edge.

Too bad I was already there.

"No clue, man. She took off before I got the chance to really talk to her." I paused, squeezing my eyes shut before I harshly shook my head. Needing to scrape this feeling from my consciousness. "It was for the best, anyway. Better to leave it alone."

Easier said than done. Because that selfish, greedy side of myself wanted to hunt her down.

Find her.

Keep her.

Take her the way I used to.

But she no longer belonged to me. I'd been cruel enough to make sure that she never would.

"What are you going to do?" he hedged, digging deeper. Wanted to tell him to fuck off and mind his own business, but considering there weren't a whole lot of topics off-limits between us, I figured that wasn't gonna fly.

Shrugging, I tried to keep the annoyance and helplessness out of my tone. "Absolutely nothing. There's nothing I can do, even if I wanted to."

I wondered if it came out sounding like a lie because that's sure as hell what it tasted like on my tongue.

"And you're saying you don't want to?" he challenged, though there was something smug riding at the corner of his mouth.

"That's exactly what I'm saying. Her life isn't my concern anymore."

Apparently, I was fuller of shit than Baby Collin.

"Really? Gave your heart to Clarissa, huh?" Sarcasm dripped from his question.

Repulsion seeped into my bloodstream.

"You know better than to even joke about that shit."

"What seems *funny* is that you keep riding that crazy train."

"She's just a hookup."

Such a fucking lie. I wondered if he bought it.

He covered his baby's ear and muttered the words, "A good fuck and settling are two different things."

I laughed out a bitter sound. "Think I settled a long time ago."

"Yeah? Maybe it's your chance to change it."

"Took a chance once, and look where that landed me."

Look what it almost cost.

He shook his head. "You're an idiot."

I went for his fridge and grabbed a beer, needing to shut this bullshit down before I spiraled.

That was just when a clatter of voices echoed through the house, getting louder before the kitchen door swung open.

Grace came in first, followed by Faith and Jace.

"There are my big men," Grace cooed, going directly for Ian and Collin, hiking up on her toes and planting a kiss on Ian's mouth. I didn't even think she noticed that her kid might as well have been wearing a toga.

"How'd it go?" she asked.

Ian grabbed her by the back of the neck, pulling her in for another kiss. "Perfect."

"What are you two talking about in here?" Faith asked, glancing between Ian and me like she'd caught onto something ulterior, her dark hair swishing around her sweet face.

Had known Faith for all my life. About as long as I'd known Izzy.

She was an incredible woman. Strong and resilient. Couldn't imagine a better girl for Jace or a better man for Faith.

They perfected the other.

But that didn't mean either of them needed to know about any of this.

"Nothing," I muttered.

At the same time, Ian was lifting his chin. "He just ran into Izzy."

The asshole.

He was lucky he was holding that baby.

Faith's attention jerked to me, something like horror in her expression. "What?"

Jace was rubbing at his chin in discomfort, and Grace slowly turned all the way around, her mouth gaping open, which was kind of unsettling considering she'd never even met Izzy, which meant Ian had been doing a little more of that tossing.

Big ol' wheels rolling right over the top of me.

And there I stood, my heart in my throat and all those curious eyes trying to get inside my head.

I twisted the cap off my beer and lifted the bottle in a nonchalant gesture. "It was nothing."

Except I knew damned well it was everything.

four

IZZY

Night pressed at the window of the same bedroom that had been mine for my entire childhood. On the second floor of the house, it sat at the opposite end of the hall as my parents' room, which had made it a whole ton easier sneaking out all those times growing up.

Dillon and Benjamin had picked a room right next to me, choosing to share because that is what they had to do back in Idaho. The two were so close and found so much comfort in the other, separating them was like prying apart chain links.

It was just better to leave it alone.

Everyone else had gone to bed at least a couple hours before, and now, I sat beneath the yellowed, hazy glow cast by the lamp on the desk where I was sitting, a journal spread out in front of me and the end of a pencil tapping at my lip as I doodled my emotions and thoughts.

I was battling to process the turmoil that was ragin' inside of me, as if I tapped into the quiet, I might be able to find the answer. That in the darkness, it might become clearer.

Fat chance of that. Because with each second that passed, it only felt more complicated.

I turned my gaze out the window. The towering tree rustled just outside, there like the sturdiest, most loyal of friends. Strong, thick branches stretched wide, as if it were inviting me to slip out into its safety, even though my daddy had screamed and ranted at me a hundred times that it wasn't safe.

I'd climbed up and down that tree so many times, I could still picture the perfect sequence of steps, each branch a rung. I wondered if it would feel the same, climbing it now, or if that tree, too, had been shaped and changed by the passage of time.

I jumped about ten feet in the air when my phone rattled on the desk and went off with a shrill ring.

"Crap," I muttered, fumbling to quickly answer. "Hi," I rushed low, praying I'd silenced the ringing before it woke the rest of the house.

"I heard you ran into you know who," Faith drawled, her country accent thick. Funny how the second I'd crossed state lines, mine had come rushing back, too.

Pushing from the white chair that matched the desk, I tiptoed over to my door that I'd left open in case either of the boys needed me during the night. I poked my head out into the hallway.

Coast clear.

I quietly latched the door shut, quick to pad back over to my bed. My room was decorated exactly the same as it'd been when I'd left—pale yellow walls and a yellow and green floral comforter, the bed piled high with fluffy throw pillows.

"Word sure does travel fast in this town, doesn't it?" I mumbled low as I crawled on top of my bed and pulled my knees to my chest. "Should have just put out a notice in the paper."

"This is Broadshire Rim. You know it does," she told me, a

tinge of laughter in her voice, though it was the concern interwoven with it that I really heard. "But I heard this one straight from the horse's mouth."

My guts twisted at the thought of her talking to Maxon. Being in his space. It just seemed . . . so wrong.

Like she was consorting with the enemy. Which was ridiculous because I knew full well they'd remained friends all this time.

"But don't worry, the gossips around here are alive and well. I did overhear you got a job at Nelson Dentistry when I ran in to pick up some things at the drycleaners. Word on the street is you're making double what poor Sandy was. Congratulations." She was holding back wry laughter.

"They know nothing . . . I'm making triple," I deadpanned.

I only wished.

She barked out a laugh. "Are you lost in some faraway fantasy again?"

"You know that's where I like to live."

"Time to come back down to reality with the rest of us, my friend."

"Do I have to?" It was almost a whine.

Because I really, really wanted to stay there. In a place where I could make up all the circumstances and outcomes, and I didn't have to deal with any of this that felt so out of control.

The teasing evaporated from her voice. "You do, Izzy. You do."

Heaviness pressed down on my chest. The sigh I released weighed every bit as much. I brought my thumb to my mouth, nibbling at the nail.

I wasn't quite sure that I'd ever felt so many emotions all at once.

Mixed, conflicted, and contradictory.

Hope floated around me, this bright, bright light at the end of a dark tunnel. Benjamin had struggled for so long, and now, he was getting his break. A bolster to his treatment. A buoy to his life.

And I'd gotten a job.

Relief billowed out at the thought.

A job that I needed terribly.

On top of that, it felt so good to be home with my parents, their love and support so strong within these walls that I felt as if I were walking around wearing a blanket of it.

But there was a dark blemish in the middle.

I could feel her hesitation before she tentatively asked, "So, how did it go? When you saw him?"

I shrugged as if it didn't matter when it mattered so much more than I wanted it to. "Probably better than I could have predicted."

"Really?" Faith's tone filled right up with surprise.

"Yep. Ran out of there as fast as I could. Fight or flight. I picked the flight. I'm thinkin' it was a good call."

Because the last thing I wanted to do was hash out the past with Maxon Chambers in front of the Broadshire Rim grocery store. If I thought news of our unlucky meeting had spread fast, that would have caught like a wildfire in the middle of a drought.

I could almost hear Faith's disapproval and worry.

"What?" I asked, chewing at my lip in discomfort.

"You know you can't ignore him forever."

"Why not?" Okay, of course, I knew. But procrastinating felt like a much safer option

"Because like I said, word travels fast."

Pricks of apprehension stung my skin, biting down.

Barbs of regret and fear.

It was loaded down by a mountain of old pain that I still had no clue how to deal with. Maybe I'd ignored it for too long. Locked it in that secret place and pretended it wasn't real.

The unfortunate part? That meant I'd been carrying it around forever. And it was always right there, lurking, threatening to break out. Accumulating in size.

I was terrified if I fully released it, let it out to run wild, it might just consume me.

Eat me alive.

Who was I kidding? It'd been eating me alive all along.

"I don't know what I'm supposed to do," I finally admitted, wisps of agony clotting my voice.

All these years, she and I had remained friends.

She, our friend Courtney who still lived in the area, and I had grown up thick. With each other every second that our parents would let us.

Over the years, I'd stayed closer with Faith, who had a quiet spirit I couldn't help but be drawn to.

Understanding.

A confidant I could trust with anything.

We'd communicated through emails and phone calls and Skype. She'd even been out to visit me once.

But I knew the burden it put on her shoulders.

That I'd asked so much of her.

Especially once she'd finally married her high school sweetheart, Jace, who just so happened to be one of Maxon's best friends.

"Are you askin' for my advice?" Her voice filled with playful speculation.

"I don't usually need to considerin' you're all too happy to dish it out," I returned, teasing her a little. She never hesitated to tell me like it was. Of course, she never judged me when I refused to agree.

"Don't pretend like you don't call me for that very reason."

"Well, that's because you're very wise," I shot back.

"I'm taking that as a compliment."

I couldn't help but smile. "As you should. You're kinda awesome."

She laughed, then sobered, waiting for me to catch up to the original question.

In contemplation, I twirled the end of my ponytail that had fallen over my shoulder. "Okay, fine, what do you think I should do?"

"I think you should tell him."

Right, right.

Just throw myself right off a bridge. My broken heart flailing out in front of me. No one there to catch it when it hit the raging water below and got lost in the waves of the river.

I'd barely been holding onto it, all along.

"And what then?" I asked, the words burning like a knife dragged up the inside of my throat.

"I don't have the answer to that, Izzy. That's a chance you're gonna have to take. And I know what he did to you was horrible. Horrible. I won't even try to make excuses for that. But he *is* a good man. I wouldn't be suggesting this if I didn't wholly believe that is the truth."

Anxiety hit me, so strong I felt some kind of attack coming on. Knowing she was right. Not wantin' her to be. My head shook fiercely. "How can I just. . . trust him like that?"

"You take a leap. It's the only thing any of us can do."

"I don't know if I can handle him hurting me any more." Grief rode out on the confession, those wounds gaping in a way they hadn't in a long, long time.

Because somehow . . . somehow it felt as if Maxon Chambers had once again gained the upper hand. My life held in his palms even when he shouldn't have any power.

"I know you don't believe it, but he's been hurtin', too," she murmured.

Of course, I knew it. That man had always bled pain. It was his biggest pitfall—his refusal to see that he could live outside of it. The belief that maybe my love could have been enough.

"I don't know if I'm ready," I said.

"You've been hiding for a long, long time, Izzy. Don't you think it's about time you freed yourself from the cell you've been locked in? You've let the past dim your light. You're one of the most brilliant, genuine, caring people I know, and you hide all of that behind your pain and fear. You can't fly if you're wearing chains."

Sorrow constricted my throat, making everything tight, my heart and my stomach and my skin. "And how do you stop being afraid of the one thing that can destroy you?"

"I don't know. Maybe you slay it."

five

IZZY
FOUR YEARS OLD

Fear crawled all over her, like ants were marching across her skin, bitin' everywhere they went. She hugged the limb tighter, so scared to let go, but the bark was rough and hard and it was gettin' harder and harder to hold on.

It hurt.

It hurt.

But it was gonna hurt way, way worse if she fell the rest of the way to the ground, and she was gonna get into so much trouble.

A breeze rustled through the trees, and the branch she was clinging to swished to the side.

Her eyes stung so bad, her tears hot where they were streaking down her cheeks, making her hair stick to her face.

Don't look down.

Don't look down.

"Help!" she cried out again, her throat hurting almost as bad as her arms from screaming for so long. "Please . . . someone help me! I want my mama!"

Her arms were shaking as bad as the leaves, and the tears were coming faster, her arms tired and weak.

Her daddy had told her she was gonna get a broken leg or a broken head the last time he'd found her climbing up and down, so, so mad, crying, too, and saying he'd never been so scared.

She'd promised she'd never, ever do it again.

But the tree—the tree was her favorite place.

"Help," she whimpered more, quieter this time. "I don't wanna be alone. Please. Someone help me."

Her stomach felt funny, like she was gonna throw up, the heat on her skin too hot and sticky, her head feeling light.

Her head flopped a little. Her hands started to slip, and she scrambled to get a better hold, before she was right back in the same position and slipping again.

She almost was giving up, letting go, because her daddy was down in his library and her mama had gone to the store and she was supposed to be in her bedroom playing with dolls and she'd been out there alone for so long.

No one was gonna find her.

"Please," she sniffled, the word not even reaching the air, knowing it was too late.

She thought her mind was gettin' lost in one of the faraway worlds she liked to make up when she saw movement at the edge of the yard. She frowned and tried to wipe her eyes on her shoulders without letting go of the tree.

It was a boy.

A boy who was running across her lawn, his hair like white flames where he sprinted across the yard beneath the bright summer sun.

His big brown shoes flopped as he ran, and he wasn't wearin' a shirt, just an old pair of ratty pants.

"Help," she shouted again, a rush of strength racing through her arms. "Help! Over here!"

He skidded to a stop beneath the tree and peered up at her. "You been yellin' up there? I could hear you all the way to my house."

Izzy's heart raced, more scared than she'd ever been, her arms close to slipping. "Yes, I need help. Go get my daddy. Hurry fast."

Except he wasn't running for the front door, he was starting to find his footing at the base of the tree. "Hold on, I'm gonna get you."

"You're not big enough."

He scoffed like that made him mad. "I'm plenty big enough. You want me to just leave you out here? You'll be nothin' but a splat of blood on those rocks if I don't get you right now."

She wailed at the sound of that. "Please don't let me be a splat of blood."

"I'm not gonna let you fall," he told her, his voice sounding like laughter, climbing higher and higher, propelling himself up with his hands and feet, so fast she thought he might be flying.

He made it all the way up to where she was, and he looped an arm around her waist and hauled her up so she could sit on a branch, freeing the weight from her arms. And it felt so good and hurt all over and she was crying again.

Relief.

She wanted to hug him and hug him and hug him.

"What you cryin' for, Little Bird?"

Hiccupping, she wiped the tears and the snot from her face. "Cuz I didn't wanna die. You saved me."

He laughed. "I wasn't gonna let you die, silly. I heard you, and I came running. That's all you gotta do. Just start yellin', and I'll know when you need me to save you."

She sniffled a little, a smile pulling to her face. "Okay. But what if you're not strong enough?"

Except, he seemed pretty strong. Maybe even stronger than her daddy. Brave to come rushing right up that tree like it was nothin'.

"Psh. What are you talkin' about? Don't you know I'm a dragon?"

He flexed his scrawny arms, his biceps the size of tangerines.

"A dragon?" she asked, curiosity making her eyes pinch.

"Dragons are the strongest and the fastest and the fiercest. So scary. Just like me. Except you don't gotta be afraid because I'm a good dragon. Even my mama says so."

"Okay," she agreed super fast because that sounded just fine to her.

Then he smiled softer. "Little Bird, Little Bird, stuck in a tree."

She giggled, her heart feeling light. "Dragon, dragon, come and rescue me."

He grinned so wide that she couldn't help but laugh again. "That's right. Just like that."

six

IZZY

"*Okay*, I'm off to go pick up Nana's medicine. I won't be long." I smacked a kiss to Benjamin's temple where he was eating a sandwich at the table, then leaned down to grip Dillon's adorable mouth at the sides, making a fishy face and pecking a kiss there, too.

He looked up at me with wide, worried eyes.

"Why does Nana need medicine?" he asked, face marring with a little frown.

"Because she's old," my mama hollered from where she was across the island, the woman grinning like the Cheshire as she whipped something in a big mixing bowl and poured the batter into a pan.

I tsked at her, not wanting her to go there.

Not when I felt as if I'd already lost thirteen years.

"You're not old. I'd call it aged to perfection."

Daddy chuckled where he was reading the paper at the table, his gray mustache dancing all over the place.

Yes, reading the paper that still got tossed onto his porch each mornin'.

The man was so old-fashioned, he still didn't own *one of those newfangled phones* as he liked to call them, and I'd had to call to get wifi installed before we moved out here, one of the reasons my account had dipped into the red.

Not that I expected them to jump through hoops or pay for the things I wanted. I was simply dumbfounded at how people managed to get by without it.

"Call it what you want. I still call it old," he grumbled with amusement.

"Daddy," I chastised, grabbing my purse from the island. "My mama is not old. And neither are you."

He shrugged. "What? You can't go on deluding yourself into believin' we're still young, Isabel. Have you seen this face?" He made a circle around his. "It's as cracked as the paint peeling on the walls. We were old enough to be your grandparents when you were born."

"Which was nothing but the Lord's blessing," my mama was quick to point out the way she always did.

They considered me a miracle baby. Mama had tried for years to get pregnant. She said when she'd finally given up, I'd decided to come along.

Daddy said it was because I was stubborn.

Mama said I'd come at exactly the perfect time.

"Well, I personally think you're as old as you feel."

"And I feel as old as the hills," Daddy said, taking a sip of his coffee and looking at me over the top of it, playfulness in his eyes.

"How old are the hills?" Dillon asked, coming over to climb onto the chair beside him.

I slung my purse over my shoulder. "Have fun with that one, Daddy. You asked for it."

I moved toward my Mama.

"What are you making?" I asked.

"Blueberry pie."

I stumbled a step, but somehow, I managed to keep it together, pasting a bright smile on my face as I continued toward her. "Oh, nice," I said because I sure wasn't gonna say anything else.

I popped up and kissed her on the cheek. "See ya."

Without saying anything else, I rushed for the kitchen archway, glancing at the clock, figuring I had plenty of time to get to the pharmacy.

Since it was Saturday, it closed at 1:00.

This was Broadshire Rim, after all. I wasn't gonna complain. I figured we were lucky there was a pharmacy.

Still, I didn't have time to dilly-dally.

Oh, crap.

Maybe I was gettin' old, too. Like I said, you were only as old as you felt.

I started through the archway when my mama's voice hit me from behind. "You know who loved blueberry pie."

It wasn't even a question.

Planned.

Purposed.

My mama nothin' but a sneak.

It stopped me in my tracks, and I paused to look at her from over my shoulder.

Okay, glare would be a more appropriate description, considering my eyes narrowed on her in offended disbelief.

She'd all but sang it where she was facing away at the counter as she spread the blueberry filling over the crust.

"Mama," I scolded, trying not to let any of that hurt I'd felt last night bubble up. To keep it down.

I'd decided for a little while, I just wanted to be. Let the boys adjust. I'd deal with Maxon soon. Hash it out. Wrap up our unfinished business and call it good.

If only it were that easy.

She glanced back at me. "Think you should invite him over for Sunday brunch."

"Are you crazy?" It was a gush of disbelief.

"I second that." My daddy waved his index finger in the air.

"Gotta happen sometime. Might as well happen over pie," she said.

My attention darted to my children, that protectiveness rising high, so big and full that my breaths started coming harder and faster.

"The last thing I want to do is have it out with that man over *pie*."

"Whatever you say." She hefted a single shoulder.

I humphed.

Mature, I knew. But I couldn't help but feel flustered. Redness crawling up my neck and landin' on my cheeks. It seemed this whole damned town was conspiring against me.

"I've got to go, we sure don't want you to die, you know, since you're old and all," I sang as I started back for the door, badgering her a bit.

Her laughter chased me out, along with her words, "Just think about it, Izzy Mae. You can't go on livin' hiding under your bed the way you did when you were a little girl."

Yeah, well inviting that man into it was the worst thing I'd ever done.

"Shoot," I whispered when my car sputtered and lurched.

Was this really happenin'?

My car chugged a little more, and I pushed down harder on the pedal, trying to coax it into action.

I tossed up a few silent prayers with it, too.

That was right when something dinged and a red light popped up on the dash and a dark cloud of smoke came billowing out of the hood.

"Oh, no, don't fail me now," I whispered under my breath, patting the dashboard. "Come on, just give me a little more."

It'd been a wonder my clunker had gotten us across the country in the first place. I'd been figuring the poor old girl was on her last leg, and I'd bargained a really nice washin' and a fresh quart of oil if she would get us out east safely.

Apparently, she thought her end of the bargain had been met because that was right when she up and decided she had no power left.

Because she was stalling out right there on the deserted road.

I was barely rolling forward, trying to at least coast off to the shoulder. My heart leapt in a jolt of fear when a car came speeding up behind me from out of nowhere, honking its horn as it flew into the other lane and whizzed by in a blur.

Like my breakin' down was doing him a major disservice.

Jerk.

I managed to get it all the way off to the side. At least I'd made it to the pharmacy in time, the little white bag with my mama's medicine sitting next to me on the seat.

I blew out a strained breath, thumbs tapping at the steering wheel as I contemplated.

The most logical thing would be to call a tow truck to get it fixed, but there wasn't enough left in the bank for that.

A little thread of worry needled my chest.

I needed this car to be working come Monday morning. Nelson Dentistry was twelve miles away, and it wasn't like there was a city bus or public transportation I could take. I could borrow my daddy's truck, but that would mean they would be left without a car.

That wasn't an option I was comfortable with.

Maybe . . . maybe I could fix it.

I gave myself a resolute nod. That was exactly what I was gonna do.

I fumbled around under the dash and pulled the latch, and I almost squealed with pride when I heard the hood pop. I got right into that thing without a hitch.

Point one, Izzy.

I pushed open the door to the sweltering heat, sweat instantly beading on my skin when I came into contact with the humid summer air. I was wishing just as fast that I wouldn't have chosen my heeled booties and a pair of fitted jeans when I'd gotten ready this morning. Carefully, I treaded the loose gravel in the three-inch heels, basically tiptoeing my way to the front of the car.

The front of the car where something was hissing like it was mad. A viper getting ready to strike.

A frown pulled to my brow, nerves rattling, and I hesitated for a second, looking around at my deserted surroundings. Nope, no help there.

Get it together, Izzy. You can do this.

It wasn't like the car was actually gonna bite me.

I fumbled around under the hood, quickly because it really was hot, and I thought it might just bite me after all.

I found the second latch and released it, the hood springing up with the smallest amount of force. It released another big plume of smoke, and I coughed and waved a hand in front of my face as it cleared.

When it was safe, I peered down at the engine and fiddled with a couple of hoses.

Problem was, I didn't have the first clue what I was looking at. Auto mechanics had never been one of my top priorities to learn.

I turned away, deciding I was going to have to suck it up and call a tow truck to take it to a shop. Maybe I could find one that would be willing to let me pay payments.

I couldn't be without transportation.

I started to head back to the driver's side to get my phone when I heard the roaring engine of an approaching car. I thought about stepping out and waving my hand to ask for help, but if it was anything like the last one that had passed, I'd be risking death, and I was so not in to playin' Russian Roulette.

I stepped farther away from the road, safely shielded by my car. I could hear it gettin' closer, coming up around the bend, hidden by the tall, skinny trees that flourished in this area.

Then that roaring shifted, and it quickly decelerated.

A siren blipped a warning.

Thank goodness, it was a cop.

I basically sprang out from behind the car when it eased off the road and came to a stop behind me.

Peek-a-boo.

I was sure I looked crazed, but I couldn't stop the smile that was splittin' my face, my arms from waving over my head as if they hadn't already seen me.

But that was just when I was realizing the cop that had come to a stop behind me wasn't just a cop.

The big white suburban with the severely tinted windows hiding the driver was unmarked. Nothing to indicate it was the authorities other than the flashing of the blue and red lights hidden in the fierce looking grill.

My mind was suspecting it was some kind of detective, while my heart was screaming out that I was getting ready to face down my worst nightmare.

Nerves rushed and sped and careened, my heart skipping beats, but that really didn't matter since it was speeding so fast.

Plenty of blood flow.

Unfortunately, all of it was flooding from my head, and I was hit with a rush of dizziness.

My breaths got shorter and raspier as the driver cracked open the door. A boot landed on the gravel, then another.

Awareness spiked. It was nothing but this crazy, frantic energy that sizzled across my skin. And the worst part of it all was how familiar that it was.

An old embrace that might as well have been a smack to the face.

Those boots moved out from behind the door, and it slammed shut.

And there he was, standing beneath the bright sun.

Maxon Chambers.

Need and attraction and the love I'd tried to squash underfoot whipped around me. A vicious summer storm in a cloudless sky.

Looking at him today wasn't any easier than seeing him the first time three days ago.

He took a step forward, and I swore, I could feel the planets shift their orbit.

Or maybe they'd shifted the second I'd crossed state lines.

Our destinies had always felt dependent on the other, though I'd never imagined it'd twist our paths up quite like this.

We had come alive in the other. A million mismatched pieces strewn between us that had magically fit.

Still, I knew he was more dangerous than any casual passerby could ever be. Dangerous to me. To my heart and my world and everything that remained the most precious.

"Maxon," I whispered, unable to stop myself. I twined my fingers together in front of me.

No place to run or hide.

"Izzy." He looked between me and my car that had gone caput. "You havin' trouble?"

I didn't think he had the first clue what kind of trouble I was in.

I gave him a tight nod. "I don't know what's wrong with it. It was running just fine, and then it seemed like it overheated."

A dose of amusement rode into his expression, one stark brow lifting in speculation. "It was running just fine? Are you sure about that? If seeing you drive off a few days ago was any indication, this thing hasn't been running *just fine* for a long time."

A smirk ticked up at one side of his mouth, that easy sexuality he'd worn like a brand making a resurgence.

My knees wobbled.

"Well, I had to rely on her to get me all the way back out here, so I can't blame her too much." I lifted my chin. Why I felt the need to stick up for my crappy car, I didn't know, but the last thing I wanted was this man to be judging me.

Maxon smiled a little more, tipping his head to the side, the guy so gorgeous it should have been a crime. "She?"

A little huff blew through my lips. "Of course, it's a she. She's a caretaker. I've been relying on her to get me around for years. Yours looks like a brute." Why in the world was I talking to him this way? Nothing but an easy conversation.

"That so?" More amusement was riding out of him, that urgency from a few days ago gone.

Like seeing each other this way was . . . normal.

Expected.

He started coming closer, a rough chuckle tumbling out, hitting me square in the chest.

Hit after hit.

There went that easiness. Blown out of the water by the magnitude of his presence.

“Mmhmm,” I managed to mumble.

He’d always been unbearably tall.

But now he seemed . . . massive.

Imposing.

Foreboding in an arrogant, powerful way.

Drippin’ with all that danger and peril that he’d warned me he was capable of.

Too bad I hadn’t listened.

“Well, I didn’t have much choice in the matter. Government issued.” He shrugged a bulging shoulder. It gave a little flop to his blond hair that was cropped at the sides and longer on top. “I guess they thought it was a perfect fit.”

God, this man. I fidgeted, trying to take a step back. Last thing I needed to do was go and get hypnotized, his nearness some kind of mesmerizing drug.

Face so deliciously rugged, his chiseled jaw coated in at least three days of scruff. I had the stupid urge to reach out and scratch my nails through it. To touch him the way I used to do.

But it was hard to stop my mind from traveling that direction. The man a fantasy I’d tucked away that had manifested as whole.

Every inch of that big body was packed with tight, rippling muscle, both arms completely covered in colors and designs that danced with a story I wasn’t close enough to read.

Still, there was something about it that felt as if he had peeled off his layers.

A book sitting wide open to confess his sins.

Maxon tipped his head, mischief playing out in those eyes, and I realized my mouth was hanging open, drool probably running out the side.

Oh god.

He’d caught me checking him out.

Could this get any worse?

Redness flushed, and everything heated, and I swiped at the dampness that gathered above my lip as he was stopping a foot away from me.

"Hot out here, isn't it?" he asked, something arrogant swimming in the depths of those blue eyes, the icy, vast color of a glacier tinged by the sea.

"Very."

Those plush, full lips twisted into the softest smile, his demeanor jumping from one extreme to the next.

Remorse and regret and affection. Things I was sure I wasn't ready to see.

"Izzy," he murmured, and his hand was reaching out. Like . . . like he was gonna touch me.

Panic sent me stumbling back, my eyes going wide. I splayed my hands out over my chest as if it could protect me.

He huffed out a frustrated sound and sliced his fingers through his hair, looking away for a beat before he was turning that powerful gaze back to me. "How have you been?"

Bitter laughter came rushing up my throat. I tried to hold it back, but there were some things you couldn't keep contained. "Are you really askin' me how I've been?"

He winced, but he didn't drop his gaze. "Yeah, I am." He edged forward a little, stealing my breath.

I tried to shield myself from it, but there I was, sucking down his aura.

An intoxicating cocktail of the woods and the sea.

All man.

All sex.

"As if you really care." God, I hated sounding petulant. Carrying around this chip on my shoulder. But he'd cracked me, left that gaping cavern right through the middle of me that throbbed and ached.

There hadn't been an ounce of me that hadn't believed in him. In his love. In his devotion.

Him throwing that away had only made it hurt all the worse.

A weighted sigh blew from his mouth, and he was slowly shaking his head, and still he wouldn't let me free of the trap of his stare. "I do, Izzy. I fucking do, and I shouldn't, but if you think I haven't been worried about you all these years, wondering how you were and where you were and who you'd become, then you're wrong."

"You never even crossed my mind."

Oh nice, Izzy. You are officially thirteen.

Amusement came riding back to his striking face. "Not even once, huh?"

"Nope."

Lies, lies, lies.

He knew it, too.

Because those lips were twisting up, all sorts of smug and far too playful. As if we were the oldest of friends, and he didn't mind if we sparred.

Ripping myself from the trance, I stepped back and hugged myself tighter, needing to get away from the draw of this man.

Or maybe I was just trying to hold back my heart that was trying to make a break for it, climbing a rib and getting ready to swing from a wayward rope.

Just another foolish, deadly jump.

"Listen, Maxon, I really need to get back to my mama and daddy's. I picked up my mama's medicine in town, and she's waiting for it. Is there any way you could take a look or maybe call me a tow truck that can take it to a shop where they might let me make payments?"

I really didn't want to be asking him for any favors, but what else was I supposed to do?

His expression both softened and hardened with worry.

But that wasn't what I wanted.

His worry.

Him thinking he needed to swoop in and save the day the way he always had.

It was far too late for that.

"Izzy," he started to say, and I put up a hand.

"About what happened the other day . . . it was no big deal. I didn't keep close track of my account when I was traveling, and I spent a little more on gas than I'd first thought. It was no big deal.

You don't have to worry."

He grabbed the wrist of the hand I had put in his face.

A gasp ripped from my lungs, and flames licked up my arm.

Hotter than the sun.

I was staggered by it, unable to do anything but get lost in the ferocity that blazed from him. "I do worry," Maxon gritted.

I managed to pry my wrist away, hugging it close, the burn too real.

"I do worry," he muttered again, shifting in discomfort, as if he was beggin' me to believe him.

I couldn't reply, all the words and confessions locked up inside, so heavy they were close to making me choke. Pain brimming and lapping and rising to cut off the flow of oxygen.

Finally, he tore his attention away, looking into the distance before turning back to me. "I'm just . . . let me take a look at your car," he seemed to settle on. He moved over to my car and tucked himself under the hood, while I just stood there, staring at him from behind.

Hating the pull he had on me.

Or maybe I was just really hating the way his snug jeans hugged his ridiculous butt.

I mean, the man was *ridiculous*.

Heck, I could probably snag a picture of that and post it up on my Instagram and get two-hundred thousand new followers.

Show him off like some kind of trophy.

The real problem was that I'd always wanted to keep him for myself.

I bit down on my lip as I watched him fiddle. He was muttering under his breath, wiggling some wires, before he planted both hands on the frame and glanced back at me.

That striking face pulled up into something that looked far too close to affection, and it made my mind twirl its way into stupid things.

It only made it worse when his lips twisted up at one side, something about it so sweet.

"I think I might be able to get this started for you."

"Are you serious?" I might have clapped in excitement. But

could you blame a girl? I needed this car fixed, and I didn't have a lot of resources to make it happen. Beggars couldn't be choosers.

A rough chuckle left him, and he roughed a hand over his face, leaving a bit of grease on his forehead.

God, why was that so sexy?

"Glad I can get you worked up so easily."

I bit down on my bottom lip, praying it would stop another rush of blood from rising to my cheeks.

Oh, if he only knew.

"If you were thinking you were gonna have to hike it ten miles in the heat and these heels, you'd get worked up, too." I managed to get it out, as if talking with him was no big deal.

"You sure that's what's working you up?"

Okay, there it went. That flush breaking free, climbing my throat and splashing on my cheeks like evidence of impure thoughts.

Maxon laughed, and then reached out and casually squeezed my forearm. I gave it my best to keep my pulse from completely stampeding out of control.

No such luck.

"I'll be right back. Let me grab some tools," he said before he sauntered back to his SUV, the guy eating up the ground as if he owned it, going all the way to the tail end.

And I stood there hugging myself and gnawing at my lip.

Contemplating.

Taken by how he maybe seemed . . . different.

More mature.

Less bitter.

He'd always been cocky, but now he oozed confidence.

As if maybe he'd risen above the horrible things that had held him back. My heart of hearts told me that was what had come between us.

The problem was, he'd allowed it to. Had chosen to believe the lies instead of the truth, cast me aside so easily when it seemed like the easiest thing to do.

I'd had to believe he'd hurt me because he didn't know anything else but pain. But that in no way excused what he'd done, either.

And there I was, back to asking the same question I'd asked Faith.

How would I ever know?

A minute later, he was back, a toolbox opened on the ground, hands swift and adept and rough, and I was getting hit again with a rush of chills.

Like a fool, I was standing there imagining what those hands might feel like gripping my hips.

Oh God, Izzy, don't go there. No matter what happened, that was not a path we'd be repeating.

But it was hard to ignore those old feelings that were begging to be acknowledged.

Dark blond hair flopped across his brow that was lined in concentration, a bead of sweat dripping down his temple, and those muscles flexing with strength as he worked to get a bolt tightened back in its place.

"Why don't you give it a whirl?" he rumbled, not looking back, still fiddling with something under the hood.

I rushed for the driver's seat as quickly as I could in these stupid shoes, thankful for the distraction. Sliding in, I inhaled deeply and told myself again that this was all gonna turn out okay.

Holding my breath, I turned over the ignition, reminding the heavens that I did, in fact, believe in miracles.

I had two of them waiting for me at home.

It chugged but didn't start.

Dang it.

"Hold on one sec," he shouted.

I waited, my knee anxiously bouncing.

Metal clanked before he called, "Try it again."

I turned the key, and the engine squealed before it chugged and rumbled to life.

Air escaped my lungs on a shot of relieved, disbelieving laughter.

He did it.

Oh my gosh, he did it.

All of that excitement and gratitude came bubbling over, and maybe I should have stayed in the car where it was safe, but I left it idling and pushed back out so I could thank him.

I stumbled to a stop when I came around the front.

Maxon had his arms stretched overhead so he could grab the hood to slam it down.

Masculinity radiated from him as if it possessed its own lifeforce.

This raw, potent sexuality that glowed beneath the sun.

Then he went and lifted his shirt to wipe the sweat off his forehead.

My eyes dropped, sight filling full of nothing but rippling, defined abs, as chiseled as that face, and it was my own stomach that was clenching.

Oh my God. Men shouldn't be allowed to be that alluring. It made common sense go flying out the window.

He dropped his shirt, and he actually had the nerve to smirk when he caught me staring.

I dropped my gaze just as fast.

"Thank you so much, Maxon . . . this is amazin'." I managed to give him my thanks while my entire being was itching to run. Or maybe what I was really itching to do was reach out and touch him.

He leaned down and gathered his tools, latched the lid of the box, and pushed to his full, towering height.

It cast me in his shadow.

A hedge of protection.

"Glad I could get it running, but that fix is only temporary. You need to get it into a shop and do it soon, or you're going to find yourself stranded on the side of the road again."

"Right," I agreed with my mouth, calculating how many paychecks it might take to be able to pay for it.

Agitation coming on, I hesitated, tapping my foot when I tentatively asked, "Any idea how much it might cost?"

He sighed, roughed a hand over his jaw. "Thinking . . . four hundred. Maybe five. You're going to need some new parts. I have a friend I can get in touch with . . . might be able to pull in a favor."

I probably shouldn't be taking favors from Maxon Chambers.

But was I really gonna be bitter enough to turn down that offer?

"That would be really nice."

He smiled. Smiled one of his soft, tender smiles. The one that moved through my senses like a cool breeze after he'd heated me up with everything else. "I'd be happy to."

"Thank you, again. Honestly, I don't know what I would have done if you didn't find me out here."

"Hoof it in those heels for ten miles?" A playful grin worked itself onto his lush mouth, that dimple showing up in his cheek just to make my life a little more miserable.

Gentle laughter rippled out, unstoppable, and I was chewing at my lip again, trying with all of me to keep from goin' soft.

We just stood there staring for a minute, gazes tangled, our tongues holding back so many words.

So much time had passed, and the mistakes littered between us were almost palpable, nothing but mountains and cliffs and caverns. Was there any chance we could find common ground?

I pushed out a sigh and shook myself from the thoughts. "I really should get going. Thank you, again."

Why was it so hard to walk away from him?

Don't do this, Izzy. Don't let your heart get wrapped up in him. It isn't a safe place.

"All right. I'll give you a call on Monday. Let you know when I talk to Dalton. He owns a shop in Charleston. Your parents still have the same number?"

I laughed out a small laugh. "Um, yeah. Neither of them even have a cell phone."

Something wistful pulled across his face. "Why doesn't that surprise me?"

I just shook my head, fighting the grin that felt more dangerous than anything.

"Hope they're doing well, Izzy. Just like I hope you are, too." He started to walk around me, and then paused, right there, looking at me from the side, though I could see the way his thick throat was bobbing in unease.

"Can't believe you're here. Never thought I'd get the chance to say sorry to you. For what I did. For being a coward. But I want you to know, I've thought about you every single day. *Every single day.* Every single one of them was spent praying that you were okay. That you were happy. Know it doesn't make up for anything, but I need you to know that."

His words were raw—grating—the pain coming from them almost knocking me to my knees.

Emotion fisted in my throat, and I couldn't say anything, only gave him a tight nod and tried not to breathe him in as he offered me another apologetic smile and started for his SUV.

Panic built up in me the farther he got away.

"Maxon," I shouted before I could stop myself.

He paused, his shoulders going rigid as he swiveled to look back at me.

"You want to come for lunch tomorrow?"

A frown of surprise pulled all over his face.

"I think there are some things we need to talk about," I said.

"You want to talk to me?" He sounded shocked.

"Yeah," I told him.

His frown deepened, and I quickly added, "My mama is making blueberry pie."

That was all it took to have an affected smile ticking up at one side of those lips. "My favorite."

I gave another nod.

Awareness spun between us, a storm that churned and spiraled and sucked me right in, the way it'd always been. What I needed to remember was that nothing would be the same.

"I'd love that," he said.

"All right, I'll see you tomorrow at one."

I climbed into my car, soul crashing against my ribs. I sucked in the deepest breath and pulled out onto the road, hoping beyond hope that I wasn't making a huge mistake.

seven

MACK

You had to wonder why some asshole always went and ruined your day.

Especially when I was in the middle of one that had sparked a hope in me unlike anything I'd felt in a long, long time. Izzy just . . . standing in front of me and making me feel like everything could turn out right. Helped a bit that she'd invited me over for her mama's blueberry pie.

She might as well have been passing me an olive branch.

But that's just the way life went, wasn't it?

You had to take the good with the bad.

And when you were a cop, you spent your life taking on a whole lot of the bad.

Proof of that was I was more than halfway home, minding my own business, when a car came blazing out of a side street just as I was making it back into Charleston.

My attention whipped that way, watching as a late model BMW blew the stop sign coming out of a neighborhood, fishtailing as it hit the main road.

They gunned it going the opposite direction.

Doing about double the speed limit.

Switching on my lights and siren, I flipped a U in the road. Could feel my skin getting sticky, hit with the unsettled feeling I got whenever things weren't quite right.

An intuition that had saved my ass more times than I could count.

I grabbed my radio. "Detective Chambers, lights and sirens, pursuing late model BMW. Requesting back up." I rattled off the license plate and my location. I got confirmation, and I floored it, the big engine of my Suburban roaring.

The white car in front of me swerved in and out of the lane, flying by two cars, not giving a fuck that he might be putting someone in danger.

Nothing I hated more than that.

My eyes narrowed, and my heart thudded harder. Was this asshole trying to outrun me? With my siren going, the two cars pulled off to the side to let me by, and I got right up on the car's tail.

Could tell he was thinking about it. Itching to push his car as fast as it would go.

Run.

I edged an inch closer, letting him know I'd be all too happy to chase him down.

Finally, he flipped on his signal, put on his brakes, and pulled off to the side of the road. I came up right behind him, adrenaline a thunder in my veins.

I'd been in this line of work long enough to smell the stench of trouble from a hundred miles away. And it was just emanating from this asshole.

Actually, four of them. Could see the car was filled, two in the front and two in the back.

Unease stirred, and I waited until the plates read clean, then stepped out of my truck into the overbearing heat. Sweat instantly slicked my flesh, and my guts twisted up in a sick sort of anticipation, at the ready for anything.

Was wearing my typical uniform—jeans and a tee and boots and my gun strapped to my side.

Never mattered if I was on duty or not. I was ready to go.

Could almost see the four kids sitting in the car gettin' antsy over that shit, looking in the mirrors, squirrelling in their seats, anxiety coming from that white metal like it'd been painted with it.

If I didn't already know I had a prick on my hands, he only sealed the deal when I got up to the side of the car and he still had his window rolled up. With the heel of my fist, I banged on it.

Reluctantly, he finally rolled it down, arrogance coming out of the inside as thick as the heatwaves sagging in the sky. My gaze swept the car, taking in the four guys that I pegged at around twenty. They weren't dressed much different than any other guy I'd come across on the streets.

It was what was underneath those layers that got to me. Something sleazy oozing from their skin that cued me in that they were up to no good.

"Problem, officer?" The driver's tone dripped with sarcasm, brow lifting like it was me with the issue rather than the other way around.

Had half an inclination to reach through the window and take him by the collar. Let him know exactly what the problem was. But I played by the books as best as I could, and this punk wasn't even close to being worth my ass getting dragged into the sergeant's office.

"Considering you were doing sixty in a thirty and blew through a stop sign, I'd say there is."

He scoffed out a laugh. "Sixty? I think your radar must be off. Wasn't doin' more than . . . thirty. Max. You can ask my friends." He almost laughed when he said it, glancing in the rear-view mirror at the two guys in the back, sketch written all over them, carload of twitchy motherfuckers with their knees bouncing a million miles a minute.

"Yeah, no chance were we going any faster than that," one of the guys in the back spouted, head bobbing so fast I wasn't sure how it didn't snap off.

"That so?" I returned, wondering if they actually thought that was reason enough for me to let them go.

"That's so." It was nothing but a sneer from the driver.

"Not what my radar said."

My head swiveled as I leaned closer, taking in the interior of the car, hunting for anything that might give me a reason to search it.

Gut telling me they were dirty.

Interior was clean, no bags or paraphernalia sitting out. Nothing that should raise any suspicion that this was anything more than a normal traffic stop.

"Where you coming from?" I asked, voice low and controlled, hinting at a growl.

"Pretty sure that's none of your damned business." This from the driver. I kinda wanted to pop him in the mouth.

A rough chuckle left me. "You been drinking? Doing drugs?"

"Do I look like I've been drinking?" Instantly, this kid was combative. Hated to say that I'd expected it, but I had, not surprised at all to find that feeling creeping up and taking hold.

"License and registration," I grated low.

A disgruntled sigh left him. "That really necessary?"

"Wasn't asking so I could find out the color of your eyes. Think you could do as you were asked, or do you need to step out of the car?"

Defiance blazed from his expression, but he finally reached across the console when he saw the cruiser marked with Police roll up behind my truck.

I kept my eyes focused as he opened the glovebox, watching for anything it might expose.

Nothing stuck out in there, either.

"Be right back. Don't go anywhere, yeah?" I warned.

I went back to my SUV to do a search after he handed both

over.

Zachary Keeton.

My computer screen populated with a slew of driving-related tickets, mostly speeding and two for reckless driving.

Shocker.

Only thing even remotely criminal was an arrest for misdemeanor theft.

No outstanding warrants.

Even though my gut was telling me these four were involved in something bigger, I was left with no option other than to write him a ticket. I moved back to his window and handed it to him.

"Drive safe."

He snatched it out of my hand, a smirk taking over his face. "I'll do my best."

I stood there and watched him pull back onto the street, fighting the sick feeling in my gut. Shouting that I should do something more. That these guys were vile and corrupt. But sometimes I had to let things go. Accept I couldn't fix everything. It just sucked when you knew something seedy was right under your nose.

"Where have you been my whole life, handsome?"

I grinned, happy to hear the familiar voice. I needed a distraction for the uncontrolled energy, my emotions in shambles. Too excited for my own damn good, and that old worry trying to steal itself a winning spot after it was supposed to be long dethroned.

I tossed my attention over to Mirena who stood at the head of the table where I was sitting in my regular booth at Monty's.

It was the same question she asked me every single time I came in, which was more often than was probably prudent to admit.

"Lookin' for you, gorgeous. What else would I be doing here?" I said, giving her my same response as well.

Nothing sexual about it.

Hell, Ian had hit that up before he'd settled down with Grace, so I sure as hell wouldn't have gone there even if I wanted to, anyway.

I didn't. Never had.

She was just . . . cool and sweet and playful, so I always played right back.

Made our favorite bar feel a little bit more like home.

Of course, my little excursion tonight was sans Jace and Ian. Assholes had better places to be. Like actually *at home*. Couldn't exactly fault them for that.

Didn't mean that it didn't bother me just a bit that I was sitting there alone. It was moments like these that made me wish that maybe I had more.

More than just living my life for the job. But I knew better than asking for more than that. I'd committed myself to making the world a better place after being a part of the problem for so long.

It was all I had to offer.

All I had to give.

My life was dangerous, and my mind was fucked up.

Soul bent.

Besides, I was the one who'd chosen to be a cop. Wasn't fair to ask a woman to be okay with that, too, never knowing if I'd make it home at the end of the day.

On top of that? Only woman I'd wanted waiting for me was Izzy. And fuck, I wanted her. Wanted her in a way that just wasn't rational. Just as bad as I had then.

Maybe more considering now I knew what it felt like to have to live without her.

So, there I sat, all spun up, craving something I knew full well I shouldn't take, knowing I couldn't risk getting involved with her again, and pretty much planning to take a bite out of her, anyway.

Mirena smiled one of her playful smiles. She'd been a waitress here for about as long as I'd been coming around.

She lifted a brow, gossip written into her expression. "Tell me all about what case you're working on right now. You trackin' down a murderer or a drug dealer or busting up some major crime family? I want all the gory details."

A light chuckle rumbled out, and I scratched at the stubble coating my jaw as I sat back in the booth, slanting her a smile. "Now why would you want me to go and drag you into my mess?"

Something wry tipped up at the corner of her mouth. "Oh, I'm pretty sure just about any girl this side of the pacific would be happy for you to drag her into your *mess.*" She waved an indulgent hand behind her. "Look at all these ladies . . . every single one of them who isn't here with someone has clocked you."

I laughed and took a sip of my beer. "Hardly."

"You just keep telling yourself that, big guy." She rubbed my shoulder, the way she always did, nothing to it, but that didn't mean I couldn't feel the ripple of jealousy that suddenly shocked through the dense, hazy air.

Anger surging, scratching its way through the atmosphere.

Bitter unease clawed inside of me, and I glanced to the side of Mirena in time to catch Clarissa pushing through the thick crowd, hips swaying from side-to-side, long, dark hair flowing all around her.

Tension knotted my shoulders, and I blew out a heavy gush of air that was nothing but guilt and remorse.

Last thing I wanted to deal with tonight was Clarissa.

Mirena followed my gaze, almost wincing when she saw her striding our way. All the easiness she'd been wearing earlier vanished.

Suffice it to say Mirena wasn't exactly Clarissa's biggest fan.

"Just let me know if you need anything else. I'll get out of your way."

She backed away, and a lithe body dressed in black leather pants and a flimsy white blouse that exposed one shoulder slipped into the booth next to me.

Clarissa sent me one of her coy, sexy smiles, like she was expecting me to be happy to see her waltzing in like this.

All sexpot mouth and curvy hips.

"Clarissa," I said, not having the first clue what I was supposed to say. Not after this week. Not after seeing Izzy twice.

Guilt climbed my throat. No. Not because I was doing Clarissa some wrong by going to Izzy's tomorrow and, like a fool, praying it led to somewhere good.

It was sitting there wondering what Izzy would think if she saw her snuggled up to my side.

"Hi, baby," she purred.

I cringed, hating when she called me that. More than ever tonight.

Not when it felt like everything I knew as my normal had been knocked to the right. Thrown off-balance.

Blood pounding with the need to get inside a tight, warm body. To feel hands on my skin. A mouth moving with mine.

To give a big middle finger to all the bullshit and questions and sum of my past, and go after the one thing in the world that had ever made me feel like I could be a better man. The person who had *made* me a better man, even when that better would never be good enough.

And it definitely wasn't Clarissa that fit that bill.

But that was my fault, wasn't it?

I'd used her just as badly as she'd used me. But I couldn't seem to stop torturing myself by going to her again and again.

Nothing but a bad reminder of every mistake I'd made.

Like I felt this intrinsic need to keep one foot firmly planted in the past.

"Where have you been?" she asked, words a flirty pout. As flirty as her hand that was suddenly squeezing my upper thigh. "I've missed you."

I shifted an inch away.

"I've been busy."

She tittered out a laugh. Everything about her was seductive. But it was the kind of seduction you knew would strike you in the end.

The girl looked like a viper.

Her bite just as deadly.

"Tell me you're not sittin' here saying you've been too busy for me? That's not very nice," she cooed, like she actually thought she was cute.

I hesitated, warring, unrest growing stronger.

How the hell was I supposed to handle her?

Thing was, I had to. No chance was I going over to Izzy's tomorrow when I had this hanging over my head.

Didn't want to be a dick, but it's not like what Clarissa and I had was hearts and flowers.

We were nothing but grudges and shame.

I blew out a sigh, scrubbed a hand over my face.

She laughed a bitter sound, her voice mocking. "Tell me you're kidding."

A frown pulled to my brow. "Didn't say anything."

She shook her head, and a smirk was curling at the corner of her mouth. "Don't even pretend like you weren't getting ready to say what you were getting ready to say. I know you better than anyone else."

Bullshit.

But I didn't argue with her. Figured she was due her anger.

"You and I both know this is going nowhere," I told her, voice just loud enough so she could hear me over the din in the bar.

She squeezed my thigh tighter, face coming up close to mine. "So what you're telling me is you want to take this somewhere?"

I reached under the table and pried her hand away. "No, Clarissa. This can't happen anymore. Never should have happened in the first place."

She was the worst mistake I'd ever made.

Her expression turned into something smug, hurt and defiance just showing underneath. "Should we count the number of times you've told me that before?"

She leaned in closer, her lips almost touching mine. "And you always, always come crawling back."

"Not this time," I grated. Disgust billowed, my regret thicker than the air in the dingy bar. Suffocating and dark.

She laughed a derisive sound. "You're so adorable. No wonder all these fools think you're so sweet and innocent. But I know better than that, don't I?"

Anger surged through my veins.

"Stick to your own kind." My father's reproach rang in my ear like the imprint of a bad dream. Funny how I hated every fucking word

that had come out of that bastard's mouth, and somehow, I'd taken that one thing as wisdom.

Seeing Izzy had me wondering if I'd had it all wrong. If maybe things had been different.

I angled down, getting in her face, making her rock back an inch. "I'm not fucking around, Clarissa. This ends now. Both of us deserve better than what the other has to offer."

Her dark eyes danced. Fucking feeding from the turmoil.

She slid out of the booth, but she leaned over the table, a hand on my chest as she dipped down. Our noses brushed as she whispered, "No, Mack, you and I both deserve exactly what we have to offer . . . nothing." She ran a fingertip down my cheek. "And you and I both know it'll only take a little bit of time before your back begging for it. You might have the rest of this city fooled, but remember, I know who you are."

"I was seventeen," I told her through clenched teeth.

"And you think that changes anything? You're still the same guy, and I'm still the same girl. Don't ever forget that. You belong to me, and you always will."

She straightened, all that sex rolling from her in waves, her hips swishing as she turned, casting me a look from over her shoulder. "See you around, Mack Boy."

A disturbance rustled through my senses. Moaning from within. The reminder of who I'd been.

And I wondered if I had any chance of escaping him.

I let myself into the sweeping darkness of my small house. It was in an older neighborhood in Charleston, mostly families and retired couples. That same silence bounded back, and all the questions I'd been hearing earlier came at me tenfold after running into Clarissa.

Wasn't like that had been a surprise.

It was our normal rendezvous.

Another fucking mistake.

I let the door drop closed behind me, and I blew out a heaving sigh as I walked into the main room that housed the living room and kitchen. The original walls that separated the two rooms had been knocked out to create a more modern vibe when I'd had this place remodeled.

What I'd wanted it to be, I didn't know.

A fucking home? Only thing it'd turned out to be was a place to sleep.

I tossed my keys to the island, trying to pull myself out of the funk I was getting sucked into, and went over to the refrigerator and grabbed a beer. I twisted the cap and flicked it into the garbage, and I drew in a long breath as I leaned back on the counter.

I looked toward the ceiling like it might hold some answers. A direction. Maybe in the texture was one of those secret mazes that led to a hidden clue, or maybe it was one of those pictures of Jesus that suddenly popped out and spoke to you.

God knew, seeing Izzy again felt like some kind of biblical miracle.

Or maybe it was just karma teasing me again with what I could never have.

Was I really going to let Clarissa continue to influence me?

Heaving out a sigh, I drained the rest of my beer, threw the bottle in the recycle, and walked out of the kitchen to the hallway that led to the back of the house.

I passed by the one guest bedroom on the right, then followed the hall as it made a ninety-degree turn to the left where the two additional bedrooms ran along the very back.

The first one I used as an office, and the second was the master.

Opening one side of the master's door, I flicked on the light. Basically, the entire house had needed to be gutted when I'd purchased it, new floors and new paint and new fixtures.

I crossed the room and went into the restroom at the back. It was all white cabinets and chrome fixtures and black accents.

I brushed my teeth and shrugged out of my tee and jeans, tossed those into the hamper.

Routine.

Exhausted, I made my way back out and climbed into my bed.

My very huge, very empty bed.

I flopped onto my back.

Excitement and dread warred inside of me. This feeling that I was coming up on something good. Worry was if I was going to taint it. Ruin it the only way I seemed to know how to do.

I tossed, trying to get comfortable, then tossed to the other side.

Yeah, sleep was not gonna happen.

It was going to be a long damn night.

Sitting up at the side, I flicked on the lamp and opened the drawer on my nightstand.

A mangle of emotions surged from that dark place hidden within. Grief and regret. I rarely let myself visit it, but tonight, I couldn't resist.

I squeezed my eyes closed for a beat before I pulled out the flimsy book that had been bound with twine, the pages made of a thick tan parchment, cut at haphazard angles.

Completely handmade.

The cover was cardboard that had been covered in more of that parchment. It was the drawings on the front that had gotten to me most.

A black dragon had been sketched like it was perched on the spine, and images of a young man were interwoven in the shiny, scaly tapestry with peeks of the sky and a volcano in the background.

Gorgeous and crude.

Agony settled over me.

The loss radiating. Screaming out from my insides. What I would never reclaim. A life I would never be able to save.

My whole childhood I'd pretended I was a dragon. Hell, I'd claimed it, insisting the truth of it to my mother and anyone else who would listen.

She'd nod along, tell me I was the best, fiercest dragon in the world, laughing under her breath as she'd shake her head.

I'd thought she thought it was silly. Nothing. Or maybe that she hadn't even listened or understood me in any way.

But then I'd found the book with my name scrawled on the inside in the shed near her things when I'd cleaned it out that last time. Like she'd left me a message. Words when she no longer had the power to speak.

And it'd spoken to me.

It was the day I'd turned my back on my past and made the decision to become who I was today.

Inside, it was filled with a story that was simple and profound and had always felt like my mother had left me a message.

This was a fantasy about a barn boy close to becoming a man. He'd been sent to slay a dragon to earn his right in the castle, only to find the dragon close to death, left with a stab wound from a knight who'd already come to do the deed.

The boy had nursed it back to health, and in the process, they'd found something in the other. A missing piece. An understanding. A realization that things weren't always as they seemed.

They'd become united. A team who'd sought out the treachery of the king who'd sent the boy in the first place.

I flipped it open to a spot at the end where the dragon had been injured again in the last battle that had brought everything to a head.

> *"Go, earn your right. Finish what you were sent to do," The Dragon rasped. Its body heaved with great lurches of pain, the wound at its side gaping as its blood spilled onto the mountain floor, running down like a red river twisting through the towering trees.*
>
> *Teno shook his head. "No. I won't leave you."*
>
> *"Go. There is nothing left for you to do here. There is nothing to gain. Prove who you are. Inside. You've already proven it to me."*
>
> *Teno looked at his truest friend. The one who was to be his enemy. A vile creature to be left as dust and ash. Teno grabbed him by the ears, dragging him close.*
>
> *Black eyes stared back, ridged in flames and surrounded by ire. But held within was eternity. "I will not leave you, my friend. We fight. We fight together. It is you who will earn your right."*

The Dragon's black eyes deepened, and it struggled to climb to its feet. Massive and unsightly. The most beautiful thing ever seen. It nudged Teno with his snout, and Teno pressed his cheek to the fire that burned from within. He ran his palm down his coarse neck. "It's you who will earn your right."

I guessed it was this passage that always made me wonder exactly who it was I was fighting for.

eight

IZZY

I glanced at the clock.

Only for the three-thousandth time this morning. In the last twenty times I'd checked, only two minutes had passed.

Goodness.

I was gonna drive myself right out of my mind.

Needing a distraction, I lifted the lid off the pot and poked at the boiling potatoes with a fork, trying to breathe around my heart that had ridden all the way up into my throat.

Or maybe it was actually floating outside of me, like a child who was misbehavin' and wouldn't do what it was told and sit still.

All night it'd been fluttering, wings wayward and wild, my night spent tossing in my bed, wondering if I'd made the worst mistake of my life.

Inviting that man to my house.

Could I be ripping myself open any wider?

Just begging for him to reach out and punch in a few new holes. Apparently, there weren't enough already.

"Would you stop it?" my mama scolded softly from where she was putting the freshly-baked biscuits in a basket.

"Stop what?" I asked, wiping my sweaty hands on the back of my pants.

Erasing the evidence.

She huffed out a dubious sound. "You've been flitting around this kitchen like a loon the entire morning. You might as well have your head cut off the same as that bird that's currently roasting in the oven." With the butter knife held in her hand, she pointed at the oven where the chicken was roasting.

"Seems about fitting, considering I put my neck on the chopping block," I muttered under my breath.

Pushing out a sigh, my mother set the knife down on the counter and moved my direction. She placed both her hands on my face, dipping down to catch my gaze when I tried to drop my attention. "Hey, baby girl. Look at me."

I did.

She squeezed a little tighter. "I know you're nervous, but you are doin' the right thing."

On a long sigh, I blew out some of the strain I was holding in. If I kept it in for a second longer, it was gonna drive me mad. I peeked up at my mama. "And what if it turns out bad?"

"Then that's on him."

My lips pursed. I knew she was just trying to give me encouragement, that I couldn't make the right choices for Maxon, but still, that feeling in my chest grew heavier with the thought. "But that's the problem, Mama. If he does turn his back? I'm not sure I can handle that kind of rejection from him again. I'm pretty sure it will crush me."

Even after all these years.

"Love always hurts, Izzy Mae. That's what makes it so important."

I shook my head, not even willing to go there with her.

"I don't still love him."

The wrinkles at the corners of her eyes crinkled. "You just keep tellin' yourself that. You think a mama doesn't know when her baby girl is in love? I knew it then, and I know it now."

"I think you're delusional," I told her, trying to play the heaviness off.

She quirked a brow. "You mean old?"

Soft laughter rolled out. "That's exactly what I mean."

She moved back to her biscuits. "Well then, I guess you should be thanking your lucky stars that your mama still has it together enough to make your favorite meal."

"And to butt her nose into my business. Don't forget that."

She swiveled a fraction, grinning wide. "Never. I'll be meddlin' until the day I die."

"Lucky me," I mumbled, going back to the potatoes, poking at them again.

"Damn right, you are." She winked.

In amusement, I shook my head, and her smile softened. "No matter what happens, your daddy and I are here for you. You are never alone."

I started to tell her how much that meant to me, but she beat me to the punch. "Of course, we don't look quite as good as that man who has you in a stir. But I guess we'll have to do."

"Way to ruin the moment, Mama." My eyes went wide with the playful taunt. Seriously, after everything, I had a hard time understanding why she still kept Mack on some kind of pedestal.

"Ruin the moment? You should be thankin' me for that visual I know just went through your mind."

I jumped a little when the swinging door banged open, and Dillon came running in. Dark blond hair flying, grin so wide my floating heart jumped back in my chest. Right where it belonged.

Because it didn't matter how *stirred* up I was over Maxon Chambers. In the end, my boys were the only thing that mattered.

My world.

My reason.

He dashed around the island. "Nana, Nana, is lunch ready yet?

I'm starving!" He threw his belly out, pounding it like a drum.

"You're starvin', huh? What have you been doin' to work up such an appetite since I made you breakfast this morning?" she asked, bumping him with her hip.

"I'm a growing boy, Nana. Five-years-old. Do you know how many inches a boy my age grows in one year? We have to have lots of food to make us grow strong. And milk. Don't forget the milk."

Nothing but serious business.

"Never." She glanced at me with a secret smile. "Good thing it's coming up on time to eat."

That was the cue for my heart that had just settled into place to jump right back into a disorder. Thrashing and flailing and doing stupid things. I searched for a breath, for clarity, reminding myself that I could do this.

I pinned a smile onto my face, crossed over to Dillon where he was standing beside my mama, and ran my fingers through his messy hair. "Remember we have company coming over?"

He looked up at me. "Your friend who really isn't a friend anymore and now gets to be a cop?" His eyes got wider. "Being a cop is so cool. Maybe I should be a cop instead of a pilot." Contemplation twisted his brow. "What do you think, Mom? You think I should fight bad guys or shoot down bad guys?"

For once, I ignored his crazy train of thought and focused in on the first part of what he'd said. Is that what he got from the explanation I'd given the boys last night when I'd been tucking them into bed and told them Maxon was coming over?

Mr. Chambers, actually.

And I sure didn't tell them what he'd been to me. I guessed I'd really mucked that one up. Basically, I'd hemmed and hawed and stuttered around a really pathetic explanation of who our guest was gonna be.

"He's not *not* a friend. He's just . . . well . . . it's complicated."

Awesome.

There I went. Another bang-up job of explaining this to my son.

"What your Mama is trying to say, Dill Pickle, is that they used to be friends and they grew apart, had a misunderstanding, which is what adults do sometimes, and now maybe they want to get to know each other again."

I sent her a grateful glance and at the same time wanted to roll my eyes about the *misunderstanding*. If only.

"Well you coulda just said that," he told me.

The door creaked open again, slowly, this time Benjamin using his side to push through the door. He fumbled around to make it through. A very strong part of me wanted to rush to his side to help him hold it open, but I knew he wanted to do it himself.

He grinned his overwhelming smile, and my spirit soared, and I couldn't have stopped the affection that spread to my face if I tried. "Hey, handsome man."

"Hiiiiii."

On his forearm crutches, he slowly made his way over, his right foot dragging more than the other, his shoulders bunched up to his cheeks. But that grin never dropped. Not once. Not for a second. "Is itttt time?"

Nervously, I glanced at the clock again. "He should be here in about five minutes."

Five minutes. Goodness. Was I really gonna go through with this?

"Do we have to wait for him to eat?" Dillon almost whined.

I tapped at his nose. "Um, yes, sir, you do. Where are your manners? We have company comin'."

"But I don't even know why you'd want to wait around for a guy you don't even like." My five-year-old smirked. Stinker.

"Watch yourself, little man. I don't want any troublemaking goin' on during lunch. You have to be on your best behavior."

I pointed between both of my men.

"Why, 'cuz he's a cop?" Dillon asked, grin too wide. God, he was just like his grandma, always stirring the pot.

I raised my brows in a teasing way. "No. Because I told you, you aren't allowed to be a troublemaker, no matter how badly you might want to be."

"No stoppin' that," my mama added, right as the buzzer was going off on the oven. She went for it, grabbing her hand mitts and pulling down the door. "Mmm-mmmm," she drew out. "Do y'all smell that?"

Dillon threw his head back and held his stomach. "Nana, what are you tryin' to do to me? Kill me? Told ya I was starving."

She chuckled. "Soon, Dill, soon. Didn't anyone ever tell you patience is a virtue?"

"What's a virtue?"

Oh, goodness. Normally, I could keep up with the constant shifts in conversation, quick to answer all of Dillon's million questions, but I couldn't focus on anything but the ticking of the clock.

Tick. Tick. Tick.

Problem was, I wasn't sure if it was a bomb.

Benjamin hobbled his way over to me, and I leaned over and pressed my lips to his forehead, breathed him in.

He angled back, the expression on his face a little confused, far too knowing, smiling at me as if he were trying to get a read on what was on my mind. "You okkkay? You seem more nerrrvous than when you went to yourrr interview."

That's because I was. Working was a necessity. And Maxon could be a travesty.

I touched his cheek. "I am, sweetheart. Don't you worry. I'm just a little nervous to see my old friend."

"Is that what the kids are calling it these days?" My mama shot me a wink.

I scowled at her.

She laughed a small laugh.

"Will I liiike him?" Benjamin asked, genuinely curious, and my heart was thumping more.

"I think you will, sweet boy."

That was right when the doorbell rang, and my heart that had been thrashing against my ribs crashed right through. A tumble across the wood floor.

I knew that's what I was doing. Laying my heart at his feet and praying he didn't stomp all over it.

Inhaling deeply, I smoothed out the beige blouse I was wearing with the delicate lace ruffles on the collar and arms. I'd matched it with my best fitted cropped black pants and a pair of heeled sandals.

Nope.

I wasn't dressin' up for him.

Not at all.

It rang again.

"Well, go on," Mama chided.

Benjamin busted out in laughter. "Whaaat's wrong, Mom? You scccared of cops?"

Just this one, Benjamin. Just this one.

I tossed a look at all three of them, Dillon at my mama's legs begging for a biscuit, Benjamin leaning on the island. "Remember, I'm gonna be a bit. I need to talk to him first, and then we'll be in, okay? I need you both to stay in here and wait. Do you understand?"

"Ah, Mom, but didn't you hear that I'm starving? I'm gonna be a pile of bones on the floor if you gotta have a conversation. What do you gotta talk about that's so important, anyway?"

"Yeah?" Benjamin added.

"Just . . . old friend stuff."

God, I'd dug myself into a hole. And suddenly I was feeling paranoid that I'd done this all wrong. Yesterday's invite had been nothing but a knee-jerk reaction. The memory of my mama saying I should invite him over paired with the thankfulness that he'd rescued me when he had.

I should have called him and asked him to meet me somewhere else.

In private.

It wasn't like Faith wouldn't have his number.

Because this was suddenly feeling like an ambush, and I'd never wanted to be the attacker.

But I'd already done this, and the man was at the door, and I couldn't keep stalling for a second longer.

I inhaled and pushed through the swinging door, legs shaking as I moved through the living room. I paused only when my daddy poked his head out of his study. "You need me, just start screaming. I've got Gretchen locked and loaded."

"Daddy," I scolded.

He shrugged his bony shoulders. "What?"

"There won't be any need for any shotguns, no matter what, you hear me?"

"Fine," he grumbled and retreated back into his study, and I set my hand on the doorlatch and the dead bolt, counted to three—inhale-exhale-inhale—before I turned the lock and opened the door.

Was stupid to be taking in all those deep breaths, considering when I opened the door, Maxon was standing right there, and I was hit with a swell of lightheadedness.

The man so stunning, I was shooting a hand out to the jamb to keep myself standing, knees going weak.

The stubble from yesterday had been shaven, his face so pretty it could make a girl weep.

Wearing dark jeans that fit him just right, a blue-collared shirt with the sleeves rolled up those muscled forearms, all the colors on his arm sending my mind into a whirl.

A spiral of patterns that sucked me right in.

I wobbled.

He chuckled. "Whoa there, Little Bird. You okay?"

My head jerked up when he called me by the nickname he'd given me the first time he'd seen me, and my shallow breaths were turning ragged.

Everything came at me all at once.

I steadied myself, pulling it together the best that I could, a weak but real smile arching at one side of my mouth.

Because I realized right then I had no shame. I'd done nothing wrong. It was time I pulled up my big-girl panties and stopped acting like this man held the power to shatter our world.

We'd been living just fine without him all along.

"I'm glad you came." It was the truth.

His lips twisted up, this perfect mesh of arrogance and sweetness, dimple peeking out.

"That's good because I'm really glad you invited me."

I chewed at my lip. "I've been needin' to talk to you."

A little frown pulled to his brow, and I thought maybe it was just then he realized that when I'd said we had some things to sort out, I really meant it. It wasn't just a simple apology. A shake of hands, an awkward hug, and the promise of starting again.

"Okay." His tone turned nervous.

I jutted my chin out to the covered porch, and he took a step back, gesturing for me to go ahead of him. Our arms brushed as I passed. Heat blasted across my skin, the man too much, his presence just as potent as the thick air that sagged in the summer sky.

Birds chirped all around, and the trees rustled in the hot breeze, and the smell of our home was coming at me from all sides.

Wild jasmine dancing in my nose, all mixed up with the scent of the woods and the sea.

His aura slipping and sliding and taking hold of me.

I shivered and took a few steps out onto the porch. I was back to crossing my arms over my chest as I stood facing away from him, wondering how in the world I was supposed to tell him this.

"Izzy." That rough voice hit me from behind, worry and concern coming out with it, and there was no resisting the lure, and I slowly spun around, hit again with the full force of the man.

"I need to tell you something before we go inside," I whispered like caution.

He raked a hand through those dark blond locks, the epitome of the description of sand. Shiny, sunny strands dappled with browns.

"Figured you might have a few things you needed to say to me," he said. "Same as I have a few things I need to say to you."

My smile teetered, and I was trying to hold on. Trying not to break down right there.

"I have children." I figured I just had to get it out before I lost the nerve.

I watched the words penetrate him. The shock and the hurt and the jealousy.

Maybe a little curiosity.

Then it was acceptance that came riding in. The man knew he had no right to any of the earlier ones. It wasn't as if he didn't know I wanted a family. A big one.

Heck, I'd dreamed of it with him right here on this very porch.

We'd sit rocking on the swing in the night with fireflies humming around us. Sometimes we dreamed those dreams sitting in my tree, and sometimes in my room which had led to bad, bad things that had felt so incredibly good.

The memories of it seemed to echo around us then, whipping and whirring and inciting those old feelings that might have been better off left dead.

His throat bobbed heavily when he swallowed, and he was back to rubbing at the back of his neck, doing his best to hold back his disappointment and anxiety.

I understood that.

Was okay with that.

I guessed in a whole lot of ways, I'd been disappointed, too. But the hurt and betrayal had outweighed all of that.

I let him process, the man looking off into the distance, his big body vibrating as he bounced a few times. Finally, he looked back at me. "Okay."

Okay.

I rubbed my hands up my arms. It was way too hot to get a chill, but I felt something cold sweeping through me.

He took a step forward, angling down. He touched my cheek.

Fire flashed. Warming me. Head to toe.

God, I couldn't let myself get lost in this man right then.

"It's okay. I get it. We've been apart for a long, long time. Never expected you not to move on with your life. It's what I'd hoped you'd do. Find something better. But I'd be a liar if I said I'm not fucking thrilled that you're back."

Moisture welled in my eyes, faster than I could stop it. I wasn't sure if it was because I didn't know if I could ever forgive him for what he'd done. If I could ever open my heart enough to go there with him again. At the same time, I wanted to so badly.

But this was bigger than what I wanted.

"Maxon . . . it's more than that."

My explanation froze on my tongue when the door banged open, and in a blur, Dillon came stampeding out onto the porch. Two feet away from Maxon, he came to a screeching halt.

It took me a second to process that he'd gone and disobeyed, and my already fried nerves were zapping and crackling. "Dillon." My voice was sharp, a little bit horror and a lot angry that he hadn't listened.

"What did I tell you about waitin' inside?"

But he didn't have time to answer before Maxon was swiveling around, and I was moving toward Dillon, too, this feeling coming over me to get in front of my son. To be right there in case I needed to protect him.

Not that I would ever think Maxon would purposefully hurt him. And in a physical way?

Never.

But it was my job to protect my children the best way that I could. To shield them and hold them and ensure the relationships they were a part of, the ones they made, were the healthiest they could be.

"Hey, there," Maxon said, so softly and with so much affection that my scrambled heart throbbed in an overwhelming bout of emotion. "What's your name?"

"I'm Dillon. Are you really a cop? Do you have a gun? Have you had to shoot anyone? Do you get scared at your job?"

There my son went, rambling his unending slew of questions, while I was struggling to stand. To remain calm. To see this out before I totally lost my nerve and asked Maxon if we could do this another time.

Maxon chuckled and glanced up at me with a smile on his face, so big that it was making it hard for me to see anything but him kneeling there.

The kindness.

The goodness.

All the things I'd thought I'd seen in him before he'd proven just how cruel he could be.

I shook it off. I had to focus. I wasn't finished. "Dillon, you weren't supposed to come out here until I was finished talking with Mr. Chambers. You need to go back inside."

"Ah, Mom. Why do you gotta be such a funsucker? I was just sayin' hi." He turned his attention back to Maxon, lowering his voice. "My mom is so serious all the time but that's okay because she's got the weight of the whole world on her shoulders. Life's hard, Mr. Chambers."

Maxon laughed, and then he wasn't laughing any more.

I could feel it.

The shift in the air.

My alarm becoming his.

His spine stiffened. This staggering wave of energy cracked through the air as he straightened.

The man stumbled.

As if he'd been burned.

Broken.

I guessed I should have prepared myself for this, for his reaction to seeing Benjamin standing at the door.

nine

MACK

Horror.

Gutting, ravaging horror.

It clutched every cell in my body, freezing me in that moment. I blinked, trying to break free, but those chains only cinched down tighter.

Was surprised I could even register it when Izzy scrambled around me. "Both of you . . . get back inside. Right now."

"But mom," the little one argued.

"Now, Dillon. Right now." Her voice was desperate, flooded with panic as she tried to get her kids back inside.

While I stood there. Hands fisted in my hair. Freaking the fuck out. Trying not to puke right there on the ground.

Wanted to pry my eyes away, but there was nothing I could do but stare at the kid in the doorway. This kid who was way too skinny and had these crutches that looked like he used every day and had the exact fucking eye color as mine.

Same as it looked like his face could have been carved out of me.

Jesus.

Reality crashed. A tidal wave. Devastating.

I had a kid. I had a kid.

And Izzy hadn't told me.

Izzy's mother was suddenly there, clambering around to help. "I'm so sorry, Izzy Mae. I was getting the chicken from the pan onto the platter and they slipped out before I could stop them."

"Just, get them inside," she pled, and finally they were wrangled in, the door slamming shut, leaving just Izzy and me on the porch.

Rage came eating up the shock I'd initially felt.

Fury and hurt.

Fury and hurt.

They cut and slashed and filleted, knives slicing deep, pain screaming so loud I could barely hear. Could barely stand. Could barely breathe.

Problem was, I didn't know who to aim the fury at.

Izzy stood with her back to me, her shoulders pumping up and down, the silence echoing between us with the force of a storm.

A storm that assuredly would decimate.

Bile rolled up my throat, and my chest was heaving, body starting to shake with a turbulence I stood no chance at keeping at bay. "Are you fuckin' kidding me?" I growled.

She whirled on me, tears streaming down her face, but there was fury on her face, too. Written on every inch. "No, Maxon, it's not a joke. Does my life look like a joke to you?"

I pressed my fists to my eyes, trying not to fucking break down right there and sob like a bitch. Was not a crying man. But considering I'd just been knocked with the reality that I had a kid and I'd missed out on twelve years of his life, I was thinking I'd earned a pass.

I dropped them just as fast. Just feeling . . . irate and pissed and fucking worried.

So confused that I couldn't see, the world spinning around me, going faster and faster. I pointed at her house. "What's wrong with him?" It was a haggard demand.

Izzy gasped and reared back, and those hazel eyes flashed with disgust. "You just saw your son for the first time, and the only thing you can think to ask is what is wrong with him?" Incredulity blazed from her, her pain as thick as mine.

It was mixing together, pouring out to become this boiling vat of animosity that roiled in the middle of us.

I scrubbed both hands over my face, so goddamned frustrated, so goddamned mad. Red flickered at the edges of my sight, that old hatred rising up fast.

Hatred at myself.

Hatred at my father.

Hatred of Izzy for keeping this from me.

"Well, excuse the hell out of me, Izzy, for not having the right words when I find out I have a kid that I didn't know about." I slammed the tips of my fingers into my chest over my heart. "That I have a kid who obviously is disabled, and I didn't have a fucking chance to be there for him."

Anguish came bursting out of her mouth, and her head swiveled from side-to-side in huge rolls of disbelief. "Are you seriously goin' to stand there and act as if this was my fault?" She took a step toward me, her face pinching up. "Are you seriously going to stand there and make accusations?"

She took another, and the air was getting thinner, and the only thing I was breathing was Izzy Lane.

"You ruined me, Maxon. You broke my heart. You betrayed me." The words were harsh. Livid. Bullets impaling me, one after another.

"And then when I needed you most . . ." Her chin quivered. Tears streamed free. "When I begged you to call me, you didn't. Tell me, whose fault that is?"

Guilt screamed. Too much. Clotting in my chest. Expanding until I was suffocating. "Mine."

Mine.

It was the only thing I could manage, and I could feel myself cracking. Coming unhinged. Before I lost it, I turned and fled.

"Don't you dare run from this, Maxon Chambers." Izzy's voice pierced me from behind.

And I wondered if she'd expected anything else.

Elbows propped on the table, I had my face buried in my hands, thinking this was a bad fucking idea, too. But since I didn't have any good ones, at least I could get tanked while doing it.

Second Mirena had seen me, she'd hauled my stumbling ass over to a secluded, darkened booth at the very back of Monty's where I was hidden in the hazy shadows.

Great place to get lost in a rage. In hatred and disgust.

What the fuck had I thought going over there? That I'd apologize really quick, sweep her into my arms, and we'd live out our lives?

A happily ever after?

Sunshine and fucking rainbows?

Sunshine, my ass, and my *ever after* was never destined to be the happy kind.

I should have known. That's what I got for hoping for a change. For something more when I'd always known I couldn't have it.

I groaned, then jolted when I felt the movement across the booth from me. Warily, I opened my eyes, not in the mood for any bullshit.

Jace and Ian slid into the opposite side, worry written all over their expressions.

Annoyed, I frowned, taking another sloppy swig of my whiskey. "What the hell are you two doing here?"

Might have been slurring.

Who knew.

Tapping his fingertips on the table, Jace angled his head.

"Mirena called my number on one of my business cards. Said Ian and I needed to get down here. Something about our brother getting ready to have a meltdown. I'm pretty sure she was just worried you were going to tear apart the place."

Asshole tried to slide in a joke. Would have smiled, too, if his comment didn't have me wanting to rip off his face.

Ian itched in this seat. "Mack, man . . . what's going on? You look like shit." He glanced at the tumbler clutched in my hand, brow twisting in surprise. "And are you drinking whiskey? Shit. It really is bad."

Humorless laughter came rolling out. "Oh, it's bad, all right."

"What's going on?" he pressed.

"This have something to do with Izzy?" Jace asked, leaning forward. No doubt, he was probably shouting over the band playing on the stage, but his words were getting lost in the din, people shouting and the crowd noisy.

I rested the side of my head on my palm, and it only spun faster, my stomach sick.

So sick.

"Izzy's a mom," I somehow managed.

Jace shifted in discomfort. "Mack—"

I shook my head to cut him off. "Two kids. Oldest one is mine."

Oldest one is mine.

I gasped out a choked sound. Couldn't breathe. Might've been dyin'.

"Shit, Mack, dude . . . what the fuck? Are you sure?" Ian stumbled around the question, and Jace was pushing out a strained breath, running his hand through his hair.

"Like looking in a goddamned mirror." My voice was a rasp, that kid's face etched in my mind like it'd been written there all along.

Fuck.

I took another swig of my whiskey and forced the acid down. It burned just as bad as when I forced out the words, "Has a disability, too. Cerebral palsy, maybe. Something like that. His legs are all . . . fucked up."

Was I able to say that and not be considered a dick? Because they were. And I wasn't putting the kid down. Problem was, it was taking every ounce of restraint I had to remain sitting the hell down and not to go rushing back over there, sweeping in to pick him up.

Hold him.

Protect him.

Right there to make sure no one ever messed with him.

His smile hit me, filling up my mind, the kid so . . . happy.

A fireball that had come from out of nowhere, crashing into my atmosphere, but not quite making it into my world.

It's your fault.

It's your fault.

Pain splintered through my chest, and a shudder of revulsion slipped beneath my flesh. I curled my hand around the glass, so hard I was lucky I didn't crush it. But maybe that's what I was hoping for.

A distraction from the unbearable pain scrambling all the rationale I kept inside. Anything would feel better than this.

"Fuck, Mack, I'm sorry," Jace said, and there was just something about his voice that had me looking up to study his face, this feeling taking me over.

It only sent a fresh round of anger surging through my veins.

This was Jace. Not my blood, but my brother. The guy who I'd trust with my life. Hell, with the shit the two of us had gotten into a few years back, it wasn't even a theoretical notion. It'd been our reality.

And there it was—guilt gripping his expression.

My head cocked to the side in disbelief. "You knew?" My voice was ragged and sharp, my existence no longer making sense.

My attention flew to Ian, and he was already putting up his hands in surrender, head shaking fiercely. "Don't even say it, Mack. You think I wouldn't tell you something like this?"

"Yeah, well your big brother didn't seem to find it fit to do me the same favor."

Jace sighed out his regret.

There was a ton of it, but that didn't make it better.

"Listen, Mack, I just found out. Barely a week ago. Faith told me after Izzy came back to Broadshire Rim."

Disappointment and betrayal pulsed and throbbed, and I sat back in the booth, blowing out a resentful breath. "Faith knew."

Of course, she knew.

She'd been Izzy's best friend.

He nodded. "Yeah. Pretty sure carrying that secret has been eating her alive. But she felt she owed it to Izzy."

A roll of bitter laughter filtered out, and I rocked my head back on the high booth, body filled up with nothing but disbelief. "Perfect."

"This isn't Faith's fault—"

"You're right, it's not. It's mine," I bit out, cutting him off because I didn't need any fucking explanations.

"I never wanted to keep it from you. I told her I wouldn't keep it for long, but I promised I would give Izzy the chance to tell you."

"Doesn't change anything, does it?"

"Uh, yeah, pretty sure it changes a lot. You're a dad, asshole. And you're over here getting hammered when you should be getting to know your kid." Jace's brow was all pinched up, guy looking at me like he didn't recognize me.

I scoffed out a sound. "Izzy was right in not tellin' me. I don't deserve to be a dad, and I sure as hell don't want that kind of responsibility."

The words slashed.

Disgust after disgust.

All of it coming fast.

All of it directed at me.

I was to blame.

I'd always been to blame.

Ian angled over the table. "So, what, you're just going to pretend like you don't have a kid? Go on with your life like nothing has changed? Keep dipping your dick in girls like Clarissa because it makes your life easy? Tell me you're joking because you are not acting like the guy I know."

Easy.

Hilarious.

Jace reared back. "Tell me you aren't still hooking up with her?"

"None of your concern who I'm hitting," I returned.

I started to push from the booth. "Now, if you'll excuse me, I'm gonna go take a piss and get the hell out of here. You two have families to be with. You don't need to babysit me."

I started to walk away, and Ian grabbed me by the forearm. "Come on, man. Don't act like this. Let's talk this out. This is a big fucking deal, and I know you have to be shocked. Confused. Angry, and on some level, I'm sure you deserve to be. But you can't just walk away like this."

I ripped my arm out of his hold. "Watch me."

I was being a prick, but I couldn't sit there for a second longer and endure their judgment. Could feel it radiating from them, coming at me, wave after wave.

Had enough judgment to cast me into the grave.

I stumbled my way down the hall and fumbled into the men's restroom. Could barely remain standing at the urinal while I took a piss, my mind and head spinning so fast my sight was blurring.

A cyclone of alcohol and agony.

I tucked my dick back into my jeans, buttoned, washed my hands, refused to look at myself in the mirror in fear that I was gonna see the kid staring back.

The kid. The kid.

I pressed my face into my hands, trying to shut it down. To shield myself from this need rising up inside of me, screaming out to do something. To stand up and be the man Izzy had believed I could be.

First sight, and I'd already fucked it up.

Izzy hated me.

Izzy.

Little Bird.

I pressed my hand to the wall when I swayed, and I shook my head hard and flung open the door and staggered out into the hall.

Feet nearly gave when I saw Clarissa coming out of the women's restroom, my sight blurry, but 99.9% sure it was her.

Speak of the devil.

God, wondered what it'd feel like to have those lips wrapped around my cock.

Torture myself with the mindless bullshit I deserved.

Her smirk was nothing less than cruel victory when she saw me standing there staring at her.

She sauntered across the space, dripping sin, backing me right into the wall. "Back for me so soon?" she purred.

My stomach twisted, nausea rising, but I was reaching for her, pushing my fingers into her hair, jerking her mouth to mine.

"Told you, you'd come crawling back," she hissed at my mouth, kissing me harder. Deeper. Her tongue slipping inside.

That sickness only grew.

Spin. Spin. Spin.

I was gonna lose it.

The girl crawled all over me right out in the hallway.

Nothing new.

It felt wrong. So goddamn wrong.

"You belong to me, Mack. You always have. Don't fucking forget it."

And I tried . . . I tried to kiss her back. Tried to fight the nausea that churned in my guts when I wrapped my arms around her waist and hauled her against my hard, aching cock.

Problem was, it wasn't aching for her.

Izzy, Izzy.

Anguish flowed.

I pulled her closer, trying to get lost, to fall into her, to block out everything except for the feel of her against my body.

The only thing I saw were three faces.

Three faces.

And I knew, I was utterly and completely fucked.

I pried myself away, stumbling back, and I pointed a finger at her. "No," was the only thing I could get out of my mouth.

She raked the back of her hand over her mouth, cleaning the lipstick I'd smeared. Or maybe her face was just distorted.

She laughed that crazed sound. Like she'd won.

"No," I mumbled again, turning around, hand darting to the

wall to keep me steady.

I blundered my way down the hall, her voice hitting me from behind. "Time to get over yourself, Mack. Why do you think you keep coming back to me? We were made for each other."

Trying to block her out, I shoved through the throbbing crowd, glancing over at the booth where I'd been sitting. Jace and Ian were long gone. No doubt, they knew the only medicine for me was blowing off steam.

That's exactly what I needed to do.

I shouldered through groups congested in front of the stage, knowing I was being a total dick, but I needed to get outside.

Get some fresh air.

Clear my mind.

I never let myself get out of control like this. Always vigilant. Always at the ready.

I finally made it to the door, and I pushed out into the night. Dingy streetlamps burned outside the rundown brick building that was a mile and a half from my house. Hardly anyone was out, only a couple getting cozy against the far wall, a single car passing on the two-lane street.

I turned the opposite direction of the couple, my feet dragging on the sidewalk as I started for home. The echo of the bar seeped through the brick walls, laughter and music and chaos. At the end of the building, I made a right down the alley toward the dirt parking lot behind Monty's.

At the far end of it, there was a trail that cut through a grove of trees and led to a neighborhood right next to mine. I'd have to hop a fence, but that sounded way better than hoofing it the extra mile.

The faster the route walking home, the better.

My boots scuffed on the dirt, when I felt the echoey silence shift. Something ominous rode on the night air.

Noises hit my ears, and I struggled to listen, to make them out in the middle of the disorder wreaking havoc on my brain.

Muted voices.

Low thuds.

I kept moving that way, shaking my head, trying to sober up.

The area was only illuminated by the dim glow coming from a light hanging from the shed at the very back of the lot, and I rounded it to get to the trailhead, eyes scanning. The fine hairs prickled at the back of my neck as awareness crawled over me from behind.

When I shifted, the same four guys I'd pulled over yesterday stepped out to box me in against the fence.

A spike of adrenaline jumped into my system, but my brain was fuzzy and soaked, and I fumbled around to get my phone out of my back pocket.

Dizziness addled my brain, and I shook my head, trying to prep myself to go up against nothing good. Wasn't exactly at 100% after I'd drank double my weight in whiskey and was at four to one.

The prick who'd been driving cracked a grin.

"Well, look who's here, big, bad cop. You been drinking?" he taunted.

Managed to at least get dispatch on the phone, even though I didn't have time to respond before they were encroaching.

"Fucker . . . you're gonna get what's comin' to you."

One guy rushed me, and I threw a punch, my fist cracking against his nose. I threw a left at a second, barely clipping him on the chin.

From out of nowhere, I took a blow to the jaw. It gave one of the pricks time to jump on my back, and an arm cinched around my throat just as another guy kicked me in the gut.

Air busted from my lungs, leaving me gasping. A torrent of fists and feet came at me from every direction.

Blow after blow landed on my back and my head. On my face and my ribs.

And fuck. It hurt. It hurt like a motherfucker.

Pain splintered against the battering that sent darkness clouding my sight. Everything dimming.

I tried to remain upright. To stand under the attack. Throwing elbows and kicking and trying to break free. Landed a few meager hits. But this wasn't gonna be a winning fight.

Someone got me at the temple, and I dropped to my knees like some kind of pathetic offering.

And I knew, with every part of me, that I deserved it.

ten

IZZY

In the dimly lit kitchen, I fought to get the wrapper off a teabag. Apparently, wrangling it was some kind of enormous feat.

Finally, I managed it, and I dipped the bag into the cup of steaming hot water, praying it might bring me some sort of relief.

My hands were still shaking all these hours later.

Shaking and shaking.

Almost as hard as my heart that rattled in my ribcage, this bleeding organ that heaved and throbbed, firing off erratic pulses of regret and anger and torment that tremored through my entire being.

The house was stilled and sleeping, darkness oppressive were it cloaked the bank of windows at the far end of the kitchen. Branches clawed and screeched at the eaves, like a physical haunting of what had transpired this afternoon.

How many times had I imagined what Maxon's reaction might be to learning about Benjamin?

The worry and the fear and this overwhelming sense of protection that would well at the thought of my boy suffering the cruelty of that sort of rejection?

My fingers trembled as I brought the cup to my mouth.

In all those nights I'd lain awake, plagued by the unknown, I'd never thought it'd go down quite like that.

Anger and resentment bleeding from us both.

"Izzy Mae." The voice hit me from out of nowhere, and a high-pitched screech streaked up my throat, just about as quickly as I flew around. One of my hands darted out to the counter to keep myself steady while the other tried to keep the steaming-hot cup from sloshing everywhere.

"Mama. What in the world are you doin' sneaking up on me like that? That's not safe. Don't you know you have a whole butcher block of knives sitting on the counter? I could have thought you were an intruder."

She chuckled a little. "Getting away from yourself there, don't you think?"

"Maybe."

Okay. A whole lot.

But I was on edge.

A very, very sharp edge.

She waded deeper into the lapping darkness, her face coming in to view. Affection marred with a frown of worry. It was the same expression she'd been wearing all day. She blew out a sigh. "I couldn't sleep. I knew I'd find you down here wearing a hole in the floors. Call it Mama's intuition."

Blowing out a sigh, I ran a hand through my hair and wished I had something more constructive to do with them. Someplace to divert the agitation.

This energy that made me want to run a half marathon.

Or maybe just crawl the walls.

"Yeah, I guess I couldn't sleep, either."

Her frown deepened, and she came closer, rounding one side

of the island. "I'm so sorry."

My brow twisted up. "What are you sorry for, Mama?"

Sadness left her on an undulating wave. "For letting the boys get out from under me. Mostly for forcing you into this before you were ready. I shouldn't have done that. I just . . . wanted resolution. For you. For Benjamin. For Mack, too."

"None of this is your fault."

It was no one's fault but Maxon's and mine.

Dillon had been playfully offended that my old cop friend didn't want to hang out with us, teasing me that the two of us must still not like each other very much if he didn't want to stay to eat, while my daddy had grumbled that some people never changed and it was time for someone to stand up and take responsibility.

But it was Benjamin's reaction that had nearly destroyed me.

Poking holes at that brittle place that had always held the remnants of Maxon's betrayal.

Home to the sharp shards of love that I was never gonna get rid of.

He'd been sitting at his window, staring out, and I'd gone over, touched his hair. He'd looked up at me with his sweet, sweet face, and my ever-insightful boy had whispered that he was sorry that he might have scared away my friend.

What was I supposed to say to that? Truth was, in a way he had, but not in the way that Benjamin was thinking.

At least, I didn't think Maxon could be so horrible and low.

My aching heart gave another pang, a dark misery rising and sloshing, threatening to take over.

What if that was what had sent him running?

"What are you thinking, sweet girl?" Mama asked, edging forward another step.

I inhaled, trying to see clearly through the pain and questions. "I just . . . I think I need to go over there and talk to him."

"Right now?" she shot out, a little horrified. "At this time of night?"

"We're long since passed worrying about what the neighbors think, aren't we?" I teased a little, though it didn't come out sounding all that funny.

"Izzy," she chastised with a click of her tongue. "You think I've ever been ashamed of you?"

"Never. You never once made me feel that way."

"Good. Because that would wreck me." She angled her head. "But do you think that's a good idea right now? Running back over there? Think maybe you both need some time to clear your heads. Come to terms. He suffered a big shock, and his reaction caused you a big blow."

The cup clanked when I set it on the counter, my entire body in upheaval. "I'm not running back to beg him for anything, Mama, but I think we both know the way he found out wasn't all that fair. I feel like I owe him an explanation. An apology. I can't stand the idea of him sitting across town thinking I tried to trick him or trap him."

Her lips pursed. "I get that, Izzy . . . you've been the one who's had to make all the hard choices for all these years. Always protectin' your family. Doin' the best for Benjamin, the same when Dillon came along."

I huffed out a sigh. "Apparently, I'm not all that great at makin' those hard decisions, am I?"

"Nonsense. You have done the best you can, and who those boys are? The love and compassion they hold? That's because of you and your heart. Don't question that for a second."

I looked at my Mama, emotion bleeding free. "There are so many things I'd do differently if I could."

A soft smile pulled to her mouth. "All of us would, sweet girl. We all make mistakes. They shape us. We learn from them. We make changes because of them. They make us who we are. And all that shapin' has made you into the most amazing person I know. Someone who is kind and good and deserves to find happiness."

"I am happy, Mama. My boys make me happy. Bein' here with you and Daddy makes me happy."

Her gaze softened. "I know that. But I'm talking about joy, Izzy. In life. In something just for you. Whether that's fallin' in love or reaching out and taking hold of what you *love* to do. You think that spark isn't still shinin' from you? Just because you're a mama doesn't mean it doesn't still glow. And I know that man broke your heart in a way that is hard to undo, but whether if it happens tonight or in a year, both of you have to resolve that, let it go, so you can move on and find your *joy*. It's been holdin' you back for too long."

A gleam came to her eye. "Unless you're not wantin' to move on."

"Mama," I chastised. God, she just knew how to get to me.

She took me by the chin, and she studied my face in the shadows. "But whose joy is forgotten is lost."

Emotion rushed, warmth pressing full as I murmured, "And whose heart is free is found."

She held my gaze, that vast, endless love shining through.

The kind only a mother understood.

She smiled slow. "Free your heart, Izzy Mae. However you need to do it. Whatever it looks like."

"Thank you, Mama."

She pinched my chin a little. "I will always support you . . . wherever you go. Whatever you decide."

She stepped back. "All right then, you'd better go before it gets too late. I expect you home before one. And don't you let that boy talk you into somethin' you're not interested in. Or is that exactly what you're interested in?"

She cocked a brow.

"Mama," I muttered through the thick emotion, light laughter breaking through. No one could flip a U as fast as her. "You are utterly ridiculous. You know the last thing I need is to go gettin' wrapped up in that man again."

Not that he even wanted me or that I wanted him.

That would be plain foolish.

"Ridiculous? I'm just keeping it real." She started for the swinging door. "Apparently, I'm the only one in this house who isn't completely delusional. You think I didn't feel that tension radiating from you two on the porch? We were all lucky it didn't blow the house right over."

"It wasn't anything like that," I told her softly.

"You just go on tellin' yourself that." She paused, her

expression going somber. "Find your heart, Izzy Mae. Don't ignore it."

Thirty minutes later, I pulled to a stop at the address Faith had given me. His house was in a quaint, quiet neighborhood in Charleston.

Squeezing the steering wheel, I peered out the side-window, trying to ignore the spike of hurt that pierced my spirit when I took in his house.

Small and charming and sweet. Hedged by a short fence that might have been considered cliché if it weren't so perfect, dainty white flowers blooming on the green shrubs that grew up the slats of the wood. Porch painted gray with white accents, the barest light flooding the space in warmth. A manicured lawn stretched in between.

Seeing it hurt.

It was the kind of home I'd hoped for as a little girl. The kind of home I'd dreamed of when I'd become that hopeless romantic as a teen. The kind I'd been a fool to tell him all about.

I nearly rolled my eyes at myself.

Hopeless, was right.

Well, I sure couldn't dwell on it then, so I sucked down a steeling breath, cut the engine, and climbed out.

In the dull light coming from the porch, my sight caught on the same Suburban parked in the driveway that Maxon had been driving when he'd saved me a few days ago. Sitting next to it was an enormous black pick-up truck that he probably took hiking or camping or hunting.

Or hell . . . it just looked like Maxon, no matter what.

Rough and rugged and strong.

Part of me wanted to run and hide from all that strength and intensity, the same way as I'd been doing for the last thirteen years. But that was no longer an option.

It was time for me to suck it up. Tell him like it was. He could hold it or trample it or laugh in my face, but all of those things were up to him.

The only power I had was in myself. My own choices. My own

resolve.

Fingers fumbling, I unlatched the gate and started up the concrete walkway, feet clumsy in the same heeled sandals I'd been wearing earlier.

My heart felt even clumsier.

Like I might tumble.

Take a fall.

Land flat on my face.

But that was a risk I had to take. I at least owed Maxon this. An explanation. An apology for my own wrongs, not that any of them negated what the man had done.

Holding onto the railing, I eased up the two steps onto the porch.

Swore, the echo of my shoes felt like gunshots as I crossed the wooden planks.

A breeze whipped through the humid night air, and my tongue darted out to wet my dried lips, and I searched for courage as I stood at the dark gray door.

I lifted my hand and rapped the wood. It sent a loud, reverberating echo through his house.

I struggled around the dread and the worry and the gross feeling that had forever whispered in my consciousness.

Whispered that I hadn't been good enough. Not pretty enough or sexy enough or interesting enough.

That insecure girl didn't matter right then.

This was about Benjamin.

Stilled silence echoed back. Well, that and the roar of my pulse that thundered in my ears.

I leaned in closer to the door, listening for . . . anything.

I looked back at the cars parked in the drive, sure that he had to be there.

A smack of panic hit me in the face.

What if . . .. . . what if he was with a woman?

Oh, God.

I hadn't even considered that. And I shouldn't. Shouldn't even contemplate it or give it a second thought. But I couldn't help it, those old memories that crept up the way they loved to do.

Ghosts that shouted and mocked.

Pain crushed my ribs, squeezing, pressing at those shards, still sharp enough to cut.

I gulped for a cleansing breath and forced myself to knock again.

Harder this time.

Nothing.

I frowned, bit my lip, wondered what to do.

Resolution brimmed within.

I wasn't going anywhere until the two of us had this out.

Talked.

Maybe found some closure.

I moved over to the steps and sat down on the top one.

And I waited.

Waited and waited.

The night drew deeper, bugs trilling in the shrubs, the hot summer breeze rustling through the leaves on the enormous tree that grew in the middle of Maxon's yard.

I got lost in the peace of it, my mind wandering far. To fantastical things that I hardly allowed myself to contemplate anymore.

I was so deep in my thoughts that I jolted upright when the blinding glare of headlights came up the road. It had to have been the first car that passed in probably an hour.

A lump climbed my throat, thickening everything when the car slowed and pulled to a stop behind mine.

The sedan gave off the same vibe as Maxon's Suburban, completely white with those blacked out windows, strange antennae sticking up on the rear window.

An unmarked cop car.

A shiver sped across my skin.

Cold and hot and sticky.

I had no idea who he was with. If he'd even want to talk to me. Had no idea what I was gonna say.

The driver's side door opened. A super tall, thin man stepped out, wearing a rumpled suit.

I pushed to standing, waiting, this worry rising up so fast, this feeling that somethin' was . . . wrong.

The man eyed me speculatively as he rounded the front of the car. "Probably not a good night for Maxon to have any company," he said, though what I really was hearing him say was *get lost.*

Discomfort crawled beneath the surface of my skin.

He thought I was there to . . . to sleep with Maxon.

God, that hurt, too.

No doubt, Maxon had women hanging all over him. Waiting for him. Wanting him.

That face and that body and those hands.

He was gorgeous. Compelling and striking and sexy.

I stood ground, refusing to back down because none of that was what this was about.

"Is something wrong with him? What's goin' on?" I tried to keep the tremor out of my voice, but I failed that task miserably.

Ignoring me, the man pulled open the passenger door, and a stir of that energy came blasting out.

Disorder and disease.

I felt it like a punch.

A blow to the chest.

Bowling me back.

Anxiety flamed, and I started to come down the steps, unable to stand still for a second longer, when the man dipped inside the door and helped Maxon out.

He held him upright, and Maxon had an arm slung around his shoulders. His head drooped to the side, his body slouched, hardly holding up any of his weight.

Wings of dread flapped in my stomach, and my heart lurched in a violent careen to the right. I reached a hand out to the porch railing to steady myself.

"Maxon?" I questioned, panic laced through my voice. "What's wrong with him? What happened?" I demanded, my voice hitching higher.

Through the shadows, I could barely make out the expression of the guy who was helping him, though I was pretty sure he was glaring at me like I was an obstacle.

An annoyance.

Or maybe like I was trash.

"Think you'd better go on your way. Told you it wasn't a good night for company."

Was it wrong that I wanted to toss it right back at him? Tell him, good, he could go on his way?

Maxon groaned. It was this . . . horrible, pained sound. Agony that cut me like a knife.

But in it contained some semblance of my name.

The sound of it enveloped and warmed.

Urges hit me.

I wanted to be the one helpin' him. The one there for him. To soothe whatever he was going through.

And I knew that made me nothin' but a fool, but it didn't matter.

I was drawn.

Shackled.

Chained.

Just the way I'd always been, unable to stand beneath the force of the man.

I was a little terrified that I might just offer myself up as a willing prisoner.

I hurried down the two steps, not even caring that the man helping him threw me an annoyed glare.

I got that he was bein' protective. But this was my Maxon he was protecting.

Oh, and that right there should have been a good enough warning for me to go running, but I just took another step toward the two of them, trying to get a hold on what was happening.

"Is he drunk?"

I mean, why wouldn't he be? I'd wanted to drink myself into oblivion, too. I'd just had two babies I had to think of first.

"You might not want to be too hard on the guy. He hasn't exactly had the best night." More frustration and spite coming from the stranger.

My attention shifted from the silhouette of Maxon to the man at his side, questions of what he meant on the tip of my tongue, when every cell in my body froze.

Because that was right when they took a lumbering step forward and came into the glow of the light cast from the porch.

Horror raced up my throat, dragging like razor-sharp claws.

A sob followed it, and my hands shot to my mouth to cover it.

Hold it back.

But it was no use.

It ripped free.

Maxon was . . . bloody. So bloody.

A gaping wound flapped open over his left brow, and his bottom lip was split wide open.

His skin was dirty . . . covered in filth . . . clothes he'd been wearing this afternoon torn and mangled.

Under it, I could almost see the purple bruises blooming on his skin.

My own pain clutched me, every cell screaming out.

"Oh my god," I whimpered.

Breaking out of the shock, I rushed the rest of the way down the walkway. "What happened to him?" I demanded. "Is he okay?"

Alarm rang through my being, horrified that after he'd left my house, things had gone so wrong.

So very, very wrong.

Maxon tried to focus on me, and his mouth hitched up at the side, words slurred together, nothing but a train wreck. "Hey, gorgeous. Musta died and gone to heaven for you to be standin' there. Fuck . . . so pretty. Why're you so pretty?"

Oh yeah, he was definitely drunk.

Hurt and drunk and saying nonsensical things.

That was all.

I looked at the guy holding him up. "What happened to him?"

He sighed, but it sounded in resignation. Guessed there was no missing the fact that Maxon wanted me there.

Wasn't about to admit to him I was pretty sure that was only the alcohol talkin'.

The guy angled his head. "Dumbass left a bar and had four guys jump him. He got lucky."

"Lucky?" The word was pure disbelief.

It sure didn't look like the man had gotten lucky tonight, and I meant that in every way.

He smelled like a pit, the stench of stale alcohol and rotting garbage coming off him in waves.

"Pretty sure he has a couple busted ribs. But this asshole refused treatment, so who knows what the fuck is wrong with him." This was anger from the man, totally directed at Maxon.

Maxon grunted. "Fine now . . . just wanna go home."

God, how did I end up in the middle of this? I twisted my fingers together, contemplating what I was supposed to do. Figured the best thing was to shove off the emotion, the reason I'd been here, and be glad that I'd come when I had.

Maxon needed help. I could give him that.

My brain shot into action. "Okay. Let's get him inside and get him cleaned up. Maybe if he sobers up some, I can convince him to go to the ER."

Going to the opposite side of the man, I wound my arm around Maxon, ignoring the rush of tingles slipping across my skin.

It just wasn't fair the effect he had on me. I should be repulsed. And I really didn't want to be anywhere else.

Maxon leaned on me more, his presence consuming, mumbling something incoherent.

Something sweet.

"We've got you, Maxon. Don't worry. You're gonna be okay. I promise," I whispered in a hush.

What was I even sayin'?

Doing?

This was crazy.

"Maxon, huh?" the guy questioned me, and I could almost hear the grin in his voice.

Shyness worked its way to my face. "I've always called him that."

"Seems like you two have known each other a long time?"

Without a doubt, this guy was doing his best to figure me out.

"All my life. And you?" I asked as we slowly made our way up the porch.

Formal introductions, and all.

"Pete. Maxon's partner."

"I really think you should have taken him to the hospital."

Pete laughed as if any of this was normal. "Know he looks bad, but believe me, he'd probably be in worse shape if our sergeant found him like this. Better for her to read the report than witness this disaster in person. Actually, saved his ass, bringing him here."

God, I didn't understand that world. The danger of what Maxon did. The life he led.

Getting sloshed at a bar and then getting in the middle of a fight.

That was just . . . stupid and reckless and made my aching heart bleed in worry and pain.

"Owed me, asshole," Maxon slurred, smiling a big, sloppy smile at Pete.

"Which is why you're here, and I didn't dump your ass at the ER instead."

"Fine. Got Izzy. Gonna keep her." At least, that's what I thought Maxon said, and my stupid heart skittered.

No, that wasn't helpin' things, either.

God, I really was getting in deep. Deeper than I should. But I didn't know how to let go. Didn't know how not to care when this man used to mean everything to me.

We made it to the front door, and I grabbed the keys that were dangling out the front pocket of Maxon's jeans, fumbled to get the right one into the lock, and opened it.

Dim light spilled out, his house only illuminated by the muted lights that glowed from under the kitchen cupboards, the inside just as quaint and perfect as the outside.

We stepped inside, and Pete moved to prop Maxon against the wall. "Can you stand?"

"Yup. Good as new." His words were almost filled with a laugh.

"Hardly," I scolded a little, not sure how these two could make light of this.

"You good?" Pete asked, moving toward the door and pointing at Maxon.

Um . . . what? Did he think he was just going to leave me there with him?

"I'm good," Maxon said, leaning against the wall, all of this attention trained on me.

Redness flared, and I tried to tamp it down, to keep this unsettled feeling from turning into something else.

"Not sure that's a good idea," I said, fidgeting with my fingers. "I mean . . . you can't just leave him here with me like this."

"Know he looks like death warmed over, but believe me, he's had it way worse than this. Drawbacks of the job." There he went again. As if this were a joke.

The man could have been killed.

"Pretty sure the only thing he needs is a hot shower and a few kisses on those booboos, and he'll be good to go. Looks like he's in plenty good hands."

That redness that'd been creeping flashed, full blown heat.

"I'm . . . I'm not . . .we're not . . . we don't . . ."

Frantically, I gestured between Maxon and me. I sounded like a blundering fool.

Maxon's expression shifted, a smirk catching at the side of that busted lip.

How was it possible that was sexy?

But it was, and trembles were taking up residence in my belly.

Those blue eyes glinted, needy and hot and arrogant, like he was standing right there, remembering all the times when we *had.*

"I just want Izzy," he grunted at his friend, and my stomach tangled in a thousand knots.

Oh, this was bad.

Bad, bad, bad.

Pete dug into his wallet and pulled out a business card. "Here's my number if you need me. He'll be fine. Just get him into bed and let him sleep it off."

"Owe you," Maxon told him, head slumping to the side.

"Damn right you do. Take care of yourself, man. Clean up. Sleep it off. Be ready for Sergeant Woods to rip you a new one when you come crawling in tomorrow."

Pete stood in the doorway, glanced back at me. "Are you cool?"

Was I cool? Did I look cool?

I looked back at Maxon who was just . . . starin' at me.

So many emotions coming off of him I didn't know how to process them all.

Those blue eyes nothing but a raging sea at midnight. Dark, lulling waves taking me under. Deeper and deeper. There was nothin' I could do but inhale and hope I didn't drown.

"Yeah. I've got him," I told Pete, while my rational side screamed out that this was a terrible idea.

He gave me a tight nod and pulled the door shut behind him.

The second he did, the walls closed in. Closer and closer. The air thick and dense.

Energy crackled, this physical entity that had always lived within us.

I got stuck in a whirlwind of it. Just starin' at the man who'd loved me like none other and then hurt me in a way no one else had ever had the power to do.

His commanding face torn to shreds. Blond hair sticking up and matted. Chest heaving with massive, choppy breaths.

Mine matched time, ragged and harsh.

He was so beautiful. So big and powerful and strong. Rippling with it as he leaned against the wall, like a warrior who'd just made his way home after battle.

Mesmerizing in a way that had captured me the first time I'd seen him.

And I knew . . . I knew he was broken in ways that were only represented by his bruised exterior.

Tonight was so much more than him simply happening upon a fight.

There was a part of Maxon that hunted it.

Wanted the pain.

Wanted the disorder.

Wanted to make himself pay.

I'd been desperate to fix those pieces for so long, but those were the parts of himself that he'd always kept out of reach. The ones he didn't let me touch.

"Should I call Jace or Ian?" I finally managed to ask, the words choked as they scraped across my raw throat.

"No. Just you," he slurred.

Air heaved from my lungs, and I squeezed my eyes for a beat, coming to the decision to be there for him.

"Okay. Let's get you cleaned up." I edged back over, wading through that energy, my footsteps slowed in that quiet ferocity.

I wrapped an arm around his waist.

Chills spread. Fire and ice skating down my spine, tingles spreading outward, touching every cell.

"Do you think you can walk?" I forced out.

"Yeah. Looks worse than it is," he rasped.

"Don't lie to me, Maxon Chambers."

He released a rough sound, pressed his nose into my hair, his mouth moving near my temple. "You're right. It hurts, Izzy. Hurt's so fuckin' bad. That's the truth."

The words staggered me, whipping through me with the force of a storm. And I knew what he was sayin', where they were coming from. But I didn't think either of us were prepared for that conversation tonight. I didn't want him saying things he didn't mean when he had alcohol soaking his brain.

When my heart was already tattered and torn and mangled like his body.

Bleeding at the sight of him like this.

I started toward the short hall at the back of the open room that housed his living room and kitchen.

He took lurching steps as we went, teeth clenching as he grunted with physical pain, and I took on as much of his weight as I could.

Tears stung the back of my eyes.

Because he was hurting.

Because he felt too good.

Because I didn't think I could ever fully trust him again.

"Where is your bedroom?" I murmured.

"Down the hall . . . last door on the right," he grumbled through halting breaths.

I got him all the way to the end of the hall, to the double doors sitting there as if they were asking for permission for passage.

A disorder blew through, the air too thin, too deep, too profound.

Gathering my strength, I reached out and turned the knob. The door swung open to a big room.

Modern and redone like the rest of his house.

Masculine and sexy.

My heart panged.

I ignored it, ignored the forgotten dreams and his massive bed and his scent that was hitting me from all sides. I led him into the attached bathroom where I flicked on the light.

He squinted beneath the harshness, and I gasped again when his wounds were illuminated this way. "Oh, God, Maxon . . . what did they do to you? You should be at the hospital."

"Don't want to."

A frown pulled at my face. "You don't have to be the tough one all the time."

He stumbled over a choked laugh. "Not so tough tonight."

I released a breath. "Four men got to you?"

"Four punk kids. I should . . . I should have . . ." He trailed off in some kind of agony. I could feel it. All the things from earlier.

"Izzy . . . I'm so sorry." He was slurring more, and I was shushing him, whispering, "We'll talk about it later."

"You came."

"Yeah."

"For me?" Vulnerability tumbled out with his question. A band pulled tight, right through the middle of me.

The part that wanted to promise that I'd be there for him forever and the other that hated him for what he'd done.

"I figured you and I had more things we needed to say to each other."

"So many things," he mumbled.

"Let's save it for when you feel better, why don't we?" I pled, sure my heart couldn't handle a thing he would say.

Maybe I should have listened to my mama when she said we both needed time to clear our heads. She was right. We needed it. But that would have meant I wouldn't have been here for him this way. And tonight . . . just for tonight, I wanted to be.

"Fuckin' hurts." His face twisted.

My stomach did the same, hating that he was in pain.

"I know," I told him, trying to soothe him. Because it did. It hurt so bad. And I wasn't sure if that would ever go away.

He reached out, and his fingertips brushed my cheek. "So pretty."

Redness flushed. I bit my bottom lip, ignoring it, knowing he wouldn't be sayin' it if his restraint wasn't dulled.

If the reality wasn't marred and distorted by the trauma of the night.

"Come on, let's get you cleaned up."

I stepped back a little so I could gather the hem of his shirt in my hands. Maxon stared down at me.

Blue eyes roiled, fierce and uncontrolled, air coming in harsh breaths from his nose.

I tore my attention away, unable to stay standing beneath the weight of it all.

"I'm going to need to take your shirt off. Is that okay?"

He grunted his approval, and I started pulling it up, over those rows of perfectly chiseled abs he'd been teasing me with a few days ago.

I tried not to look. Not to let my mouth water or my body trip into need.

I tried all the harder not to cry when I saw the purples and blues rising under the red scrapes, some of them pitted with tiny rocks where his shirt had torn, a big scrape over the scar that remained on his side. One that I would never, ever forget.

And I was picturing him a ball on the ground.

People hurtin' him. I hated it. Hated it so much.

"Oh, God, Maxon."

"It's okay."

"No, it's not. I hate that this happened to you."

"Deserve it. Deserve it all."

"Please, don't say that," I begged as I lifted his shirt higher.

It exposed his chest, and I was struggling for air.

Fighting my senses.

The sorrow at him being hurt this way. The love that had

refused to die. The arousal that stirred just being in his space.

I wanted to reach out. Touch him. Caress his flesh. Kiss it better the way Pete had implied.

The man was magnificent. Wide, bristling strength. Solid muscle carved from a stony cliff. Jagged and hard, destruction below if you didn't hold on tight enough.

But it was the wounds covering almost every inch of him that shook me to the core.

"Tell me these assholes got arrested?" I peeked up at him, praying he couldn't read everything I was thinking. "I can't believe what they did to you."

He gave me a grim shake of his head, and his body slumped a little to the left. "No. I'll get 'em. Don't be scared, Izzy. Won't let nothin' happen to you. Never."

I didn't want to point out that he'd hurt me worst of all.

Swallowing down all the confliction, I peeled his shirt the rest of the way over his head, careful of the gashes on his face. I tugged it free, dropped it to the floor.

My eyes drifted.

Catching.

Hooking.

It pulled a gasp out with it, and I tried not to gape, tried to keep my eyes from racing to take in every inch of his bare shoulders and upper arms. The designs he'd marked there.

The man a hardbound book.

Grief almost cut me in two.

I ached, and I wanted to reach out and turn the pages.

Read everything that was inside.

"Izzy," he grunted, feeling the fever of my gaze.

I shook the reaction, fought to maintain a semblance of control. Of decency in this moment. "Why don't you sit on the toilet so I can tend to your wounds."

A frown pinched his brow, but he nodded, backing away as I stepped toward him. My trembling hands reached out, tentative, hovering, before I wound them around to his back to support him.

His massive arms wrapped around me way up high.

I could feel his heart. The pound, pound, pound.

While mine ached and ached and ached.

He eased to sitting, and his arms that had been around my upper back slid down, hot hands landing on my sides.

Tugging me close, the man searched my face before he leaned in and ran his nose along the exposed flesh above my blouse.

Shivers flashed.

A river of gooseflesh that ate up my body.

"So good, Izzy. You smell so good. Like a field of wild jasmine. Want to lie in it."

Oh, he needed not to be sayin' those things to me.

"Don't, Maxon. You're drunk," I begged, trying to quiet him, to stop this from happening, my mind from taking a jaunt into lurid thoughts

I set my hands on his shoulders and peeled myself away. I fumbled over to the sink and turned on the faucet so I could warm a washcloth under it, trying to gather myself while I was there.

You can do this.

You can do this.

I edged back over to him, and he lifted his face, those eyes on me.

Energy sizzled in the tiny space.

I swallowed around it and focused on cleaning up his wounds.

Gingerly.

Tenderly.

What he really needed was a shower, but I knew there was no way I could hold him up, and I had an inclination that getting this man naked would be a bad, terrible idea.

So, I just kept rinsing the cloth, ringing it out, going back time and again.

Caring for him, a stupid part of me wishin' it'd always been my job. That he'd returned it. Been there for us when we needed him most.

A heavy sigh pushed from his mouth, and his head kept sagging forward, the man close to passing out. I was pretty sure that was more from the alcohol than any of the injuries he'd sustained.

Tipping his chin up, I dabbed at the biggest cut over his eye, his striking face right there.

He opened his eyes when I did.

Potent blue gazed up at me. Intense and wild and running to places neither of us could afford for them to go.

"Izzy Baby," he grated.

I struggled to swallow around the lump.

"You've got to stop." The words shook as fiercely as my hand.

His head rocked to the right side, and his mouth was tweaking up again, arrogance sliding free. "You remember, Little Bird? Bein' with me?" Big hands gripped me by the thighs. "Sneaking away so we could get lost? How fuckin' perfect I fit in this body?"

A flashfire of memories sped through my mind. Incinerating everything. All rationale. All logic.

He grunted. "Never have had a woman that felt so good. Nothin' has ever felt so good as Izzy Lane."

Redness clawed and streaked, a fire lapping higher.

I struggled to fight them. To extinguish the flames.

"Almost finished," I grated, words so rough I didn't even know how I managed to force them out.

"But I wasn't good to keep you. Wanted to keep you. Fuck . . . Izzy, I wanted to keep you." His confession was slurred, edged in sorrow, hinting at desperation.

I had to stop this. Stop this before he said things we'd both regret.

We needed to talk.

But not like this.

Not when our defenses were shot and our sanity had fled.

I moved to the cabinet, inhaling cleansing breaths as I rummaged around for a bottle of alcohol. Unscrewing the cap, I covered the opening with a cotton ball and tipped it over, and I tried to prepare myself for when I turned back around.

But he was still there.

Looking at me like he wanted to devour me. Like he wanted to cry.

God, had we gotten ourselves into a mess. And I tried to remember all the hurt inflicted as I swabbed the cotton ball over the gashes on his face. To remember the way it'd felt when he told me he didn't want me anymore. That picture of him with her engrained in my head as I bandaged the wound.

"Never good enough, Little Bird. Wanted you to fly," he rumbled, as if he were hearing every single one of those thoughts. But even if he had, that wasn't reason enough for him to do what he'd done.

He'd broken me.

Shattered me.

Left me weak.

I'd struggled for so long to be strong. To be the kind of mama I wanted for my boys.

He didn't get to negate that by still claiming that stupid belief that the two of us didn't belong together because we were from opposite sides of the proverbial tracks.

"Can't believe we made a baby," he kept on, though it was choppy, getting caught on barbs of grief.

Could feel them penetrating both of us.

Arrows piercing deep.

"We made a baby," he whimpered.

Agony blistered from his body, seeping from his skin, and he dropped his face to my stomach. Those hands that had felt seductive shifted in possession, digging in like a plea.

"I didn't get to hold him. I didn't get to hold him, Izzy."

The magnitude of his pain almost dropped me to my knees.

Gutting.

Obliterating.

"Please . . . stop, Maxon," I begged. Begged desperately because I couldn't handle what he was sayin'. The truth that he hadn't had the chance. The choice because of the bad choices we'd both made.

"You're breakin' my heart." I ran my fingers through his hair, wishing I could take away something—some piece of what we'd both been through. "We'll talk about this when you're sober. When we both can think straight."

But he wasn't stopping.

A groan left him, a low wail of mourning that rippled through my body. His hands cinched tighter. "What happened to him,

Izzy? What happened? What did I do wrong? What did I do wrong? I'm so sorry. I'm so sorry."

His words turned into a mumble of disorder, mind fading in and out of coherency.

Anguished.

Tortured.

I reached out, prying his face away from my stomach, and forced him to look at me.

"You didn't do anything wrong. It was my fault."

My fault.

Grief blistered through my being. The reality of my naivety.

He grabbed my wrist and pressed his mouth to the inside of my forearm. "No. Perfect."

I trembled under his caress, and I squeezed my eyes closed to break the connection, unable to take it a second more. I pried my hand away and tried not to look at his eyes as I finished applying his bandages.

I had to stop what was happening in this bathroom before I had no chance of escaping it.

"Come on, let's get you into bed."

I helped him into his room, trying to keep my distance, which was basically impossible considering the way the man leaned on me as he staggered across the floor.

I sat him down on the edge of his bed, and he flopped onto his back, so close to passing out.

Which was exactly what I needed him to do. Close those eyes and that mouth and let us both rest.

It'd all become too much.

I leaned over him, hating that I felt even an ounce of attraction right then. That my belly would tighten with need, a fire blooming when it should have been left to ash.

Hands shaking out of control, I flicked the button of his jeans and pulled down his fly.

The muscles on his abdomen rippled and danced.

"Izzy Baby."

"Shh," I told him as I dragged his pants down his thick legs, tossing my gaze to the far wall to keep myself from looking at him in his underwear, hating that every cell in my body felt heavy and needy at the thought.

I managed to wind them off his feet without peekin' like a creep.

I pulled down his covers. He rolled into them with a sigh, and I covered him up.

"Little Bird fly," he muttered, close to incoherent.

Still, I heard it somewhere in my soul.

One second later, he was passed out, and I sat there in the muted light, watching him breathe.

The steady rise and fall of his chest.

The man so beautiful it wasn't fair to my broken heart. My mind so conflicted and confused I had no idea where we stood.

My gaze caressed over him.

Like a fool, I reached out and traced my fingertips down the dragon he had tattooed on his left arm.

It appeared as if it were perched on his shoulder, the tail wrapping down and around his arm, the monster's eyes red and confused.

Beautiful and deadly.

"My dragon."

I knew if I got too close, I was gonna get burned.

eleven

MACK
SEVEN YEARS OLD

Mack darted through the forest, moving tree to tree, hiding behind their fat trunks as he stalked around the perimeter of the meadow.

Stealthy and fast.

He crouched down, peering out behind a big oak, her sprawling, spindly branches twisted and gnarled. Some stretched toward the sky before they drooped to the side, and others crawled along close to the ground, like fingers reaching out to dip into the yellow flowers that grew wild in the clearing.

Streaks of sunlight sheered through the sky, touching down like glittering darts on the toppled trees and gurgling stream.

Movement rustled in the middle of it, and Mack jerked, shooting to attention, before he went running to pounce.

Sprinting as hard as he could, he hurdled over a downed log, splashing into the water, coming up fast on the other side.

He dove, just barely missin' the rabbit that went scurrying away.

He flopped onto his butt.

Dang it.

He wasn't ever gonna be a hunter, especially if the only thing he could hunt with was his bare hands.

He froze when he heard the rustle from above. The tinkling laughter that filtered down, impaling him like those laser-beam rays of light.

He peered up into the dense tree that sat at the edge of the meadow. Already knowing what he'd find. Or who he'd find.

Her face peering down just as intently as he was peering her direction, the girl at least twenty feet up in the tree, and his chest was clutching in a strange way.

In a way that made him want to shout at her to get down.

"You missed it," she said, like he didn't know.

He scowled, not likin' it one bit that she'd seen it. "What are you doin' followin' me? Thought I told you not to come down around here?"

It wasn't safe.

There were snakes and spiders . . . and . . . and his dad.

Something ugly crawled under his skin. He had to stop himself from climbing that tree and hauling her down himself.

But there she was, perched in her nest.

She laughed, shifting around to sit on the branch. "Who said you get to tell me what to do?"

"Well, your pa sure isn't gonna like it if he knew you were up in that tree."

He was always yellin' at her that she was gonna break her neck. Mack promised himself he wasn't ever gonna let that happen. But he wasn't sure how he was supposed to stop it if she never listened.

She was always going on, doing her own thing, singing and laughing and playing.

Free.

Following him everywhere. He couldn't ditch her, no matter how hard he tried. She was a pest, a tag-along who wouldn't leave him be and made him feel strange in a way he wasn't sure that he liked.

Her eyes went wide from her roost. "You wouldn't go and tell him?"

He crossed his arms over his chest. "And why shouldn't I?"

She started to scramble down, faster than she should, her foot going for a branch that was too thin.

She stepped on it, and Mack's heart lurched. He raced to get under her right as it snapped.

She screamed.

He stretched out his arms, trying to stop her fall, and her body hit his with a smack. It was nothing but a blur of her wild, wild hair, her flailing arms and thrashing legs.

He held her tight against himself as the impact sent him tumbling back onto the meadow floor.

Arms wrapped around her as fiercely as he could.

Protecting her.

Ignoring the pain when his head struck the ground.

Ignoring the way his chest felt funny when she scrambled around, her hands planted on either side of his head as she stared down at him. "You saved me again."

"Told you I would."

She smiled. Smiled this smile that was brighter than the sun that cast her head in a halo. "That's because you're my best friend."

He frowned. "You can't be my best friend."

She frowned right back, still pinning him. "Why's that?"

"Because I'm a boy and you're a girl."

"So?"

He hurried to think of a better reason.

"Because I'm a dragon and you're a bird. I might eat you."

She laughed, her face twisting up in joy.

He felt it, too.

Joy.

He couldn't help but smile back at her.

"Doesn't matter if you're a dragon. You're still my best friend. We can fly away together."

"But what if I'm mean?"

She sat up, pushing off him. He sat up, too.

"You're not mean."

"Mack!"

They both cringed when his daddy's voice cracked through the heavens. Coming from the direction of his house.

His house that was so much different than Izzy Lane's.

Hers was like a castle.

His mama called theirs a shack.

But it hadn't felt so small until his daddy had gotten back, out of prison for doin' something bad, but his mama wouldn't never tell him what it was. The only thing he knew was now everything felt different. Wrong and ugly and black.

"Mack!" his father shouted again, and fear slithered down Mack's spine.

Izzy bit down on her bottom lip and grabbed his hand. He realized it was shaking. That his whole body was shaking.

She weaved her fingers through his, and she whispered, "Don't worry, my dragon. I'll save you, too."

twelve

MACK

Harsh rays of light impaled my face. I squeezed my eyes against them, desperate to cling to sleep.

Oblivion.

That's right where I wanted to stay.

Reality danced at the periphery of my mind. A haze of blurred and distorted memories taunting me from the sidelines.

Getting ready to jump into the ring of chaos at the center of my brain.

Lying on my chest, I pressed my face into my pillow, trying not to groan out loud at the pain that splintered through my body.

Head to fucking toe.

What the hell happened last night?

Felt like I'd been put through a meat grinder.

Skin raw. Body stiff and brutally sore.

But none of that came close to the torture I could feel eating at the deepest depths of me.

No chance I could keep it at bay.

Nothing I could do to stop that face from slamming into my consciousness.

A wrecking ball.

Demolishing the foundation I'd built.

That kid. That kid.

My reason. The sacrifice I'd had to make.

No longer did any of it make sense.

Groaning low, I rolled onto my side. I had to drag myself out of this bed and face the boatload of bullshit I'd gotten myself into last night.

Was gonna be lucky if I didn't find my ass chained to a desk job for the next six months.

Then I froze.

Awareness gripped me everywhere. A million tiny needles prickling across my skin.

Pained pleasure.

I pushed onto my hands and tried not to fucking toss what was left in my stomach at the punch of agony coming from my mangled body.

I ignored it, instead swinging my gaze to the side, breath fucking hitching in my throat as everything came rushing back in vivid colors and dramatic scenes.

She'd come to me.

Had been waiting for me.

Had stayed.

My gaze fixed on the oversized lounge chair that was usually under the window that had been pulled up close to my bed.

Girl curled up on it. Fast asleep.

Locks of that hair a shiny river cascading around her shoulders, a mess of blondes and browns that glinted in the light and had me wishing I could reach out and touch it.

Fist my hands in it.

Use it to hold her close.

Her tiny body—way too thin, still too goddam perfect—was contorted where she'd clearly been trying to find a comfortable spot.

A throw that barely covered half of her was twisted around her torso.

So pretty that looking at her hurt like a bitch, too.

Regret hurtled at me.

I'd felt it before, but never quite like this.

Never where I'd thought that maybe . . . maybe I should have made a different decision. Always thinking I'd been doing her the best that I could do her.

Ruining her in a way that would set her free.

Because I'd always known I couldn't keep her.

My dick didn't get the memo, though, fucker hard as steel where it was pressed to my bed. I pushed up to sitting, readjusting myself, trying not to moan.

Pain and need.

Pain and need.

Story of my fucking life.

I started to stand so I could slip into the bathroom when she stirred.

Those hazel eyes blinked open, intensity building as she came to the realization that she was right there.

With me.

Probably the last place that she wanted to be.

She scrambled to sit up, discomfort and uncertainty coming off her in waves. Slamming me. Ricocheting back.

Two of us lost to that power that cinched down tight.

The connection that had only been ours.

I scratched at the back of my neck, cleared my throat, barely peeked over at her, afraid that I might scare her away. "Hey."

She heaved out a sigh and gathered the throw against her chest, clutching it like protection. She was still wearing the same pants that had made me want to come in mine from yesterday, her blouse wrinkled, her tiny feet bare.

Her eyes were sleepy and her lips were pouty, shyness creeping across her pale skin.

Sexy as fuck.

"Hey," she whispered back. "How are you feelin'?"

A rough chuckle left me. "Like shit."

"I'm thinkin' after what happened, we should be looking to the bright side and being thankful that at least you're here to feel that way."

There was something in it, something sweet and serious. Something tender that tightened my chest and made my heart beat harder. This boom, boom, boom that was taking to the air in the room.

I dropped my attention to the floor. "My job's dangerous, Izzy."

"I know," she murmured, edging forward, "but it seems to me you went looking for trouble last night."

Resting my forearms on my thighs, I looked over at her. Full of regret. Not having a fucking clue what to say except, "I'm sorry."

"I'm sorry, too." Those hazel eyes were wide and sincere.

I struggled to swallow around the rock lodged in my throat. "I have a son."

It wasn't so much of a question. Just a clarification. Just needing her to look at me and tell me what the fuck had happened. How I didn't know.

"Yes."

I forced myself to keep my gaze steady on her. "What's his name?"

"Benjamin." She squeezed her eyes closed when she said it while her confession nearly sent me toppling back.

My heart clutched, stalling out, grinding to a standstill. My head started to nod, pain leaking out.

Benjamin was my middle name.

"You named him after me."

"You're his father." She said it like it made sense. Like my entire world hadn't been tossed upside down.

I sucked in a staggered breath.

Izzy inhaled deeply, sitting forward, and then started to rush,

"I know this is so much for you to take in, and you shouldn't have found out the way that you did. I came here last night . . . to apologize for that. It was wrong. Wrong that I invited you over for a family dinner like you could just slide right into the table like you'd been there all along. I'm sorry that I didn't find a way to tell you sooner."

"Why didn't you?" I asked, that hollowed out space inside of me howling like a bitch.

Unease had her shifting in the chair. "I tried. You know that I tried."

My mind flashed to the calls I'd ignored. Close to a hundred of them. All coming in within the first six months after she'd left. Then . . . I'd received one . . . a couple months after she'd stopped calling.

My spirit sank. Was pretty sure straight to the pits of hell.

"You called me the night he was born?"

Silence bounded around the room. The pain radiating from her flesh vivid. Like fresh blood gushing from a cut to her soul that had never stopped bleeding.

"I . . . I needed you that day." Her face pinched in agony. "He almost died. His umbilical cord had been wrapped around his neck. I waited too long because I was scared to be alone and wanted to pretend I wasn't in the position that I was. I hadn't told my mama or my daddy . . . I'd just . . . left. Told them I needed a fresh start. That I couldn't stay in Broadshire Rim after what you'd done to me."

Those lips trembled in agony. "I didn't go stumbling into the ER until I was holding my belly, screaming because he was almost there."

Torment spun around us. Drawing us together. Pushing us apart. "All I remember was them getting me into a room and shouting at me to push, then the doctor shouting at me not to, but I couldn't stop. He wasn't breathing when he was born. He was . . . blue."

Her face twisted in horror, like she was right back there, reliving the moment, the words vibrating with emotion. "Completely blue. Not moving. Not crying. They finally got him breathing and rushed him to the newborn ICU. It was the middle of the night . . . I was . . . terrified. Absolutely terrified. And the only thing I wanted was to hear your voice. For you to tell me you'd save me. Save us. The way you'd always done."

"Izzy." It was a sob. A shout. I didn't fucking know. Only thing I knew was I wanted to bang my head against a wall. Make it go away. Stop it. Turn back time.

Sadness took to her features, and she was chewing at her quivering bottom lip, trying to keep herself from crying. "My mama and daddy came as soon as I called them. I wasn't alone for long."

"Don't make excuses for me."

Her shoulder lifted at one side, that tenderness that was this girl right there. "Oh, I'm not, Maxon. There's a very big part of myself that has hated you all this time. Hated what you did to me."

"If I could—"

She gave a harsh shake of her head. "I'm not here for you to make apologies or excuses, Maxon. I came back to Broadshire Rim because Benjamin was accepted into a study here in Charleston. A study that might be able to help him fully walk again. Have his independence. I came back for him. Not for us."

I gave a tight nod, my fingers clutched together, squeezing to keep myself from flying to my feet and putting a fist through the wall. "What's wrong with him?"

A lumbering sigh parted her lips. "He has cerebral palsy. No one knew until about nine months after he was born that he'd suffered a brain injury from the oxygen deficit at birth. He just . . . wasn't progressing normally. Wasn't crawling or playing with his toys the way an infant would at his age."

Indecision had her shifting, glancing at the floor before she finally looked back at me. "He's an amazing child, Maxon. Amazing and smart and he works so hard that just watchin' him breaks my heart. Makes it bust up with pride. I was warned he might not ever walk, might not ever talk, but after seven surgeries, he took his first step."

That was it.

All I could take.

I sprang to my feet, welcoming the searing pain that sheered through my body.

A thousand knives slicing me into pieces.

Aggression curling through me, I pressed both my fists to the wall, like it could absorb the brunt force of the hatred I felt right then.

Arms shaking with restrained exertion.

Teeth gritting.

I flew back around, jagged breaths surging out before I was dropping to my knees at her feet.

Shock rocked her back, and I grabbed her by the face. "I'm so sorry. I'm so fuckin' sorry. And those words don't mean a goddamn thing, but I am."

I knew I'd spewed a bunch of shit at her last night. That she didn't believe a fucking word I said. But I was going to prove to her that she could.

Tears blurred her eyes, that mesmerizing dance of browns and greens. "I should have come back sooner. Told you. But it was easier for me to stay away than to have to face you. I'm sorry for that."

"Don't apologize to me, Izzy. I was mad . . . shocked yesterday . . . but you don't have anything to be sorry for."

It was on me.

All the blame.

All the fault.

Just like it'd always been.

"I want to know him."

She blinked hard, and a slew of tears slipped down her gorgeous face. There was nothing I could do but gather them up, my thumb tracking up the path of the moisture.

"I'm not sure you're ready for that, Maxon. I . . . I can't have you comin' into his life and then deciding it's too hard. I should have given you time to figure it out before. I realize that now. I just . . . got back here and saw you and got carried away."

I tightened my hold on her face. "I want to get carried away."

Fuck. I wanted to get carried away.

Run ahead and behind and in between. Be there for them,

every step of the way, racing a few extra million laps to make up for what I'd lacked.

A bluster of dread and worry flickered at the back of my brain.

Had anything really changed?

But there was no chance in hell I was gonna turn my back on my kid.

"He's my priority. Not you. Not me. It's my job to protect him."

"Let me protect him, too."

There was my answer—*everything* had changed.

I wasn't about to let my past railroad me any longer. Fear holding me hostage. Look what good that had done.

A war played out on her face, those teeth going to town on her bottom lip.

My guts twisted, wanting to dip in, kiss it away.

She glanced to the far wall, contemplating, before she looked back at me. "You really want to get to know him?"

"More than anything."

"Why don't you come back over tonight for dinner? But I . . . I'm not ready for us to tell him who you are. You're my old friend. Nothing more. Not until we both can be certain you can handle this."

Relief gusted through my soul.

So heavy I sagged forward and pressed my face to her heart that thundered in her chest. I wanted to reach out and touch it, carry some of her weight.

"Okay."

"Okay," she said.

She leaned back, searching for space. For distance. I had to fucking pry myself from the lure of that sweet body. Wanted to pick her up and pull her onto my lap.

Undress her fast and kiss her slow.

Hold her and fuck her and love her and keep her.

The way I should have done all those years ago.

Discomfort wound its way back into the atmosphere, and she looked at the clock before she angled those eyes back on me. "I need to get home and get a shower. I start work this mornin'. Do you think you'll be okay to take care of yourself?"

"Yeah. I'm okay."

Fucking lie, but it didn't have a thing to do with my busted to shit body.

I pushed to my feet and stretched out my hand. She hesitated for a second before she accepted it.

Every cell in my body tightened, the brush of her fire, the warmth of her hope.

"Thank you, Izzy. For coming here last night. For telling me. For giving me this chance."

"Don't mess it up." Of course because it was Izzy Lane, there was no hardness to it. Just sincerity.

I scratched at the back of my head, not wanting to let her leave. What I wanted was to drag her into the shower with me and have her take care of me the way I really needed her to.

But I was pretty sure she wasn't going to be up for that.

"I'm going to have your car looked at today. Where are you working?"

How pathetic was it that I didn't know a thing about her? Where she'd gone and how she'd truly been. Only knew these few minor details that were so major that my head was still spinning, nearly as fast as my spirit was reeling.

"Nelson Dentistry," she answered.

"All right," I told her, calculating how I was going to make all of this happen today.

She stood a foot away, itching, the air between us alive. "All right. I'll see you tonight at seven."

"I can't wait."

She grabbed her shoes from where she'd left them on the floor and threaded the straps through her fingers. Her hair fell all around her, those lips and those eyes so dominant in her slender face.

So goddamn gorgeous I wanted to reach out and touch her again.

She looked up at me with the full force of that beauty.

"Just . . . be careful with him, Maxon. That child has endured enough pain for a lifetime."

She turned and started for the door, and the second she did, a million questions started coming at me. Faster and faster. Blow after blow.

Finally, couldn't keep it in, and the words were getting loose from my tongue. "Dillon's dad?"

Jealousy burned on my skin.

Had no right to it. But it was there. Wound up in that cute kid who'd been bouncing around, nothing but a pistol.

She froze at the doorway, spine going rigid. Slowly, she turned to look back at me. "That's not somethin' I want to talk about, Maxon. This is about you and Benjamin. That's it."

"You sure about that?"

Couldn't help but exert it.

This.

Us.

The fact it was going to happen.

She held me with nothing but nostalgia and regret in that mesmerizing gaze. "You hurt me, Maxon. You hurt me somethin' fierce. I'm not sure I can handle that kind of hurtin' again."

Then she left me there, my fists clenched at my side, a silent promise on my tongue.

She was mine.

And I'd never let a fucking thing hurt her again.

thirteen

IZZY

"You spent the night at his house?" Faith screeched through the line.

My attention went darting around my surroundings, and I lowered my voice to a hiss as if it were the world's most sordid secret. "Would you be quiet? Someone might hear you."

Light laughter rolled out of her. "Like who? Your conscience?"

"This isn't funny," I said. "You know it wasn't anything like that."

Except for all those stupid feelings that had kept rising to the surface the whole time. The turmoil that spun, his and mine, the need that had become partner to it all.

Not to mention, having to sleep in that chair next to where he was lying, the man moaning throughout his sleep, whimpering my name the whole time.

It'd done a number on me.

"You're the one who told me I needed to tell him, and look what happened," I accused without an ounce of anger.

I could almost feel the shift of her demeanor, her mood sobering as she exhaled in what sounded like sympathy. "You knew it wasn't gonna be easy, but you knew it had to happen. Living with that weight was nothin' but a burden to you, Izzy. It was time. Way past time."

"I know." Exhaling long, I pressed my trembling fingers to my forehead where I stood beneath a tree trying to hide out from the blazing sun.

I'd slipped out for my lunch break and called Faith, needing someone to confide in.

Get this disorder of emotions off my chest.

"I'm proud of you for going back over there. That took a lot of courage," she added.

I paced a circle. "I just . . . I'm terrified of what happens now. He's insisting he wants to be a part of Benjamin's life, but he doesn't have the first clue what that really means. I mean, God, you should have seen the way he took off runnin' when he saw Benjamin. The man was the definition of a cowardly cat with his tail caught on fire."

"Did you expect anything different? You knocked that man for a loop . . . Jace and Ian got a call to go down to Monty's to talk the guy down, he was so distraught. Shocked. He deserved that time, and it didn't take him all that long to come to his senses."

"Whose side are you on?"

"Yours. Mack's. Benjamin's. Love's. Whatever you want to call it."

Sometimes her belief was infuriating.

"Can't you just man bash him with me for a little while?" I all but begged. Still, the hint of a tease was weaving its way into my tone.

I could almost see her pursing her lips, not sure if she wanted to laugh or chastise me. "Is that what you really want? To bash that man more after what he went through last night? Not to mention the fact that you walloped him a good one, too."

Regret churned in my spirit as I let myself grasp how serious this was.

The man could have died.

What she was so conveniently forgettin' was that he'd walloped *me* a good one first.

And that was the crux of Maxon Chambers.

He'd give. Give and give and give. In all the wrong ways.

Believing his own safety wasn't of worth. Making all the wrong decisions when he thought he was bein' noble.

And I couldn't help but worry that was exactly what he was doing now.

Doing the honorable thing and trying to do right by his son. That was all good and well except for the fact our hearts were tangled in the middle of it.

"No, it's not. Of course, not. Doesn't mean that makes it any easier."

Faith pushed out a slow sigh, and I could hear her wavering, struggling with what to say, and I knew she was getting ready to lay it out the way she always did.

No holds barred.

"Think you need to ask yourself what it is you're really scared of, Izzy."

"You know exactly what it is I'm scared of," I whispered bluntly.

No use in hiding it.

I blinked away the moisture that threatened my eyes.

Truth was, I was terrified. Terrified of the way he made me feel. Terrified of the power he still wielded. Terrified of those blue eyes that screamed sincerity.

The man just standing there with that beautiful body, begging for my trust.

And trust?

It was the pinnacle of loyalty.

The culmination of hope.

Grace given in love.

He'd held all of mine in the palms of those hands.

Fisted it so tightly that he'd crushed it.

I knew it.

Knew it in my gut.

That man could wreck me anew, and I couldn't afford for that to happen.

"And maybe that is exactly what makes it worth it, taking this chance," she urged in her soft way.

"I have to be strong for my boys." It was nothin' but a defense.

"And sometimes strength reveals itself in our vulnerabilities. In our willingness to lay ourselves on the line. Maybe that's exactly what he's doing."

"Well, I guess we're going to figure that out pretty quick since I went and invited him over to dinner tonight."

I almost rolled my eyes at myself. I couldn't even make the man suffer it out for a day or two before I was inviting him back through my door.

Nothing but a masochist.

But there'd been no resisting the sorrow that had been clear. The truth of it. The intensity of it.

Maxon was broken over this. But he'd been broken all his life. And I just prayed that brokenness didn't destroy us all in the end.

Heaving out the weight of the worries, I glanced at my watch. "I better go. Lunch is almost over. I need to get back inside."

"Okay, call me later and let me know how it goes tonight."

"I will," I said before I ended the call and peeked over at the office door where I'd started my new job little more than four hours before.

Luckily, I'd taken to it quickly, the software they used the same as at my old office. Suffice it to say, Helen had been pleased, going on about how I was going to work out just fine while I'd been struggling to focus on work at all.

Leaving the shade of the tree, I jogged across the parking lot and hopped onto the sidewalk running the front of the strip mall.

I was just getting ready to pull the door open when Dr. Nelson popped out of the fancy car that had pulled into a spot in the front, wearing another pair of scrubs, smiling his bright white smile.

He rounded the front of his car, tossing his keys in the air and catching them as he approached.

"Isabel."

"Hello, Dr. Nelson," I managed as I stepped back in his direction, nervously tucking a strand of hair behind my ear as I tried to turn my attention to the job rather than the disorder I'd left whirling back under that tree.

Problem was, it was doing its best to follow me.

"How did this morning go?"

"I think it went pretty well."

He tipped up a smile. "Pretty and modest."

My brow lifted. "Excuse me?"

Did he just call me pretty?

He chuckled under his breath, waving me off. "Sorry, ignore me. I was just thinking out loud. What I meant to say is you're being modest about it only going *okay*. Helen has told me no less than ten times that you're the perfect fit for the office and basically saved her life."

There was nothing I could do to stop the flush that rushed to my cheeks. "Well . . . I think she might be exaggeratin' a bit."

He grinned, leaning back. "I doubt that."

More redness. This time rushing all over. "Well . . . I . . . thank you," I finally settled on, not exactly sure what to say, feeling a little unsettled with the way he was appraising me.

"Thank you for stepping up the way that you have. We needed someone like you in the office."

"I'm really happy to have this job," I told him, right before my attention was getting hooked. Stuck on the roar of the big truck that rumbled into the lot.

My breath snagged in my throat when I realized who was driving, Maxon's face so gorgeous when he pulled into an open spot and hopped out.

My heart that had barely leveled since I'd left his house this mornin' shifted into overdrive.

This out of control pound, pound, pound that beat in time with every overconfident step he took. As if my entire being was emitting a thundering signal that begged him to come my way.

He wore jeans and a tight-fitted tee, just innuendos of those tattoos I'd seen last night peeking out the bottom of the sleeves, the rest of the innocuous shapes winding down into the art on his forearms.

The grime from last night had been washed away, but the butterfly bandage over his eye was still intact.

It only made him appear sexier.

Rougher and rawer and everything that shouldn't be making my mouth go dry.

Dr. Nelson turned his focus in the direction mine had gone, and he reached out and set a hand on my arm as if he thought he needed to offer protection.

"You know this guy?" His voice sounded with speculation and distrust.

"Yeah," I barely managed.

Maxon's easiness faltered when he saw Dr. Nelson touching me.

His chin lifting and those eyes flashing possessively. If I didn't know better, I would have been sure there was smoke puffing from his nose.

"Maxon, what are you doin' here?" The words were a rasp.

"Told you I was going to get your car taken care of today. You didn't think I'd forget, did you?" Confidence rode out with the question, and that strong brow lifted as his eyes dropped to Dr. Nelson who was still gripping my arm.

The problem was, I didn't have the first clue what to think when it came to him.

What to say or what to do.

So I just stood there staring with my mouth hanging open.

Maxon cocked his head, waiting. Then he put out his hand as a smirk twitched up at the corner of that lust-inducing mouth. "I'm going to need those keys, beautiful."

I nearly had a stroke right there. It was bad enough last night when he was mumbling those sweet things incoherently. But out in broad daylight? In front of my new boss?

Every cell in my body was seizing.

He edged forward, and I was inhaling, sucking down the

overwhelming presence of the man. "Izzy . . . your keys?"

"Oh, right, right," I fumbled, snapping out of the spell he had me under. Apparently, I went stupid when I had two very gorgeous men loomin' over me.

Sucking in a breath, I stepped away from Dr. Nelson without drawing too much attention to the act and turned all my focus to digging around in my massive purse I had slung over my shoulder, kind of wishing it was big enough for me to crawl into so I could hide. Disappear.

I finally found them and pulled them out, and I held them up like a prize. "Here we go."

Maxon sent me a smile. One of those smiles that had my tummy tumbling and my pulse going haywire. Dimple denting on one side of that cheek and those blue eyes dancing.

Oh lord. What was he tryin' to do to me?

He stuck his hand out under them, and I dropped them into his waiting palm.

Kind of like he was asking me to do with my trust.

"Thank you," I told him honestly.

Wholeheartedly.

His expression softened, and his lips pressed together. "It's the least I can do."

I bit down on my lip to try to keep the wash of emotion from floodin' my eyes, and I simply nodded, taking a step back toward the office.

He seemed to take the hint that I needed to get back to work, though he hesitated, looking back at Dr. Nelson who seemed to be staring him down.

What in the world was happening?

But there was no missing the tension banging between the two of them.

Some sort of challenge being thrown.

Mack's eyes narrowed before they slowly shifted back to me. "I'll have this back before you get off."

"Thank you again," I whispered.

He nodded, then glared back at Dr. Nelson before he turned and started across the lot toward my car. He paused to glance over his shoulder. "Can't wait for tonight, Little Bird."

The oxygen jumped from my lungs, and my chest heaved at the outward affection, knees wobbling with the way he was lookin' at me.

And I knew right then that I was in so much trouble.

Taking my discomfort all wrong, or maybe he'd gotten it exactly right, Dr. Nelson set his hand on the small of my back. "We should go inside."

I nodded around the lump in my throat, and I let him open the door and guide me in, more than thankful for the blast of cold air on my face.

Anything to cool the burn.

God knew, I'd be a fool to stand in the flames.

fourteen

MACK

I pressed the button to accept the call on Bluetooth in the Suburban. Didn't even have the chance to say hello before Pete's voice was coming at me through the speakers.

"You're alive!"

He sang it like he was a cast member of some terrible Broadway show.

"Feel like death. Does that count?"

He laughed outright. "You were beat to shit, man. Have to be honest—you scared the piss out of me when I rolled up on the scene and you were flat out and facedown. Thought I might have lost you."

"Apparently, Baren and Dominguez got there right as one of

those pussies found themselves a nice steel rod. They'd have shown up a few seconds later, and it would have been lights out for me. Too bad the rats scattered before either of them had made it out of their cruiser."

Regret tightened my throat like a noose.

What if yesterday on Izzy's porch would have been my only chance? The one time I'd seen my son? His one memory of me splitting like a bitch?

Sickness clawed, and I forced it down, hands cinching on the steering wheel.

Instantly, I wished I hadn't done that, either.

Truth was, every movement was brutal. Every inhale agony. Ribs burning like a motherfucker, and my skin feeling like I'd gotten up close and personal with a cheese grater.

Funny how I didn't think I'd ever felt so alive.

The sensation of Izzy's presence still wrapped me like an embrace.

I inhaled, and I could still smell her.

Closed my eyes, and I could still feel the tender caress of those fingers. Could still hear the soft cadence of her voice.

Girl had taken care of me like I was something that deserved to be cared for, same way as she always had. Filling me up when I was nothing. Maybe that was the reason I'd gotten greedy.

Just like I was feeling then.

Because I was dealing with another problem when I closed my eyes—I saw that pompous fucker wearing scrubs with his hand on her like he thought he had every right to put it there.

Took everything I'd had not to rip it clean from his body since it'd been clear he was staking some sort of claim. Figured that wouldn't go over all that well. All I needed was a headline about a local detective going rogue and coming unglued on some poor, unsuspecting nurse or whatever the fuck that he was.

Except I was pretty sure the asshole would be *expecting* it.

Gauntlet thrown.

"How'd it go with Woods?" Pete asked, breaking me out of the haze of anger.

Unclenching my locked jaw, I somehow managed a grin. "You

know she loves me."

Could almost see the disbelieving smile crack his face. "You asshole. Don't tell me you got off scot-free again."

Wanted to roll my eyes. *Again* was a stretch. Sure, I'd gotten into a few situations that weren't exactly protocol. But I toed the line the best that I could. Respected the rules and my sergeant.

"Seemed she couldn't be too mad at me when she was looking at me beat to crap. Four to one. There was nothing else I could have done. Of course, she has me on the desk for four weeks so I can heal, and my ass is off the case."

Not that I was going to just sit aside and let someone else take care of this bullshit. Still, I'd agreed like the good cop I did my best to be.

"Any idea why they jumped you? Why they found you?"

"Guess they thought it'd be good fun to kill a cop. Sport. Or maybe the prick was just pissed he had to pay the fine. Who fuckin' knows."

"Why's it seem like people get more twisted every day?"

"Because they do," I responded.

Though, I had to admit I wasn't 100% sold on that idea. I'd seen enough depravity and cruelty as a kid to know that sort of sickness had been around for a long, long time.

"Remember the good old days when kids were fighting over drugs and turf?" he mused.

I let loose a short laugh. "Think you still have plenty of that to go around."

"Seriously, though . . . these senseless crimes . . . don't get it, man. It's starting to wear."

I grunted. "Aren't they all senseless?" I asked as I took a left from the main road and started to head toward my house.

A pulse of anxiousness jumped into my veins. Been pulsing the whole day, really, even though I'd been trying to keep it cool.

Knowing I was going to get the chance to really meet my son. Praying that old saying that we only got one first impression didn't count in this case, considering I'd blown that one to shit.

Another shock of apprehension blistered beneath my skin.

Couldn't wait to stand in front of him. Look at him. Maybe

even get the chance to wrap him in my arms like I was aching to do.

Whole time hoping I could be a better man than the one I'd become. The one I'd been bred to be.

A coward who acted out of fear.

"Guess so," Pete continued. "It's hard for me to process bullshit like that at all . . . but when there's nothing for them to gain but life in prison? What the fuck is that?"

"I'm with you, man."

"Any leads?" Pete asked.

"Car from yesterday was abandoned down on 5th. Baren and Dominguez went to the prick's house this morning. Loser lives in his mom's basement. Of course, she claims she hasn't seen him since yesterday."

"Typical."

"Yup. But we'll get them."

These cases were easy. Four idiots. One of them would make a mistake. Wouldn't be all that hard to hunt them down.

"So, who's the girl?"

My heart thudded with his abrupt change of subject, and I took the last right into my neighborhood.

"Izzy." Her name was like a rough stroke of lust running off my tongue.

"Know her name, asshole. I want to know what she means to you."

She means everything.

Couldn't bring myself to say it. Not when I knew she wasn't ready. So, I gave him the most basic truth. "My oldest friend."

He barked out a laugh. "Your friend? Didn't look like a friend to me. Thought I was going to have to stop you from humping her leg."

I blew out a strained sigh. "Not like that."

"Really."

"Nope."

He sobered. "Ahhh," he finally drew out. "Always wondered."

"Wondered what?" Came out harsher than I intended.

He chuckled in disbelief. "Come on, man. You think it's not

obvious something's haunted you? The way you live your life like it doesn't matter? Tell me, does it matter now?"

Last thing I wanted was to get into this with him. Jace and Ian blowing up my phone with texts all day was bad enough.

Both of them stricken that they'd left and I'd been jumped. Then the speculations had started firing when I'd finally admitted that Izzy had come.

"Listen, I've got to go."

"Hot date?" he razzed.

"You want your ass kicked?"

He laughed again. "Whatever, Mack." He paused, tone sobering when he said, "That girl seemed sweet. She's not anything like Clarissa. Be careful."

No. He was right. She wasn't a thing like Clarissa.

"Talk to you later." I ended the call before he could get in another word.

I jumped out of my Suburban, getting ready to race inside so I could change my clothes.

Excited.

Antsy.

Nervous as hell.

Spent my life thinking I couldn't have this kind of joy, coming to terms with the fact that I had to live with that hollowed out vacancy that howled inside of me.

With the pain of letting her go.

With the regret of the way I'd done it.

Now, that *joy* was right there, waiting for me to reach out and take it.

It was the kind of joy I'd only ever found in that girl.

Starting up the two side steps that led onto the porch, I came up short when I noticed my truck in my periphery. I blinked, thinking I was seeing things.

What the hell?

All the side windows were busted in, metal beat to shit, but it was what was spray-painted on the side of the truck that had a cold slick of apprehension seeping beneath my skin.

Pigs get slaughtered.

Disquiet billowed in the late afternoon air, and I instantly had my hand on the gun strapped to my side, eyes darting everywhere as I slowly edged back down that way, pulse speeding and boots crunching on the gravel.

Warily, I peered into my truck.

A rugged gray brick sat in the seat among the tiny squares of broken glass.

Awareness prickled at the back of my neck, hairs lifting as those dark places heaved.

Ominous. Menacing.

Threat written in black scratch.

Die cop, die.

Disgust knotted my stomach, and my throat locked up tight.

I slowly let my gaze move over my shoulder and across my front yard. Hot air whipped, and the trees rustled.

My ears filled with the echo of children playing down the street.

Innocent.

But I could feel it.

Something sinister rising in the air.

Knew it had to be the fuckers from last night. Had no idea how they'd found me. Why they'd be so stupid to come around here. Only thing I knew was I was going to track them down. Make them pay. Stop them before they had a chance of getting close to me or my family.

For the first time in years, I truly had something to lose.

fifteen

MACK

I did my best to cool the fire in my blood as I rounded the last turn up the bumpy lane.

A million emotions had chased me down as I'd taken the thirty-minute drive to her house.

Anger and rage over the threat that had been made, purposed and directed at me.

A stark reminder of my life.

The danger that lurked at every fucking corner.

Another reason I'd committed to not having a family, refusing to drag anyone into my mess.

Fact that I already had a family waiting at that house and those boys didn't even know it only doused that disorder in gas.

Izzy the match.

A slew of questions whirled, heart heavy with dread, nerves frazzled with this eagerness all at the same damned time.

Fuck, I was gonna lose it before I even got there.

Two seconds later, that big house came into view.

I pulled my Suburban to a stop behind Izzy's car, considering my truck was toast. A tow had come to haul it away so they could dust it, confirm my suspicion of who'd been responsible.

Before I let myself spiral any farther, I jumped out and strode across the bricked walkway. I took the porch steps in two bounds.

Heart knocking at my ribs, I rapped at the door.

Uneasily, I shifted on my feet, trying to beat back the anxiety.

But I could feel it rising. Reaching a boiling point. Getting ready to blow.

Once I walked through that door, nothing in my life was going to be the same.

The feeling only escalated when metal screeched and the lock was turned, and I felt myself close to losing my mind.

The door a cracked open. Izzy slipped out of it and quietly clicked it shut behind her.

A spike of that energy streaked through my blood, and my guts twisted in want, nothing but a steely need that hardened every cell in my body.

Swore to God, she nearly bowled me over.

My eyes raked over her, head to toe, and the girl was fighting one of those blushes, all nervous and agitated, the same way as she'd been earlier at the office.

Took everything I had not to reach out and stroke the color with my fingertips.

Caress it with my mouth, tongue thirsting to get a taste.

She'd changed into this flowy, black dress that had tiny yellow flowers all over the print, soft and sexy and fitted just right, a little plunge at the neckline that revealed next to nothing but teased me into next week.

She peeked up at me, teeth working at that bottom lip, nerves rolling through her slight body.

Emotion held fast to those hazel eyes, and I was pretty sure she was every bit as terrified as me.

Two of us standing at a precipice on the opposite sides, getting ready to take the dive together.

"Hey," she whispered beneath her breath, and I was wanting to lean in, inhale the word, her breath and her light and the sun.

Shit.

I was completely fucked.

I needed to get my shit together before I did something stupid like drop to a knee and ask her to marry me.

Bet she'd love that.

"Hey," I murmured back.

Smooth.

But there I was, tongue tied, heart fisted.

"You came." Hope twisted through the lines bunched on her forehead, and she tipped her face up toward me, studying me like I might be a riddle to solve.

I itched, wanting to reach out and trace the shape of her face.

That jaw and those lips.

Maybe dot a kiss or two to her eyes.

"Didn't actually think I wouldn't show, did you?" My voice hinted at a growl.

At the desperation I could feel lining my bones.

Her throat trembled when she took an uneasy swallow. "I guessed after yesterday, I thought you might have some reservations."

I edged forward, erasing almost all the distance between us, our hearts a thunder in what was left, the bare space alive.

Energy kicking.

I angled my head. "And after what happened last night and this morning?" The words dropped to a promise. "After I came by your work?"

There was something to that one, the jealousy I couldn't seem to keep contained, no matter how hard I tried.

Okay.

Wasn't trying at all.

Figured I'd better make my stance known before some slippery asshole snatched up the best girl in the world.

She released a trembling roll of laughter, although there didn't seem to be a whole lot of amusement to it. She peeked up at me. "So maybe it's my own questions that had me worried you might be having second thoughts."

"You don't trust me." It was a statement.

Of course, she didn't. She didn't have a reason to.

Not yet.

Just prayed I'd be good enough to prove to her that she could.

Lines dented her forehead. "I think the real problem is how quickly I'm offering that trust to you."

Some shape of relief filled my exhale, and I leaned even closer, this girl coming on like a drug.

Intoxicating.

Wild jasmine and the sun.

I sucked it down, and she was shivering as I pressed my mouth close to her temple and whispered, "I'm fucking scared, too."

She leaned back against the door, like she was searching for space. Only thing it did was make me want to press her to it, slide my palms up the bare flesh of her thighs barely concealed by that dress.

Her head rocked back on the wood, and it put that striking face on full display, her mouth a mere breath away. "We don't have the luxury of bein' scared, Maxon. This is real life. My children's lives. My children who are my entire world. And if you step through this door, that means I'm allowing you to be a part of it. That I'm taking that risk. Do you understand what I'm saying?"

Fear stretched tight across my chest. More glaring was the determination and devotion that covered it. "There's nothing more that I want than to be a part of that world."

I wavered for a second before I asked, "What did you tell them about what happened yesterday?"

"I told them that you weren't feelin' well and had to go home, but you were doing better today."

Her voice was a wisp. Close to a plea.

A flutter of soft amusement pulled at one side of that mouth that was making me crazy. "Dillon thinks we don't like each other much."

Couldn't help the draw, just . . . needing to touch. I reached out and took the first two fingers on her left hand, and I swung them between us.

A simple touch that was nothing but a wildfire.

Goddamn.

My heart leapt, spirit all too quick to get on board.

This was the way it was supposed to be.

She gasped in surprise—because I'd had the audacity to do it or from the shock of energy that went racing, I didn't know. "Problem's never been how much I like you, Little Bird."

Flustered, Izzy shifted, pulled her fingers away, and cleared her throat. "This isn't about us," she reminded me, though I could feel the need radiating from her soft, flushed skin.

"Isn't it?"

"Maxon . . ."

Blinking a bunch of times, she glanced away before she looked back at me, a shield visibly coming up, the girl trying with everything to block me out.

"We'd better get in there. The boys are probably bouncing from the walls by now. Can't believe they actually minded this time and stayed inside."

Softness filled her gaze. No doubt, that expression was reserved for her boys.

"They're really, really excited to meet you, Maxon. Please, don't let them down. I know Benjamin is your son, but Dillon doesn't know anything different than Benjamin does. Try . . ." Her brow pinched. "Try to treat them the same, if you can, if only for tonight."

A growl rushed up my throat, and I pushed forward, eclipsing her as I towered over her tiny body.

Shock had her gasping a tiny sound, and it was taking everything I had not to grab her.

Hold her.

Let loose all the words that were burning on my tongue.

Figured there were only a few that were appropriate right then. "They're your children, Izzy. Yours. A part of you. How could I not love them both?"

Redness flashed across her defined cheeks.

I wanted to kiss her so damn bad my guts hurt.

Her head shook.

"Don't stand here and make promises you can't keep."

"I want to be in my son's life, Izzy. Be the kind of father he deserves." It was a groan, and I was pressing closer, so close that I could feel the erratic thrum of her heart.

I nudged her jaw with my nose, inhaling as I went. "Want to be the man you deserve."

"Maxon," she whimpered.

"Let's go inside, Izzy Baby. I'm about two seconds from getting very, very distracted, and meeting my son needs to be my priority right now."

"Damn you, Maxon Chambers."

I grabbed her hand and pressed her knuckles to my lips. "Was damned without you. Took my first real breath in years the second I saw you standing in that store."

She stared at me, that connection pinging between us, the air thin.

"Let's go inside, Izzy." My voice roughened. "I want to meet my son."

Trembling, she reached back and turned the knob, and she ducked her head as she pushed it open and ushered me inside ahead of her.

A surge of warmth covered me.

Remembering this place.

These walls.

A sanctuary.

Peace.

It was all clouded by the last time I'd been in this room. The horror of what had gone down.

I gulped around the memory of it, knocked out of the stupor when the little guy who'd floored me yesterday came barreling down the steps from the top floor, inciting a riot with every step.

Kid had a messy mop of dark blond hair that bounced around his chubby face.

Joy radiated from his spirit.

And it was clutching mine, holding me in a tight fist.

Emotion sloshing like a flood.

Coming at me from every direction.

Bright and dark. Beautiful and ugly. Hopeful and sick.

Standing there, it all fell over me, why I'd pushed Izzy away in the first place. Wondered what had changed. Petrified I wasn't any better than I'd been then.

But I was determined to be, whatever it took.

Izzy was clearly worrying over the same thing, the girl chewing on her thumbnail as she shifted on her feet.

Ready to intervene at a second's notice.

Become a physical barrier between me and her kid if that's what it required.

Hurt, but I got it.

Accepted it.

Dillon had his hand on the railing as he flew down. Somehow, his words flew faster. "Mr. Chambers. You came! Are you feeling better? Mom said you got sick. Do you hate being sick? Nana said that old people get sick all the time and need medicine. Are you old? You don't look old. Do you need medicine?"

Halfway down, he skidded to a stop, and his brown eyes grew wide with shock when he caught sight of me.

Bruises littering my face. Bandage over my eye. With everything else, I'd almost forgotten about what had gone down last night.

He gaped at me for a second before he shot back into action. "What happened to you? Did you get in a fight? Did you have to arrest someone? Were they bad?"

Felt like I'd been swept up in another one of those tornadoes. A perfect disarray touching down, kid shifting everything in his path.

My insides were a tangle of emotions I wasn't even close to being able to put my finger on. "Might have gotten into a fight with a couple bad guys."

Left out the part that they were still out there.

He came to a stop a foot away, a massive frown wiping the happiness from his expression. "Did they hurt you? Nana has a special bag in the freezer that makes it better, but I really think it's the love she sends with it that does the trick. Do you want me to get it for you?"

Fuck, there went my heart, banging in my chest.

An uproar that didn't know where to land.

"That's okay, little man. Looks worse than it is."

It was everything else that was making me feel like I'd gotten a fist through the chest.

Izzy moved to his side and ran her fingers through his hair.

"So, I know you two sort of met yesterday since this one decided to disobey."

She was looking at him with a gentle reprimand when she said it, her mouth tipping up.

Guilt took hold of his face. "I'm really sorry. I just wanted to meet your friend who is a cop." He turned his attention to me. "Except you don't really look all that much like a cop."

Dillon was clearly speculating as he took me in. "Where's your uniform?"

I stood there, trying to keep up, this kid shifting from one topic to the next without so much as a blink of his eye.

"I'm a detective which means I should probably be wearing a suit like my partner likes to do, but I think this looks better, don't you?"

Pretending to play it cool usually wasn't too much of a stretch, but I was having a bitch of a time managing it right then. I forced a grin around the agitation, trying to win a few extra points with the kid.

Could anyone blame me?

"You look pretty cool to me."

Then his eyes doubled in size when a thought struck him.

"Are you undercover?" He whispered it, looking around all covert-like, kid all-in at keeping the secret.

Fucking cute.

"You do kinda look like a bad guy," he said even lower, and he looked at his mom in awe. "Your friend *is* the coolest."

If only she could be that impressed.

"Boom. Bang. Bam! Sneak attack," he whisper-shouted as he

launched into a couple karate chops and a side kick that was nothing but awkward.

My chest tightened.

Shit.

This was almost too much, and I set my hand to the achy spot that was pressing firm.

I glanced over at Izzy.

She sent me a wistful smile that nearly bent me in two. Hazel eyes shimmering under the light, brimming with soft encouragement.

Different than it used to be.

But still there.

Taking her expression as a go, I knelt down in front of Dillon.

This kid who I didn't have a clue where he came from.

What her life had been like. If she'd been happy or hurt.

Envy shivered, a vicious pulse through my blood. I beat that shit down, and instead stuck out my trembling hand. "Glad to meet you, Dillon. I'm Maxon, but all my friends call me Mack."

His smile stretched wider, two rows of tiny white baby teeth, two big ones on top.

Enthusiastically, he placed his hand in mine. "Nice to meet you, Mr. Mack. Is it okay if I call you that? Am I your friend? Do you want to be mine? Are you and my mom friends now?"

I glanced over at Izzy who was clearly fighting her own war. Chin trembling and moisture glistening in those eyes.

"Yeah, Dillon. I'm really hoping she and I can be friends again." I was looking at her when I said it, and her teeth clamped down on her bottom lip.

I sent her a look that I hoped would convey how fucking sorry I was. For ever hurting her. For doing her so wrong. Wishing I could go back in time and change it all.

"Then she can call you Mack instead of Maxon, like all your friends, right?" Dillon asked, breaking the connection.

"Well, thing is, your mom was a special friend, so she gets to call me Maxon," I told him, words raw, filled up with all the need I was feeling right then.

I glanced back at her just in time to see the pink touch her cheeks, and I could only imagine what it'd be like to get to pink her up everywhere.

Watch heat rise to that silky flesh.

I pushed down the greed when I heard the swinging door creak that I knew led to the kitchen.

Or maybe it was just those final cracks working their way through my spirit.

Soul crashing.

Slowly, I straightened to standing, doing my best not to crumble to the ground as the door slowly opened.

Nothing but a pile of bones. Broken and brittle.

Emotion clotted off the air when the kid with my face struggled to make it through the door.

He did his best to maneuver with those crutches, his legs so goddamn skinny and the toes of his right foot dragging on the floor.

His ankles and knees were bent at an odd angle, his arms and shoulders a bit off, too, but not close to being as affected as his lower body.

And fuck, he had this crooked smile that melted a crater through the middle of me.

A fist of sorrow squeezed my being, and I felt every fucking thing I thought I'd known shatter.

Splinter into nothing.

Devotion rushed in to take its place while a slew of taunts and teases played out in my mind.

Picture after picture.

Izzy alone. Her belly round. A tiny baby in her arms. A lifetime I hadn't known.

I didn't know if it was helplessness or sheer determination that lined my body that had me going for him.

Fuck boundaries.

Izzy's hand shot out. Her touch froze me to the spot, fire spreading up my arm. My attention whipped to her.

She was pleading with her eyes not to make this transition harder.

Not to go in blazing.

Reminding me I hadn't earned the right.

"Izzy," I all but choked, and I inhaled a jagged breath, fighting with all of me to keep standing still.

She squeezed my arm, the girl just getting it the way she always had.

She knew I was floored.

Staggered.

Slayed.

Benjamin started to hobble my direction.

My heart burst right there. Nothing but mangled bits crawling for the kid.

With each lumbering step he took, my chest tightened more.

Compressing and swelling.

Energy lashed in the middle of it.

Different but the same.

Could feel Izzy's anxiety where she stood at my side, and Benjamin shot her a careful, searching glance before sliding his gaze back to me.

And I wondered if he could see it, too.

Feel it.

Bleeding and spilling out.

The way every cell in my body seized in awareness.

Did he recognize me the way I recognized him?

And I wondered if this was what it felt like when a man first held a newborn in his arms. What it felt like to hear his child's first gurgling cry. Destroyed.

Knocked down so he could be rebuilt.

Become a better man.

Izzy moved to his side. Discretely, she swiped at the tear that had gotten loose and streaked down her cheek.

She cleared her throat, but it didn't do anything to unclog the emotion that hung from her being, the pain riding out on her introduction.

"Maxon, this is my son, Benjamin." She set her hand on his shoulder, her voice a song when she whispered near his ear, "Benjamin, this is my friend, Maxon."

"Hiiii, Maxxxxon," he said.

The words were elongated, like the letters were getting piled on top of each other. His mouth stretching open wide, jaw wrenching to the side to get the words out.

My lungs squeezed.

He let go of one crutch and awkwardly stretched out his hand, his arm a little disfigured, too.

In it, I saw his perfection.

"I'm glllllad you came," he warbled.

And I knew right then, nothing else in the world mattered.

Nothing but them.

sixteen

MACK

Dillon made a beeline for the kitchen, not even pausing as he threw open the swinging door. "Dinnertime!" he shouted.

Sweat beaded at the base of my neck, and I anxiously rubbed my hands together, nerves rattling as I thought about having to stand in front of Izzy's parents.

People who'd been nothing but kind to me growing up. People who I'd stumbled into a few times over the years, but like a coward, I'd always turned my head, dropped my gaze in a shame that I didn't want to face.

Acting like a punk who didn't give a fuck.

It couldn't be farther from the truth.

Time to man up because there would be no avoiding them any

longer.

Benjamin slanted me a wayward smile before he turned around and started toward the door, a whole ton slower than Dillon had gone.

Izzy stepped up behind him, her footsteps slow and tentative. At the doorway, the girl stopped and tipped that gorgeous gaze back at me.

Waiting.

An uncertain invitation on her face.

I forced myself to just . . . move.

To beat down the age-old insecurities. To ignore the scars that felt like they'd been ripped open wide.

Raw and bleeding.

I bypassed Izzy who held open the door. When I did, our arms brushed.

Fire spread.

She sucked in a breath, and my spine went rigid.

God. That was going to be a problem.

The attraction that blazed, barely contained.

Doing my best to ignore it, I stepped the rest of the way into the kitchen and right into the middle of the chaos going down.

AKA: Dillon.

He was running circles around the gigantic island, flapping his arms, shouting the whole way, "Nana, that smells so good. I want all the potatoes. Wait, did you make potatoes? And gravy? You can't have potatoes without gravy. That's a rule, right?"

He didn't even slow for her response, diverting paths and clambering onto a chair at the table where Izzy's father was reading the paper. He leaned on his forearms, getting right up in the old man's face. "Right, Grand-Pop? No gravy—no good, baby."

The old guy grunted, lowering his paper an inch to look at Dillon from over the top.

He was doing his best to front annoyance, but there was no missing the affection swimming in his eyes. "Whatever happened to kids eating what was put on the table in front of them?"

"That's called old-fashioned, Grand-Pop."

"Old-fashioned, huh? Nothing wrong with that."

"You shush, Mr. Grumpy Pants," Mrs. Lane was saying with a chuckle from where she had her back to everyone, whipping something that no doubt was going to be delicious in a bowl.

My mouth watered just thinking about it.

"I finally get the chance to spoil my grandbabies, you can bet your bottom I'm gonna do it."

"I'll bet my botttttom," Benjamin added in that voice that twisted through me with a force unlike anything I'd felt before.

Razor-sharp or a caress, I wasn't sure. Only thing I knew was it cut me wide open.

Another grunt from the old man who still had his face buried in the paper.

That was right before awareness spread.

Thick and hot and clammy.

In discomfort, I shifted on my feet, sucking in a steeling breath when the door stopped its slow sway behind us, the stillness casting us in a spotlight.

No longer able to hide.

Izzy's father slowly dropped the paper and pinned me with a glare, eyes dark and narrowed.

If looks could kill and all of that.

Or maybe he was just calculating how fast he could get to his gun.

End the threat he was viewing me as right then and there.

Had never had the courage to talk to him after what had happened. He had to think I was a complete asshole.

Wouldn't be that far off base.

I roughed a hand through my hair, itching in the tension that bounced from the walls, gaining speed with each pass.

Mrs. Lane clearly felt it, too, because she slowed her mixing and shifted around. Her eyes softened, and my heart squeezed in the middle of my chest.

"Why, it's Maxon Chambers," she mused. Her expression twisted in something I couldn't quite read.

I wasn't sure how the hell I was supposed to stand under the scrutiny.

Welcoming the judgment because God knew I'd earned it.

"That's Mack to his friends, Nana," Dillon piped in from the table. "Unless you're a special friend like Mom. Are you a special friend, too?"

Izzy choked at my side.

Mrs. Lane busted up laughing, and Mr. Lane grumbled something that sounded a whole lot like, "Special friend, my ass," under his breath.

Izzy cleared her throat. "Mama, Daddy . . . I'm sure you remember Maxon?" She peeked over at me when she said it, redness still lighting on those cheeks.

Girl trying to be a proper hostess in the middle of what had to be the most uncomfortable situation either of us had ever found ourselves in.

You know, since I was only a *friend* coming over for a *friendly* dinner.

"If only I could forget." This from her father.

Apparently, I should have worn my bullet-proof vest. Hell, full on riot gear would have been safer with the way he was looking at me.

This was a man I respected fully. He was the first man I'd met who fit the image of what a father should be. Ian wasn't the first man I'd thought deserved father of the year.

Loyal and protective. Loved his wife.

Playful, too.

Watching Izzy with a soft smile, losing his mind when she was doing something dangerous that she wasn't supposed to do, but never in a million years would he lay a hand on her.

Was terrified of him at first, but I soon understood the difference between a gentle discipliner and a tyrant.

Night and fucking day.

And standing there, I hadn't done a thing to deserve that kind of respect. I got it, but that didn't mean it didn't leave me feeling like an intruder.

I glanced at Izzy, and my spirit stretched tight.

Emotion gushed in all those vacant places.

A direct reminder of why I was all too willing to stand in the fire.

She was willing to take this chance on me, and that was worth any amount of unease or unrest. Any amount of judgment or speculation.

"Jack," Mrs. Lane admonished, shooting a scowl at her husband and waving him off like it was no big deal before she was sending a welcoming smile to me. "Ignore him."

"Ignore that Mr. Grumpy Pants," Dillon was all too eager to agree. "He might act mean, but he's got all the love."

Benjamin cracked up like it was the funniest thing he'd ever heard, though those blue eyes were keen on me the whole time.

Watching.

Like he was digging for the answer to a mystery.

"Come here," Mrs. Lane said, gesturing with her hands at herself as she ambled over. She stretched her arms out in welcome.

The woman had aged in the last handful of years, though she still had that lightness she'd worn like a signature color. Tenderness oozing from her demeanor with a dash of sass that kept you on your toes.

God knew, she'd welcomed me like a son but didn't hesitate to chase my ass out of here in the times when I was getting unruly.

You know, like when I was climbing into her daughter's bed.

She wrapped her arms around me, and I let her, fighting the overwhelming bout of sadness I felt at her touch.

The kind that could completely take me under.

Stepping through the doors of this house had always reminded me of what I was missing.

Made me feel like an outsider.

A beggar looking in from the fringes and wishing I belonged.

A family where I didn't quite fit.

I gulped around the magnitude of it as she hugged me tight.

Urges hit me.

This need to confess a million things. Tell her I was sorry that I'd let her down. Tell her how damn bad I hated that I'd hurt her daughter.

Hated that I hadn't been there for Benjamin.

She beat me to the punch. "I'm really glad you're here,

Maxon."

Pulling me closer, she hiked up on her toes and murmured quietly in my ear so only I could hear, "Now don't go and do something stupid like hurt my daughter. I'll hunt you down and cut off your balls. Know it took some big ones for you to show up here today, so use 'em wisely."

Wow.

Woman was not pulling punches.

I pulled away and cleared the uneasiness from my throat. "That's the last thing I want to do."

She patted my cheek. "Good boy."

"Good boy!" Dillon parroted, and Mrs. Lane turned around and smacked her hands together. "It's dinnertime, my favorite little men. Let's get some food in those bellies. Who's hungry?"

"Meeee," Benjamin stammered, and Dillon was shouting over the top of him, "Me, Me, Me!"

Entire place was straight chaos. Only the very best kind.

Benjamin shuffled for the table. "I ggget to sit by Mmmack."

My spirit clutched.

Fuck.

Didn't know if I was ever gonna get over that.

"No way, no fair. I get to!" Dillon argued, and he scrambled to spread himself over the empty chair next to him while remaining seated on the other.

Kid was a handful, that was for sure.

"I told you, bein' a troublemaker is not allowed," Izzy said, angling her head at her son in tender exasperation as she started for the table, clearly preparing herself to break up a fight.

Dillon turned up a sour-patch face from over the top of the chair. "Ahh, Mom. I was gonna call it, fair and square."

"Your brother called it first," she told him, voice firm.

"Don't you two know dogs sit on the floor?" Izzy's father offered way too light.

Izzy gasped. "Daddy."

He raised his shoulders, mock innocence on his face. "What?"

"You know very well what. I already warned you that you need to be nice. He's our guest," she urged beneath her breath, like she could shield me from the clear irritation her father was feeling at my presence.

Thing was, he was the one who had it all right.

"Seems like Grand-Pop is the troublemaker to me. Why you troublemakin'?" Dillon asked.

"Mind your own beeswax," the old man said with a tease.

Too bad Mal-Pal wasn't here to skewer him for that one.

Seemed Dillon's joke standards weren't quite as high, considering the kid howled with laughter.

"I don't got no beeswax!"

I stood there in the bedlam, attention pinging from one spot to the next, not having the first clue how I was supposed to mix.

Where I stood.

Hiding out by the kitchen door wasn't exactly going to cut it.

Benjamin's gaze darted between Izzy and me. Questions played out in those keen eyes.

Kid reading deeper.

Between the lines.

Clearly catching onto the fact that there was a whole lot more to this thing than some weird guy standing antsy off to the side.

Wondered if he knew that for me, everything was hanging in this precarious balance.

Time to suck it up.

I pushed out the strain and forced my heavy feet in the direction of the table. "How about I sit between both of you, then you both can sit by me?"

"Aren't you the good guy," Mr. Lane grumbled.

"Daddy," Izzy chastised again.

"Fine, fine," he mumbled, shooting me daggers before he sent his daughter a winning smile.

"Oh, great idea! See, Mom, we can totally share," Dillon said, all too quick to vacate the middle chair so I could sit next to him.

I waited until Benjamin climbed into the chair on the left before I slipped into the seat in the middle.

Izzy took the seat directly across the table from me, hands shaking with her nerves, girl clearly feeling just as frazzled as me.

"I'm sorry," she mouthed.

My head shook.

I wasn't sorry at all.

She smiled. Smiled a soft smile that might as well have been an embrace. Her presence sure. Like fingertips tracing my skin.

My muscles ticked, flexing with ripples of need.

Hardening with want.

Desire fisted my guts while my mind whirled with questions and worry and possibilities.

Heart game but not quite prepared for this.

Scrambling to catch up, rushing double-time and somehow permanently lagging behind.

Mrs. Lane set a platter piled high with roast and potatoes and carrots in the middle of the table, following it by a big bowl of gravy.

Clearly, she didn't want to send Dillon into a tailspin.

"There we go." She squeezed my shoulder. "Eat up . . . blueberry pie is for dessert."

"Bluuueberry pie is my favvvorite," Benjamin said, shifting in his seat so he could grin up at his grandmother.

Emotion pulsed, and I was struggling to breathe, to make sense of all of this, trying to process how it was possible that I was there.

Right in the middle of something so amazing.

And again, I was feeling like an outsider, someone who didn't quite fit in.

Desperate to be a part of a family but remaining an outlier.

Too fucked up to really belong.

Mrs. Lane eyed me, nothing but knowing. "Huh, what do you know, Benjamin. It's Maxon's, too."

seventeen

MACK
NINE YEARS OLD

Mack heard something shatter inside the house. His spine stiffened, and anger came at him like one of those storms that hit from out of nowhere.

Full force.

"Where do you think you're goin', bitch?"

Prickles of hate crawled across his skin as he tuned his ear that direction, and he dropped the stick he was carving out over by the shed and tucked the switchblade in his pocket.

This building with the big padlock on it was where his mama grumbled that his daddy did all of his dirty work.

Mack didn't agree.

He thought there were plenty dirtier things happening inside those shabby walls.

Sucking in a breath, he forced down the tremors of fear that made him want to run and hide in the forest.

He was no coward.

His daddy called him that all the time.

This time, he was going to prove him wrong.

He inched beneath the shimmery rays of light that streaked through the breaks in the dense trees toward the rickety cabin he called home.

Planks on the porch rotted, trash littering the yard that was almost completely closed in by overgrown shrubs and trees.

Ugly.

Inside and out.

His insides rolled with sickness.

That ugliness didn't have a thing to do with what it looked like.

His old shoes scuffed on the dirt, and he heard a scuffle, his mama's gasps of surprise and fear.

But that was the way it always was. They never knew what they were gonna get. A good guy or a bad guy.

His mama told him everyone was made up of a little bit of both, but Mack knew for certain he didn't want to be made up of any of that.

"To work. Where I go every Wednesday," he heard his mama say, though it was close to a cry, and Mack slipped up the wobbly step onto the tiny porch, hoping the wood didn't creak beneath his feet.

Beside the front door, Mack pressed his back to the wall. He held his breath when he leaned around so he could peek through the mesh of the screen door.

His mama was in the kitchen, and his daddy was looming over her, wearing no shirt and his jeans ripped, hair matted from staying up all night. Beer cans littered the living room floor, and Mack could smell the stench of it coming at him like a warnin'.

Dread knotted through him, tightening his chest and closing off his throat.

He tried to swallow it down. To blink it away. He didn't want to be afraid the way he used to be.

"Let me go," she said, trying to yank her wrist from his hold. The only thing it did was make him squeeze her harder and tug her fast up against him.

For a beat, Mack squeezed his eyes closed, making a wish that he really was a dragon.

That he could fly.

That he could swoop up his mama and they could fly away to a better place.

"Told you before, I don't want you anywhere around them. Fillin' your head with that bullshit. Think they're better than everyone."

"And I told you, it's my job. They pay me good to clean their house. Besides, they were kind to us while you were away. I'm not gonna just go and forget about that now."

His mama's face looked all pinched up. Eyes wide with terror.

A cruel sound came from his daddy's mouth, one that Mack knew too well. "Are you fuckin' kidding me, Dee? Whose fault was it that I got sent away in the first place?"

"Yours."

Mack wanted to shout for his Mama to stop. Not to say a word. God, she knew better than that.

But sometimes his mama wanted to fight, too.

When his daddy reached back his hand and smacked it across her face, the crack of it like thunder in the air, Mack felt it like a need.

The fight.

The ugliness burning bright.

This bottle of fury that lit.

Maybe he couldn't fly, but he was sure he was breathing fire.

His mama shrieked, trying to guard her face, but it was too late.

She fell to her knees, and his daddy knelt down in front of her. "Don't fuck with me, Dee. You know what good that's gonna do you." He grabbed her by the hair, and she yelped as he dragged her across the dingy floor. "Told you to stay away from those rats. Know it was them. They're gonna get what's comin' to them soon. Soon as I take care of you."

That was the last straw that Mack could take.

He bolted through the door, praying for courage. For strength.

If he could fly, he would be doing it then. He rushed his daddy, clawing at him, throwing kicks and fists. "You asshole!"

His daddy tossed him off like he was smacking at a gnat, and Mack's butt hit the floor with a thud, his attack not even making a dent. His daddy only grinned.

Coldness crawled down Mack's spine. A bucket of ice dumped down his back. He started to scramble back, shaking, though the words were coming free. "I hate you. Mama hates you. I want you to die. I'll kill you myself."

Laughter rolled from his daddy, pitch black. "That so, boy? Seems you need to be reminded of who you are. Of who you belong to. You actually think you're somethin'? Somethin' special? Those pig fuckers fillin' your head with lies, too?"

His daddy snatched him off the floor by his shirt, and Mack kicked to get free, but his feet weren't even touching the ground. "Get mad, boy. Show me that hate. That's what I like to see. You are just like me."

Mack was almost crawling along the lawn as he moved beneath the moon. His body screamed in agony, but he didn't care. He had one place to be. Lights burned from the bottom-floor windows of the pretty white house, and he kept to the outskirts of the property, feeling like a dirty thief like his dad, but he didn't care.

He needed to see her.

He got to the base of the tree, and he bit back the groans that wanted to rip up his throat as he began to climb. He got to her window.

Her light was on, and he could see her at her desk, talking to herself with a big o' smile as she drew something in a notebook.

He smiled in return, his chest feeling light. Funny in a good way for the first time that day.

He tapped at the window, and she shrieked, her hands flying to her mouth before she was laughing and crawling to her window, setting it open wide. "Mack! What are you doin', you crazy boy? It's too late to play. I already brushed my teeth."

"I just needed to see you."

It was the truth.

He already felt better.

"Well, you better get in here."

He wasn't gonna argue. He slid through, glancing at the drawing she was making of a dragon and a bird. Somehow, it made his smile go sad. She flipped the notebook closed. "Whatcha wanna do?"

Cry.

Die.

Scream.

All of the above.

He flopped on the floor. "Just wanna lay here with you."

She snuggled down next to him. "Want me to tell you a bedtime story?"

"Yeah."

He jerked up to sitting when the door flew open. Mrs. Lane stood in the doorway, her hand on the knob and her eyes narrowed thin. Mack's heart ran harder than it ever had. He knew he wasn't supposed to be in that tree, let alone come in through her window.

"What in the world is goin' on in here?"

Izzy grinned like they hadn't been caught doin' something bad. "I'm just tellin' him a bedtime story so he can sleep better, Mama. He's got bad dreams."

Something flashed through Izzy's mama's eyes. Something soft and tender and sad. "You know he's not supposed to come in through your window, Izzy Mae. We have a door."

"I'm sorry, ma'am," Mack said, gulping, shaking, more scared than he was earlier that day. Last thing he wanted to do was make Izzy's parents hate him. They were always so nice. Good to his mama. Good to him. And he was pretty sure they liked his daddy about as much as he liked them.

She sighed. "It's okay. Just . . . use the door the next time, that's what a real man does."

"Yes, ma'am."

She sighed again. "Well, come on, you two, I just made one of those blueberry pies Maxon here seems to like so much. Guessed I sensed you comin'."

His belly rumbled. He hadn't had dinner, his mama in her room all day.

He climbed to his feet slowly while Izzy jumped to hers. "I already brushed my teeth, but I'll do it again."

Izzy flew out of her room and down the stairs. Her mama was in front of him, casting him glances as he slowly made his way down. His stomach was tight, his nerves scrambled, feeling like he wasn't supposed to be there but wanting to stay forever.

They went into the kitchen, and Izzy's daddy was at the table, reading something in the paper. He dropped it low, confusion at first, his eyes darting to his wife who sent him some kind of look that Mack couldn't make out.

Only thing he knew was Izzy's daddy smiled a soft smile. The kind his own dad had never worn. "Hello, son. You smell my wife's pie from across the way?"

Mack couldn't stop his smile. "I might've."

"Get up here, get yourself a slice. Next time, though, use the door. Wouldn't want to mistake you for an intruder."

He should've apologized again, promised that he would, but he wasn't sure if it was gonna be a lie. Instead, he sat down on the chair next to the man.

Izzy climbed into a chair on the other side of him, rambling about what they were gonna play tomorrow. Her mama dished them each a big helping, steam coming up, the scent hitting his nose.

Maybe he'd died after all, and he'd flown right into heaven.

Her mama ran her hand down his back. He tried not to flinch, but he couldn't stop it, and he tried harder not to cry when she whispered at his ear, "You have a place here, always, Maxon. You remember that. You get scared or in a bad spot, you know where to come. You can always, always tell me or Izzy's daddy anything. You hear?"

He nodded tight, but he knew all the things he wanted to say would never fall from his mouth.

eighteen

IZZY

"*What* did I get myself into?" I whispered where I stood at my mama's side at the sink, cleaning up after dinner. Maxon was with the boys on the far side of the room.

Benjamin had wanted to show him his reading nook.

Of course, he had.

Did I expect anything different? Did I expect that bold presence wouldn't make an instant impact on my boys? As if they were not going to notice him walkin' through the door.

Hardly.

From behind, Dillon tackled Maxon who was sitting on the floor on the rug. My son roared like a monster, laughing uncontained as he wrapped his little arms around his neck. "Sneak attack! I got you! I told you that was the best kind."

Maxon roared back, dragging Dillon over his shoulder, flipping him upside down before he started to gently wrestle with him against his chest. Like he'd been doin' it for all these years. "Oh, you think you're sneaky, huh?"

Dillon howled with laughter as Maxon tickled him.

"Get himmmm, Mack," Benjamin cheered from his spot next to the window.

There he was, already rootin' for Maxon.

Just awesome.

"Well, whatever it is, it sure looks good," my mama said so only I could hear, her words full of suggestion as she snapped my hip with the dish towel.

"Mama," I scolded, sending her a frown. "This isn't about me and Maxon. This is about my boys."

Apparently, neither she nor Maxon were gettin' that. He'd left me completely rattled the whole dinner, watching me with that intense stare, as if he were contemplating doing wicked, bad things.

A shiver trembled through me at the thought.

She almost rolled her eyes. "Tell me you aren't fool enough to believe that. That started with the two of you." She pointed at Benjamin whose face was shining pure joy. "Can't take yourselves out of that equation."

"Thank you for the reminder," I said, words dripping sarcasm. "I'd totally forgotten where babies come from."

Or maybe that was exactly what I needed. A reminder to keep my panties on and my knees locked tight. Maybe order myself a nice chastity belt. Anything to keep myself from falling into the arms of that man. God knew, it would be far too easy to do.

"All's I'm sayin' is you can't ignore the past, Izzy Mae. If he's gonna be a part of your son's life, that means he's going to be a part of yours. It's going to come to the point where you have to decide what role that is going to be. Think he's makin' it plenty clear where he stands."

I glanced back over my shoulder when my mama peered that way, and I wasn't all that surprised to find him looking back, watching intently, that face so gorgeous and eyes filled with something I wished I could avoid.

Sorrow and regret and his own kind of hope.

Dillon took the opportunity to jump him again.

"Got you!"

Maxon let him completely tackle him to the floor.

I wanted to cry out for him to be careful considering I'd seen the damage that had been done, but Maxon didn't seem to mind at all.

Or maybe he was just welcoming the pain.

Tearing myself away from the scene because it hurt too bad to watch, I turned back to my mama.

Her expression softened. "Would say tough for him if it was all one-sided, but I know my child well enough to know when she's missin' something. When she's wanting something, but she's too scared to reach out and take it."

"There are a lot of things we want in life that aren't good for us, Mama."

"I guess that's the problem I'm havin'. He was so good for you, and you were so good for him. Together, you were something amazing, right from the start. Had a bond like few people ever get to experience."

I sent her a playful scowl. "I think you have a crush."

She laughed a soft sound. "Wouldn't call it a crush, but I guess your old mama is one of those hopeless romantics." She looked over at Maxon who was listening intently as Benjamin read him something from one of his books. "Or maybe I'd just always hoped for something better for that man."

Heaviness filled my chest when I looked back that way to see the way he was tenderly interacting with my boys. God, had I ever wished for that, too. That he'd have seen himself the way the rest of us did.

Pushing out the strain, I tossed the rag I'd been using into the sink. "Better get them into bed." I popped up and kissed her on the cheek. "Thanks, Mama. Tonight was really hard, and you doing all of this means the world."

"Well, your daddy sure didn't make it any easier."

A soft smile pulled at one side of my mouth. "He's just bein' protective. I kinda like it."

Mama chuckled. "Older he gets, the ornerier he gets."

"Boys love him to pieces."

Mama sobered, angled her attention to where Maxon was now reading the boys a story, both of them piled on him. "Just who are you talkin' about?"

Ignoring the implication, I forced myself to walk that way, my heart rate kicking with each step. His presence gettin' bolder the closer I got.

"Bedtime," I whispered quietly, somehow not wanting to break up the tranquility.

"Ahh, do we have to?" Dillon complained.

"Yes, you do. We have a big day tomorrow. Benjamin has his first therapy appointment. It's gonna take a lot out of him."

Even though I knew he tried to hide it, Benjamin cringed, fear taking hold of those blue eyes that told their own kind of story. One of courage and determination and a life filled with pain.

The kid my hero.

When he turned his face away, I knelt down in front of him. He was sitting right up next to Maxon, and my pulse tripped.

Jumped at the proximity.

I tipped my son's chin toward me. "Hey, brave boy. I know you're nervous for tomorrow, but you are going to do great. More than great. You're gonna blow them away. And just think of all the things you're gonna achieve there. You are amazin'. Absolutely amazin'."

Grief panged at my ribs when his crooked mouth twisted with a smile of timidity, this child never wanting to make me worry about him.

"It's okkkay," my sweet son promised in his fearless way.

I could feel the anxiety and questions coming off of Maxon, the way he stiffened as he angled the full weight of his attention on Benjamin.

He looked at him as if he were a stranger.

As if he'd known him forever.

As if he got it and didn't have the first clue of what to do about it.

He glanced at me, gutted, at a loss.

Maxon slowly shifted and climbed onto his knees, and carefully he edged all the way in and wrapped his arms around Benjamin.

He hugged him close.

Pressed his nose into his hair.

Inhaled him as if he were meeting him for the first time.

Benjamin didn't reject him or hesitate. He wrapped his scrawny arms around that fierce, strong neck, and hugged him back.

Emotion raced my throat, thick and sticky, and my hands started trembling, unsure of what to do as I knelt there on the floor as he hugged the child that I'd fought for. The child who'd caused me so much pain and so much relief.

A thousand sleepless nights and a whole, beating heart.

Maxon stood the rest of the way up and helped Benjamin adjust his forearm crutches, the man standing next to him as if he were meant to be his protector. As if he were the one fighting for him, too.

I was a fumbling mess when I climbed to my feet and swung Dillon into my arms in the hope that this whole thing might seem halfway normal.

Who was I kidding?

There was no chance of that.

Not when Dillon was uncharacteristically quiet as we started out of the kitchen.

I caught my mama's eye as we went, her expression wistful.

Maxon followed right behind, his hand on Benjamin's shoulder, standing guard over him the whole way up the stairs.

"Brush your teeth."

I set Dillon down at the bathroom door. Benjamin sent me a confused, heartbreaking glance when he passed.

The child sensing the disorder.

The reality that our lives were coming up on a change.

A big, big change.

They brushed their teeth and got ready for bed, and Maxon followed us around as if he wanted to be a part of the process but had no idea how he fit.

The man lurked in the shadows.

Watching.

Too intent.

So much for him being nothing more than a friend who had come over for dinner.

The whole time, I struggled not to break down. Not to drop to my knees and cry with the weight of it all. To issue up a thousand prayers that I wasn't makin' a horrible mistake.

That I wasn't putting my children in the line of fire.

Leaving their hearts unguarded.

Benjamin climbed onto his bed across the room, and I scooted Dillon toward his on the opposite wall. He scampered up. "Here we go," I said, dragging his covers to his chin and pressing a kiss to his forehead. "Goodnight. No more troublemaking for tonight," I whispered softly.

He grinned a sleepy smile. "Don't worry, I'll save some for tomorrow."

"I'm sure you will."

I pushed to standing, crossed the room, kissed the top of Benjamin's head, brushed my thumb over his cheek.

"Goodnight, brave boy."

Shyness bled into his cheeks. "Night, Mmmmom."

I turned, unprepared to take in the sight of Maxon standing in the doorway. So gorgeous. Stunning. Completely broken down.

Our eyes met in a tangle of questions, and I slowly stepped back and gave him the permission he clearly was seeking.

He edged in, big body taking up the space, filling it full. I gulped around the force of it, shivers raking my flesh.

He inched by, and he made his way over to Dillon. He towered over his bed. Tension curled through the muscles on his arms.

Cautiously, he leaned down and ran a hand over the top of Dillon's head, pressing a kiss to the same spot on his forehead where my lips just had been. "Good night, Lil' Dill. Thanks for letting me hang out with you tonight. It was the best night I've had in a long, long time."

His voice was grit. Rough and choppy. Overflowing with all the things he couldn't say.

"Will you come again?" Dillon asked.

"I hope so."

"Tomorrow?"

A soft smile tugged at one side of Maxon's mouth, that dimple peeking out for a beat because I just needed one more thing to make me weak. "I'm not sure about that, but I'll talk to your mom and see what I can do. How's that sound?"

"Deal," Dillon said, sticking out his hand. Maxon shook it, then he brought it to his mouth and pressed a kiss to his palm.

Oh, my stupid heart.

My stupid, wayward heart that was beating wild. Getting way out there where it shouldn't be.

It only got worse when he straightened, and he moved with slow, measured steps over to Benjamin who was sitting up on his bed.

His gangly legs hugged to his chest, his body thin and his teeth as crooked as his grin.

Maxon sank down onto his knees in front of him and reached out and took him by both shoulders.

Emotion crashed.

I wasn't sure I was gonna make it.

"I'm going to be thinking about you all day tomorrow. I know you're scared to start something new, but you have this. I know you do."

Benjamin's brow furrowed in a sweet, curious way. "But you dddon't even know me."

No doubt, my smart boy knew this wasn't a random encounter. That all of this *meant* something, even though none of us had any idea where it was going to lead.

He could feel the currents. A riptide. The crosswinds coming in from the opposite direction.

"I don't have to have met you before to know you, Benjamin. I can *feel* you. I can *see* you. You are brave and strong."

"Likkke you?"

Maxon winced, and those hands tightened. "Braver. Much, much braver."

This man was going to wreck me. Wreck it all.

I cleared the sob I could feel working its way to my throat and forced out the words, "All right, lights out. It's going to be a really long day tomorrow."

Maxon waited for me to head for the door, and his gaze swept the room as if he were making one last pass. Ensuring its safety.

Sheer, unmitigated protection in his stance.

I got to the doorway, and he seemed to have to pry himself from that spot.

"Goodnight," he said at the door, his gaze shifting between the boys, hesitating before he flipped off the light switch.

Reaching around him, I pulled the door almost all the way closed.

I shifted back around, and Maxon was right there.

Stealing the air.

Filling it.

Oxygen.

The man a lifeforce that I'd always believed would sustain.

I dropped my attention before I got lost there. "It's late."

"Yeah. I should go so you can get some rest, too." He didn't necessarily seem all that enthused by the prospect.

I started down the stairway, my hand on the railing to keep me from stumblin' beneath the pressure. But that pressure only increased, Maxon right there, two feet behind.

His breath on my neck.

His presence on my soul.

I swore every single one of his steps sent a vibration scattering beneath our feet, a tremor along the floor.

Downstairs, it was quiet, most of the lights turned out except for the bare glow beneath the kitchen door. My daddy had retired at least two hours before, claiming he was wiped, but I was pretty sure he just couldn't tolerate the tension any more.

Couldn't blame him a bit.

I was in the exact same boat.

A prisoner to the tension that just grew and grew.

Maxon said nothing. But I could feel it. A thousand words. A million confessions. Insurmountable regrets that I wasn't sure either of us could topple.

I opened the door to the surging, summer night.

Humidity clung to the darkness, the threads of it almost visible where it whooshed through the trees.

I stepped out onto the porch, and Maxon followed, and I could feel the heaves of his chest.

Distress and misery.

Slowly, I turned around. I kinda wished I hadn't. I was struck by the expression on his face that was illuminated by the porch lamp hanging next to the door.

Agony was etched into every line. "Does it hurt?"

I blinked, caught off guard, not even sure how to answer considering everything did.

"Benjamin," he clarified, taking a step forward.

His aura was overwhelming. Pure inundation.

The woods and the sea. Power and sex.

It was enough to make my head spin.

"When he goes to therapy? Is that why he's scared? Because it hurts?"

I barely nodded when I realized what he was asking. "Yes. Some sessions more than others. And he knows this study is going to be gruelin'. They already prepared us for that. It's going to require all that he has."

Maxon surged forward, closing in, and I froze, completely trapped by the fierce gaze of the dragon that had awoken. The man volatile. Close to unhinged. "I want to be there for him. I need to be."

"I'm not sure that's a good idea. You're movin' fast," I stammered.

In a flash, he had me pinned to the wall, the man a barely-contained fire.

"Moving fast?" His voice was incredulous. "I missed twelve goddamn years, Izzy."

I gulped, trying to see through the nearness. Through the haze of attraction. Through the force of who he was to what I was supposed to be fighting for. I found the will to look up into that fierce, destructive beauty.

"He doesn't know you, Maxon. He needs time to adjust. And

so do you. You've got to be sure you're ready for this."

A groan pulled out of him, something guttural, something raw. He pressed both of his fists to the wall above either side of my head. The man writhed in physical pain. "I can't stand the idea of him hurting, Izzy. I can't. It wasn't supposed to be like this."

His words were razors, cutting him deep.

Old, old love leached from my spirit, flooding my bloodstream. I tried to convince myself not to do it, but there wasn't a thing I could do to resist.

Nothing I could do to stop that overwhelming feeling from taking hold.

My dragon.

My dragon.

My hand was shaking when I reached up and traced my fingertips along his sharp jaw and down over his chest to his pounding, shattered heart. "It's not the same as what that man did to you. Not at all."

Maxon's eyes slammed shut, misery twisting him in two. "I should have protected him against anything bad happening to him. I swore, that if I ever had a kid, he or she would never go through what I did. And then I promised myself I'd never have one because I couldn't take that risk."

"He's not," I croaked through the promise. "He might be in pain, but he's got love. So much of it."

"I had it, too, Izzy Baby. I had it, too. But I had to let it go." He dropped his forehead to mine, and I was sucking down his ragged breaths, breathing his pain, wishing there was a way for me to bear some of it.

But the man was bleeding from the wounds that I'd never had the power to heal.

His head rocked back and forth, his body shaking, shoulders pumping up and down.

"Izzy," he murmured, so low, my name a needy groan.

"Maxon." I shouldn't have said it because it came out sounding like a plea.

"Little Bird," he whispered, his lips featherlight where he painted the words along the length of my jaw.

A gasp left me on a breath as a riot of sensation erupted. Tingles streaked, gooseflesh rising in an undulating wave.

"So pretty," he mumbled.

He exhaled a breath that became mine.

Our noses brushed.

Back and forth.

Back and forth.

Oh, God, what was he doin'?

Flames flickered beneath the bare caress. The man my fire, my cold body begging to come alive under his scorching touch.

I whimpered, sagging against the wall when he stroked his hands down my sides and slipped them under my dress, palms riding up the outside of my thighs.

Better question was what I was doing. But there was no reason. No sanity in the middle of this.

No logic where heartbreak and hope met.

"You are so fucking sexy." His confession was a growl. Deep and dark. "Do you have any idea what it was like sitting across from you all night? What it was like waking up with you asleep in my chair? Like staring at the sun, knowing you'll go blind if you look for too long, and knowing taking in that beauty for even a second would be worth it."

He nudged forward, erasing the space between us, and his hands spread wider.

Desire raced. A flashflood of need that shivered across my flesh.

His mouth traced the shell of my ear. "Want to stare at you forever. Get lost. Take you. Possess you. How's it possible you're here, Little Bird? You came back to me. Feel like I'm dreaming."

"It was you who didn't want me."

His hands tightened on my thighs, tugging me forward against his hard body, eyes pinned on me. "There's never been a single day in my life when I didn't want you. We are endless."

That was the last thing I heard before his mouth crushed against mine. All senses failing except for the one that registered that Maxon Chambers was kissing me.

It was a reckoning.

Lightning.

A crack of thunder in the air.

I moaned a low sound of pleasure, a groan of pain.

His kiss was fevered.

A demand.

Push. Pull. Take. Give.

A promise.

An apology.

Sensation rushed my body.

This old love trying to bust free.

To climb out.

Reach for him.

Endless. Endless.

I whimpered.

"Izzy," he raked at my mouth, his hot tongue stroking out in search of mine.

There was nothing I could do. Nothing but open to him. Our tongues met in a dance of greed.

Desperate in their play.

As desperate as our hands that began to fumble and grasp. Both of us searching for what might have been.

His hand fisted in my hair, tugging as he kissed over my jaw and down my throat.

A fever pitch.

Our bodies ignited, grappling and groaning and begging to get closer.

He licked down to kiss at the flesh that my dress exposed above my breast, and then he was palming it over the fabric, thumb tracing circles over my nipple that immediately puckered into a hard peak.

It'd been so long since I'd been touched this way. So long, and it felt so good, so right.

Urgency burned in my blood, reaching a boiling point, and I let my hands slide over his wide shoulders.

Holding on.

Fingers digging in to beg for more.

I was losing control.

This moment that was spinning out of our grasps and given to something bigger.

Sweeping me from my feet, he hiked me up and pressed me against the wall, winding that big body between my thighs.

Second nature.

The skirt of my dress bunched around my waist, and I was gasping, making all these sounds that I didn't recognize as he rubbed against me, his hand on my breast, his fist on my soul.

He dove back into my mouth, and in the same beat, both of his hands moved to my bottom.

The man took two handfuls of bare flesh.

A spike of pleasure tore through the middle of me, and I jerked and arched, and he was pressing himself to me, the hot, hard length of him seeking my surrender. "Nothing has ever felt as good as you. Nothing. Want to get lost here, Izzy. In this body and this sweet, sweet heart."

Oh, was that heart speeding, sprinting out ahead, and I was lettin' him wrap an arm around my waist, the other hand slipping around the front and nudging my panties aside, fingers sliding through the throbbing flesh.

"So wet," he groaned, and I was trying to get closer, welcoming the intrusion when he pressed two big fingers inside my body, and I had the craziest thought that I wished it was his cock that was pushing inside of me instead.

Good judgment demolished.

He drove his fingers deeper, the man groaning as he devoured my mouth.

Sparks of pleasure lit behind my eyes, and my hands were clutching. Tugging. Fingers digging in. Trying to find a place. To remember the way we'd been before our treasons had been committed.

I wanted to go there. To run in our meadow. To fly in that blue, vast sky. To trust. To tumble through the atmosphere and know he'd be there to catch me when I reached the end.

And I was already there. Standing in the shadow of a blue moon. Shooting with the stars.

Flying.

Streaks of pleasure. Jolts of ecstasy.

I cried into his mouth, and he swallowed the sound down, as if he were feeding off my bliss.

"Mom?" Dillon's voice broke through the insanity, coming from the other side of the door.

I froze.

Maxon jerked back a fraction, lust raging in his eyes.

Jagged breaths spiked between us, our bodies vibrating, our pulses racing in the distance.

Crashing together where our senses were just out of reach.

As hard as reality crashed over me at what I'd just done—what I'd been about to do—and a tiny sound of horror bled from my mouth.

I pushed at his chest, and reluctantly, Maxon settled me onto my feet.

Stealing glances at me, he helped me to resituate my dress considering I couldn't seem to get my hands to cooperate.

Oh God.

What did I do?

My body felt achy and needy, sated and still throbbing with the kind of want I didn't have the luxury of feeling.

Maxon's shoulders heaved with barely contained aggression. Like he was two seconds from coming back for me.

"I need to go inside." The words clanged with regret. Ricocheted with my stupidity.

"Izzy." He reached for me.

I whirled back around. "Please . . . Maxon . . . don't. That . . ."

Remorse shook through my spirit, and I looked at the spot where he'd just had me pinned, so easily, as if I hadn't learned a single lesson at all. I warily shifted my attention back to him, voice a rasp of fear. "That was a mistake. That cannot happen again."

I wouldn't survive.

"Mom? Where are you?" Dillon called again, and I tried to force back the overwhelming emotion.

Frantically, I straightened my hair, but I was pretty sure there wasn't a thing I could do to straighten out my heart.

Stupid, stupid heart.

I started for the door, praying I could make it there without fallin' apart.

I should've known better. I knew exactly what coming back here was gonna do to me. Make me that same naïve girl who just wanted to fall into the hands of the boy that she loved.

The boy who'd become a man.

That man who edged up behind me. A dark shadow. A wraith. "I might have made a ton of mistakes in my life, Izzy. But you and me? We've never been one of them. And I promise you, I'm going to be here to do right by my son. Do right by you."

My head dropped, and I stared at the ground, inhaling a breath that was purely man.

Sex and desire and dominion.

I tore myself from it and rushed inside, not stopping to look back.

Terrified of what I would see on his face.

nineteen

IZZY

"What did I do?" I groaned, leaning on my elbows and burying my face in my hands.

Faith reached over the bistro table where she'd met me for lunch and pried my hands away, trying to talk me down from the ledge where I was teetering.

She'd come running the second I'd sent out a distress call.

I hadn't gotten a lick of sleep last night, body twisted up in the remnants of pleasure that streaked and clutched and throbbed, teasing my sanity, while my mind had raced with the implications of what I'd done.

She angled herself closer to force me to look at her. "You let yourself feel. There isn't a thing wrong with that."

Oh, I'd felt plenty, all right.

"Are you crazy? There is a ton wrong with this. I invited the man over for dinner to meet his son, not for a quickie out on the porch."

The hint of a smile played around her mouth. "Sounds to me like you were the only one who got the quickie in."

I pouted at her, hating the picture she'd evoked, the man hard and needy and left wanting, while I'd been tucking tail and fleeing. "That was his fault."

Her brows lifted in speculation.

I released a heavy sigh. "Fine. It was both our faults. But if he hadn't gone and stirred up all those memories . . . made me hurt for him . . . it never would have happened."

She chuckled out a disbelieving sound. "I'm sorry, Izzy, but whether you want to admit it or not, the two of you clearly have a ton of unfinished business."

"Yeah, well, I'd do best to shut it down."

Hang up a nice sign that read *Closed Indefinitely* to go along with that chastity belt I should have ordered.

Expedited.

"Really?" she challenged.

"Absolutely," I returned.

Letting myself get lost in Maxon Chambers was nothing but a fool's game.

She angled closer and lowered her voice. "How did it feel kissin' him? How did it feel with him touchin' you?"

Chills streaked across my flesh. I would totally blame it on the weather if it weren't for the searing southern heat blazing from the blue, blue sky.

I wavered, fiddled with a wrapper, studied the logo on the napkin. "Like I was flyin'," I finally admitted without looking up at her.

"And when's the last time someone sent you flyin'?"

I sent her a glare. "I *was* married."

Her expression turned dubious. "Yes, I do remember. So, I'm gonna ask you that question again."

I huffed. "Fine. The last time someone sent me flyin' was the last time Maxon Chambers touched me. There. Are you happy?"

It was always, always him.

Her tone softened. "It's not a question of whether I'm happy or not, Izzy. It's about whether you are."

"I'm . . . satisfied," I settled on.

She grinned. "After last night, I bet you are."

"Faith," I scolded, redness rising to my cheeks.

"Stop bein' such a prude."

"I'm not a prude. I'm just . . . cautious."

"Maybe that's your problem . . . you're bein' too cautious. Maybe you need to let the chips fall where they may."

"You know how that worked out the last time."

"And I also know you both were young. Naïve. Made choices that neither of you would make today."

My lips pursed, knowing she was right, but not sure of what the outcome would have been if I had done it differently.

In the end, Maxon would still have been the same man.

Faith tipped her head to the side. "What was he like with the boys?"

I sat back in my chair, my heart in my throat at the memory. "Amazin'. They took to him like he'd been there all along. Like he was their best friend."

She took a bite of her salad, hesitating before she asked, "And how did that make you feel?"

I hiked a shoulder. "Scared. Ecstatic. Hopeful and terrified. Everything in between and all at once."

Pausing, I looked out over the shopping center that was in the same plaza as the dental office, trying to process the convoluted emotions that had stalked me all night.

I returned my gaze to her. "The hardest part was watching him struggle. Seeing how Benjamin's disability was affecting him. I know him well enough to know that he wants to make it right. Like it's somethin' that can just be fixed or a burden that he can shoulder. I'm not sure he's really grasped what taking care of a child like Benjamin means."

"And you don't think he's up for the responsibility?" she asked.

If I had the answer to that, things would be so much easier.

"He says that he is. That he wants to be there for him. I'm not sure if I can trust that or not." I met her eye. "He asked if he could be there today for Benjamin's first appointment."

She nodded like she wasn't surprised by that at all. "What did you tell him?"

"That I didn't think he or Benjamin were ready for that."

She gave me a look that promised she wasn't surprised by that, either.

Worry trembled through my being, and I chewed at my lip, trying to put the feeling into words. "It's more than just him being there at his appointments for support. This is a man who has been hurt so badly, and I'm not sure he can differentiate what is caring for a child, loving them wholly, and thinking he's directly responsible for every single thing that child goes through. He was devastated when he realized that Benjamin would be in pain during his therapies. Nearly lost it when I told him the number of surgeries he's had."

"Can you blame him?"

"For hurtin' for his child? Wishin' his life was easier? No. But I'm not sure he can handle watching him suffer."

"Like you do it just fine?" she challenged.

I blew out a short breath. "It kills me, Faith, but it's part of our lives. Our everyday."

"What if Maxon wants to become part of that life, too? He hasn't had all those years to accept Benjamin's disability. He wasn't there. And before you say it, yes, I know full well that was his fault. But the man can't make a change if he's not given a chance to do it."

My words took on a tone of desperation. "And what if he fails? What if my boys fall for him, and he walks away when it gets too hard? I'm not sure I can take that risk."

Something that looked like pity traipsed across her pretty face. "You can't control everything in your life, Izzy. You have to know that by now. There are gonna be sharp turns and detours and straight up dead ends. Ones you never saw coming. But there are also gonna be wide open roads, too. The kind where you put the top down and let the wind blow in your hair and you don't care where you're going. You're just along for the ride."

Oh, Maxon Chambers would take me for a ride, all right.

"I have children to worry about."

"And I had Bailey," she told me, looking at me with an expression that said *so what?*

"Don't you dare tell me you sat back and didn't worry about a thing when Jace showed back up in your life. I know you were terrified," I pointed out.

"And what if I'd let that fear and worry stop me from finding my heart's joy? My dream? There are times in our lives when we have to trust that things are going to turn out right."

"I just don't want my boys to get their hearts broken when he lets them down."

Faith pointed her fork at me with a wry grin taking hold of her mouth. "I think it's someone else's heart that is in the clutch."

I started to tell her that I couldn't let his big fingers get any tighter around it when I heard someone calling my name.

I turned in the direction of it to find Dr. Nelson climbing out of his shiny red car. He lifted his hand in the air, sunlight shining around him as he sent me a big smile.

I sent him an awkward half wave.

"Who is that?" Faith all but hissed, angling down low as if we'd stumbled upon some sordid secret.

"My new boss."

"*That* is Dr. Nelson? Millie Tomson said he was a looker, but I'd figured she was comparing him to that poor old widower, Mr. Sneed."

"Oh, he's no rumor," I told her.

He strode our direction. Cool, calm, and collected.

"How's lunch?" he asked as he approached, far too casual, sliding his fingers through his brown hair

"It's great," I managed. "Enjoying the day with my best friend. This is Faith." I gestured to Faith who was pretty much gaping. Good thing she was happily married and her husband was just as much of a *looker*.

"Nice to meet you, Faith. I'm Trevor." He shook her hand.

"Nice to meet you, too."

He turned back to me. "We'll have to do this sometime. I feel a little left out."

"Oh . . . I . . ." I stammered, not having the first clue how to respond to that.

He just smiled and shook his head. "I'll let you two get back to your lunch." He glanced at his watch. "I'll get my time with you in a few minutes."

A sly smile took to his expression.

I sat there stupefied, watching his back as he turned and walked away, just as confident as he'd come.

"Oh. My. God," Faith whispered. "Someone's got themselves a crush."

I turned back to her. "Stop it. He's just bein' nice."

"And you're just bein' naïve," she shot back. "That man was doing nothin' less than undressing you with his eyes."

I shifted uncomfortably. "He's my boss."

She waved me off as if it were nothing. "It happens all the time. Throw two people together in the workplace with chemistry, and they go boom. Doesn't matter the societal tiers this world puts us in. Boss or employee. Superior or inferior. Aren't we all people at the end of the day? I mean, unless he's holding the fact he's your boss over your head, using it against you, then that is an entirely different story."

"He's not. Not at all. He's been nothing but kind."

"So?" she pressed.

"So what?"

"Are you interested in him? Does he make you feel anything like you felt last night when Mack was sending you flyin'?"

I blinked at her, almost wishing I could say yes.

"You know what they say, never settle for anything less than butterflies," she added, taking a sip of her tea.

Truth be told, they were completely missin'.

My phone pinged on the table next to me, and my eyes went wide when I saw the text that bleeped through as a tingling flush went slip-sliding through my body.

Maxon: I can't stop thinking about you. Haven't in

thirteen years. My life never quite made sense without you. Now I know exactly why it was meaningless.

Oh, there were the butterflies she was talkin' about. Taking flight. Swooping and flapping. Divebombing my good sense.

Faith narrowed her eyes. "Is that him?"

I could barely nod through the lump that formed in my throat.

"Well, I think that's your answer right there. I should take a picture of what's on your face right now to save for your wedding day."

It all just went downhill from there.

Maxon: Did you think about me last night when were you falling asleep?

Maxon: Was I on your mind this morning when you woke up like you were on mine?

Maxon: I know you hate me, but there's a part of you that still loves me too. Do you remember that guy?

Maxon: I want to be him.

Hate him?

No.

Not even close.

That was part of the problem.

Two hours later, after I hadn't responded considering I didn't have the first clue what to say, his tone had shifted, and I got the feeling he was just texting me every time he had a thought that he wanted to share with someone. And he wanted that person to be me.

Maxon: How's work? My day is long, counting the minutes and not knowing when I get to see you again.

Maxon: What time is Benjamin's appointment? Tell him that I'm thinking about him.

I wavered, not sure I should respond, knowing there was no chance I could keep from it. Not when he was wearing me down.

Minute by minute.

Word by word.

Fingers poised on my phone, I peeked around the office, as if I were gettin' ready to commit the most shameful of acts.

Me: I'm getting ready to leave in a few minutes. He has to be there at 3:30.

Scandalous, I knew.

Maxon: You have to leave work early?

Me: Yes. Mondays and Thursdays. I've already worked it out with the office manager.

Maxon: Or I could always take him one of the days? I want to be here for him, Izzy. For you. You don't have to do this alone, anymore.

God, this man. Did he have the first clue what he was doing to me?

I left work, and my mama was outside with Benjamin so I could take him the rest of the way into Charleston.

My son was both agitated and excited. He was quiet the whole way, and I had to stand outside the facility with him for ten minutes, whispering words of encouragement before they finally seeped in deep enough and he was ready.

"You are brave," I whispered to him, holding his hand as we

stepped inside to the welcome of the doctors and therapists. The whole thing was really an introduction to what was going to be happening, almost a celebration of sorts for the twenty patients who would be a part of the study so they would be familiar and comfortable with their surroundings.

The children played in the therapy gym without any instruction, and I watched from the sidelines, his smile wide and his laughter free.

By the time that we left, my heart was soaring with hope.

I was pretty sure Benjamin's was, too, with the way I kept catching his crooked smile through the rearview mirror as we drove back to the house.

Dillon came flying out the door, asking his brother a million questions.

My mama, the sweet caretaker that she was, had dinner ready for us to eat.

I knew so easily this could become our routine.

But it was what was pushing at the boundaries that made it all so difficult. The reminder that nothing was settled. An upheaval that I didn't know whether to welcome or shun.

Maxon: How was Benjamin's appointment?

The only thing I knew was that my pulse took off with a roar when that one came in two hours later while I was in my bedroom. And I realized I was excited to share this news with him.

Me: It was wonderful. The doctors and therapists are so welcoming. It's going to be a good thing. I can feel it. Benjamin left with a smile on his face. That's all that mattered.

Maxon: Can I see it?

Me: ???

Maxon: His face. Your face. Dillon's face.

Two seconds later, my phone was ringing with a video call, Maxon's name coming up on the screen.

Nerves raced, and I looked around my room as if I were looking for a place to hide before I finally told myself to suck it up, pull up my big girl panties (and keep them there) and answer the stupid phone.

"Hey," I said, though it was wispy when his gorgeous face came on the screen.

God, why did the man have to be so appealin'?

"Hey, gorgeous."

Redness flushed. "Maxon."

It was a reprimand.

Caution.

His smile was nothing but a smirk. "Just telling the truth. Figured you didn't want any lies."

"Maxon," I said again, and he just chuckled.

"Let me talk to Benjamin."

Chewing on my bottom lip, I pushed down the agitation and moved out of my room and into the one next to it where the boys were putting on their pajamas. "Hey, Maxon wants to say hi."

"Mr. Mack!" Dillon shouted. He hurtled across the room like his pants were on fire. He jumped up to get into the camera. "Hey! What are you doin'? Are you coming over? Did you work today? Did you know my Nana made lasagna for dinner? It was so good. Do you like lasagna?"

Maxon laughed at Dillon's erratic train of thought. "Doesn't everyone love lasagna?"

"Not crazy people," Dillon said, far too serious.

"Guess I'm out of the woods then because I love lasagna," Maxon replied, rubbing at that jaw that was sending my mind into a tailspin.

A nosedive right into ideas of reckless things.

"Are you comin' over?" Dillon pushed.

"Not tonight, Lil' Dill, but really soon."

"Did my mom say so?"

"Not yet, but I'm working on her." He was lookin' at me with that smirk when he said it, something about him so arrogant tonight, his expression promising he was *working* on more things than a simple visit to see the boys.

"Hard work pays off," Dillon said.

Awesome.

All the character I'd been trying to instill in my boys was coming back to bite me in the butt.

"I'm nothing if not a hard worker," Maxon said, and even through the phone, I could see the way those eyes were glintin'.

I bit down on my bottom lip to stop the spark of need I could feel lighting up in my belly.

God.

This was bad.

"Go on and get ready for bed," I told Dillon, needing to cut off the direction of this conversation and fast, and the man had barely said anything.

I turned to Benjamin who fumbled to get his pajama shirt over his head.

"Someone wants to talk to you," I all but whispered, tiptoeing that way.

Benjamin smiled. "Maxon?"

My heart leapt, praying that didn't make me a fool. Nodding, I shifted my phone around so Benjamin was in view, and I could see Maxon's expression do its own foolish things.

Leaping and jumping.

"Hey, there Big Ben."

My heart clutched.

Big Ben.

Oh, no.

Now he was giving my boys nicknames.

This really was bad.

"How was your session?"

"Good. Not hhhard today but next tiiime the real work starrrts."

It was basically verbatim what his therapist had told him.

"Are you ready for it?"

Benjamin nodded.

"That's my boy."

Oh God.

I had to put my hand on my chest to keep my heart from physically spilling out onto the floor.

"It's bedtime. You better tell Maxon goodnight," I barely managed, my emotions all over the place.

Wanting to just . . . give. Terrified of what might happen if I did.

"Goodniiight," my sweet boy said, and Maxon just stared for a beat before he finally whispered, "Good night, Big Ben. I'll see you soon."

"Okkkkay."

I pulled the phone away, and Benjamin gave me the strangest look. One that asked too many questions. One that made me have to turn my back so I could slip out of the room and into mine.

"I've got to go tuck the boys in," I rushed, words a ramble to match the shaking of my hands, the memory of last night too raw and fresh.

Too tempting to repeat again. Because God, looking at him? I wanted to. I wanted to run straight to his door and into his arms.

"Izzy—"

"Goodnight, Maxon," I told him before he could get in another word. Before he made me stumble. Before he made me lose all reason.

I tossed my phone to my bed and scurried back out to get the boys into bed.

As if I could outrun that man so easily.

Because when I got back to my room, a slew of messages were waiting.

Maxon: Let me take him to his appointment Thursday.

Maxon: I can switch my work schedule around easily, and you won't have to worry about taking the time off.

Maxon: Let me be there.

Maxon: I'm going crazy over here, Izzy Baby.

Maxon: Fuck, I can still taste you on my tongue.

Maxon: I can still smell you on my fingers.

Maxon: I want you, Little Bird. So fucking bad.

Oh God, that shifted gears and fast. A complete one-eighty. It sent my pulse scattering, draining from my head and rushing to areas where I sure as heck didn't need my blood pounding.

I fumbled with my phone, quick to respond, needing to get it over with before I let myself get caught up in something foolish.

Me: Fine. Thursday. Come pick the boys up here at my mama's. He needs to be there at 3:00. You can bring them to my work by 5 after.

Then I quickly shut it off completely. Needing to cut the interaction. As if when I climbed into bed it would stand the chance of escaping him.

Because when I closed my eyes?

He was right there waiting for me, too.

twenty

MACK

"Wait, let's get this straight before we move on any farther—you're actually calling me for advice?"

I could almost see Ian's smug smile from across the miles, the asshole.

I grunted at him as I accelerated through traffic on my way back to my house after checking in at the precinct. "Fine, get it over with. Rub it in. And then tell me what the fuck I'm supposed to do."

I'd basically begged Izzy to let me take that kid to his appointment this afternoon. Now, I was sweating bullets so thick I might as well have been in the middle of a 10-70 with shots fired.

"If I had the answer for all the nonsense going down in your brain, I would be a very rich man," Ian razzed.

"Cut it, man. You are rich. You wanna rub that in, too?"

Wouldn't call his life golden, but the fucker had sure gotten lucky when it came to the dollar signs.

Ian laughed, and then his tone sobered. "Here's the thing, Mack, you're calling me for the answer, and you and I both know you already know what that answer is."

"And what's that?" I challenged, changing lanes and passing a couple of cars.

"You know this lands right back on your father's doorstep. You've got to stop worrying that you're going to follow in his footsteps. Make his same mistakes."

"Already made plenty of them, haven't I?"

The chokehold he had on me still felt like steel lining my ribcage. Memories of the path I'd been traveling. Who I'd almost become.

"Yeah, and you were a kid. A teenager who didn't have a whole hell of a lot of a different choice. And you've been running around for the last twelve years, this badass cop, putting every criminal behind bars so you can prove that you're nothing like him. Denying yourself happiness, thinking your life is what you owed."

Ian's voice twisted in emphasis. "Now it's time to prove you really are nothing like him. Know you're scared, and this fatherhood thing came from out of nowhere. Believe me, I get it. But the only answer to any of this is to step up and become the man you were meant to be. The man every single one of us know you are."

The lump I'd been fighting for the last three days bobbed heavily in my throat. Every question I'd had about pushing my way into their lives rising to the surface.

"And what if that man isn't good enough? What if I fail? Those boys . . . they're . . . amazing."

Affection and fear buzzed through my being.

"Not sure if I can risk bringing them into my life."

"You really think there's a chance you're going to make their lives worse rather than better?"

"You really think I won't?"

"Uh, yeah," he shot back.

"You say that so easily. Look what I almost got you wrangled into when I first met you."

"Again, you were fucking seventeen. And I think it's pretty clear I went looking for any trouble I could find. It's not like you dragged me into the sordid life. I was already there. And that was a long time ago, and you don't come close to resembling that same guy. Hell, you didn't then. Why do you think you raged against it so hard? Why do you think your father is behind bars now?"

"Izzy." Answer to that was easy. I would have done anything for her.

"Izzy," he dished right back, though he served it like a solution.

I sat there silent until he pressed, "Izzy's here, man. Right there. What are you going to do about it?"

My head barely shook, guts knotted up in the lust that I hadn't been able to shake since the first day I'd caught sight of her. Had only gotten worse with every interaction. With every pass.

Sunday night out on her porch had very nearly done me in.

"Want her," I admitted, voice rough. "Want her in a way that's not even reasonable."

There I went, cutting myself wide open. But this was Ian. The guy who got me better than anyone else.

"And the boys?"

"Want them, too. In my life. Permanently."

With Izzy right by my side.

Ian laughed like it was completely obvious. "Then it seems to me the only risk you can't take is not fighting to have them in your life."

"Wish it were that easy."

"It is, man. It is exactly that easy. You go after what you want. You fight for it. You take it. You protect it with everything you have. It's the only thing that we can do."

I started to give him shit for being so goddamn sappy when my attention snagged on someone walking along the main sidewalk. He was turning into an alley that ran behind houses in a neighborhood about two miles away from mine.

Maybe it was the color of his hair or the demeanor of his

stance, but I knew it the second I caught sight of him in my periphery. "Gotta go."

Without saying anything else, I ended the call and made a quick left into the neighborhood while I called for backup. I jerked my Suburban to the curb and jumped out, heartrate ratcheting high.

I jogged as quickly and quietly as I could between two houses, eyes darting everywhere, keen, beating back the fury that wanted to come unleashed. Did my best to remain concealed and level-headed, hand on my gun strapped to my side as I slinked along.

A dog started going wild at the fence of the house on the left, barking and growling like a raging beast, paws digging under the wooden slats.

Fuck.

So much for remaining inconspicuous.

I continued moving in the direction of the disturbance, sweat gathering at my nape and dripping down my back.

The feeling hot in the summer air.

Instinct kicking in.

I got to the alley just as the prick was disappearing around the corner along another row of houses.

I started running that way, increasing my pace, caution in every step.

At the corner, I slowed, and I peeked my head around to find the asshole strutting down the alley with his back to me.

Zachary Keeton.

I edged out, keeping close to the back fence, gun clasped in both hands. I tried to keep my breathing controlled and my footsteps quieted as I rushed that way.

Didn't matter.

Kid's spine went rigid. Awareness spinning through the dense, dense air. Like he felt me the same way that I felt him.

A clash of convictions.

A collision of creed.

His attention flew over his shoulder, and I was lifting my gun, shouting, "Freeze."

For one long moment, a blink of an eye, he stayed there, our eyes locked.

Something moved through that link.

A deep-seated hatred that I couldn't process, even though I felt it to my bones.

Then the asshole took off like he'd been poised at the starting line of a 400-meter dash.

Feet pounding the dirt.

I took off after him, shouting the whole way, "On the ground. Get your ass on the ground."

Dust kicked up behind him, and he broke right, scaling a fence and hopping over the top of it in a second flat.

I went after him, hiking myself over and dropping to my feet in someone's yard on the other side. Swings on a swing set swayed, and what couldn't be more than a two-year-old boy had his face pressed to the sliding glass window watching the action go down.

Fuck, fuck, fuck.

Not how I ever wanted things to play out.

Innocents in danger. Minding their own business when some disgusting prick decided to get unruly.

Rage burned hot in my blood, and I shot back into action, racing for the fence where the asshole had gone. I followed the chaos, going for the next yard where I heard a dog start yelping in agitation, and I was pushing over the top just as the punk was skating over the opposite side.

I sprinted, pulse racing hard, pants raking out of my throat as I gave everything I had to chase this fucker down.

But by the time I made it over that fence, I'd lost sight of him.

Vanished.

"Goddamn it," I shouted, chest heaving.

Within minutes, two patrols showed. We scoured the neighborhood for a full hour before I had to call it, refusing to be late to pick the boys up for the first time, wondering all over again if I wasn't making a huge mistake.

I made it to my house, wary and on edge. After I searched high and low and found no sign of anything awry, I jumped into the shower, quick to dry off and pull on new clothes.

The bruises from the other night were still evident on my body, but it was the dread of who I was, of my life, that was aching in an unbearable way.

Feeling the weight of it, I edged over to my bed and sank down onto the side, and I dug into my nightstand drawer and pulled out the book that always brought me comfort.

The drawing on the spine to match the tattoo I'd had done on my arm and shoulder.

Both scared and fierce.

I opened to one of the passages that I had marked.

> *The Dragon puffed, smoke coming from its massive snout.*
>
> *"You set out on a journey you believed your purpose. Your only option. To prove your loyalty to the king. Yet your heart stumbled on that path, knowing it was unsound. Now you tremble in fear?"*
>
> *Teno rocked, legs curled to his chest where he sat next to the fire, struggling to find warmth in the wrath of the winter. "How can I stand against an army when I am but one man? No more than a stable boy?"*
>
> *"You stand because you are brave. Because you've known all along who you were meant to be."*

For a moment, I let my eyes drop closed, inhaled the words like a buoy, and then I stood to go and pick up my son.

twenty-one

MACK
FOURTEEN YEARS OLD

Beneath the silvered light of the moon, Mack quietly climbed the tree. The tree that was an escape. A stairway to his own personal heaven.

Little Bird's nest.

With his shoulder, he swiped angrily at the tears clouding his eyes, hating that they were there. He wasn't a wimp or a coward.

But he wondered if maybe he really was as he rushed to make the ascent as fast as he could.

Every inch of his body hurt.

Inside and out.

Inside and out.

There was only one thing that could make it feel better.

He scaled the limbs, palms of his hands burning as he carelessly grabbed and pulled and hoisted himself higher, desperate to get up that tree as fast as he could. He was almost weeping when he got to the darkened window on the second story of the house, and he crawled on the branch that reached it so he could lightly knock at the glass.

Darkness radiated from within, and he could barely make out the hint of the wispy white curtains that hung at the sides.

Relief stretched like a band across his chest when metal screeched, and the white-framed window was pushed up.

Little Bird poked out her head. Blonde hair fell around her shoulders, her skin soft and pale, hazel eyes wide as she stared back at him through the shadows.

Or maybe she was just an angel. A figment of his imagination that had been sent to rescue him.

"Maxon, what's wrong? What happened?" she whispered, her words worried and sweet.

He wanted to fall into the comfort of them.

Close his eyes and forget.

"Let me in," he begged, glancing down and behind him, listening for anything. For any indication that he might be comin' for him. Or for Izzy.

He wasn't about to stand for either one.

"Okay," she agreed without question, and she scrambled to get out of the way.

He slipped through, and he climbed on top of her desk before he slipped all the way in.

The second he did, he dropped to his knees on the carpeted floor.

No energy left.

She slowly knelt down in front of him. She was wearing a nightgown that was pink, and her legs were bare, and Mack felt guilty that he kept thinking dirty things. Things her mama and her daddy definitely wouldn't like.

Things he was sure she wouldn't like, either.

"What's wrong?" she asked again, the green of her hazel eyes glowing in the muted light.

"I just needed to see you."

Something good. Something good.

Relief.

A frown tore through her expression, and she slowly reached up and ran those tender fingertips across his cheek.

"Are you missin' your mama?"

Grief clutched his chest.

His stomach.

His mind.

Knives and whips and chains.

His body felt like it was on fire.

Incinerating.

Eaten alive.

If this went on any longer, he was sure his heart was going to fail.

He grasped her hand and pushed it closer to his face. "I want to die, too."

A tear slipped from her eye, and she leaned up higher on her knees, angling his direction. "Don't say that. Please, don't ever say that."

"Why not? What's the use in livin' when it always ends?"

Her head shook emphatically. Desperately. "Because I'm here, and you belong here with me. We belong together. Always, Maxon. Always."

He slumped to the floor. So tired. So tired.

Rolling onto his back, he stared at the darkness that danced on her ceiling.

Tingles spread across his skin when she snuggled against him.

She rested her head on his chest.

He winced.

He regretted it the second that he let his weakness show because she scrambled to sit up and jerked at his shirt.

"Did he do it again?" she gasped in horror.

Frantically, her little hands tried to expose him. To lift the fabric. To show off his vulnerabilities.

He didn't want her to know how weak that he was.

He grabbed at her, trying to stop her frenzied search. "Please. Don't."

His *daddy* had gone on one of his drunken rages, coming after Mack when he hadn't gotten the wheels off a car he'd been stripping in the shed fast enough.

Instantly, the tirade had gotten physical, the vicious words coming from his father's mouth turning to the loss of Mack's mama, the way they always did.

The way she'd died in that fiery car crash.

Blaming it on the Lanes for making her pack her things and run.

It'd been Mack's idea, though. His fault. He'd begged his mama for them just to go.

To go somewhere else. Somewhere better. Somewhere where he could keep her safe.

Even if it meant being away from Izzy for a while. He would have gone back. Found her.

His mama had been on her way to get him at school. His backpack stuffed with his things had been hidden in the woods behind the schoolyard, ready to go.

She'd never shown.

Only a police officer had been there hours later when he'd finally gone back to his house, there to tell his daddy that his mama was gone.

"I hate him, Maxon. I hate him, I hate him. I'm gonna tell my mama."

This time, he gripped Izzy's wrists. Hard. "You can't do that. You know the only thing it's going to do is make him madder, and he'll just hit me harder."

It wasn't like anyone was gonna do anything about it, anyway. It didn't matter how much people acted like they cared. In the end, they always turned a blind eye. A lame excuse enough to explain it all away.

It'd been that way his entire life. Except for the Lanes. They were the only ones who'd really cared. They'd tried to get custody of him when his mama had passed. Funny how that judge had declared his daddy fit.

Izzy slumped down, her voice going soft. "It's not fair."

No.

It wasn't.

Guilt beat a path through his body.

Lying there, he had to wonder if he really was meant to be there with Izzy at all.

Lately, sneaking through her window had started to feel wrong.

She was so much better than him. So much better than the thoughts that kept coming on stronger every time he was around her.

She was going to have a better life than the one that was set out in front of him.

Taking over his *daddy's* business.

He almost rolled his eyes.

Like his life was normal. Like his daddy might brag to the other parents that his son would be the next successor in line.

How proud he'd be.

No.

Mack didn't belong there beside her.

The princess and the pauper.

But right then, he didn't care, and he snuggled her closer, let his fingers flutter through her silky hair, and begged his body to stop the way it wanted to react.

Izzy wasn't like anyone else. Not one of those girls who let him touch them and touched him, too.

She was better than him.

He needed to remember that before he got lost and forgot who he was.

Who he was always gonna be.

"You're my best friend, Maxon," she whispered.

He leaned over and kissed her temple, inhaling her scent.

Wild jasmine and the sun.

She sighed. Touched his chest.

"Little Bird," he whispered. "Let's fly away."

"Okay, my dragon, just tell me where you want to go."

twenty-two

MACK

"You did it, Big Ben." Barely managed to get the words out as I knelt in front of my son who had just wrapped up his appointment.

"Did you seeeee me?" he asked hopefully, smiling his crooked smile, and my heart that was already wrung out squeezed.

Squeezed so tight that it wrenched out this soggy feeling that I couldn't fully process. This feeling that left me gutted and overjoyed.

Aching and full.

Like I was on the cusp of something bigger than I ever could have imagined and the weight of it was already too much.

"Yeah, buddy, I was watching every second. You did amazing.

Just like I knew you would. Dillon and I were cheering for you the whole time."

His grin widened, and the kid blushed, his bony shoulders going up to his ears. Like he was shy that I was giving him praise and hungry for the attention at the same time.

There went my heart again.

This bam, bam, bam that was making my head spin.

"You did so good, Ben-Ben! You're going to be so strong. Stronger than any of us! I bet you aren't even gonna need those crutches." Dillon leaned on me, his arm around my neck where I knelt down, kid glued to my side.

I was pretty sure that was right where he'd always belonged.

"Watch out Dilllon, I'll be fasssster than you." Teasing pride billowed from my boy.

Dillon's eyes bugged out with the suggestion. "Well, maybe the same fast. I don't think you should be too fast. How about that?"

It was the first time all hour I almost had the urge to laugh. This sibling rivalry that was all too sweet.

Relief coming on after the battering storm.

Izzy had warned that Benjamin's session was going to be grueling.

I wasn't close to being prepared for what that really meant.

For an hour, I'd had to sit and watch my son cry tears of pain and frustration.

Kid had been pushed to the limits.

Pushed to the extreme.

The whole thing had been about recording his baseline so they could set goals and parameters for the direction they were going to take his treatment. See where his strengths and his weaknesses were. Where the improvements could be found and where the focus needed to be.

I got it.

Understood it.

At least my brain did.

Thing was, my spirit had so not been on board with any of that shit.

Whole time, I'd sat there with my knee bouncing a million

miles a minute.

Soul raging.

Banging at its confines.

Had to stop myself about fifteen different times from jumping out of my seat and demanding that they stop.

Never expected my heart to ache this way. In a crazy way that didn't quite make sense.

No, it didn't come close to coming from personal experience, but I thought it was safe to assume most parents wanted to protect their children. Shield them from pain.

Shelter them from suffering.

But this? It had been fucking brutal. Every second he'd been through slowly killing me.

What only confused it was the massive amount of pride that had soared in me every damn time he'd cheer in victory. When the therapist would shout encouragement that he was doing great.

Talk about not knowing how to stand under the upheaval. I had all but dropped to my knees when the therapist had given him a high-five and told him he was finished.

"We have about an hour before we need to meet your mom. I think a celebration is in order," I said, glancing between the boys. "What do you think?"

"I love celebrations!" Dillon was all too quick to agree. "What kind of celebration are we going to have? A trip to Disneyworld?"

A chuckle left me as I looped an arm around the kid's waist. "I was thinking something more along the lines of ice cream. Getting a little ahead of yourself, aren't you, Lil' Dill?"

"Mom says I'm always getting ahead of myself, but I run really fast, just like Ben-Ben is gonna. And I just really wanna go, and we've never been, and it looks so super cool. Please, can we go? I got a piggy bank, and it's almost full. I can give you some dollars."

Laughter rolled out, and I ruffled his hair. "Maybe another time, Lil' Dill. Pretty sure your mom wouldn't be too happy about that idea right now. Besides, we only have an hour. Don't think we can quite squeeze that in."

"Ah, man, why's she always gotta be a funsucker?"

Could feel the force of Benjamin's smile. "Because we're

tttroublemakers. She's gotttt to keep us in llline."

"Troublemakers? You two? I don't believe it."

"Believe it, Mr. Mack," Dillon claimed. "I mean, not *bad guy* troublemakers. Wait, is that the same thing? Oh man, I hope not. I don't want to get arrested."

"So far, I think you're fine. Just don't push it," I teased, and then I pushed to standing, taking Dillon's hand and winding an arm around Benjamin's shoulders to lead them out.

We stepped out into the late afternoon, three of us together, walking along like we were a family.

Family.

I gulped around the thought of it. The agony of it.

Something I'd never really had. Something I'd witnessed with Izzy and her parents, so close, but always out of reach.

I got them into the truck that I'd rented while mine was being repaired, and ten minutes later we were standing at the ice cream counter with a slew of flavors beckoning from behind the curved glass.

"Pick your poison," I said.

"Poison? That sounds like a bad idea. Maybe you're really the troublemaker." This from Dillon, except he was grinning up at me with his hand still clinging mine.

Kid razzing me.

My chest tightened, same as my hand did on his. "You have no idea, Lil' Dill."

No idea at all.

Wished I could erase it. The bullshit I'd done. The things I'd kept hidden. What still haunted me today.

"Do they have bluuuuberry?" Benjamin tumbled through the question, hobbling on his crutches to the glass, peering down.

I couldn't do anything but reach out and feather my fingers through his hair that was the same color as mine had been at that age, heart beating overtime at the contact. "Might not be as good as your grandma's pie, but it looks like they have it."

"I'll take bubblegum," Dillon exclaimed. "Can I have a cone with the chocolate and the sprinkles on it, too?"

Izzy was probably gonna kill me for sugaring them up before I took them to meet her, but I was with Mrs. Lane—if I got the chance to spoil them, you could bet your bottom I was going to do it.

"Sure can. How about you, Big Ben? You want one, too?"

"Cannn I have two scoops?"

I looked at the teenaged girl and gave her our order, paid, and carried our ice cream over to an open table.

They immediately went to town, digging in. I took a bite of my plain vanilla, looking at my son who was lapping at his cone like it was the fountain of life, watching me at the same time, his little brother babbling on, stitching his little spirit to me just as quickly as his brother was.

Impossible but right.

I fought the fear that wanted to climb into the atmosphere, instead smiled and nodded along as Dillon launched into a million questions about what it was like when I was growing up *in the olden days*.

Apparently the 90s was way back when.

"And my mom was your best friend?" Dillon asked.

"She sure was."

He scrunched up his nose, wiping some of the ice cream smeared all over his face with the back of his hand. "But she's a girl." He said it like it was the weirdest thing.

Funny how I'd once tried to give her the same excuse and she wasn't having it.

I gave him the same response as she'd given me.

"So? She's still my best friend."

"So, you're friends again?" he pressed.

"I hope so," I answered, roughness making its way into the words.

"Special friends?" His brow rose in speculation.

"Yeah, special friends," I admitted carefully.

His brow managed to rise higher. "You mean, the kissin' kind?"

Shit. Nothing like a kid putting you on the spot.

Rubbing the tension at the back of my neck, I wavered, glancing between the two of them.

Benjamin was studying me with those keen, deep eyes.

Uneasiness twisted through my being, not sure what to say or how Izzy might want me to answer. But the last thing I wanted was to mislead these kids on my intentions.

I nodded slow. "Yeah. The kissing kind. If she wants me to be. Would that be okay with you two?"

There I sat, asking my twelve-year-old son who didn't know he was my kid and his little brother for permission to kiss their mom.

Just awesome.

"Eww," Dillon cried, acting like he was gagging.

Benjamin dropped his head in embarrassment, redness blooming on his cheeks.

"What do you think about that, Big Ben?" I prodded.

He lifted his head. "You want to beeee her boyfrrrriend?"

"I do."

I wanted to be her everything.

Didn't say it out loud.

Didn't think anyone was ready for that.

He stared over at me, that fierce, brave little man I was coming to know surging to the surface. "Did you know both our dads didn't lovvvvve her enough? They llllleft her. She dddoesn't think I hhheeear her, but ssssometimes she cries at night, and I know whhhhy. Because I maaake it that she has to be allllone."

Pain slammed me, as intense as the hurt and shame that contorted my son's expression.

A crushing, devastating blow.

I couldn't breathe.

"Maybe they were just cowards. Not brave enough to stay," I forced out, words choppy.

"Are you a cowwward?"

"I don't want to be. Not anymore."

It was a confession without divulgence.

"My mmmom is ggggood," he told me, and there was a warning woven in it.

"And so pretty," Dillon added, mouth covered in ice cream.

"Your mom is amazing," I told them, words rough. "She's perfect to me. She's always been. And I want her to know that."

"Okkkay then," Benjamin said, his nod slow, like he was asking me to agree. Trusting me that I got it.

"Deal! Are we on the same team, now? Mom said we gotta stick together. Be a team because we only got each other."

Heart in my throat, I nodded at Dillon.

"Would be the best thing in the world for me if I got to be on your team."

If I got to love you.

Protect you.

Keep you.

All those things scrambled around in my chest, calling out their claim.

Overcome, I cleared the emotion from my throat, knowing I needed to change the subject and get the hell out of there before I admitted things Izzy didn't want me to admit.

I glanced at my phone. "We'd better get you two cleaned up. We need to be at your mom's work in fifteen minutes."

Dillon shoved the rest of his ice cream cone into his mouth, barely able to chew around the mess, grin stretching wide around the pink smeared all over his face. He held his hands out to the sides.

"All done."

I managed to laugh. "Think I'm going to have to dunk you in the sink."

He giggled the cutest sound.

Everything clutched and sped.

Fuck, I'd gotten in deep. So deep. Sinking in surrender.

Slipping out from behind the hard booth, I helped Dillon jump down and reached out for Benjamin. He took my hand, and I helped him slide out, kneeling down in front of him so I could help him put on his forearm crutches.

"There we go," I whispered low, glancing up at him, time freezing for a second when I met the depth in his eyes.

Did he know? Could he feel it?

Sucking it down, I straightened and led them both to the restroom to wash their faces and hands. Then I led them back out to the truck where I helped both of them buckle into their booster seats, Benjamin's a special one with about fifteen latches.

Whole time I was clicking him into his seat, I could feel a thousand questions coming off of him.

I drove out of Charleston and headed to Broadshire Rim. The shopping center where the dentist's office was located was in the newer area closer to Charleston, and the drive went by fast, even faster with Dillon chattering the whole time.

Kid nonstop.

Perfect in his disorder.

Just like his mom.

Just like his brother.

Benjamin laughed at something he said, and lightness weaved its way into the air, and I was shaking my head with a chuckle as I turned on my blinker and slowly pulled into the parking lot.

I started to whip into a spot in front of the building.

Second I did, my spirit chugged.

Nothing but an assault of jealousy that flamed and lashed.

Coming on bright from that dark, dark pit.

Possession slammed me, a jumpstart in my veins that made every inch of me shake.

Izzy was outside the door, key in the lock.

The prick who'd been all up on her on Monday was leaned against the wall with his arms crossed over his chest.

Looking like a pompous douche.

Eyes grazing her flesh like he was figuring out how long it was going to be until he got to taste it.

He reached out, touched her arm as he said something that I wished I could hear, and she swiveled her head that way, that blonde flowing around her back and a smile on her face as she said something back.

Would pay a pretty penny to hear that, too.

Head craned to the side, his mouth moved as he adjusted the strap of her bag on her shoulder where it had started to slip.

"Oh, fuck, no."

"That's a really bad word, Mr. Mack. Don't tell me you really are a troublemaker, too. Mom's already got her hands full with the two of us."

Shit.

Didn't even realize I'd said it out loud, but I couldn't stop it.

Anger surging. Jealousy rising. Teeth grinding to dust as I put the truck into park.

I wasn't about to sit there and watch this go down.

"Who is that cock—" Shit, I was slipping again. "—roach?" I fumbled to add on.

Great.

There I was, winning all kinds of points.

Dillon quickly unbuckled and flew forward. He held onto the headrest in front of him as he peered out the windshield. "That cockroach is Mom's new boss. He's a dentist. Do you like going to the dentist?"

That was her boss?

"Mom always thinks it's sooooooooooooo good," Dillon continued to ramble, "but I don't like it one bit. That noise? Whaaaaaaaaaaaa." He tried to mimic the sound of the water drill. "I don't like it, Mr. Mack. Not one little bit."

"Yeah, buddy, I don't like it, not one little bit, either."

And I wasn't fucking going to let it happen.

No dentists for Izzy.

I hopped out, the engine still rumbling and roaring, and I strode their direction.

"Hey, Izzy," I said as cool and calm as I could muster, a veneer to cover up the greed seething underneath.

Cockboy saw me first. His eyes narrowed in annoyance.

Perfect.

I grinned. "Boys are all buckled in my truck. Do you want to change cars or do you want me to take them home? They're going to need baths. We stopped for ice cream after Benjamin's appointment."

Unease moved through that tight little body, Izzy swinging her gorgeous face toward me.

Could almost see her mind jumping right back to Monday night.

Knew she could still feel it, my touch burning on that lush, pink skin.

Knew she could still taste my kiss on her tongue, same way as I could still taste her.

I'd gone to sleep every night swimming in the remnants of the girl.

This stunning girl who was watching me like she was terrified to take one step closer because when she did, there was going to be no going back.

What she needed to know was we were unstoppable.

"Oh," she squeaked, caught off guard as I got closer.

I just smiled.

"Um . . . well . . ." She fiddled and tucked a loose piece of hair behind her ear. "We'd better get them shifted. I need to swing by the store on the way home for milk."

Wanted to offer to do it for her, but the asshole beat me to the punch.

"I actually have to stop at the store. I don't think I live that far from you. Want me to drop some by?"

Was he serious? Her motherfucking boss? I wanted to knock him in the mouth.

"Oh." This time she was slanting that surprise at him, stumbling around her thoughts, the poor girl getting tossed from one rope to the other in a wrestling ring. "Oh-oh . . . I don't think that's a good idea. That's very nice of you, though, but I can manage. I'll see you tomorrow."

Dropping her attention to the ground, she turned around and started in the direction of her car, not even slowing as she passed where I stood, though she cut me a look that told me she knew exactly what I was doing.

Good.

I stared down the prick who was watching her go, the guy grinning at me like he was up for the challenge.

"Hi, cockroach!"

I flung my attention over my shoulder to catch Dillon with his head stuck out the back window that was rolled halfway down, hands gripping the top of it, shouting at his mother's boss.

The guy's smug smirk faltered, and I reminded myself to give Lil' Dill five bucks later.

“Dillon,” Izzy scolded, horrified, moving for her car. She tossed her bag into the front seat.

“See ya,” I told him, backing away with my hands stuffed in my pockets, not even giving a shit that I was acting like an asshole.

I moved up behind Izzy. Her spine stiffened as I approached, and she straightened and whirled around, shooting me the sweetest little daggers from those big eyes.

I grinned.

“Don’t you dare go grinnin’ at me, Maxon Chambers,” she hissed low.

“What?” It wasn’t even meant to be a denial.

She huffed. “You know what I’m talkin’ about. You think I don’t see what you’re doin’? You might as well pee all over me.”

I inched closer, leaned in, inhaled jasmine and sweet and the sun. “First off, that’s illegal. I’m a cop, remember? Unless you want to do it in private. Then I might be game.”

Okay. No. Totally wasn’t into that shit. But I loved seeing her feathers get ruffled.

She gasped and a bright shade of fuchsia took to her cheeks. “Maxon Chambers,” she reprimanded like I was one of her kids.

“Izzy Lane,” I returned, laughing under my breath like I was one, too, loving how fucking cute that she was when she got all frustrated and didn’t know what to do with me.

Flustered, she shook her head. “You can’t do this. You can’t come around here acting like you are a part of who I am.”

I angled close, tucked a wayward lock of hair behind her ear, tried not to dip my nose in to trace along the delicate flesh of her neck. Still, I whispered the words at the shell of her ear, “Not a part of you? You couldn’t scrape me from who you are if you tried. Come to dinner at my house tonight. You and the boys. I want to feed you.”

Apprehension moved through that sweet body. “You know that’s not a good idea.”

"I think it’s a great idea.”

“Well, kiss her if you want her to be a kissin’ kind of friend,” Dillon shouted from the window.

Izzy’s eyes went wide, and I had to stifle a laugh.

Now I owed the kid a ten.

At this rate, he really was going to earn that trip to Disneyworld.

I inched closer to her, backing her against her car. "What do you say? Come to dinner."

"Maxon . . . this is gettin' complicated."

"And you should know, I have every intention of complicating you." Our mouths were almost touching when I murmured it, and I could feel the thud of her heart hammering at her chest.

Took everything I had not to press myself against it. Feel it beat.

That energy alive.

"Please, Mom! I want to eat at Mr. Mack's house! I've never been there before."

If he kept it up, I was going to have to sign my bank account over to him.

She looked at me like she wanted to throttle me. Only it was soft and adoring.

My stomach tightened. Before I did something stupid like actually kiss her in front of her kids, I backed away and smiled. "I'll drive the boys. See you there."

She huffed, and if I didn't know any better, would have sworn she stomped her foot. "Fine," she said, all exasperated like, but I was pretty sure there was a smile behind it.

twenty-three

IZZY

I followed Maxon and the boys into Charleston, my senses still a thunder as I dialed my parents' number.

Relief hit me when the old answering machine picked up.

Call me a coward, but the last thing I wanted to do was explain to my mama or daddy on the phone why we weren't going to be there for dinner.

No doubt, my mama would have plenty of questions later. The whole problem was I seemed to be lacking all the answers.

Never had I felt so out of sorts.

So uncertain.

I mean, what was that whole kissin' thing? What had he told my boys?

God, I was in trouble. I knew it to my core.

When the answering machine beeped, I left a message. "The boys and I are having dinner at Maxon's tonight. We'll be home by eight or eight-thirty. Hope you have a nice, peaceful evenin'." I quickly tacked that onto the end, as if maybe I could convince myself that the only reason I was staying out tonight was to do them a favor.

Wishful thinking.

Because my nerves had gotten themselves into a tangle.

Anticipation knotted in my belly.

Hands sweaty where they clung to the steering wheel.

I just knew agreeing to come over here was changing everything. I was coming up against a wall.

A deadline.

A decision.

And it was all happening too fast.

Taillights flashed as Maxon pulled into his driveway.

I pulled in behind him, and Maxon hopped out.

The man looked like a reckoning when he gave me a look that told me to sit tight in my car.

Confusion twisted across my brow.

What was he doin'?

I watched him stealthily move around his front yard.

Slow yet sure.

He climbed to the porch, unlocked the front door, and peered inside.

At least I got one answer.

One thing of which I was sure.

He was checking for safety.

His posture rigid and imposing.

A protector.

A fighter.

My dragon.

Sorrow clogged my throat and moisture filled my eyes with the realization of the fear that this man still held onto so tightly.

As if it'd been etched into him as part of his being.

I wanted to reach out and stroke it away. Hold it. Bear a portion of it for him.

I just wished he would have let me.

He disappeared inside for a minute, and when he returned, his shoulders were relaxed.

He started back to his truck to help out the boys, and I slipped out onto shaky, unsteady feet.

"Is this your house?" Dillon asked as Maxon swung him down from the truck, holding him from under his arms. "How long have you lived here? Do you have a dog?"

"Sure is. About four years. And nope, no dog."

One thing I could say about the man, he kept up just fine with Dillon's erratic train of thought.

"You don't have a dog?" Dillon asked as if it were some sort of crime. "Why not?"

"Wouldn't want it to be alone all day while I'm at work."

"Because you live alone?"

"Yeah, Lil' Dill. Because I live alone."

He sent me a look that nearly broke me in two when he said it.

The starkest sort of loneliness bled out.

Most unsettling part was the hope brimming in the middle of it, as if maybe he had the intention of changing that.

Oh lord, I could feel that fork in the road coming up fast.

Left or right.

Dillon went scampering up the side steps and onto the porch while Maxon ducked back into the truck. He murmured a bunch of words that I felt more than heard, so gentle with his son as he unbuckled him from his special seat and helped him get his crutches adjusted after he settled him on the ground.

"There. How's that? Are you steady?"

"I'vvvve got it."

"Watch out for the gravel. It's loose," Maxon warned softly.

"Stoppp worrying so much." Benjamin sent him a sly, knowing grin from over his shoulder, and Maxon sent him an adoring one in return, and my world was trembling on its axis.

So close to toppling over.

Benjamin slowly made his way up the steps.

I stood beside Maxon and watched our son go.

That feeling rushed over us.

Attraction and want. Flickers of old affection that had become somethin' new.

Awareness and regret.

I forced the words out beneath the pressure of it. "Thank you for takin' him today. I hope it wasn't too much trouble."

I realized my arms were hugged over my middle when I said it. My stance and my words nothing but a defense.

Because I could sense it all slipping away.

"He's my son, Izzy." His words dropped low in emphasis. "My son."

A shiver raced my spine, and my voice came soft. "Sometimes, I watch him just . . . walkin' . . . and joy explodes in the middle of me. I spent so many years worried that he wouldn't be able to run and play. Seeing him like this? It feels like a miracle."

"He is a miracle." Maxon's tone was as jagged as the gravel under our feet.

I glanced over at him.

The sight of the man was nothing but a thief sent to steal my breath.

"Maxon—"

"Need to tell you something." He cut me off.

Anxiety pulsed through his body. It sent a hammer of dread assaulting mine.

My teeth clamped down on my bottom lip, and I struggled to prepare myself for what he might say. That yes, Benjamin was a miracle—wonderful and inspiring and kind—but that it was all too much.

Nothing I hadn't heard before.

I could handle it, right?

"The day you left when you came and took care of me?"

My brow pinched.

Not what I was expecting.

Fury blackened his expression, rage bustling beneath the surface of his skin. "Found my truck busted up that afternoon. A slur spray-painted on the side of it. Think I'm being targeted."

I whirled around to face him.

"You think whoever hurt you that night was responsible?"

They knew where he lived?

Terror raced.

Taking over.

The thought of something horrible happening to him more than I could process.

His hands curled into fists. "Don't know for sure, we're still waiting on the prints, but my gut says yes. Could just as easily be some neighborhood kid playing a prank. But I won't take the chance. Won't let my guard down."

He inched forward. "Need you to know what's happening before you walk through that door. What being around someone like me means. Last thing I ever wanted was to drag you into my mess. Never wanted this for anyone. And when it comes to you, I don't know how to stop myself."

There was his fear again.

Though, in that moment, I was feeling it, too.

Fear for him.

For the life he led.

The danger he faced at every turn.

Respect seeped from my pores. Respect for the decision he'd made to turn his back on the path he'd been slipping down when he'd been getting caught up in the ugliness.

But I had to wonder if he were doing it for the right reasons.

"I'm not afraid for me, Maxon. I'm afraid of you racin' toward danger just because you think that's what you deserve. That you have to pay a price. Prove who you are. I think that's pretty clear."

What was I sayin? Did I mean it? Could I look at him and see who he truly was.

But I was sure that I always had. I hadn't been the one who was blinded. It was Maxon who'd gotten lost.

"That's because you were the good in my world. The light that chased out the dark. You never wanted to acknowledge what was hidden underneath."

There was a warning in the rumble of his words, and I turned my attention away, needing a breath.

Not sure how we were ever gonna meet in the middle.

If he'd ever get over his past. If I could ever forgive him for living it.

Where did that leave us?

He blew out a sigh. "Come on, let's go inside."

I cast him a soft smile, unable to stop myself. "We'd better. The boys are probably raiding the refrigerator by now."

I took the hand he extended. Heat sizzled up my arm at the contact.

I didn't know whether to chastise myself for thinking it felt so right.

He ushered me inside, and Benjamin was on the floor in front of a console with a huge TV sitting on top of it, pulling out a video gaming system.

"Maxon said we could play, Mom! He's got Mario Cart. It's the coolest game in the world. You want to play with us?" Dillon shouted.

I glanced at Maxon. Feeling out of sorts. Wondering how I was supposed to fit into the shape of his world.

He nudged me. "Go on, sit down, relax. I'll start dinner."

"You don't have to take care of me." Another defense.

He inched closer, his breath a warm caress across my face. "Let me. I want to."

For a moment, I hesitated, and then I gave, toeing off my shoes and settling on the couch.

Tucking my knees to my chest, I tried to pay attention to the boys who started playing a video game.

But my attention kept getting caught up on the man in the kitchen, his big, powerful body adept there, too.

Dicing the vegetables, tossing them in the heating oil, the scent of garlic and onion rising to the air.

His face intense yet at peace.

Shoulders rigid but demeanor welcoming.

I found myself standing, drawn, the way I'd always been, moving that way.

Energy washed, a lap across my bare feet, throat getting wobbly as I edged up to his side and leaned my hip up on the counter beside where he worked.

"Miss me?" He lifted a brow, half his attention on me and the other on the food he was prepping.

A light giggle escaped.

Talk about a shift in the mood. But I loved that about him. The lightness he could wear when the heaviness threatened to pull us under.

"Not even for a second," I teased right back. "I just came over here to make sure you knew what you were doing. Wouldn't want your cooking to make my kids sick or anything."

Something coy played all over that sexy mouth, dimple denting at the side. I had the stupid, reckless urge to reach out and taste it.

There was that fork. Coming up faster.

"Huh. I would have sworn your heart just started beating harder. You sure it's not something else that has you coming this way?"

"Nervous about the food," I retorted, though my words were getting low and wispy. I blinked through the haze of need that was suddenly clouding the air.

I cleared my throat. "Who knew you could cook. That smells delicious."

"All kinds of things you don't know about me." He winked.

Okay, so that was kind of what I was worried about. The unknowns. Who he'd become. Was he different than this beautiful surface that he was showin' me?

He tossed in some strips of chicken. "I hope you like stir fry. Easy and fast."

"Anything you make would be just fine."

"How long have the two of us been settling for just fine?"

The shift in his tone came out faster than I was prepared for. This easy, cocky boy flipping a one-eighty.

Blue eyes flashed.

Savage possession.

I reared back in surprise.

And there was nothing I could do but whisper the admission into the dense air.

Unable to stop it.

Not sure I wanted to keep the reality of it from him. It needed to be said. "I've never been just fine, Maxon. Though I'm sure you were. Plenty of company to keep you warm at night."

I didn't mean for the bitterness to come through. But it was there.

Before I could make sense of it, he had me by the upper arms, and he spun me around, backing me into the counter and out of view of the boys. He towered over me, so powerful, muscles of those arms twitching with restraint.

Heat instantly exploded in the middle of us.

Flames raking at my skin.

I struggled to find a breath beneath the impact of him, but the only thing I managed to do was gulp down his presence, overflowing my lungs with the promise of sex and dominion.

"You think I was ever fine for a second without you? That my heart ever beat right? That my spirit was ever at peace?" He edged even closer. "Not for a second, Little Bird. Can't fly without you by my side."

My head shook slowly. "You're wrong. You could always fly. Soar higher than anyone."

My moon in the darkest sky.

"You just forgot to remember you had wings. That you had the power. I believed in you. Believed in us. You gave me away, Maxon. Why? For what?" I almost begged, moisture clouding my eyes with the way he was looking at me, with the scars that he'd left ripped open wide.

A patter of footsteps came scurrying our way.

I froze, not sure what to do, realizing I was pinned.

Dillon groaned. "Oh, man, is this what it's gonna be like all the time now? You two kissin' away? Sheesh."

He was all childlike outrage.

Maxon's eyes fired, still pinned on me for a beat, wrought with something so severe my knees nearly buckled beneath the force of it. Then he fixed on a bright smile, turned around, and swept Dillon off his feet.

And then he was . . . oh God . . . he was peppering a million kisses all over Dillon's sweet, chubby face, making my son shriek with laughter.

"What? You don't like kisses?"

"Kisses are gross!"

"You better get used to them."

"Why, 'cause you're a part of the team now?" Dillon asked, still howling between the kisses Maxon was smacking all over his face, trying to deflect the assault and desperate for more of it at the same time.

Maxon shifted his gaze back to me, slowing as he tucked my 5-year-old to his side. He held him tight, as if he wasn't ever gonna let go.

"Yeah, Lil' Dill. Because I'm a part of the team now. No getting rid of me."

"In you go," I told Dillon who crawled into the backseat. "Buckle up."

"Do we have to go?"

"We do, it's late."

"But we don't even got school yet, not for two whole weeks," he argued, his eyes begging like a puppy dog's as he stared at Maxon who was lingering around by my back.

"You might not have school, but I have work."

"Come on, Mr. Mack, tell her it's early. We could play Mario for like . . . fifteen more minutes. That's it. I promise."

I could feel amusement riding off of Maxon, his hands going up in surrender. "If your mom says it's time to go, it's time to go."

"Ah, man, always a funsucker."

"Always a troublemaker," I shot back, playfulness pulling at the corner of my mouth as I bantered with my son who always had something to say.

The quiet one was just smiling soft, content and happy after the amazing night we'd spent inside the walls of Maxon's house.

Dinner so easy.

Light.

Laughter and conversation coming from the four of us. As if we'd been simply catching up at the end of a day that was just like any other. Funny, when it felt completely monumental.

As if we'd just shared our first real meal as a family.

That in itself was terrifying.

I needed to get out of there before my body settled right in.

Straightening, I backed out.

Of course, because I was fumbling and nervous, I had to go and bump right into Maxon.

His big hands went to my waist to steady me, and he pushed his nose into my hair at the back of my neck, and oh God, a shiver was flashing across my skin.

"Whoa, there," he murmured, rough voice sending another rash of chills skatin' free.

I managed a feeble smile as I stepped out of the way, and Maxon dipped down so he could lean inside the backdoor of the car. He reached across and ran his fingers through Dillon's hair. "See you soon, Lil' Dill."

"When?"

"As soon as I can."

"Promise?"

"Promise."

Maxon's attention swept to the seat closest to him, and Benjamin was just sitting there, smile so bright.

"Pppromise?" he mimicked, his blue eyes wise and aware.

Maxon dipped down and pressed a kiss to his forehead. "I promise."

He seemed reluctant to stand up, but he finally did, stepping back and shutting the door.

The light dimmed within, leaving us in the shadowy darkness out in front of his house, the light from the porch barely making it this distance.

I swallowed around a lump the size of a grapefruit that had taken up residence in my throat. A chaotic disorder of what I wanted and what I knew would be so reckless to give in to.

"Thank you so much for dinner," I managed. "It was wonderful. The boys had so much fun. I'm sure my mama and daddy were happy for the break from the noise, too."

There I went, assigning this a different meaning.

But it felt so much safer than taking on the meaning that was roiling through Maxon's expression.

"I'll see you later," I said, floundering around for the doorlatch.

Needing an escape.

But there was no escaping the impact of his words that hit me from behind. "Could you see it, Izzy? Us doing this? Every day?"

I whirled back around, and my back hit the door. I was sure it was the only thing that was keeping me standing.

And there it was.

That fork in the road.

A decision to be made.

He was so beautiful, staring back at me, his shoulders heaving with the exertion I could see him using to keep himself standing there.

From not surging forward.

Taking me the way we both knew I wanted to be taken.

I blinked at him, moisture hazing my sight, my heart lumbering with the savage force of the memories that broke free.

The question that remained.

My own fears this man had etched on me.

Scars that screamed.

"I don't know, Maxon. I don't know what to make of any of this. You're movin' so fast, and I'm not even sure what you want from me."

He surged forward, body eclipsing me in shadow. "I want you. Want you more than anything I've ever wanted before. I want to tell Benjamin I'm his father. Ask Dillon if I can be his, too. Want a family."

His throat bobbed with turmoil. "A family, Izzy Baby. Never had one before. And the only person I have wanted that with is you."

It was crazy how he was speaking the exact words I'd spent years dreaming of hearing.

Verbatim.

The man a match to my soul.

But that's what it'd been—a dream.

And my soul had spent thirteen years achin'. Achin' with torment. Misery meted at his hand.

I struggled for a breath. Struggled to find reason. To make sense of the chaos of what I was feeling.

Words started pouring free.

"I loved you, Maxon. I loved you with every part of me. With every breath. With every heartbeat. I did since I was a little girl. And you shattered that in a way I don't know can ever be repaired."

I clutched my hands over my chest, voice cracking with the confession. "I'm terrified to believe in what you'd refused to believe in. Terrified of feeling all those things again. I don't think you understand all that I've been through. What it feels like to be alone. Scared. But I did it . . . I did it because I had to. For my boys."

I glanced at them and cringed when I found their attention locked on the shadow of us.

I prayed they couldn't hear what I was saying, but I turned back to Maxon, anyway, opened up, spilling my guts all over the ground.

"I don't know if I can afford to put myself in that position again. Not when their hearts are on the line, too. Not when I'm not sure that you fully understand what love is. And loving you when you don't love me back? That's the worst place I've ever been, and I can't condemn myself to that kind of hell again."

He looked like I'd struck him.

His body bowed.

Stricken.

I took the opportunity to jump into my car, fingers fumbling as I turned over the ignition, desperate to get away.

A sharp turn left.

Veering off this collision course.

Fleeing the flames.

Knowing I had no chance of outrunning them anyway.

twenty-four

MACK
SEVENTEEN YEARS OLD

Music thumped against the walls, and the entire house vibrated with a dark, greedy energy.

Voices were elevated, pitched to be heard above the din, a throbbing crowd that chased ecstasy.

Tossing back shots and lining their noses with whatever they'd managed to score.

Like they could stand a chance of flying away from this depressing reality.

The loudest of the crowd was by the sink in the kitchen, a ring of morons chanting, "Chug, chug, chug," as they did keg stands, cheering in pride like they'd brought home a gold medal.

Sitting at the round table at the back, Mack kept his voice low, his focus turned toward Ian who sat sideways on his chair facing him, angling his ear Mack's direction.

"A thousand bucks, man. Your only job is to drive those parts across state lines and not get pulled over."

Mack tried to ignore the bitch who straddled him, wanting to get up close and personal with his dick, Clarissa thinking this was her damn business, too.

"Simple as that," he added.

Simple.

Hatred spun through his being.

Last thing he wanted to do was bring Ian into his mess, this scraggly kid who'd shown up in town about a year before. Even though Ian was a year younger, the two of them had become instant friends.

He guessed the broken-down always gravitated toward the sleaze and shade.

Thing was, Ian had come to him.

Desperate.

Desperate for money. For food. For a goddamn break.

Wanting an in on what was clearly going down in Mack's backyard.

Ian nodded. "That's it? I don't have to do anything else?"

Clarissa laughed. The sound of it curled through him like a disease. "You sure he's got the balls to do it?" she cooed her insult, pressing her tits against his chest.

He had the distinct urge to toss her from his lap.

He ignored her, instead, ignored the tussle of unease that moved through his stomach and focused on his best friend not getting his ass nailed for grand theft. "That's it. Drive slow but not too slow. Fucking pay attention and make sure you aren't drawing attention to yourself. Drop it at the address and get your ass back home."

Anxious laughter rumbled from Ian. "Yeah, I can do that."

"Good."

Ian looked up at him. "Just . . . don't tell my brother, man. Jace will have both of our asses if he catches wind of this. He's been riding me and Joseph about keeping our noses clean."

"Yeah, well Jace should be the last of your worries." Mack hesitated. "You sure you're up for this? You want out, just say it, and you're out."

"Aww, so sweet." Clarissa toyed her finger in the collar of Mack's tee.

God, he despised her.

Mack knew bringing Clarissa's father into the gig was a mistake. Knew it the second his *daddy* showed up with the prick ambling behind him, bringing another into the fold.

Just one big happy fucking family.

But Mack did what he had to do.

What he had to do to survive.

Funny, how he'd fought his father forever and then slid right into the position like he'd always belonged.

Heaviness clanged through his chest. Shame and dishonor. But it'd been stupid to think he'd been purposed for anything else.

Like he was better.

Destined for great things.

What a fuckin' joke.

"Nah, man. I'm in. Better than selling dope for my ma's prick boyfriend," Ian said, driving an agitated hand through his hair.

"Yeah," Mack started to agree when his breath hitched.

It got locked somewhere between his lungs and his throat and the sun.

A prisoner to the shift in the air.

Nothing but a crack in the atmosphere that let a lightning bolt of energy come speeding in.

His attention jerked up, jumping over the faces packed in the sordid house, coming to the one that was breaking through the crowd.

Izzy.

What the fuck was she doing there?

She didn't belong.

His heart started to thud, this thunder that pulsed and screamed with its demand.

"What time should I meet you?" Ian's question was nothing

but a blur in his mind when his eyes tangled with that hazel, unforgettable gaze.

Then Mack was fully losing his mind when he saw Sean say something to her, grab her by the hand, and try to get her to follow.

Mack knew firsthand the asshole was a dickbag.

Izzy seemed frozen, though, and her eyes widened with shock and rejection. That was right before her expression shifted to gutting pain when she focused in on the girl on his lap.

Mack's spirit fisted.

He'd stopped going to Izzy about six months before.

It was the fucking hardest thing he'd ever done, but the sacrifice had been necessary.

Their worlds had grown farther and farther apart. Their differences becoming too apparent.

Guilt had begun to eat at him every time he'd steal through her window like a thief, feeling filthy when he'd gather her up and hold her close, his dick pushing at his jeans and begging for him to take her, even though he promised himself he would never stoop that low.

Every time she whispered encouragement, told him he was going to be something great, filled his ears with all her good and belief, it'd only underscored the fact that she didn't recognize the shame written on him.

The things he'd done. The things he was bound to do.

She was so much better than him. She was the great one. The one going places.

His Little Bird with the biggest, brightest wings.

Then the day had come when he'd had to accept it fully—that their worlds could no longer mesh.

It'd been close to dawn when he'd slipped out of her bed, his heart clutching all over the place as he'd stared down at the girl who was fast asleep, that blonde strewn all over her pillow. He'd left with that picture of her emblazoned on his mind and the memory of her fingertips tracing shapes across his bare shoulders etched on him like a tattoo.

Five minutes later, he'd stumbled through his front door.

His *daddy* had been awake.

Didn't matter that he'd denied it, his father knew where he'd been, spewing his old, misguided hatred at the Lanes through his drunken stupor.

Mack didn't care. He'd turned his back and headed for his room so he could crash, until his father had said it.

"If she's so good, maybe I should take her for a ride. Maybe her old mama, too."

Rage had spiraled through the middle of him. Hatred bigger than it'd ever been.

But really, his father had only been pointing out who Mack really was. An example of their sick, depraved world.

It was the last time he'd climbed that tree.

Like he'd just told Ian, don't draw attention to what you wanted to keep hidden.

To what was important.

To what was good.

And Izzy Lane was the only good thing in his life.

Sean started to pull her through the crowd in the living room and through the kitchen, smug smirk on the bastard's face as he was leading her outside.

Izzy's attention was locked on Mack the whole time.

Uncomfortable and scared.

She cast him one last glance over her shoulder as the door shut behind them.

That was all it took to send that whole philosophy flying out the window.

"Off," Mack demanded.

Clarissa clawed her way closer, pouting like she thought it was sexy. "Where do you think you're going?"

"Don't worry about what I do," he grated, shoving her off.

Rage buzzed from Mack's body when he stood.

He might as well have been on autopilot with the way he moved, no sense or reason, just one destination.

Pushing through the crowd, he ignored anyone who tried to get his attention, and the second he had his hand on the door handle, he flung it open and surged out into the deep, black night.

A firepit blazed in the distance, the heavens dense and darkened.

His gaze scanned the silhouettes of couples and groups that were sprinkled throughout the yard.

But there was only one who mattered. The one who'd gone off the far side of the deck with that asshole, over by a hedge of overgrown shrubs, close to out of sight.

Didn't matter.

Mack was sure he could find her blind.

"Sean, don't. Let's just go. I want to go home."

"No, you don't. You want to stay."

"No, I don't."

"I think you do."

"Let me go."

Fury split through the middle of Mack.

A physical rendering.

He ran across the deck and hurled himself over the railing, dropping to the ground, a rampage of violence skating through his veins. Every muscle hard. Possession riding high.

Fucker was so invested in defiling his Little Bird, he didn't even notice when Mack streaked up behind him, unaware Mack was even there until he had an arm around his neck and was yanking him back.

"What the fuck?" he shouted, hands scratching at Mack's arm and trying to get loose.

"Did the girl tell you she wanted to go home?" It was nothing but a threat at the prick's ear.

"Mack." Izzy sagged forward, pain and relief in his name.

"Why are you here?" he demanded, fear slicing through him, a hot, jagged knife at the thought of what might have happened had he not been there to protect her.

And he'd promised that he would always, always protect her.

Hurt and disbelief churned through her features, and Mack's stomach was twisting in that fucked-up way that he couldn't let it.

"You don't get to tell me where I can go."

"So what, you want me just to let this skeeze touch you when you don't want to be touched? Turn my back? Is that what you want?"

She slipped out from the spot where she'd been pinned. Mack kept Sean locked, dickbag kicking and flailing like he thought he stood the chance to bust free.

Izzy spun on her heel to face him. The tears streaking down her face glimmered in the light. Torment was written on every inch. "No, Maxon. That's not what I want at all."

She started backing away, moving for the deck stairs, her head shaking. "But isn't that what you already did?"

Mack watched as she turned and fled. He kept hold of the prick until she was safe and out of sight. Mack tightened his hold, kid choking, Mack's threat low at his ear. "If I ever see you anywhere near her, they will find your body buried in the forest. You got me?"

Mack released him, and Sean surged forward, whirling around and holding his throat. "Are you fucking crazy?"

He guessed he'd always been when it came to Izzy Lane.

"You get one warning." He pointed at the asshole who was still choking, and Mack backed away before he turned and jogged back into the house, his eyes darting everywhere.

But Izzy was gone.

Mack killed the engine of his car outside the shack that he called home. It plunged his world into darkness. Into an unbearable silence.

Just the whoosh of the trees and the howling of ghosts.

His mama's voice in his ear.

Vapor and mist.

"You are better than the world you were born into."

Groaning, he rocked his head back, squeezing his eyes closed before he forced himself out of the car.

It was a car that had been bought on the solid. Too bad every penny funding it had been dirty money.

Guilt lanced through his spirit, and he dragged his feet toward the house, only to freeze when that feeling rushed him from behind.

Overwhelming warmth.

A cold that chilled him to the bone.

Each sensation at odds.

Every muscle in his body hardened in awareness, and his guts tangled when he slowly edged around to find her hidden in the shadows.

He moved that way, until her face was coming into sharp, plain view.

Cheeks blotchy and red, eyes so big and round, mouth quivering.

"What are you doing here?" The words were grit. Fear and need.

Fuck. He wanted her so bad he could taste it on his tongue.

"I miss you," she whispered. "I miss you so bad it hurts. God, it hurts."

Tears streaked down her face, her lips wet with them, and she angled her head as if she was begging him to look closer at her. "Do you have any idea how horrible it is to be waitin' for you to come, and you never do? Night after night, lying there, my heart so empty? You left a hole inside of me, Maxon, and that hole just keeps gettin' bigger and bigger every time I see you with her."

Mack dug deep to find the strength he was going to need to get through this. To keep himself from hurtling himself at her. Sweeping her up and holding her close and taking her hard.

She was better than all of that.

Still, emotion raced his throat. Thick and needy. As desperate as his hands he was curling into fists. "I'm no good for you, Little Bird."

"And she is? Good for you? Meant for you in a way that I'm not?"

Shame and regret crawled beneath his skin. "She's nothing to me."

Izzy choked over a gasp of pain. "If she means nothin', then what does that make me?" She was pleading, taking a step toward him, her trembling hands pressed in petition to her chest. "I wanted it to be me, Maxon. I wanted to be yours. Your first and your last and your everything. You are my best friend. You've always been. But I can't go on pretendin' that I don't ache for you.

Need you. Want you in a way that has only ever belonged to you."

She was killing him.

Word by word. Breath by breath.

"I'm in love with you, Maxon. Don't you see that? I love you so much. So much that it is ruinin' me. Tell me that you feel the same way."

Her confession penetrated like spears. Stakes of grief. He nearly broke beneath the weight of it. Mouth dry, no words on his tongue because he couldn't form a lie that big.

He just stood there like a bastard, watching heartbreak crack across her face.

She barely nodded, crushed by the understanding.

She shifted her attention to the shed for the barest beat before she looked back at him.

Her voice shook with its own sort of ferocity. "No matter what you feel for me or not, I need you to know, you are so much better than this. You have always been destined for greater things. I hope one day you realize that."

She pointed her finger at the ground.

At his world.

At his life.

Then she turned around and disappeared into the trees.

Agony clutched his spirit, driving a knife right into his soul.

Empty and vacant as he watched the only person who could ever fill it walk away.

Her presence fading.

He tried to force himself to go into his house. To turn his back. But panic was taking over. He couldn't stand for her to leave with that look on her face.

He needed . . .

Fuck, he had no clue what he needed. The only thing he knew was he started running, dodging trees and branches as he cut through the forest. He burst through the thicket and out onto the meadow.

He skidded to a stop, chest heaving from the exertion. From the turmoil. From wanting something so bad and not being able to have it.

Izzy whirled around, and those mesmerizing eyes went wide with surprise.

"Maxon," she rasped.

He hesitated, torn, but then he found he was unable to stop the words from bleeding from his heart. "I feel it, too, Izzy. I do."

Pain followed the admission. "But this can't work. You know that it won't. We come from two different worlds. Are two different people."

She blinked at him through the wetness in her eyes, and she started to move back in his direction. "Two people who belonged together. It doesn't matter where we come from just as long as we end up in the same place."

He swallowed around the thickness in his throat. "I'll ruin you."

"You already have."

He started moving for her, drawn, unable to stop. "I'm terrified of this, Izzy. Of what it means. The only thing I know is my life means nothing without you in it."

She started running for him, and he was running for her, too.

They met in the middle, and he swept her up.

Relief.

He pressed his face into her hair as he spun her around. Breathed her in. Wild jasmine and the sun. "I love you. I love you so fucking much. So fucking much."

He held her close, listening to the rapid beat of her heart. The fluttering that promised to carry him away.

"My dragon," she whispered.

"Little Bird," he murmured back, chest stretched tight as he stared up at her. "Let's fly away."

"Just tell me where you want to go."

And he was taking her mouth, kissing her soft and slow and with everything he had.

Twirling her around.

Together, they soared.

twenty-five

IZZY

With a dull lamp lighting my way, I sat at my desk, hand brushing in frantic strokes over the paper in the notebook I was drawing in. A jumble of designs were bleeding out, all my confusion and hurt and anger at odds with the massive amount of need and want the man had evoked in me.

How could I just let go?

Believe?

Chewing furiously at my bottom lip, I colored and shaded, slashed and sketched and hoped that the images would come to life.

That a story would arise.

Make sense.

Give me an answer.

Gasping in surprise, I nearly fell out of my chair with the light tappin' that came at my window.

It was a sound that was so familiar but I hadn't heard in so long that for a moment I was wondering if I were imagining it.

But I knew. I knew because it resonated like a drum in the depths of me.

A call.

A plea.

Heart stampeding, I slapped shut the notebook and lifted my head.

A dangerous, darkened silhouette came into view out in the tree.

Massive and distinct.

Beautiful and destructive.

So compelling that I could do nothing but push off the chair and lean over the desk, my hands shaking like crazy as I fumbled to release the latch and slide up the window the way I'd done a thousand times before.

In all of a second, Maxon had pushed through, and I was stumbling back, struck by the force of his blistering presence as he climbed over the desk and onto his feet.

Body towering. Expression fierce.

Overwhelming.

For a moment, we just stood there staring at each other, pants heaving from our lungs as our spirits caught up to the point of the meeting.

An intersection.

His eyes pinched in despair.

"You think I don't know what a family is? That I don't understand what love is?" he demanded in a desperate sort of disbelief, voice rough and raw as he took a step forward, every word scraping with the magnitude of what he was saying.

My spirit clenched, and I sucked in a shattered breath as I stared up at the devastation written in his expression.

There I was, right back at that fork in the road.

Only now, it felt like there was only one direction I could go.

Reaching out, he took me by both sides of the face, those big hands stretched across my cheeks and dipping under my jaw.

Forcin' me to look at him.

As if I could look anywhere else.

A shudder ripped down my spine, and need rushed like wildfire through my body.

"Loving you was the *only* truth I knew," he grated. "The only thing I ever did right. The only thing that has ever been real."

I could feel the thunder of his heart, this rioting pound, pound, pound that ricocheted against the frantic beat of mine.

Oh God. I didn't know if I could handle this. What he was sayin'. What he was implyin'.

"I don't want to go on living this life without you in it." There he went, tearing me up more, his tone deepening in emphasis. "Don't want to spend one more day without you by my side. One more night without you lying next to me. Let's love again, Little Bird. Love me, the way I love you. And I promise, I will never let you go."

I was nothing but a shaking mess at his admission. All those broken pieces he'd left me with toppling to the ground.

"Maxon," I whimpered.

He tugged me forward. "Do you love me? Do you still feel the same, or am I too late?"

My attention raced across his face, looking for any trace of insincerity. For any reason not to believe this man. To keep on fighting what clearly was a losing battle.

Because this man had won me over long, long ago.

My soul shivered in awakening.

Reservations sheared away.

The cold eclipsed by the heat of the flames that came alive between us.

There were no boundaries left. No barrier so high. No fear so great.

None that could compete with what was taking me over.

"Tell me," he demanded low, his nose brushing mine.

My hands curled around his wrists, hanging on for dear life, and I let the deepest confessions of my heart pour out.

"I have loved you since I was a little girl and you came runnin' to rescue me. I have loved you since I first saw that tender smile and had the honor of meetin' that fierce, brave heart. I loved you when I didn't really know what it meant, and I loved you even more when I grew into the fullness of it."

My voice slowed in significance. "Never for a day did I stop. I love you, Maxon Chambers. I'm so in love with you."

His kiss was swift and all-consuming.

Dizziness swept through my mind, knees going weak. It didn't matter at all, considering the man was sweeping me into the security of those sure arms and pulling me to the warmth of his rock-hard body.

His tongue stroked mine, and my arms locked desperately around his neck.

"Every day, I loved you," I muttered into his mouth, and he grunted back, splaying a big hand over the small of my back and sliding down to grip me by the bottom.

The other wrapped up in my hair in the same moment my legs were wrapping around his waist.

Basic instinct.

Belonging there all along.

Never breaking that kiss, he carried me across the room, keeping hold of me as he crawled with me on top of my bed and laid me down in the middle of it.

The springs squeaked, and Maxon cringed with something that looked close to guilt, as if he were remembering all the times he crawled into this bed and tried to stay quiet, and I was somehow grinning against his mouth.

Lost to this moment. Lost to this man. All sanity given, offered to his willing hands.

Because in that moment, nothing else in the world mattered.

Nothing but us.

"What are you grinning about?" he asked with a quiet, playful huff, the man grinning, too, though there was so much affection woven in it that the force of it was stretching my chest tight.

Joy pressing full.

"At you. That you're here. That you came back to me." I

reached out a trembling hand and stroked across his gorgeous face. "That you're lookin' at me that way."

He grabbed my hand and pressed my knuckles to his lips, mumbling at the flesh, "And how am I looking at you?"

"Like you love me. Like you're gettin' ready to devour me. Like you'll be all too happy to do it again."

Rising up higher, he planted his hands on the mattress as he dipped his face down to whisper his mouth across mine. "Again and again. Forever."

"Endless," I murmured back at his lush lips, so soft, so sexy in their pluck and pull as he kissed me slow.

Reverently.

His hand slipped over my cheek, cupped my jaw, my chin. Maxon glided it down to palm my breast over the fabric of my shirt, chills spreading in the wake of his adoring touch.

I arched. Released a tiny moan.

"God, I love the sound of that," he rumbled, getting onto his knees and sitting back so he could reach down to gather the hem of my tank in his hands. He peeled it up, cool air hitting my flesh, goosebumps flashing across my abdomen and scattering over my arms as he tugged it over my head.

I wasn't wearing a bra, and my nipples were tingling, pebbling to hard, needy peaks as I sank back onto the pillow.

Maxon stared down at me.

Desire sparked. Little bursts lighting up in the space. Excitement and greed.

"Shit," he hissed, and he leaned forward onto one hand so he could trace the tip of a finger around the aching flesh. "So goddamn sexy, Izzy Baby. You have any idea what you do to me? Years I spent dreaming about you, fantasizing about this body. No memory could ever do you justice."

He dipped down and grazed his teeth on the lobe of my ear.

Chills streaked, and I whimpered, hips jerking from the bed.

I wanted to feel every inch of him.

Rediscover and reclaim what I'd been missin' for so long.

"Can't wait to get inside of you. Take you the way I've been dying to. Going to prove to you that I can be the kind of man you deserve. I promise, Little Bird. I promise you."

I could feel the tremor of fear come rolling out with it.

The little boy who'd been marred by brutality.

Fed the lie that he would never be good enough.

Heart clutching in a fist, I rocked my head back on the pillow to make sure he understood what I was saying, my gaze seeking his.

"You've always been the kind of man who deserved me. Right and good. Just like I always hoped I'd be good enough to deserve you. Maybe you just needed a little time to come to terms with that. With who you really are. The man I saw."

Blue eyes flashed with regret and devotion.

I ran my thumb along the hollow beneath one of them.

"I'm so proud of who you became. I knew it. I knew it all along."

And that seemed to be all that Maxon could take before he broke.

Restraint gone.

Chains busted.

He dove for me, his kiss as desperate as his hands that searched my body, palms pressing firm as they roamed my flesh, cupping my breasts before they were riding down and his mouth was taking their place.

Sucking and licking and driving me wild.

Little teases of pleasure of what was to come.

My fingers twisted in his hair, cinching down tight, and I tried to silence the whimpers that were escaping my mouth as he kissed a path down my belly.

Tried to contain the blaze that burned across my skin when he tucked his fingers into the waistband of my sleep shorts.

Tried to quiet the shout of my heart when he angled back and peeled them down my legs.

His gaze fire.

Complete annihilation.

Completely bare to him, my stomach trembled and shook, my knees quaking as he eyed me like he was watching the sun rise and set at the same time.

A collision of colors.

Complete and utter awe.

And I could take it no longer, either, and I shot up, ripping at his shirt to get it over his head, and oh my God, I was sure I died a little when I got the full impact of his fierce beauty when I tugged the fabric free.

Those shoulders wide, muscled arms nothing but intimidation and strength. The colors and designs vibrated across his skin, that dragon perched on his shoulder and wrapping down like a reminder of who he was.

I caressed it, felt my spirit leap into the sky where I met with him.

The second I looked back to the intensity in his eyes, we were an instant, frenzied tangle.

Maxon kissed me mad while I touched him everywhere that I could, hands on his massive pecs and riding down the carved planes of his abdomen.

"You steal my breath, Maxon. Steal it right out of my lungs."

I yanked at his fly, and he jerked back. "Goddamn it, Izzy. You're gonna kill me."

He ripped his zipper down and shoved his jeans and briefs over his hips, winding out of them as his eager pants rose into the air.

Mine escalated to match, desire racin' through my veins as he freed himself.

A tremble rolled, and I was swallowing around the nerves that flickered through my senses.

Sensation heightened.

My mouth going dry.

His thick, hard penis bounced at his belly, straining for me as he kicked his jeans from his ankles and climbed right back between my thighs.

I was gasping, feeling lightheaded, unable to see.

Blinded by this lust.

Blinded by this love.

I swatted around for the drawer on my nightstand, silently thanking my mama for constantly meddlin', even though I'd wanted to crawl under a table when she'd shoved the big box of condoms at me the other day and whispered, "Just in case."

He tore into the box and had his massive length covered in a flash.

Just as fast, he crawled back over me, and my thighs were gripping at his hips, anticipation wracking through the middle of me.

Oh lord. Was this really happenin'?

Our breaths mingled and our hearts careened, tempos lost to the urgency that struck in the air, and Maxon was running his nose along my jaw, inhaling as he went, as if he were looking for some sort of control that had long since slipped.

But I was so tired of fighting this truth.

The truth of who we were.

No longer could I lie to myself.

And I was issuing his name like praise.

A promise.

A plea.

"Maxon."

Because it'd been too long, and every second that he wasn't mine seemed like a complete waste of time.

And I was pretty sure that Maxon agreed because he took me in one quick stroke.

One that sent the oxygen gushing from my lungs and exploding in the air.

One that filled me so full that the only thing I could feel was him.

Every molecule taken.

Captured.

A low groan rumbled in the depths of Maxon's chest, something dark and deep and desperate. His forehead dropped to mine. "Izzy Baby. Fuck . . . you feel so good. Never thought I would get to feel you like this again." He nuzzled the side of my face. "Motherfuckin' heaven."

Those eyes met mine, so intense, and I swore that I could feel him sinking all the way inside.

"Little Bird." It was his own prayer. An appeal.

He gathered me up, and I dug my fingers into his back.

Holding him to me.

Fiercely.

Knowing there was no chance after this that I could ever let him go.

He began to take me.

Wholly.

Without measure.

Letting himself go.

Hips rocking in rough strokes that sent my mind spinnin'.

They grew with each thrust of his body. A drive of desperation as we raced for the top.

This war of give and take.

And I could feel it, riding high, coming together

Coalescing. Gathering to a breaking point.

"You're so gorgeous. So fucking beautiful. Do you have any idea?"

"Maxon, please."

"Shh . . . Little Bird . . . I've got you. I won't let you down. Not ever."

Vibration shook through my body.

He reached between us, stroked me where I was achin'.

"Oh, God." I almost sobbed it.

In an instant, he sent me soaring.

Ecstasy shattering me into a billion unrecognizable pieces where I became partner to his dark sky.

A scatter of stars strewn through the heavens.

And I was whimpering, fingers clutching his hair as he took me higher, the intensity almost too much, my body stretched taut as he drove into me again and again.

Kept me there.

Refused to let me fall until he met me.

Until we were flying.

High, high above the trees.

Where we'd always belonged.

Where he was my forever.

Endless.

twenty-six

IZZY

I bolted upright in bed, and then I was scrambling to clutch the covers to my chest when I realized I was naked.

Naked.

That was all it took for an onslaught of memories to assault me. Picture after picture. Heat flashed across my flesh as if he were still touching me, and with a trembling hand, I reached out and brushed my fingers over the vacant spot on the bed where I last remembered him being.

Sheets cold, and somehow, every part of me was still on fire.

Sunlight spilled in through the window that was cracked open, and I wondered when he'd gone. When he'd slipped out into the rising morning the way he used to do.

He'd held me last night, that gorgeous man curled around me from behind.

Quietly.

Soundly.

Nothin' but our spirits whispering the weight of our thoughts.

Of course, that had been after he'd taken me time and again.

Every time I'd drift, he'd be reaching out. Every time I opened my mouth, he'd kiss the questions away.

For that sacred moment in time, it'd just been us. Our bodies. Our hands and our hearts.

Loving.

Adoring.

Putting everything else aside.

There was nothing like the morning sun to shine a spotlight on all the questions that still pervaded my mind.

It wasn't like I regretted it. At all.

That didn't mean there weren't traces of worry flickering around in my mind. Warning me that we had no plans. That I had no idea where we were going to go from here. And that tiny, tiny seed of dread that Maxon wasn't ready.

That he still harbored so much pain, and it was liable to come busting out at some point.

There was an even tinier sprout of alarm that he might have woken up to second thoughts and used that window as an escape.

My gaze moved to the window, drapes fluttering on the breeze, and my mind filled with all the times that he'd come in and out of it.

Coming to me.

For me.

My fingertips stroked over my bitten, swollen lips that were splitting into a grin.

I refused to worry about all of that right then.

Slipping out of bed, I pulled on my tank and sleep shorts from the floor, trying not to blush like mad remembering him peeling them off.

Barefoot, I rushed out to find my boys.

Their bedroom door was already wide open, and I could hear

laughter wafting up from the kitchen.

I padded downstairs, holding onto the railing, mouth tipping up in affection as I listened to their joy filling the air.

It filled me full, too.

This.

This was what was important. The happiness of my boys. The very thing I'd dedicated my entire life to echoing from the kitchen.

No matter how I was feeling right then, no matter the questions that stirred and the old fears that tried to push to the forefront, I could rest easy in that.

I pushed open the swinging door, doing my best to stride right in like I hadn't spent the night rolling around in the hay with the very man I'd promised would never have the chance to break me again.

Then I was stumbling, inhaling a shocked gasp when I saw he was there, at the table with Dillon on his lap.

My youngest son was howling with laughter as Maxon tickled him.

Benjamin clapped where he sat beside them, cheering, "Get him, Mmmack!"

I didn't know when they realized I was there, but suddenly Maxon slowed, shifting to look at me from over his shoulder.

The energy shifted.

Intense and alive.

The rest of the eyes in the kitchen turned to land on me.

Nothing but a target.

I stood there fidgeting, sure it was written all over me that I'd dipped my fingers into the cookie jar one too many times last night.

Dillon popped his head up my direction, hanging onto Maxon's shoulders. "Mom, you're awake! About time. It's almost time to eat. Breakfast is the most important meal of the day, don't you know that? Grams is making pancakes and eggs because we need our protein, too. And Mr. Mack is gonna eat with us!"

Right. Right.

Mr. Mack was gonna eat with us.

I struggled to readjust my image of how I'd imagined this

morning would play out, wondering just how it was that Maxon had ended up sitting there at the table.

Redness crept to my cheeks as my gaze swept the faces staring back at me.

My daddy pretended as if he were reading the paper, but there was no missing the concern in his eyes when he sent me a questioning glance over the top of it, and Benjamin was shooting me one of his crooked, happy grins.

And Maxon—he was looking at me as if he were contemplating throwing me over his shoulder and carrying me back upstairs.

A shiver rolled down my spine.

Oh, this was not good. So not good. Because my mama was at the stove, slanting me a sly smile as she took me in. "Yes, look who showed up at our door, bright and early. What a nice surprise."

Her eyes went wide with the implication.

"Oh . . . I . . . hi." I sent him an awkward wave. "Good mornin'."

Maxon smirked, that dimple peeking out.

My belly twisted.

Oh God, this really was bad.

"I . . . um . . . coffee." I flailed a hand in the general direction of the coffee maker, and I dropped my head, making a beeline for the other side of the kitchen. Hands shaking, I fumbled to get a cup from the cupboard, and I was surprised I even got a drop into the cup with the way the carafe trembled when I poured it.

"Need help with that? You seem a little . . . flustered," my mama teased, voice lowered to remain out of earshot, grinning a conspiring grin.

I groaned a panicked sound, peeking over at the table, wetting my lips as I sucked for a cleansing breath. "Help. Yes, yes, I need help."

Because I didn't have the first clue what I was supposed to do right then.

"Something bothering you?"

I pressed my face into my hands, and then I was peeling them away, leaving them up at the sides like a shield. My voice dropped to a mortified hiss. "I slept with him, Mama."

No need to give her the detail that it'd been five times.

"Well, that's plenty obvious. Have you seen your hair this mornin'?"

My hands flew up to the ratted mess.

Oh God.

She chuckled.

"This isn't funny, Mama."

I smoothed out my tank, as if it could smooth away the agitation and embarrassment.

"Did he just waltz in here from upstairs?" I questioned in horror, peeking over there again and wondering how I was supposed to explain an impromptu sleepover with my boys. For a beat, my attention got wrapped up in the easy way Maxon leaned over and drew something with Benjamin, talking with him as if being there was the most natural thing in the world.

"Well, I know he came crawling out your window and sneaking down that tree like he used to do. I was out back when I heard a racket, and I peeked around the corner to see what was goin' on. But don't worry your pretty face. He came around the front of the house and up the steps, knocking at the front door, just like a perfect gentleman would do." It was purely a tease.

I pressed a trembling hand to my forehead.

I was gonna pass out.

"Stop frettin'."

I went back to my coffee and dumped in a couple spoonfuls of sugar. "How am I not supposed to fret when he is here after what happened last night?" I rushed out of the side of my mouth.

"Seems to me you should be glad that he is."

I was.

God, I was.

But that didn't mean my nerves weren't racing, sure my boys knew something was up. My daddy sure knew it, with the way his glare was cutting between the two of us, though it was different somehow.

Softer and less angry, though he appeared a thousand times

more worried than before.

This really was a mess.

"Go on, I'll feed you," Mama said, transferring the huge skillet of scrambled eggs into a serving bowl. "You've got to be to work in an hour."

Oh, that was right.

Work.

It was the last thing on my mind.

I shuffled over to the table, my bare feet scooting on the worn floor, trying to play it cool and casual and like Maxon wasn't affecting me at all.

I started to round to the free chair, and I yelped out when he snagged an arm around my waist and hauled me to his side.

Right out of the blue.

He squeezed my hip in one of those massive hands.

"Good morning, gorgeous," he said in that grumbly, beautiful voice.

Dillon laughed and a blush the same color of mine was lighting on Benjamin's face.

"I . . ." I attempted to clear the disorder from my throat. "Um . . ."

He grinned. "Sit."

Blowing out a breath, I did, and he set a hand on my knee under the table.

With my head dropped, I peeked over at him, catching the adoring expression on his face.

And there was nothin' I could do to stop the sappy grin.

An hour later, I was rushing out to my car. This whole surprise of a morning had made me late.

Of course, I knew it was only gonna get worse when I felt the presence swallow me from behind, his footsteps heavy as he came out the door and jogged out toward my car.

He was on me in an instant, spinning me around, pinning my back to metal.

Kissin' me with a passion I'd never known before.

God, this man was gonna do me in.

"I thought you already kissed me goodbye?" I teased, teeth raking my bottom lip as I peeked up at his gorgeous face.

A smirk took hold of his mouth. "So, I wanted another one."

"Hmm . . . can't get enough?"

He tucked a strand of my hair behind my ear, fiddling with it as he angled his head, his expression soft. "Never."

Then that expression shifted, something somber and bold coming to caress the lines of his face. He traced over the angle of my cheek. "We need to tell him, Izzy. It's time. I can't keep sitting beside him and keeping this secret. Feels like I'm lying to him."

My gaze drifted off in the distance, processing, the fears there but quieted. Because I knew I could no longer be that person. Someone who was bitter and scared and letting the past hold her back.

I couldn't go on living like it was yesterday.

I looked back at him and slowly nodded. "Okay."

The smile splitting his face nearly knocked me to my knees, so bright and brilliant.

So free.

"I'd like to do it, if that's okay?" he asked.

I nodded again. "Okay. Just . . . you have to allow him to have his own reaction. Process it all. He's gonna be shocked."

Grief struck across his face. "I know that. I know. I deserve for him to hate me, but I will be there, even if he does, until he sees that he doesn't have to. That he can trust me."

He cupped my face, and I leaned into the warmth. "When do you want to talk to him?" I asked.

"Maybe I can take him to his appointment on Thursday? Afterward, I'll take him to the park or for ice cream or wherever he wants to go."

Heart shuddering, I peered up at him. "And what about Dillon?"

Determination steeled those strong features. "Wasn't playing when I said I want us to be a family, Izzy. For the first time in my life, I have a family, right here. I don't want to be separate from any of them. Not ever again."

Emotion surged, so thick that it was pricking tears at the back of my eyes. "I want that. So much."

He brushed his thumb over my lips. Softly. Reverently. Though there was hesitation behind it. "Last thing I want to imagine is you with another man, but I need to know about his father. Where he is. What happened with him."

As if I wanted to imagine him with another woman. I cringed with even the thought, tucking it down, refusing the remnants of betrayal from clawing its way out.

It didn't have a place in my life any longer.

I hiked an indifferent shoulder. "There's not a whole lot to tell. His name was Jon. He left me when things with Benjamin got too rough. Dillon was two months old, and Benjamin had just had another surgery. It was a rough one. Benjamin was up all night crying with his pain, needing me to hold him, while I was trying to take care of a newborn at the same time. Jon told me he was sorry, but he couldn't do it. He didn't want to spend his life in doctor's offices."

Fury raced through Maxon's being. Hatred so fierce I swore it darkened the sun.

"Did you love him?"

I blew out a strained sigh. "I did, Maxon. Differently than you, but I did. He was a friend that had grown into more. Then he let me down. He didn't love us enough. And it breaks my heart to think that maybe I didn't love him enough, either."

There'd been a ghost that had always lived in the middle of us—in the perfect size of Maxon Chambers.

Standing in the way of me ever fully giving myself to Jon.

I was staring up at Maxon when I said it.

It was soft and tender.

But I thought maybe it came with an ultimatum.

His forehead dropped to mine. "You questioning whether I love you enough? There's not enough time in eternity for me to use up the love I have for you."

twenty-seven

MACK

I glanced over at my cell ringing on my desk to find Pete's name lighting the screen. He was out hunting down monsters while my ass was stuck at a desk for four weeks.

Two down, two to go.

"What's up?" I rocked forward and leaned my elbow on my desk, ignoring the commotion and clamor of conversations going on around me.

"Fingerprints are in," Pete said, caution in his voice.

Figured he realized he was about to set me off.

"Yeah?" I pressed, preparing myself for the news I was about to receive while trying my best to ignore the agitation that stirred in that dark pit that writhed deep inside.

The place that reminded me whose side I was on but never let me forget where I'd come from.

His voice lowered like he wanted to keep me from the truth. "It was definitely Zachary Keeton. Seems he didn't do a whole lot to hide it, either. Prints were all over your truck and on the brick."

Aggression jumped into my bloodstream, seething and violent, and I ground my teeth to keep from coming out of my chair.

"Got any clue why this punk has it out for you?" he asked.

Unease rippled through my body. Something taunting at the edge of my mind but remaining out of reach. "Other than giving him that ticket? No."

He sighed in frustration, worry weaving into the middle of it. "You think it's because he's found a cop to point his aggression and animosity at?"

I shrugged, but it wasn't in acceptance. "Maybe."

Gut told me it was more than that, though.

He hesitated, clearly not wanting to broach what it was he was getting ready to say. "Have you checked into your father?"

Hatred spun, and my jaw clenched. "Yeah. Fucker is still sitting behind bars. Where he belongs."

Kept close tabs.

Always.

But the second Izzy had shown up in town, I'd doubled those efforts.

"Fuck, I hate this. Crime for nothing. I can't handle this. I'm going to have to go into an early retirement before I have a heart attack at forty. Live on a deserted beach somewhere. Sipping piña coladas for the rest of my life."

"I thought it was me with my ass in the hot seat, and you're the one who's trying to hightail it out of here?" I attempted to go light. Not wanting to give into what was pressing at me.

Fear and rage and darkness.

I wasn't that guy. Not anymore.

Couldn't give myself over to it.

Not with what I now stood to lose.

"Maybe I was making a suggestion. Two of us run away together."

"Sorry, dude, but you're not my type."

He laughed. "Yeah, and how is that going with that sweet thing? Tell me you locked that down. Your ugly ass isn't ever going to get another chance like that."

I blew out a sigh, scrubbed a hand over my face. "I'm going to marry her, man."

Silence echoed on the line, and then he muttered, "Really?" It was nothing but speculation.

Maybe he'd heard me spouting my mouth about it being selfish for a cop to settle down so many times that he didn't believe what he was hearing.

"Told you she was my oldest friend. Also the mother of my son. She has another little boy, too."

This time his silence was deafening.

"No shit?" he finally said.

"No shit."

"Well, fuck. Was not expecting that. Seems we're going to have to get us a bigger island."

A rough chuckle rolled out before I was turning serious. "Have to nail this bastard, Pete. Can't risk someone coming after me like that when I've got Izzy and her boys to worry about. Won't take that chance."

"Understand that completely. Believe me, there isn't a soul in the precinct who isn't watching, waiting to take that fucker down after what he did to you."

"Yet, he's managed to remain at large for two weeks."

"We'll nab him. We will."

"All right. Keep me posted."

"Will do, man. Just . . . hang tight. Watch your back. We'll be looking out for you."

I ended the call to find a text had come through.

Hatred and disgust curled my guts.

Clarissa: Two weeks. Aren't you missing me? Think it's time you come visit. I'm feeling . . . neglected.

Rage tightened every muscle in my body, the chains of her

manipulation yanking at my insides. Twisting me apart. Knew that whole neglected bit meant she wanted me to bring her money, too. I no longer knew if it was her blackmailing me or I was bribing her to keep it quiet.

Me: Told you I was finished with you toying with me. It's over, Clarissa. Sink your claws into someone else.

Clarissa: Aww. I'm sorry to hear that. I'd hate for one of Charleston's finest to be found to be nothing but a criminal. Even worse that his cute little girlfriend was involved.

A frenzy built in my body. A storm that raged in my soul.

She knew Izzy was here.

Shit.

She knew it.

Dread pulsed, and I didn't know how the screen of my phone didn't shatter when I fired off my response.

Me: Stay the fuck away from her, Clarissa. Away from me. I am warning you, you don't want to mess with this. I will make sure you regret it.

I tossed my phone to the desk. Hostility boiled in my blood, and my knee was bouncing, trying to find a direction to focus my aggression.

I looked at the clock.

I needed to pick Benjamin up in thirty. Needed to cool it. Get it under control before I did something that I *would* be regretting.

I grabbed my phone and called Pete back.

"Yo," he answered.

"I've got to run, but do me a favor, will you?"

"Anything."

"Get whatever you can on Clarissa Pelter. Bank records. Cell records. Anything you can."

"Shit . . ." Could feel him stirring on the other end of the line.

"You don't think she's involved?"

"Don't know. But I am going to find out."

"Big Ben, buddy," I murmured softly, heart gripping as I glanced in the rearview mirror of my truck. Benjamin rode in the back.

He'd just finished his session.

This one . . . this one had been brutal. He'd worked so goddamn hard, but there had been no missing the agony that had been written all over him. The frustration and the discouragement, just like what dimmed his spirit now.

His attention cast out the window.

Child silent.

But it was a different kind than his typical quiet observation.

This was . . . sad.

Fucking sad.

And I didn't have a goddamn clue how to fix it.

He shifted his attention to me, meeting my eye through the rear-view mirror. He didn't answer. Just looked at me. Blue eyes glistening with unshed tears he was trying to hold back.

"What's wrong, buddy?" Could barely force the words out around the torment crushing my ribs.

A tear got loose. He tried to hide it when he said, "Don't worrrrry. It's okkkkay."

He seemed barely able to form the lie over the thickness in his voice. A lie I knew wasn't done maliciously, not in any way, but to pretend like everything was *okay*.

Some days I knew it just couldn't be.

I could feel my heart rioting against my ribs. "You can tell me anything. Did you know that? You can tell me *anything*." My words deepened in emphasis, close to desperate. "Confide anything. If you're hurting or scared, you can come to me. You don't ever have to be ashamed."

That blue gaze flashed hesitation before he was forcing out the response, "I dddon't think I'm strrrong enough."

Everything tightened. "Strong enough? You're the strongest person I know."

I was trying to get my voice to come out positive because fuck, it was the truth, but it was wobbling.

His crooked mouth hung open in the most heartbreaking sort of surrender. "It huuurts too bad."

God.

I couldn't handle this.

Couldn't handle the desperate need to make this right and being completely powerless to do it. This kid's plight was one I couldn't undo no matter how bad I wanted to.

"I'm so sorry, Benjamin. I'm so sorry that you have to go through this. I wish I could change it." My words were a tumble of grief.

He just stared at me, like he was trying to make sense of why and what this meant. Trying to process the awareness that clawed between us, a fierce force drawing us together.

Making a decision, I took a right and headed in the opposite direction of Izzy's place and back toward my house. We rode in silence, and my attention was snapping around the yard as I pulled into the drive, a swelling of hostile protectiveness rising up within me at the thought of me putting this kid in danger by bringing him here.

Benjamin shifted in his seat, edging up to get a better look, confusion in his expression.

"What are we ddddoing here?"

"Want to give you something," I told him.

He didn't respond, just sent me a look of trust.

That kind of gutted me, too.

Ensuring nothing was awry, I returned to the truck and unbuckled this kid who had gotten so deep under my skin that I hardly recognized myself anymore.

I pulled him into my arms.

Holding him because I got that was what he needed right then.

Support and unwavering encouragement.

And suddenly, I was getting all the warnings that Izzy had given. The fact that this wasn't easy—not in the least—but it was the most important job I would ever have.

He exhaled a shaky sound and wrapped his arms around my

neck.

Devotion pumped.

Intense.

Overpowering.

Blinding.

Could feel it streaking my veins and settling as a firm reality in my soul.

I carried him inside my house and carefully set him on the couch. "I'll be right back. I want to show you something."

He nodded, curiosity filling his expression, the kid all bony and angled, the sight of him hitting me so perfectly.

Emotion clawed my throat. Anxiety and hope going on a rampage. I rushed to my room. A couple seconds later, I reemerged at the end of the hall.

Benjamin remained on the couch. The glow of the evening light flooded in around him, and he cast me a timid smile. Unsure of what was going on.

And I was praying silently that I could explain this to him right, that I might be able to make him understand the position I'd been in when I'd made the worst decision of my life—praying harder that he wouldn't hate me—as I slowly approached.

I was carrying the book with the dragon drawn in stencil on the spine.

The one that I'd found in my mother's things. The one that had always felt like it meant something. Held a power beyond the pages of a book. Magic in the words. Life in the illustrations.

Carefully, I sank down on my knees in front of him. "I want to give you something."

He angled his head, eyes scanning the crudely, gorgeously drawn cover. "Whhhat is it?"

Could barely swallow around the massive lump in my throat. "It's a special book. It's a special book that my mom made for me, and I found it at a time in my life when I felt like I couldn't go on. When I felt like it was hopeless and everything in my world *hurt* too bad. When I didn't want to go on any longer. When I wanted to give up."

His brow pinched, and I edged up on my knees a bit and set

the book on his lap. "Inside, it's a story about a boy who felt the same way. Like he didn't have the strength to become who he was always destined to be. But he found a friend in what he thought was supposed to be his enemy, and through that, he learned who he was. He found power in that. Even though it was hard and seemed impossible."

I reached up and brushed my fingers through his hair, cupped the side of his face. "This boy reminds me of you, Benjamin. He's as strong as stone and as fierce as a lion, yet, sometimes he gets scared. He doesn't yet understand that he is meant for *great* things."

My tone dropped close to desperation on the last.

Overcome. Past and present and the future toiling in the middle of me. Spinning through the space.

Regret and faith.

Is that what my mother had seen in me? What she'd hoped for? Her little boy who'd run around claiming he was a dragon. Powerful when he had no will? I fought the crushing thought that she would be ashamed with the direction I'd gone then. Devastated that she would never know who I was trying to become.

Loss curled through me in a way I hadn't allowed it for so long. Memories of her had been shoved aside. Buried. Too much for me to bear or face or acknowledge.

Now they flooded.

Wave after wave of grief and sorrow.

"You tttthink I'm meant for ggggreat things?" Benjamin's weary voice hitched in hope. Expanded with courage.

Affection tightened my chest, so overwhelming that I was finding it hard to find air. Knowing what I was coming up on. What I had to give him.

The coward in me wanted to deny what I'd done. And the rest of me? The part that would do anything for Izzy and her boys? He pressed on.

"I think you're meant for very great things. I think you were sent to show this world what it's like to really hope."

Hope.

It struck like a monsoon. A bluster of power and violence.

Terrifying and beautiful.

"Ccccan I read it?" he asked in his sweet voice.

That lump throbbed. "How about you keep it?"

He blinked at me. "But yyyyour mom ggggave it to you."

I ran my thumb over his cheek, a fucking rock in my spirit when I thought about confessing it.

But it was time.

Long since passed time.

I prodded him to look up at me when I murmured, "And now, I'm giving it to my son."

Time stopped. The past and the future colliding.

He blinked more, those eyes moving over me like he was looking at me for the first time. Or maybe he was realizing why we'd shared that connection. Why it never had felt like we were standing in front of a stranger. Spirits recognizing the other.

Still, he asked, "Whhhhat dddo yyyou mean?" His words lurched more than normal, his tongue getting tied, agitated and confused and somehow laced with a thread that said he'd known it all along.

"I'm your father, Benjamin. Your dad. Your mom and I—"

Sadness moved through his face. "I know where bbbbabies come frrrom. I'm not stttupid. Peoppple might think I am, but I'm smmmart."

"I know you're smart, Benjamin. So smart."

He studied me, though for the first time it was done with distrust. "I look just liiikkke you." He shoved his fists into his eyes like he was angry for not recognizing it immediately. "Youuu . . . youuu left us."

I watched as the rest of the reality of it came speeding in. The confirmation more than he could handle. Tears leaked out from behind his fists.

Agony gripped my conscience. Devastating. Sickening.

What was I supposed to do?

I wavered for a second, trying to remain calm, reminding myself that he needed space.

Time.

Could only take that for about two seconds, needing to reach him, to make him understand.

Carefully, I took him by the wrists, my hold light when I pried his fists from his eyes.

Big blue eyes blinked back at me. Swept in sorrow.

"Big Ben."

His chin quivered. "Was it bbbecause of me? Bbbbecause I'm brrroken? Likkkke Dillon's dad ddddid?"

I was pelted with a sucker-punch of shame.

"No. God no."

Fiercely, he shook his head. "It's my fffault my mmmom is always alone."

Misery wound.

A blackout.

I could barely remain upright as I knelt in front of him.

On my knees. Begging for forgiveness.

I reached out and gripped him by the face, making sure he was looking at me when I said it. "No, Benjamin. No. You are perfect. You are the most perfect thing I've ever done. That and loving your mom."

Awareness spun between us. A strike of energy. Different than what I shared with Izzy yet somehow the same.

Connected intrinsically.

Moisture clouded my eyes and clogged the words that started rolling off my tongue. "I loved your mom more than anything, Benjamin. More than *anything*. But I wasn't a good guy then. I was still hopeless. I thought she was better off without me."

Protecting her in the only way that I could. I'd known dragging her into my mess was dangerous. I'd had to cut her free.

"Butttt she neeeeeded you," he whispered through his pain.

More pain that he didn't deserve.

"I know. I know that now. I just didn't understand it yet."

"That means you ddddidn't love us enough."

"I didn't know about you. I didn't. I didn't know about you until the first time I saw you. The *second* I saw you, I knew it. Think my heart recognized you with the way it leapt out of my chest. It's not an excuse, but I need you to know there wasn't a day in all those years that I was without your mom that I didn't think about her. That I wasn't praying she was happy and living the kind of life I'd always hoped that she would have."

My head angled, and I filled my gaze with my son, hands splayed across his precious face. "And I have to wonder if all that time I didn't sense that you were out there, too. Maybe my thoughts could never get that far from her because you *both* were pulling at my heart."

Tears blanketed his face. "Then why didn't you ffffind us?"

"I don't know the answer to that, other than I was afraid. Afraid of loving someone the way I loved your mom."

"Do you still llllove her?" His question cracked, broken in his throat.

"So much, Big Ben. I love her so much. And I love you."

God, I loved him. Loved him so much it physically hurt.

My ribs expanded. Too full. This massive feeling taking over.

"Do you understand? I love you. You are *my son*, and I am never letting you go."

A timid smile curved the corner of his mouth. "You won't llleave us?"

"Never."

He swiped at the moisture on his face. "It would hhhuurt bad if you llleft. Wwwwe need you."

I hugged him to me. Desperately. "I need you, too."

His little arms wrapped around my neck. "I llllove you, Dadddd. I thinkkk I knnnew it, too."

I pulled back. "Knew what?"

"That I belonnnged with you."

I took his hand and pressed it over my thundering heart. "You do belong with me. You are right here. Forever."

With that crooked, adorable grin, he took my hand and spread it over the thrumming of his little heart. "Forrrevvver."

twenty-eight

MACK

It was strange when you spent your entire adult life feeling like an outsider, on the fringes peering in and wishing for something better when you knew you had no chance of ever attaining it. You got content in your own weird way because you had to accept that was as good as it was going to get.

Then the roof gets blown clean off that conviction. That resolve blown to smithereens.

You're left splayed wide open. Feeling things you'd never thought you'd get the chance to feel again.

Couldn't say I was complaining.

Ian lifted his tumbler of scotch into the air where we were all gathered around a booth at the back of a trendy bar downtown where we'd met for dinner and drinks.

Couples' night.

Me and Izzy.

Jace and Faith.

Ian and Grace.

Well, we had a plus one. Courtney was flying solo, an old friend of both Faith and Izzy's who wanted to tag along.

"This one goes out to these two love birds right here," Ian said. "May Izzy never stop blushing every time our boy Mack here smiles at her, and may he never stop looking at her like he wants to eat her. That's what real relationships are made of."

My shoulder was slung around both of Izzy's so I could hold her close, and there was no missing the heat radiating off of her as she buried her face in my chest, her flustered grin pressing right at my heart.

Ian and Jace had been razzing us nonstop since we'd shown up. Okay, they were razzing me. It just meant Izzy got in the middle of it.

Welcome to the family.

I lifted my beer. "I'll drink to that."

Grace swatted at her husband, nothing but love beaming from her smile. "Of course, you would think it's all about the sex."

He leaned in and nuzzled her face. "Uh, yeah. Get to live my life in you. What could be better than that?"

She grinned and leaned in for a quick kiss.

"Ha, isn't that the only thing all men think about?" Courtney added, laughing. "Take away their boy bits, and they wouldn't know what to do with themselves."

"Faith here sure doesn't seem to be complaining." Jace winked at his wife.

"Nope, not at all," she agreed.

My chest stretched tight. Overflowing. All things right. I leaned over and stole a kiss from the side of Izzy's head, breathed her in, felt the satisfaction in my soul.

"I love you," I murmured, knowing she'd feel it rather than be able to hear it.

Izzy turned that sweet face up to me. Tonight, she wore that blonde hair up, pieces all over, the girl so fucking sexy I didn't know how we made it all the way over here without me taking a detour to my place.

But it was more than that. So fucking much more because I knew I'd never felt happier than when those hazel eyes flashed with our truth. "I love you. So much. I'm so glad I'm here. With you."

She touched my face, and I swore, I was going to get lost in it. Or maybe scoop her up and get her out of there.

Could feel the eyes on us, and when I pulled back, Ian was lifting his glass again. "Seriously, you look the happiest I've ever seen you, Mack. You two hold onto that. That feeling right there."

He pointed at us with his index finger that was curled around his glass. Like we could take a photo and forever remember exactly what experiencing this moment was like.

No problem there.

It was unforgettable.

This time, we all clinked our drinks in the middle.

The waitress came by, asking if she could get us anything else. Ian and Jace both ordered another, and Faith asked for a refill of her water.

Grace swiveled her gaze over to Faith who was tucked in close to Jace's side. Her mouth dropped open on a gasp, like she'd caught her in the middle of doing something salacious. "Why are you drinkin' water? You have been all night."

Faith's eyes went wide, and then Izzy and Courtney were gasping, too.

"No," Grace drew out the word, having a secret conversation with her sister-in-law.

Faith nodded, and Jace kissed her temple in a tender way. "We're pregnant!" Faith drawled like she was shouting surprise.

"Oh my God, this is amazin'!" Grace whispered though it was a shout over the din of the bar. "I get to be an auntie again!"

A tear slipped down Izzy's face, and I almost panicked, a second from asking her what was wrong, but she cut off the action with the way she was smiling and reaching for Faith's hand across the table. "I'm so happy for you."

"Thank you."

"Gah, I can't believe it," Courtney cheered.

Sitting back in the booth, I took a swig of my beer and sent both of them a smile. "Really happy for you both. When do we get to meet this new little thing?"

She pressed her hand to her flat stomach. "In February."

Faith had called me last week, and we'd had a long talk about her guilt for keeping Benjamin's existence from me. She asked me to forgive her. I told her it was me who was working on forgiving myself. She was the one who had done what was right.

Izzy sent me an adoring look that knocked me sideways.

Right into eternity.

"So sweet," she said. She pressed her hands to her chest. "My heart feels so full, Maxon. I couldn't be happier than right now."

Couldn't do anything but drag her the rest of the way onto my lap, poor girl completely squished between the booth table and me, but she was laughing free, the sound so right, enveloping me.

She curled her slender arms around my neck.

"Mine," I muttered to the side of her fucking delicious flesh that was making me insane, ensuring she could hear it. That she understood what I meant.

Both her and the boys.

My family.

And I was kissing her. Kissing her deep and desperate. Hands in her hair and my heart in her hands.

A bunch of ooos and awws went up around us.

And fuck, we had an audience.

Ripping myself away, I peered out from behind her as Izzy pressed her embarrassment into my shoulder, girl shaking with self-conscious laughter when she realized we were getting carried away.

"Shut it, assholes. Whole lot of you." I pointed between my closest friends. Zero irritation behind it. Couldn't have fronted it if I tried. Was too goddamn happy for any of that.

An 80s song came on the speakers that not a soul in the world could seem to resist, and Grace jumped out of her seat.

"Oh my God, this song. On your feet, girls. We're dancing."

"I'm pregnant," Faith deadpanned, completely droll.

"Pregnant, schmegnant." Grace waved her off. "We only live once, and all that livin' has to happen while we're momma's, too. Every moment, guys. Every moment. Big and small. They all count."

It sent the words of my mother's book skimming through my mind.

"We are the moments we share. We are the moments separating us that draw us together. We are the vacant space between. We are the culmination of love that has been waiting for us to grasp it in our fingers since before time. Since before we existed but were purposed for this day. Now is when you reach out and take it in the palm of your hands. Now is when you breathe it into fruition."

Now was the time.

Courtney didn't need to be asked twice. She climbed right out, wearing a sequined dress, shimmying her shoulders. "I'm cutting loose tonight. Who is with me?"

I squeezed Izzy's hip. "Go on, Little Bird. Fly. Have fun. I'll be right here waiting for you when you get back."

Grace squeaked in excitement, and Faith just laughed in resignation. "Fine, fine. I'm coming."

Couldn't peel my eyes away as the four of them hit the dancefloor to the Prince song.

Jace rocked back in the booth, all kinds of smug as he sipped at his beer.

"What?" I challenged, though there was a knowing smirk tugging at the corner of my mouth.

He lifted his mug. "You look happy, man. So goddamn happy. It looks good on you."

"Guess I'm not going to die alone, after all. Going to have to clear that up with my Mal-Pal, aren't you?" This, I tossed at Ian who was laughing behind his tumbler of scotch.

"All right, all right, I'll admit defeat. But seriously, asshole, do you really think I was that off base? You're just lucky that girl is as sweet as she is to put up with a bear like you."

I gruffed. "Lucky is right."

Jace angled closer, gesturing to Izzy with a flick of his fingers. "That all went down fast."

I leaned my forearms on the table. "Think we've been barreling down that road toward each other for a long, long time. We were bound to collide. Some things can't be stopped, no matter how hard you try."

He hesitated for a second. "How's it with her boys?"

I looked between them both. "Incredible. Incredible and terrifying," I added on.

Ian laughed. "Uh, yeah, exactly that. Hardest thing you'll ever do, and some days you're going to think you're never going to get through it, but you wouldn't trade it for all the money in the world."

"Guess at least I won't have any diaper escapades," I told him with a forced laugh, itching a little.

Wondered if it was sympathy that went traipsing through his expression. "No matter what time you come into a child's life, it matters, Mack. Doesn't lessen your importance in their lives. Hell, I'd venture to say it makes even more of an impact. Thomas, Mallory, and Sophie are every bit my kids as Collin is."

A couple days ago, Izzy and I had sat Dillon down and tried to explain to him that I was Benjamin's biological father without having to give him all the sordid details that went along with that.

Kid had fuckin' wept.

Not because he was pissed that I hadn't been there, but because he wanted me to be his "biological" dad, too.

I'd just dropped to my knees and told him it would be my honor if I got to be his dad.

Definitions didn't matter.

It was the heart's commitment that counted.

My head shook, and I contended with the regret that vibrated in my being, wondering if it would ever fade. "I believe that, one-hundred percent." I lifted my beer like I was giving them a toast. "Both of you taught me that."

For a second, I hesitated, trying to process. "I just . . . wish I could go back. Do it all different. Erase who I was."

Self-condemning laughter rocked from Jace. "Don't we all? But that's not how life is, Mack. You know that. You keep living in the past? You're gonna repeat it. Only thing you can do is wake up each morning and give thanks you have that day. Spend it wisely. Love entirely. Don't look back. You can only ever move forward."

I started to respond when my gaze got tripped up on the movement on the dancefloor.

Oh, fuck no.

A streak of possession blazed through my blood.

A full-blown fire.

Savage and fierce.

Cockroach was winding his way through the throbbing crowd, greedy eyes set on my girl. For the first time he wasn't wearing scrubs, and instead some preppy boy suit.

Where was Dillon when I needed him?

My hand curled around my beer, fisting the glass like a lifeline. An anchor, only it was what was keeping me from sinking to the pits of that ugliness.

Ian swiveled around so he could see where my attention was pinned. He cracked a wry grin, sitting back like the cocky bastard he was in the booth. "How's it feel, man? Loving someone so much that you always feel like you're right on the cusp of losing your mind?"

"Exactly like that. Like I might lose it."

Only got worse when cockboy slinked up to her like a creeper, not even taking it slow when he set a hand on her shoulder.

Way too familiar.

She whipped around. Her face lit in a stroke of white light.

Staggering beauty.

A wide, welcoming smile split her face when she realized it was him, and those plush lips moved as she responded to something that he said.

He tipped his ear her direction, and motherfuck, I was gettin' sweaty.

Hot and bothered and not in a cute way.

He angled back, mouth at the shell of her ear, and Izzy nodded along.

And that was it, all I could take. I drained my beer and slammed the empty on the table. Pushing out of the booth, I rose to stand.

Ian laughed. Smug as all hell.

Asshole.

But I didn't slow, just strode across the floor, eating up the ground, going after what I refused to ever lose again.

The crew of the band that were playing tonight were setting up. A DJ spun canned music from the speakers, amping the crowd into a frenzied anticipation.

The throng pulsed on the packed dancefloor, shouting their excitement as a guitar screamed with a strum, the clatter on the stage only adding to the intensity.

Alive and vibrating with energy.

I shouldered through the mob.

Every footstep quivered with need.

Shivered with possession.

From the distance, I watched as Izzy introduced him to all the girls, handshakes going up all around. Dr. Dickbag smiled his sleazy, white smile, pretty boy nothing but manners.

Strange how it left me feeling not so *polite*.

I prowled up behind her and wound an arm around her waist. Pulled her flush to my front.

She didn't even tense when she leaned back into my hold, like she already felt me coming, the girl perfection in my arms. She rocked her head back on my chest, and those hazel eyes were glimmering with mischief in the light, sexy mouth hitching up at the side.

I grunted, pressed my mouth to the side of her face. "Izzy Baby. You trying to drive me out of my mind?"

A giggle rippled out of her, one I felt rather than heard. "Whatever are you talkin' about?"

It was a taunt. A tease of that mouth.

I shifted my attention to Izzy's boss, and I shoved out my hand.

All *friendly* like.

"Don't think we've officially met. Mack Chambers. Izzy's

boyfriend."

Could feel the knowing stares of Faith and Grace, two of them knowing exactly what had sent me sniffing around over here.

Busted.

Fine.

I didn't even think to care.

Courtney continued to dance, oblivious the way that she always seemed to be.

Apparently, this asshole didn't get the clue. He looked between my hand and Izzy's face, wary, before he shook my hand. "Trevor Nelson. Good to meet you."

"You, too. Izzy tells me she loves the new job."

Did my best to sound gracious.

Pretty sure it came out sounding like I was a hot second from tearing him limb from limb.

He looked at her. "We love having her there. She's saved our asses in more ways than I can count."

"She is pretty amazing." Okay, maybe that time I came off as halfway sane and not some controlling prick, which was the last thing I wanted to be.

But fuck.

This was Izzy we were talking about.

Little Bird.

A flood of self-consciousness rippled across that pale flesh, heat rising. Lust tightened my guts because I would never, ever get enough.

"And I love workin' there. I'll forever be grateful for the opportunity."

He glanced away before he looked back at her with a sly smile. "Think I'll be forever grateful, too."

Anger surged, and I was assaulted with another rush of jealousy. Teeth grinding at this prick who was outright flirting with my girl. I tucked her closer, and just then the song playing skipped, and the DJ changed beats, his voice coming on the air.

"Who is ready for Carolina George?"

A bunch of shouts went up around us, a wave of excitement sending a swell of energy moving through the crowd.

Everyone turned that way—Faith and Grace, Courtney, Cockroach, too.

Couldn't forget about him.

All except for Izzy and me.

Slowly, she shifted around to face me. A coy grin danced on that delicious mouth.

She pressed her hand to the jackhammer wreaking havoc on my chest and lifted up onto her toes, those lips so close to mine. Driving me wild. "Are you jealous, Maxon Chambers?"

I grunted again, my dick all too eager, hips surging forward to meet with hers. "Yes," I growled along her jaw.

No use in denying it.

An uproar lit around us, and I didn't have to look away from my beacon to know the band had taken the stage.

"Hey, hey, Charleston. I'm Emily, and I'm pretty sure all you ladies know Richard here on guitar, Rys on bass, and Leif on drums, and we are Carolina George!" The lead singer of the band shouted into the mic.

It almost caused a riot.

Izzy and I were lost in it. I let my arm slip around her waist, and I wedged my knee between her thighs. She groaned a tiny groan. My dick jumped. "You were doing it on purpose, weren't you," I rumbled over the bedlam that had struck up around us.

"Maybe you just needed a little reminder of what you'd been missin'."

I spread my palm out over her hip. "None required. Living without you was enough. I won't stand by and let some guy who just met you try to make his move."

She tickled her fingers over my lips. "Awful possessive."

I nipped at her fingertips. "Is that what you want? Me to let you go? I'll fight for you, Izzy Lane, but if you really wanted to walk? If you really didn't feel this burning between us? Then I would let you go. Only because I want you happy. It's all I've ever wanted."

"How am I supposed to be happy without you?" It was a breath.

A wisp.

A plea.

She tipped her chin up at me.

Our mouths collided.

Tongues and teeth and hands as we spun in the middle of the crowd.

Blissfully unaware of anything but us.

I tangled my hand in her hair, tongue taking all I could get.

Could feel the racing of our hearts, speeding faster, this feeling coming over us that demanded more.

So fucking much more.

I spun her through the crowd, edging her back and away. Needed to get her alone and fast.

Desire screamed. Wrapping us in these chains I never wanted to be freed from.

We stumbled out of the crowd and into the darkness of the hall. I pinned her against it. She gasped, arched, fingers digging into my shoulders. "Maxon."

"Little Bird. You make me crazy. You know this, right? I lose all control, all rationale when it comes to you. Could kick that guy's ass simply for looking at you. That's so fucked up."

She giggled. I swallowed it down, demanding more.

"Take me to your place. I need to feel you, my big, bad dragon."

"Are you mocking me?" Could feel my grin beneath the press of her lips.

"Never," she whispered, but she was grinning, too.

Happiness rushed through me, thicker than the jealousy.

I grabbed her by the hand and dragged her down the hall. We burst out the backdoor and into the drone of the night.

In a second flat, I had her against the wall again. The beat of the band vibrated through.

Thundered and pulsed.

With one hand, I thumbed into my Uber app while the other dug into her hip, my mouth consuming the sweetness of hers.

"Ride's here," I grunted through the kiss, not bothering to set her down as I carried her around the back and onto the sidewalk out front. Holding her with one arm, I opened the door.

The driver glanced back at us.

"Mack Chambers?" he asked for verification.

"That's us," I said, slipping into the back and dragging Izzy onto my lap.

The girl took it upon herself to straddle me.

I groaned as the car jerked into motion. "Shit, baby, you are in so much trouble for teasing me. You knew exactly what you were doing, didn't you?" It was all a rumble between our frantic kisses, the girl starting to writhe, the heat from her pussy radiating against my dick.

"If you would paid attention for one second, you would have seen I was introducin' him to Courtney. I told him to come to meet her. Faith suggested it. And you should have seen the electricity that struck up between them the second they saw each other. They're gonna be good together, I can just feel it. Of course, you might have missed the sparks with the fire you were puffin' from your nose."

Oh, shit.

God, she left me out of control.

"I'm sorry," I rumbled, really not sorry at all because I'd fight for this girl until my dying breath.

She was grinning more, her hands on my cheeks as she controlled the kiss.

"You think I wouldn't feel the same if someone were going after you? You are my heart. The one I ache for. The one I need. The moon in my sky." She murmured the last.

Nothing but seduction.

Our bodies ground, frantic, the intensity between us rising.

Unstoppable.

"No sex in the backseat of my car." This from the driver, his voice spitting his irritation.

I squeezed both of Izzy's ass cheeks, grinding her against me. "Clothes are on, man."

At least for five more seconds.

He pulled up in front of my house, and I already had the door open, scooting out with Izzy still in my arms.

Door slamming shut, I carried her up the walk and onto the

porch, fumbling to get the key into the lock at the front door. It banged open to the darkness, and I kicked it shut with my shoe, carried her down the hall and into my room.

She was giggling when I tossed her onto my bed, that sweet body bouncing, hair falling out all around her, tender smile on her face.

I stood over her. Overcome. Seemed impossible that this could now be my life.

"Izzy Baby," I grated.

She climbed onto her knees and came to the edge of the bed, and she spread her hands under my shirt.

Flames.

She began to pull it up, that sweet gaze locked on me as she did, her mouth parting with need as she let her eyes rake over me.

Loved that, too. That she shook when she looked at me. A prisoner to this energy.

She tugged the fabric over my head. "You are so gorgeous, Maxon Chambers. Do you have any idea what you've done to me? I'm so over settlin'. So over bein' alone."

I stroked my thumb over the angle of her cheek. "You're not alone. Not anymore. Not ever again."

I slipped just my fingertips along the line of her delicate throat, riding it down to brush the swell of her breasts exposed by her slinky green shirt.

"So fuckin' pretty."

She shivered, then I was gathering the silky fabric, dragging it up. She was bare underneath, perky tits pebbling up, rosy flesh begging for a bite.

I dipped in to lick my tongue over one.

She yelped and wound those fingers in my hair. "Maxon."

"Yeah, baby?" I murmured, lips caressing over the flesh.

"I need you."

"I've needed you my whole life," I told her, though my voice was turning somber.

Filled with awe. With respect. With this girl who had always believed in me even when I didn't come close to deserving it.

She prodded me to look up at her, a tender hand set on my

face. "Who knows what love is if he hasn't experienced grief?"

Familiarity pricked at my senses, and I frowned as I was rushed with a memory, the meaning of it just out of reach, and then she was pleading, "Take me, Maxon. Take me the way you've been dying to." She leaned in and whispered at my ear. "There's no one around to hear except for me. Let go, my dragon."

I kissed her hard, our tongues claiming the other. Our breaths short and choppy.

Our hearts thundered, a rage that only increased with each lash of our tongues, nothing but a frenetic batter at our ribs.

Those delicate hands fluttered down my stomach. Every muscle twitched in anticipation, tightened in greed.

She flicked the button of my fly, and she shoved my jeans down over my hips, freeing my dick that was already painfully hard, pointing for the sky, dying to get inside of this girl.

I kicked them the rest of the way off, and then I was pushing her onto her back.

She heaved a needy breath.

Without slowing, I unfastened the clasp on her black pants and dragged down the zipper.

The sound of it echoed through the dense air.

Her belly trembled, and I adored the silvered marks on her stomach with my tongue as I dragged her pants and underwear free.

It left her completely bare, writhing on the bed.

She spread her knees, eagerly.

Her pussy was pink and pretty and throbbing for me.

She ran her hands up her quivering legs, and fuck, I just about passed out at the sight in front of me.

"Beautiful," I groaned. "You are stunning, Little Bird."

I ran my fingers through her perfect slit before I leaned down so I could get a good taste of it with my tongue.

Nothing but throbbing, hot woman, wild jasmine, and the sun.

A desperate breath jerked from her lungs, and she curled her hands in my hair. "Maxon."

A needy growl raked up my throat. "Want to stay right here forever."

I nipped at her folds, dragging my teeth over the flesh, licking into her cunt. Teasing her into a needy mess in the middle of my bed.

She squirmed, begging for me to get closer, all these sweet little pleas coming from that mouth. "Please, Maxon."

Pulling back, I gazed up at her face, at the girl who'd been my everything. My greatest love. My greatest sacrifice.

Now, I was giving her everything.

"I've got you, baby. I've got you."

I climbed onto the bed and hovered over her, staring down at her sweet face.

At my life.

At my reason.

I traced my fingertips down the sharp angle of her cheek. "I love you, so much, Izzy Baby. I hope you know that."

She gazed back. "Every piece of me belongs to you."

I couldn't stand it any longer, and I pushed into the cove of her tight, sweet body.

Bliss.

Being in this girl was sheer, straight bliss.

I groaned, and her head rocked back. It forced her tits into my chest, every inch of us plastered against the other.

And still, I could never get close enough.

Our connection glowed between us.

White hot light.

I could see every muscle in her body trembling, mine quivering with its match.

"You are mine, Little Bird."

She exhaled a sound, like she was preparing herself for me, like she knew she was going to need it.

That I needed this moment. To be a little reckless. To show her exactly what she did to me.

I started to pound into her, my cock slick with her as I pulled back and drove back in.

Mewls of pleasure slipped from her mouth with each stroke of my dick.

The pace was punishing, hard and demanding. She bucked up

to me.

Hard.

Her body open.

Desperate in its own demand.

"Oh God, Maxon," she was whimpering, beginning to shake more.

Heat blistered between us, our skin slick, our names pouring like praise from our tongues.

I gripped her by her bottom, my hands taking fistfuls of her sweet flesh, wanting more.

"Endless," I whispered.

She went off.

Lightning.

Thunder.

The most brilliant kind of storm.

Cries bled from her mouth and her back arched, so goddam sexy, girl riding her orgasm.

My balls tightened and pleasure stalked my spine. My thrusts became erratic, desperate, my face buried in her neck.

Pleasure burst in every cell of my body.

In my heart.

In my spirit.

The girl possessing every inch of me. I poured into her, holding her tight, groaning through the kind of ecstasy that only Izzy had ever been able to bring to me.

Pure and right.

Everything. Everything.

"I love you," I whispered into her hair.

She clutched me tighter. "Endless," she returned.

I set my elbow on the bed next to her head so I could stroke my fingers across her face, not even shocked when the question rolled out. Like it was always meant to be. Or maybe I just should have uttered them a long damn time ago.

"Marry me."

A soft sigh left her, and the green rim on those hazel eyes glowed. "Maxon," she murmured.

"I'll do it right later. A ring and all the words. But right now, tonight, I need to know you're forever going to be mine."

A smile trembled all over her mouth, emotion filling my room to overflowing.

I'd happily die getting crushed by that feeling.

"Yes. A million times over, I would say yes. Nothing could ever make me happier than bein' your wife. Don't you know that's what I always wanted?"

A memory weaved between us.

The two of us had been out in our meadow, the girl wearing some ridiculous white dress she'd taken out of her mama's closet that was fifteen sizes too big, a bough of wild jasmine flowers in her hands.

Our fake wedding out in the meadow.

Should have known then it was real.

She chewed at her lip, fighting the emotion. "You rememberin' that day?"

I nodded. "Yeah."

"I meant it then, and I mean it now."

I gathered her hand and pressed it to my mouth. "I'm going to take care of you, Izzy. Be the best husband I can be. The best dad I can be."

Tears leaked out of the corners of her eyes, and I kissed them away, and she wrapped her arms around me tight.

We sat there in the glow of it for the longest time.

Finally, she pulled back. "I need to get going."

Reluctantly, I nodded, edged off of her, taking her sweet body with me as I stood. She yelped as I carried her into the bathroom, the girl giggling, the vibration of it moving through my being.

I tucked it down.

Held it tight.

I took out a hand towel and cleaned her up a whole lot like the way as she'd done for me that first night.

Carefully.

Adoringly.

Except tonight, all the pain and questions had been erased.

Just the future stretched out in front of us.

We dressed, and hand-in-hand, we went out the front door, my attention scanning the area, making sure everything was in the clear.

"I hate that you worry," she whispered, sensing my angst, and I pinned her against the door of her car, kissed her slow, and edged back to brush the hair back from her face. "It's my job to worry about you."

Tenderness filled her expression, and then reluctantly, she opened her car door. I helped her inside, and I dipped in to steal one more kiss.

"I'll see you soon."

"That is if you don't come sneakin' through my window in the middle of the night." It was nothing but affection.

I laughed.

She knew me well.

I would definitely be coming through that window.

"Are you telling me you have a problem with that?" A smirk lifted at the corner of my mouth.

"Never," she said.

I nudged her chin with my knuckle. "Drive safe."

With a nod, she put her car in reverse, and I stepped back and shut her door.

I watched as she backed out. Meeting her gaze through the windshield, I held both of my hands over my heart.

Her head tipped to the side, and she blew me a kiss.

Then I chuckled as I went directly to hop into my rental truck so I could follow her home.

Did she actually think I was going to let her drive home alone at night with all the shit that had been going down?

Not on my watch.

The girl was my duty.

And my family was my life.

twenty-nine

IZZY

Night pressed down from above, hugging the car like a warm, summer embrace, and a peaceful silence hummed in the air.

Trees rose up on every side, and I wound through the backroad that led to my parents' house, the spray of my headlights lighting the road. An unendin' grin had taken up residence on my face, refusing to let go.

Wings fluttered soft and slow in my belly, flappin' and flickin' to touch my heart that was overflowing with love when I glanced in the rear-view mirror.

Maxon.

Affection tightened my ribs. He loved me. I knew it. Knew it to my soul.

He was gonna marry me.

Love raced. So full. So big.

It was only amplified with the way I could feel his presence washing up from behind.

His protection covering.

His love surrounding.

I wanted to swim in it. Get lost in it. Dream in it.

I guessed that's really what this felt like.

A dream.

Headlights glowed from a way back, Maxon giving me my space, and I was smiling slow as I took the sharp curve that followed the small river that ran this side of Broadshire Rim.

I glanced in the rearview mirror again, squinting when I saw the flash of bright lights that swung around Maxon.

A car sped around him, passing him like a maniac.

I tightened my hold on the steering wheel, hatin' it that people drove like fools on these country roads. They could hurt someone.

At least Maxon was there to get the license plate. Maybe call for backup and pull him over.

A skitter of worry slicked across my skin when I saw the car swerve fast. That worry jumped into a choked horror when I realized they cut right in front of Maxon.

"Oh my God."

Maxon's headlights shifted in a severe lurch to the right.

"Oh God, Maxon."

A gasp ripped out with my cry, and I was gettin' struck with a bolt of terror. My whole body taken hostage to this nightmare.

I guessed that's what they were made up of—the people you loved in danger and nothing in the world you could do to stop it.

My heart stalled out when Maxon's headlights fully disappeared, nothing but the blinding high-beams closing in faster than I could process.

I jerked the steering wheel to the right to try to get out of the way and put pressure on the brakes, trying to see through the tears that were instantly clouding my sight.

Panic squeezed from my lungs when my wheels skidded on the pavement. I almost righted it when the car came at me, forcing me to the left so it could pass me on the right.

A scream ripped up my throat when it cut in front of me and slammed on its brakes.

Cutting me off.

No place for me to go.

A purposed attack.

I tried to stop it.

The way my tires skidded and the backend fishtailed to one side, and I was jerking the steering wheel the other direction, trying to correct it as the car blazed right on by.

But they'd already enacted their damage.

The intention clear and unavoidable.

My car careened off the left side of the road. Jumping and bouncing through the dirt at high speed.

A big tree came into sharp, distinct view.

I rammed on the brakes a half a second before I slammed into the massive trunk.

Glass shattered and metal twisted, and I was screamin'.

Screamin' and screamin'.

Pain splintered across my chest and my shoulder, across my face, and I felt wetness dripping down the side of my head.

Silence hovered in the air, or maybe it was the buzzing clouding out all sound that hissed in my ear, the airbag suffocating where it was pressed against my body.

Adrenaline pumped through my veins, my heart beating so hard I could feel it in my head.

Fear and horror slashed.

Hands shaking, I managed to free my seatbelt, and I felt around the door, touch fumbling, finding the latch.

Maxon.

Oh, God, my Maxon. I wouldn't lose him again.

No.

Never.

That panic blazed as I struggled to get free, and I yelped out in relief when the door opened to creaking metal.

I stumbled out into the night.

Disoriented.

Only one person on my mind.

My heart. My heart.

Then he was shouting. "Izzy. Oh God, Izzy."

A shadow of the man fumbled into the overgrown brush, running beneath the faint wisps of the moon.

Towering so big.

So powerful.

My dragon.

I swayed to the side, struck by a rush of dizziness, overwhelming relief and searing pain.

Strong arms wrapped around me.

"Izzy," he shouted.

And everything went black.

thirty

MACK

I knew it. I fucking knew this was going to happen.

A doctor hovered over her, talking low and with a calming, practiced voice as she asked Izzy questions.

Where she was experiencing pain and how severe it was, if she were lightheaded, or if she felt weak.

While I paced the small space like a caged animal.

Rabid.

Ready to attack.

Couldn't believe I let that go down right in front of my eyes. I'd been right there to protect her, and still, I'd failed. Failed fucking miserably.

Rage and disgust clamored through my body, and I struggled

to breathe through it. Struggled to see through the haze of red that crowded at the corners of my eyes and threatened to take over all sight.

All reason.

Violence slinked right in to take its place.

"I feel very positive about your exam, but I think we'll send you for a CT scan to make sure you don't have any intracranial swelling since you did have loss of consciousness at the scene. I'm also going to order an x-ray of your shoulder to make sure there is no break, just to be safe."

Safe.

What bullshit. No one was safe. Not when they got involved with me.

My hands curled into fists and sweat beaded on my nape as a cold, clammy dread crawled beneath the surface of my skin.

What the fuck was I going to do?

"Thank you, Dr. Chen." Izzy's voice was subdued. Quiet and tremoring with the fear I could tell she was trying to hide.

Killed me a little more each time that she released it.

"You're welcome. Someone will be in to take you down when they're ready for you."

The woman eyed me with outright speculation when she turned and swept passed. Got the feeling she was wondering if maybe she should call security.

Sensed a clear and imminent threat.

She wouldn't be wrong.

The second the curtain fell behind her, I flew over to Izzy where she sat up on the edge of the bed, and I knelt down in front of her.

She wore one of those ridiculous hospital gowns that this girl still managed to make look good. Long locks of blonde and brown twisted up in a haphazard tie on the top of her head, pieces sticking out everywhere.

But it was the cut above her eye that was close to being in the same place as the one I'd sustained that gutted me.

That and the way terror swam in the depths of her hazel eyes. The way it was muted with her love. This girl too good. Too right.

I pressed my face into her lap. "Izzy Baby, I'm so fucking sorry," I muttered through the riot of torment laying seize to my insides.

Fire and fury.

"I tried to stop it. I did."

She threaded her fingers through my hair. Leave it to Izzy to be the one to comfort me. "You were in the same position, Maxon. The very same thing happened to you. Us. And we're both fine. That's what I'm grateful for."

I looked up at her, and my lips pursed into a grim line. "You could have been killed."

She touched my face. "But I wasn't."

I grabbed the hand she had on my cheek, pressed her palm to my mouth, and breathed the beauty of her in. Tried to use the connection to her to calm myself.

I only shook with another rush of rage.

"I won't stop until I hunt down whoever is doing this and put an end to them. Until they are no longer a threat to you or the boys."

"I trust you."

Anguish seethed in my spirit, and I jolted when the curtain moved. I was riding a razor-sharp edge, teetering between the clear-cut instinct to protect her and completely coming unhinged.

My shoulders sagged when I realized it was a male orderly coming in with a wheelchair. "Your chariot, madam."

He was all easy grins as he kicked it into a wheelie.

Izzy released a soft giggle. Only she could find any sort of serenity in the middle of this disaster. "Why, thank you."

He helped to get her adjusted, and I pushed to standing, itching, urges slamming me to fly out of there and do something.

End this.

Only problem was I didn't know what direction to go.

He started to wheel her out, and I followed close behind. Our footsteps echoed as we moved down the narrow, hollow hall, questions spinning in the distance that separated us.

Nausea swirled when I sensed that distance becoming greater. A crack riding up the middle.

Not sure how I would repair this.

Fuck.

I had to stop this. I'd promised I would never let anything happen to her. Another lie that I'd meant well by. Again, one I couldn't control.

The orderly swiveled around just as they were approaching the double doors that read *Radiology*. "You'll have to wait here."

Hesitation had my muscles twitching, hating the idea of being separated from her for a second, but I finally conceded, realizing it was an argument I wasn't going to win. I moved around to the front of the wheelchair and dipped down to place a soft kiss to Izzy's lips, lingering as I whispered, "I love you. So much."

"Always," she murmured back.

Straightening, I stuffed my hands in my pockets. "I'll be right here waiting."

"I know."

He pushed a button on the wall. The doors swung open, and he wheeled her in.

My heart panged with the separation. Anxiety firing, shooting bullets of aggression screaming through my veins.

Blowing out a heavy sigh, I leaned on the wall, rocked my head back and stared at the design pitted in the ceiling. Time slipped by in a blur as I tried to make sense of all this bullshit. Puzzle the pieces together.

I was a detective.

This was my job.

I nearly crawled out of my skin when I sensed the disorder at the head of the hall, and I jerked my attention that way to the sickening sight of Clarissa coming toward me. Black hair tossed over one shoulder, skin-tight white jeans, five-inch heels that she wore like a weapon.

And I knew exactly what this was. A battle. Another clash in this unending war. One I was going to end.

She had the fucking nerve to smile at me when she met my eye.

"Oh my God, I heard what happened to you. Tell me you are okay. I was so worried about you." I didn't know if it was faked concern or if she was completely delusional.

When she got close enough, I snatched her by the wrist. "What the fuck are you doing here?" I demanded, getting up close to her face and keeping my voice low.

Not wanting to cause a scene. Probably was in vain. Clearly, one was about to be had.

Staring down at her, there was no missing the vileness.

The evil and the twisted greed.

"What did you do?" I grated, teeth grinding so hard I could feel them close to splintering, jaw cracking with restraint.

Her dark eyes flashed. "What did I do? I didn't do anything, Mack. Question is, what did you do?" she challenged.

"If you're responsible for what happened tonight, I will end you."

She laughed a salacious sound. "So angry, aren't we?" She dragged her fingertip down the side of my face.

Revulsion sliced through my body.

"Tell me if you had anything to do with this."

She pursed her lips. "I have no idea what you're talking about. Shouldn't it be me who is angry? You are the one who is running around on me." She said it with all the ownership she possessed and like it didn't matter at the same damn time.

It wasn't like the two of us hadn't been with other people.

The only thing it came down to at the end of the day was that she controlled me. All of me. A noose around my neck. The way it'd always been.

I tightened my hold around her wrist. "I told you it was over. I warned you to stay out of this with Izzy and me."

"And you should know better than that. There's a reason you and I are together. We fit. Belong. Didn't you agree all those years ago?" It was pure seduction when she said it, like me going back to her again and again was because I wanted her and not out of obligation.

Out of this fucked up world we'd created.

She pushed up on her toes, venom in her tone. "I saved her, and I saved you. Remember? Now, she needs to go. Send her away, Mack, before it's too late. She doesn't belong here with you."

"She's not going anywhere. I'm finished with your games. I

don't give two fucks about that agreement. I was seventeen, and it was the worst decision I ever made. I'm finished covering for you. Finished turning a blind eye. It's over, Clarissa."

Disbelief lined her face. "You are such a liar, Detective Chambers." She used my title like her own threat. "You have been covering your ass for all these years. You begged me, remember?"

My hold tightened. "I was doing it for her."

Her face split in a malicious grin. "Really?"

"Really," I spat.

"And what do you think changed? I would think you'd be all the more concerned about her since she has those two sweet little boys." She cooed it the way she liked to do.

Old rage billowed from that dark, dark place. Fear and disgust and regret.

"And that sad, pathetic one with the disability." She tsked. "Poor thing. Someone should have put him out of his misery." Her expression was filled with forged innocence as she stared up at me, a dare on her face.

Urges slammed me. The need to wrap my hands around her throat and squeeze. Took everything I had to refrain from doing it. "That is my son." I angled closer, darts of hatred flying low from my tongue. "They are my family. And I will do whatever it takes to protect them."

She hiked up on her toes and ran her mouth up my jaw until she was whispering the threat at my ear. "I know you will. Nothing has changed, Mack. You owe me."

It was just then that I felt it. The battered crash of energy against the floor. Deafening against the cold, stark-white laminate.

A shocked, horrified gasp ricocheted in the stagnant, sticky air.

I jerked to look over my shoulder. Izzy had been wheeled out, and the girl's chin trembled as she struggled to process the sight in front of her.

Shame shook through my body. A landslide. A landmine.

"Isabel. It's so nice to see you again." Clarissa smirked, her cheek still pressed to mine, her claws firmly planted in my soul.

thirty-one

IZZY

"Why didn't you tell me?" I stood behind Maxon where he stared at a blank wall in my bedroom.

Bare morning light poured in through the window. I'd been released from the ER, and we'd just gotten back to a sleeping house.

During that whole time, I hadn't stopped shaking.

Shakin' and shakin'.

Tremors rose from a well in the middle of me and overflowed through every cell of my body. I still wasn't sure if it was from the crash or from finding Maxon out in that hall with Clarissa.

The sight of the two of them from all those years ago had been engrained in my mind like a blemish.

Carved on my spirit like a scar.

Seeing them there like that had ripped it wide open.

Maxon roughed an agitated hand over the hair at the back of is head, flinching with my question.

He'd hauled her out of that hall so fast when he'd seen me standing behind them that I'd almost gotten whiplash. I was sure my achin' head had throbbed more with the memories of the betrayal he'd meted when he'd broken my heart thirteen years before than with the actual injuries I'd sustained.

Of course, he hadn't really cheated when I'd gone running all that time ago, unable to stay in this town any longer if it meant I'd have to see the two of them together.

He hadn't really betrayed me in the common sense of the word.

He'd already told me he didn't want me. That it was over. That we couldn't *be*.

The problem was, my heart had known it had been a blatant lie.

He'd returned to my ER room with so much aggression and anger boiling in his body that I hadn't been able to see straight. In it, he'd been silent. Raging without sound. Hovering over me like I might up and go missin'.

His terror palpable.

His fear real.

It made all of this so much harder—my need to run to him and ask him to wrap me up and hold me while I held him—at odds with this feeling that made me want to do a little raging of my own.

"Why didn't you tell me?" I demanded again. "Have you . . ." I swallowed hard, barely able to get the words to form on my tongue. "Have you been with her this whole time? Are you still—"

God, I couldn't even say it. Revulsion slipped across my skin like a sickness. A disease.

Maxon whirled around, disgust and horror gripping his expression. "God, no. Fuck, I would never do that to you, Izzy."

My face pinched. "But you did. You did it before, and it destroyed me. Destroyed me in a way I'm not sure you fully understand." I pressed my hands to my chest as if it could stop my heart from bleeding this pain.

Guilt and remorse filled his eyes, and he took a single step my direction.

His energy moved like a shockwave through my room. "I hate myself for hurting you. Hate myself. But I couldn't keep you, Izzy. It wasn't right. And I'm terrified that I'm doing it all over again. Dragging you into a world where you don't belong. You have always been too good for me."

My head shook with the refusal. "No, Maxon. That's a lie you've always told yourself. One you've got to get over. One I'm not going to let you use to turn around and break me all over again."

I blinked at him, tryin' to make sense of this. "What . . ." My tongue darted out to wet my dry lips. "Tell me what she was doin' there."

His thick throat bobbed as he swallowed, and a blister of guilt moved across his skin. "I thought she was what I deserved, Izzy. A reminder of why I could never be with you. A reminder of why I had to let you go. And fuck . . ."

His upper body angled for me, as if he wanted to reach me, but his feet remained planted on the floor. He pressed his fingertips over his heart. "I wish I could take it back. Every horrible choice I made. But I can't, Izzy. I can't take back anything. But you have to know, the second I touched you, I never touched her again. I wouldn't." Remorse trembled through him. "I couldn't."

"Why, Maxon? Why did you choose her?" My biggest insecurities came flooding out. The feeling of not bein' enough breaking free.

Agony carved every inch of that gorgeous face. My heart clattered against my ribs.

"I couldn't stay with you then, Izzy. Couldn't drag you into the mess I was in. I thought . . . I thought I would end up in prison, too. And even if I didn't, I wasn't a good guy. I never would have asked you to live that life. I shouldn't have brought you back into this disaster now. Seems my heart doesn't know how to resist you. How to stop loving you."

His head slowly shook, and I felt the confession before he

spoke it. "And yes, I was with her for those years you were away. Not because I wanted her, Izzy, but because she was what I thought I deserved. She was a representation of my shame. She was a penalty for not getting to spend my life with you."

Tears blurred my eyes. "You saved us. *Saved us.* How could you ever think you weren't enough? You were *everything.*"

The plea broke on the sob that worked free of my throat.

He erased the space that separated us. A storm surge. A tsunami. The impact of him had always been devastating and whole.

He reached out and gripped me by the face with those big hands.

"I was responsible for it in the first place. I was the reason you needed saving."

"No, Maxon, you weren't. Just because he was your father doesn't make you responsible for his actions. It was on him. It was always on him, and I will hate him until my dying breath for stealing you away from me."

My head shook as it all began to make sense. To come together.

"You loved me the whole time, didn't you?"

Guttural pain pinched his face. "Of course, I loved you."

Blue eyes churned with misery. A toiling sea of regret and love. "From the first time I met you, I promised I would be there to protect you. And that's what I had to do in order to do it."

Hurt squeezed my ribs. "That's not what I ever asked of you."

A frown creased the corners of his eyes. "I would have done anything for you, Little Bird. You knew that."

"Anything but stay with me," I whispered, coming to the full truth of the matter.

I guessed that made me angry, too.

"And what . . . are you just gonna walk away from me now because you think you're not good enough? Go back to her? Because that woman thinks you belong to her in some sick way?" I challenged, giving this man my whole heart.

"Convince yourself that your life is too dangerous? When are you gonna stop punishin' yourself? When are you gonna see you are worth it, too?"

Guilt streaked across his face, flickers of that old disbelief. The lie that he wasn't good enough.

He squeezed my face tighter. "I'm trying to be, Izzy. Fuck, I'm trying. But I don't know how I'm going to fix this. End it. But I can't allow for you or the boys to be in danger. I can't, Izzy. *I can't risk you.*"

I wrapped my hand around one of his wrists, tears soaking my face. "I won't pretend like what you do isn't dangerous. That this threat isn't real. I was terrified last night. So scared. But do you know what I was scared most about?"

A blanket of tears ran sticky on my cheeks, my sight blurred by this crater I could feel splintering through the middle of us.

"I was scared that I might have lost you. That's the real risk." I gathered up his hand, splaying out his palm, pressed it at the thunder battering my chest. "Of losing this. Of losing us."

"What if the boys lost you because of me?" Grief cracked on his words.

My lips trembled, and I shook my head. "That's not gonna happen. You will always find a way to protect me. You always have. You have always heard me callin', even when you were out of earshot."

He dropped his forehead to mine and rasped out an anguished breath. "I want to be that guy. I do, Izzy. I'm not sure I know how to be."

He straightened, and panic roared through my nerves. Wild and uncontained. I grappled to get his hand back into my hold. "Don't you dare leave me, Maxon Chambers."

One of the boys started moving around in the next room, waking with the day, most likely Dillon with his endless energy.

Maxon stiffened, as if he had no idea where he was supposed to go. If he should stay or if he should leave.

"I'm going to fix this. Whatever it takes, I promise you, you and your boys will be safe."

He started for the window, and that panic screamed.

I moved for him, wanting to reach for him, grab him, beg him not to go.

He was halfway out when I whispered the words, "Your love

isn't selfish, Maxon. Lovin' someone isn't selfish. The most selfish thing you can do is live for your fear. To live for your past. Live for us, instead. Love for us. Give your courage to us. That is all you have to do."

"Mom?" Dillon called, and Maxon gazed at me through the window.

He sent me the saddest smile before he was gone.

thirty-two

MACK
SEVENTEEN YEARS OLD

"I'm out."

Mack watched the words penetrate his father where he was leaned over a car he was parting out. His spine stiffened, and he slowly swiveled around to face him.

He might as well have stayed with his back to him. Wasn't like Mack couldn't feel the hostility vibrating through the monster, anyway.

Clarissa's father, Kiel, grunted his disgust from the other side of the car.

Mack didn't give a shit what either of them thought. He just let his hatred blaze back.

His father's blue eyes flashed disgust as he took a step toward him. "What did you say?"

"You heard me. I'm out. I'm not doing this anymore, and I sure as fuck am not dragging my friends into it."

Things had gone south for Ian and his brother Jace. The two of them had gotten into a fucked-up tangle of greed and pride with their piece-of-trash-mother's boyfriend. Jace had taken the fall. Mack knew it. Knew it all the way to his core. He wasn't going to let Ian get embroiled in the middle of something just as corrupt.

Desperation equaled destruction.

Mack knew that now. Too well. And he was ready to stand for something. Something better.

His father cracked a malignant grin. "What, you think you're better than this? You think you're different than me?" His tone was mocking when he asked it.

Anger constricted Mack's chest, and he lifted his chin. Maybe he did. Izzy promised night after night that he was. When he'd lie tangled up in her arms and legs, bare flesh against bare flesh, she'd whisper that he was better than the trash he'd been bred to be. That he was better than following in his father's debased footsteps.

That he had something so much better then a wicked, worthless heart.

He wondered if his father saw every thought play out in Mack's mind because that grin turned into a sneer. "That little bitch has been after you again, hasn't she?"

A cyclone of resentment twisted through Mack.

All the beatings.

All the words.

The loss of his mama.

The agony. The grief. The hatred.

Through all of that, Izzy had been the one good thing that remained.

Mack took a violent step forward. "You don't get to talk about her like that."

Kiel growled, asshole pushing up to his feet, wifebeater stained and his teeth yellow and a big-ass wrench in his hand.

He was nothing but a bad joke.

A cliché.

Just like Mack's father.

His father who was chuckling a cruel, dark sound. "And what do you have to say about it?"

"I'm saying I'm done with this life. With you. As soon as I graduate next month, I'm leaving with her."

With a shake of his head, his father scrubbed a greasy hand over his face and smiled.

Mack didn't make the mistake of thinking he might be offering him his congratulations.

A second later, his father was pressed up in his face, two of them chest to chest, aggression sparking between them.

"Warned you a long time ago about them, Mack. Told you to stay away. They've messed with my life enough. You let her fuck with your mind? I'm gonna fuck with her body. See how she likes that."

"You touch her, and I will kill you. You won't see the next day. I promise you."

Smugness held fast to his father's expression. "You are who I say you are. You do what I tell you to do. You sit pretty, shut your fuckin' mouth, and do your job. Or else it's gonna be you who ends up in the ground. Got me?"

Mack climbed out of his car. Late afternoon light glimmered through the lush leaves, the only beautiful thing about this place. He looked around when he sensed that something felt . . . off.

Like the peace he was breathing was artificial.

An undercurrent of upheaval riding on the atmosphere.

A knot climbed his throat, and he was struck with the same rage and revulsion that took him over every time he stepped foot on his father's land.

Though today, it was intensified.

Following that unsettled sensation, he ducked into the house.

Empty.

He ducked right back out and strode over to the shed. He yanked the sliding door and pulled it open, metal track and wheels grinding their protest.

His eyes scanned the interior of the squalid shack, hatred spilling from him as he stepped inside.

Clarissa was on a stool in the corner where she always sat, texting someone on her phone. Her attention immediately snapped to him, her dark eyes flashing with something he didn't want to read.

He ignored her the way he always did. Refusing to give into her ploys to get him back. Like she could ever come close to comparing to his Little Bird.

Kiel was in a Mustang, removing the stereo system. Just another day on the job.

"Where's my father?" Mack grated.

Kiel edged out, and he looked at Mack from over his shoulder. A grimy smile stretched across his mouth. "Takin' care of something he should have taken care of a long time ago."

Unease shivered through Mack's being.

"Yeah? And what might that be?" Mack said, voice twisting in a low threat.

He hated this prick just about as much as he hated his father.

Kiel's expression hardened. "Don't worry about it, boy. Get your ass over here and get to work, way you shoulda been doin' all along. Know that delivery didn't make it to Florida two days ago. Think your pa wasn't gonna notice? 'bout time he taught you a lesson."

Panic screamed across Mack's flesh, and he was no longer playing games. He surged forward, ready to fight the answer out of him if he had to. "Where the fuck is he?"

Kiel's eyes gleamed. "Made a little trip into town."

Mack's head spun, furiously trying to figure out what angle his father was gunnin' for, which sick, twisted scheme he was playing next.

Clenching his teeth, he backed away from Kiel whose expression turned smug.

He wanted to knock it from his face.

He stared down the bastard for another beat, trying to get a read on him, before he slipped out of the shed and started for his car. That unsettled feeling blazing. None of it sitting right.

He started to jump into his car, not even sure where he was heading, but knowing he'd spend his whole fucking day hunting down his father so he could put an end to whatever the fuck he was up to.

Clarissa's voice whispered from behind. "Wait."

Dread prickled the hairs at the nape of his neck, and he wanted to ignore her, but there was something about the agitation in her tone that had him turning around.

Skittish, she looked over her shoulder, clearly checking to make sure her father was still inside. Then she rushed over to Mack's side, her words coming at him in a lowered hush, "He didn't go into town."

That dread spiked, barbs pricking his flesh. "Where the fuck is he?"

She peered through the woods in the direction of Izzy's house before she set her gaze back on Mack. "You don't belong with her, Mack, not at all. But I don't want anything bad to happen to her, either, and I'm pretty sure your daddy is up to somethin' real bad right now."

He knew his father was a monster, but also, a coward. A fuckin' coward who would take his fists to his wife and his little kid, hiding behind the cover of his shitty walls, never doin' it out in the open.

She was agitated, rubbing her fingers together nervously. "Don't tell my daddy I told you."

Fuck. He wasn't taking the chance. Didn't give a fuck if Clarissa was messing with him the way she loved to do. Wielding her manipulation.

He just had to see her, his Little Bird, make sure she was safe and okay. Unharmed. Then he was going to hunt his father down and beat the fuck out of him, once and for all. Show him where he really stood. That he no longer had any control over his life.

Izzy's father was away on a business trip, and he knew that left Izzy and her mama alone.

He bolted through the thicket of trees, taking the trail carved out by his nightly visits to her, the earth packed down, a pathway leading to his sanctuary.

He flew across the meadow and the tall copse of trees that separated their land on the opposite side. He burst out on the expansive lawn, and the massive house came into view, the scenery picture-perfect.

In it was a disorder.

A riot of distress.

He could feel it, and fear bottled up tight across his chest.

Immediately, he knew Clarissa hadn't been spouting her normal BS.

He streaked across the lawn, as silently as he could, attention darting everywhere, searching for anything amiss. He glanced up at their tree, her window closed tight, and he rounded the front of the house.

Quietly climbing the steps, he crossed the porch and carefully, slowly tried to turn the knob.

Locked.

Fuck.

He angled his head back, for a second thinking Izzy and her mama must have went into town, but the feeling that sucked the peace out of the air promised they were there.

That something was very, very wrong.

Heart thundering in his throat, he jumped off the porch and wound around to the far right of the house where there was a side door that led into the kitchen.

Terror clutched his spirit when he saw one of the small square windows had been busted out, a few shards of sharp glass still hanging in the frame.

The door was partially ajar and resting on the jamb.

Dread curled around his being, and he drew in a breath as he inched up the two steps and nudged the door.

Creaking, it slowly swung open to the rambling kitchen. Rays of sunlight streaked in through the bank of windows at the back, almost blinding. Everything was completely still.

Too still.

Sweat lined his brow and dripped down his back, and he quieted his footsteps as he crossed the kitchen, his lungs locked tight when he barely opened the swinging door and peered out into the main room.

Oh God.

He almost buckled at the knees.

Disgust and hate and horror stabbed him in the gut.

Izzy's mama was on her knees facing away from him. Her wrists tied behind her back. His father leered over her, a knife at her throat, spouting all the bullshit he'd spouted to Mack for all those years.

"You fuckin' whore, puttin' your nose in my business where it doesn't belong. You really think I wasn't gonna pay you back for puttin' me in prison? For taking my wife away? Now my son?" He leaned in and growled the words up close to her face.

She trembled, and a low, terrified moan escaped her mouth.

"Debt's come due, bitch."

Rage clotted Mack's blood, and he peered through the crack, desperate as he scanned the room for Izzy, petrified of what he might find at the same time.

Fear clouded his eyes when he didn't see her, and the shame and horror that he had done this to them rose up so fiercely that he could no longer breathe.

Could no longer see anything but what he had to do.

His mission.

His reason.

His father leaned over Mrs. Lane from behind, blowing more vile threats in her ear.

He had his back turned to Mack.

Mack didn't hesitate.

He barreled through the door and flew at his piece-of-shit father.

At the destroyer of beauty.

Hate and disgust and violence streaked through his veins, every cell coming to terms with his purpose.

His father whirled around with the movement, the glint of the blade he held in his vile hand sparking in Mack's view.

He didn't care.

He bashed his shoulder into his father's stomach. A shocked grunt scraped from his father's mouth.

They crashed to the hard floor, the knife clattering on the wood as his father lost hold.

Mack dove into the disorder, his fists flying as he began to shout, "Run, Mrs. Lane. Get Izzy. Get out of the house!"

Whole time he prayed that she could hear it, too. That she was capable of running. Hate ratcheted higher at the thought that she might not be able to. That this perverted, depraved man might have touched her.

Hurt her.

His fists flew faster and harder as he fought to get the upper hand on his father who was fighting back just as hard.

With just as much hate.

Fury rioted between them.

Years of disgust and abhorrence.

Mack could feel it all spilling out.

Insanity taking over, an ugliness coming at him so fiercely that he couldn't see.

He wanted his father to die.

Wanted to end him himself.

Feet and fists flew, their bodies surging and grappling, grunts coming from their mouths as they struck each other.

Blow after blow.

Kick after kick.

Mack could hear Izzy's mama trying to get to her feet, the sheer terror that radiated from her soft, pure spirit as she struggled to get away from the demons that had been unleashed.

His father nailed him on the chin. Mack would have seen black if it wasn't for the adrenaline pumping through his veins.

The intrinsic need to end this.

"I'll kill you," Mack growled, throwing his father back and scrambling around to pin him to the ground.

He pressed his forearm to his father's throat. "I warned you I'd kill you."

His father spat in his face. "You little prick. You gonna fight for these rats rather than your own blood? You forget who you are?"

An elbow rammed into Mack's ribs, and he choked over the splitting pain. His father took the opportunity to break loose, tossing Mack onto his back and jumping to his feet, sweeping up the knife from the floor.

Mack flew to standing, ignoring the pain splintering through him.

It wasn't like he hadn't taken a beating before.

This time—this time he was doing it for a reason that mattered.

The only thing that mattered.

Roaring, he rushed his father again.

His father lashed out faster than Mack could process, the gleam of that knife flashing before pain ripped across Mack's side.

A strangled sound gurgled up his throat, and he staggered. He tried to ignore the searing blaze, and he battled to get to him.

But he was weak. Too weak.

He dropped to his knees, gripping his side.

Blood covered his hands.

He didn't even care that his father was wielding that knife in his face, that he was seconds from passing out, he tried to crawl for him.

His reason.

His reason.

He would sacrifice it all.

"Stop!" That voice trembled from the other side of the room, and Mack's father wheeled around at the sound of it. Izzy stood just on the outside of her father's study.

Arms shaking like mad as she aimed a shotgun in his father's direction. "You move, I'll shoot," she warned, though it came out sounding small.

Terrified.

Part of him wanted to yell at her for exposing herself. For revealing her hiding place. The other part of him screamed with pride. At her courage.

His father cracked a grin, and he started to move for her. "You think you're gonna actually pull that trigger?"

Izzy's mama whimpered where she was pressed to the wall beside her.

"I will," Izzy said, "I will for all the things you've done to him."

His father started to go for her, and she held the gun steadier, and he wavered before he completely froze when the sound of sirens started to scream their approach.

Izzy had called the cops. Izzy had stopped it.

Relief blasted through his spirit. It sent the adrenaline draining from him just as fast as the blood drained from his side.

Coldness crept over him, and his head spun with a rush of dizziness.

His father turned toward him, the same kind of hatred Mack watched him with radiating back. "You're gonna pay for this, Mack. One day, you're gonna pay."

He didn't care.

He didn't care.

The only thing he cared about was she was safe.

His Little Bird was safe.

Mack slumped facedown on the floor.

The next night, Mack climbed their tree one last time. Excruciating pain tore through is body. He didn't know if it was coming from his side or if it was the crushing of his soul.

He made it to where the dim light glowed at the window, and he peered inside, his heart ripping and tearing.

So full and so empty.

He tapped at the window, his throat bobbing the heavy affection when she smiled like she'd been expecting him and reached over and pushed up the window.

"Maxon. Your side. You should have come through the front door. God, I've been so worried about you," she whispered in a rush.

Everything clutched, agony cinching down on every cell in his body.

He slipped through, and she stood from the chair, and her slight, delicate body rocked toward his.

Drawn.

"Izzy Baby," he said. Sorrow filled his smile. Just looking at her hurt.

Her lips trembled, and he could still see the remnants of terror darkening those hazel eyes, the trauma that had been written on this girl.

"I'm so sorry," he murmured, wishing he could take it away and knowing he would be forever responsible for the scar that would forever deface her spirit.

"You don't have a thing to be sorry for."

Bitter laughter pulled up his aching throat. "Don't have a thing to be sorry for? You were almost killed, Izzy. You and your mama. Because of me."

She blinked in refusal. "No. Because of your father."

"Don't you get it, Izzy? That man is me. He's in my blood. You have any idea the things I've done?"

All his sins came blistering through his memory.

"You haven't done anything but protect me. Protect my family."

His lips pressed into a grim line. "They're investigating. They're gonna take me away. Like I deserve to be. And even if they don't? You deserve so much more than I could ever offer you."

Agony pinched her gorgeous face. "Don't you dare say that. Don't you ever say you don't deserve me. We are meant for each other. We've always been."

"No. We aren't."

Those little hands came out for his shirt, fingers curling in with the plea. "Yes, we are. I love you. I love you so much. Don't do this to me."

He felt himself crack right down the middle.

Pieces strewn far and wide.

Littered across the space.

"Maxon . . . my dragon . . . you saved us. You did. You have to know that."

Unable to stop himself, he gripped her by the outside of her shoulders, just needing to feel something.

The connection that he could feel getting ready to snap.

Forever severed.

"Someday you'll realize it. You'll realize you are so much better off without me. I can't give you the life you deserve."

"I love you." It was a deep, reverberating cry that echoed against her walls.

A plea whispered from her soul.

Mack gave into the selfishness that screamed through his veins. The greed that had gotten her into this mess in the first place.

Only one more second.

He needed one more second.

He gathered her close, felt the beat of her heart, breathed in her spirit.

Wild jasmine and the sun.

"I will always love you, Little Bird." He pressed his mouth to her forehead and whispered, "Endless."

He ripped himself away. He could feel more of those pieces breaking loose. Crumbling to the ground. Scattering.

He couldn't breathe.

He forced himself to back toward the window, watching her as he did.

Tears covered her face, and she pressed her hands to her chest like she was trying to hold those pieces in. "Maxon . . . don't do this. Please, don't do this. I know you. I know you better than anyone. You are amazin'. Wonderful. Good. My dragon."

Sorrow curled the corner of his mouth, and he knew he had to let that fantasy go.

This . . . this was his reality.

"Fly, Little Bird. Be free."

He wouldn't clip her wings any longer.

Rage had taken him over. An ugliness that darkened his spirit and clouded his thoughts.

Loss unending. Vacancy throbbing through his being.

The taillights of the officers' cruiser that had shown at his porch blinked through the evening. But he found no solace in their words.

"We're sorry for what you've been through. For what it's worth, he'll be gone for a very long time."

The man had tipped him his hat, backed away, and climbed into his cruiser.

Mack was a free man.

He hadn't been implicated.

But he knew he would always be in chains.

He stumbled over to the shed and threw open the sliding metal door to the emptiness that echoed back. All the cars were gone, the parts that had littered the space taken as evidence. His mama's things were still piled in the corner near the door, sifted through but left when they were found not important to the case.

He felt a presence roll over him from behind. Though this was different. Sticky and ugly.

Just like him.

"I stopped my daddy from going after you," Clarissa murmured from behind.

He heard the click of her high heels on the cement floor two seconds before she ran her hand up his back. "Of course, when he heard the sirens coming up toward the house next door, he cleaned up his tracks good."

Chills skated his skin, and not the pleasant kind.

"You didn't tell them about us? About my daddy's involvement?" She purred it, winding around him, her fingertip running the line of his jaw.

"You might be the only reason they're still breathing," he told her, teeth clenched.

She smiled in her coy way. "I'm not evil, Mack. I just know my place. Just like you should."

He did. Understood it fully.

Don't mix light with darkness.

Beauty with ugliness.

Selflessness with greed.

"My daddy's gonna get back down to business once things settle down. You have your place with us."

He gripped her by the wrist. "Don't want any part of it."

She just wound her other arm around his neck and pressed herself to his body. Her voice turned low with the seduction she wore like her own personal brand. He finally got that was her way of existing. How she persevered in this sordid world.

They'd both done what they had to do to survive.

"Of course, you do, Mack. It runs in your blood. Stop pretending you're someone you're not." She hiked up on her toes and whispered in his ear, "You are just as guilty as your daddy. How many cars have I personally watched you take across state lines? I know you, just like you know me."

His hold loosened on her wrist, and she grinned wickedly when it was freed, and she wound that one around his neck, too. "I'll keep your secret if you keep mine? We fit, Mack. Belong together. Don't you agree?" She pouted like she thought it was appealing, like he was supposed to ignore the threats weaved through her words.

Stitching through him like a rusted needle.

She held the truth over his head.

It didn't matter. And he didn't give a fuck if she turned him in.

He knew his place.

She hiked herself up and pressed her mouth against his.

He felt nothing but hatred.

Hatred in the kiss that he returned.

Hard and full of spite.

It felt like a branding.

Chains of condemnation that wrapped around his soul.

Because this was who he'd always been. Pretending he'd been anything better was nothing but a cruel, sick joke.

thirty-three

MACK

I climbed down our tree. As soon as my feet hit the ground, I got sucked into a spiral of rage and turmoil. A battering to my heart and mind.

Anger seethed in overpowering waves.

Dragging me under.

Fuck.

I should have been upfront with her. Just . . . laid it out instead of being a pussy.

A coward.

I should have warned Izzy about Clarissa. Come clean. But that's what shame did to you—it made you want to hide it. Sweep it under a rug. Pretend that you weren't guilty.

But the bitter truth remained that I was.

Fucking guilty.

Guilty all along.

My heart screamed to hit the porch, knock on the door the way I did every morning, and have the smiling, excited faces of those boys jerking open the door to wish me a good morning.

But I couldn't do that.

Not until I fixed this.

Found a way to ensure they were safe.

I trudged across the rambling lawn and away from the house as the sun climbed for the sky.

Needing to get away and knowing I couldn't go far.

So goddamn unsure of my place and what I was supposed to do that I couldn't see straight.

Couldn't make sense of the war raging inside of me.

Torment unending.

Grief stunning.

All the while, devotion blew through me with the force of a hurricane.

I started to twist through the hedge of trees that rose up like a wall surrounding Izzy's property. Got the sense that maybe they stood like soldiers to protect this place.

A shroud to cover their home in grace.

Or maybe they just existed as a barrier to separate our two worlds.

I'd let that disconnect divide us for thirteen years. How could I allow it to happen again? But I could feel that choice fading away, joy slipping through my fingers.

I trudged over the overgrown grasses and through the tangle of limbs before I stumbled out into the meadow that had been ours. The brook babbled as it tumbled over its bed of smooth rocks, and rays of morning light slanted through the leaves and tossed the meadow in gold and silver glitter.

The distinct scent of wild jasmine filled my senses with the warmth of her.

It'd always felt like a fantasy.

A fairy tale.

I stood in the middle of it. Breathing it in. Trying to calm the rage that rioted within.

To find a direction.

An answer.

I froze when I felt a faint presence looming from behind.

Warily, I looked over my shoulder. Suffocating guilt struck me when I saw Izzy's father standing between two trees at the very edge of the meadow.

This was a man I'd respected. One I'd let down almost as badly as I'd let down Izzy.

Last night, Izzy's parents had freaked the fuck out when I'd called to let them know what had happened. Rightly so. Izzy had begged them to stay home. Be with the boys. Told them that was what she needed most—for the boys to remain unaffected and unaware.

The girl protecting them. Just like I should.

He stood in the distance, holding something that I couldn't make out. After last night-- after every fucked-up thing I'd done—I was surprised it wasn't that shotgun.

Unease whirled through my being. "I'm so sorry," I grated loud enough so he could hear, voice cutting through the morning.

It was the truth. I was so damned sorry for dragging that incredible family into my sordid world.

Time after time.

Maybe I never should have crossed that bridge segregating us in the first place.

"You seem to have a lot you're sorry for, Maxon." His voice warbled a little, filled with emotion and old age. But there didn't seem to be a whole lot of anger lacing it.

Disappointment, maybe.

Affection, too?

A frown pulled across my brow. "Have plenty, don't I? All the things I put your daughter through?"

His head slowly shook, and he took a step deeper into the meadow. The man was short, and his shoulders had started to hunch, but there was no missing the conviction and strength in his voice. "Only blame you wear was walking away."

My frown pinched in disbelief, and bitter laughter ripped free. "My only blame? I got your daughter caught up in a world where she didn't belong. Right from the get go. Thinking I could somehow fit. And look where that got her. Where it got your family. My father hated you all because of me. It was my fault you almost lost them that day. What other choice did I have but to walk away?"

He took another step forward, lifting his chin. "Your father hated everyone, Maxon, because that's what he was—hate and cruelty. Long before you came along, I tried to get through to him. Hoping he might find something inside of himself that was good. But that man didn't possess a kind bone in his body."

Get mad, boy. You are just like me.

My father's taunt wound through my spirit.

I flinched against the assault of it.

Izzy's father made a soft sound of dispute. "Think your first mistake was thinkin' you were like him. You think your good didn't always shine through? You think we didn't know it all along?"

"You should hate me."

"Hate you? Don't like you much right now, honestly, messing with my daughter's heart. The way you're contemplating runnin' again."

I started to refute him, but wavered, the words dying on my tongue.

"Wanted to hunt you down myself after I found out about Benjamin," he continued. "Knock some sense into you. But hate you? That's not possible."

He took another step closer. "We wanted you, you know . . ."

Confusion had me squinting, and my hands started to shake with uncertainty. Or maybe it was just my spirit trembling with the fear of what he was getting ready to say.

He took another feeble step forward, his voice low. "Tried to convince your mama to let us adopt you when we finally got your father sent off to prison when you were a baby. Of course, that was after we tried to convince her to leave that monster, but she refused. Said she loved him. Think she was always a bit confused by what that meant."

Agony gripped my chest when he mentioned my mother.

Horror and hate.

The love I had for her.

The loss that would never be repaired.

My failure to be better. To save her.

I'd been too weak. Too weak.

Reeling, I angled my head. "It was actually you? You were responsible for him getting arrested?"

I blinked, trying to process. They tried to . . . take me away from him?

"Your mama always denied the beatings, always making up absurd stories that a child wouldn't even believe. But my Brianne heard it going on one day. You were screaming bloody murder, just a tiny thing, and she ran over there. Got in the middle of it. Got beat up bad. But she wasn't afraid to sit on that stand and testify against that monster."

"You actually think you're somethin'? Somethin' special? Those pig fuckers fillin' your head with lies, too?"

He took another step closer while I stood there frozen. "We woulda done anything for you, Maxon. Our house was your home. Didn't approve so much of you going through our daughter's window, but we saw that bond. You were family. Through and through."

He shifted, drawing attention to what he held in his hands.

Emotion crushed my ribs.

The book. My mother's book.

Mr. Lane frowned, his scraggly eyebrows pulling together. "You know, it was funny when my grandson wanted me to read this with him last night before we tucked them in. Said something about it being from his dad's mother, that it was special."

He glanced down at it before he looked back at me. "It is special, Maxon, but it wasn't from your mother. Izzy made this for you with a little help from her mama. After you saved them. She believed it held the truth of who you were. That it might show you what you meant to her and the way she'd always seen you. How we've *all* seen you. You'd been too blinded by self-hatred to see it for yourself. Never got the chance to thank you for that . . . for you savin' them."

Agony ricocheted through my spirit, pinging from one side to the other. My head spun. I reached up and grabbed two handfuls of hair to try to make sense of it.

"No . . . my mother . . . it was in her things."

I blinked, trying to see through the disorder.

He shook his head. "Izzy brought this to you the night she took off, Maxon. She couldn't go on a day more without you knowing who you'd always been to her. Who you'd been to us. The faith we had in you. She dropped it there on the ground when she found you with that girl. Pretty sure she left her heart with it."

Oh God.

Izzy.

She'd seen me with Clarissa. That was why she'd run so far. I knew she'd hear about us, but the last thing I'd wanted was her to have to witness it.

Pain lanced, and those pieces that had been scattered between us shivered.

Strewn between thirteen years and two thousand miles.

Could sense them rushing to come back together.

"You're everything to them, Maxon. To Izzy and those boys, and I'm not gonna stand aside and let you mess that up again without sayin' my piece. You've messed up. Messed up good. But I've always known you belonged. Always considered you my son. A part of our family. Don't get stupid and ruin that now."

Benjamin's crooked smile flashed through my mind, and Dillon's laughter echoed in my ear.

I felt the pressure of Izzy's hand on my heart.

It was her all along.

I'd told Benjamin I'd found that book when I'd needed it most.

It was the truth.

It was on what was probably my darkest day.

I'd found out Izzy had left town, and the little bit of light left inside me had gone dim. I'd been close to giving in, two seconds from following in my father's seedy footsteps.

Kiel had been bugging me to get back on board. Told me I

owed it to him and Clarissa. That it was stupid to resist because I was just going to end up there anyway.

I'd found it, my heart in my throat as I'd turned the pages and read the story, as I'd felt the illustrations. The message of it had been so staggering that it'd dropped me to my knees.

It was the day I'd made the decision to join the force. To commit my life to making a small bit of the world a better place. To give rather than take.

A penance. A punishment.

To prove to my mama that something good could rise out of the ashes.

That I was the dragon, after all.

My dragon.

Izzy's tender voice swamped me.

Her belief.

It was her. It was her.

I jumped when my phone went off in my back pocket, and it jerked me out of the memories and the realization that pierced me like an arrow.

Invading.

Cleansing.

Little Bird.

All along, it had been her who'd been my savior. The one who had made me want to be better.

Different.

I dug out my phone. Pete's name lit the screen. "Yeah?" I answered, voice clogged in desperation.

He didn't hesitate. "I found the connection. Had to dig pretty deep, but Zachary Keeton is Clarissa's third cousin. That car that ran you and Izzy off the road last night? It had been reported stolen. Driver ditched it in midtown Charleston."

It was instant.

The threads coming together.

A tie.

This kid had been working with Kiel and Clarissa.

Their fucking scheme had been going on for years. Even though I had no details, my gut had known it, and out of some fucked-up obligation, I'd turned a blind eye.

I'd assigned her credit for saving Izzy that day.

And I wondered if that had been Clarissa's plan all along.

Clarissa's warning from last night threaded through my being. *"Now, she needs to go. Send her away, Mack, before it's too late. She doesn't belong here with you."*

"Get me two officers here, now," I grated, a disquiet unlike anything I'd felt before rushing through my spirit.

Ending the call, I met Mr. Lane's worried gaze before I was shouting, "Go around the back of the house, make sure it's clear. I'm going through the front."

Then I was running. Sprinting across the meadow and through the trees and out onto the lawn.

Fear in my throat. Protection lining my bones.

I would never allow anything to happen to them. They were my destiny. My purpose. My right.

And I was finished letting my past dictate that.

I would ensure everything was safe at the house, wait for the officers to show, and then I was ending this.

Clarissa and Kiel and this punk kid were going down.

Pulling my gun from its holster, I broke out into the clearing, only to stumble with the force of the unrest that tumbled through the heavens.

Same as it'd been that day.

A quiet violence that skimmed and shivered through the sky.

I started running for the house. That sensation only amplified with each thud of my boots.

I scanned the area, eyes bouncing around as I started for the porch steps, only to freeze when I felt the sickness claw over me from behind.

The disorder that rippled through the air.

Intense and thick.

"Well, if it isn't our favorite cop. Been looking for you." The words were nothing but a sneer, a rip of hatred.

Slowly, I turned around to find that prick slinking out from where Mr. Lane's truck was parked on the far-left side of the yard.

Zachary had a gun on me. Hatred curled his expression in

disdain.

The feeling was mutual.

This was the guy who I'd instantly sensed a darkness in. Gut telling me something was wrong. Now, that vileness crawled across the ground, like the spindly fingers of a demon clawing in the dirt.

Sinking in.

Staking ground.

I started to run for him until I saw the barest hint of movement against the wheel of Mr. Lane's truck.

Panic hit me like I'd smacked face-first into a brick-wall.

Izzy.

Little Bird.

Agony squeezed my chest as a bout of rage came speeding in.

Fierce and uncontrolled.

She was on the ground behind him, wrists and ankles bound, a gag in her mouth.

Hazel eyes flashed, swimming with a plea.

My soul screamed, horror wrapping me in vicious chains.

It hit me so hard, I nearly tripped.

Sweat gathered on my hairline, quivers rising up from that dark place, the brutal instinct to protect.

I refused to let this happen. Refused to let him hurt her.

"Drop the gun," I shouted as I lifted mine, edging off to the side of the porch steps.

I aimed my gun at this sick motherfucker, terror locking up my throat and narrowing my sight.

Everything focused on taking this bastard out.

Ending this.

He didn't even flinch, just grinned as he took a step my direction. "You weren't supposed to walk away that night. And here you are, still standing. Looks like we're going to have to fix that."

"Put the gun down," I ordered again, words harsh, my finger firm on the trigger.

He laughed, letting the gun swing at his side, in the general vicinity of Izzy.

Almost sent me flying at him then.

But I had to remain steady.

Smart.

Couldn't mess this up.

"What, this make you upset? That someone's got an up on you? Your future in their hands rather than the other way around?"

Izzy whimpered and writhed on the dirt.

I calculated if I could get in a hit without putting her in the line of fire.

The risk was too great.

Violence gathered like a physical entity, cords wrapping my limbs, flames of aggression eating up my body.

"No idea what Clarissa sees in you," he spat like the little punk he was. "Protecting you all this time. Done with you gettin' in our way."

"What the hell are you talking about?" I demanded. I was desperate to draw attention to myself. To take it off Izzy. Asshole needed to forget that she was even there.

He laughed and rushed an agitated hand through his hair, and it was then I realized he was tweakin', kid methed out, antsy and irritated.

Made this whole situation a million times more dangerous.

"Come on, asshole, you think I don't know you're just waitin' on the perfect moment to screw us? Not going to jail because my cousin is in love with your dick."

Hostility raged, and I tried to keep it cool when I was being incinerated by this fire consuming me from within.

To remember my training.

Knowing what was at stake when the only thing I wanted was to rush this fucker and bash his face.

"If you go to jail, it's because you put yourself there, not because of me," I rumbled, trying to ease to the side.

To draw him closer.

To make him forget the girl he was standing too close to.

He barked a laugh. "Fuckin' cops, thinking they own us. Not today. Clarissa just wanted me to scare this bitch." He jostled the gun at Izzy.

Whimpering, she pressed her face into her shoulder, desperate to hide and chained in plain sight.

"Make her see you aren't worth the pain. Chase her back to wherever she'd come from. She's pissed I decided to take this farther, but she's gonna learn real fast she doesn't get to control me, either. No one does. I do what I want. Kiel's gonna know I'm his main man."

Fuck.

This kid was nuts. Fucking delusional. Capable of anything.

I inched another step to the right. Only thing I needed was one clean shot.

"This is a mistake, man." Did my best to sound placating. Convincing. To talk him down. "You don't want life for this. Think about it. Look how long they put my dad away for what he did. You hurt her, and you won't see the light of day."

He'd started to edge to the left, natural instinct to get away from the barrel of a gun.

Exactly what I needed him to do.

"That's glory, man."

Pete was right.

This crime for the sake of crime was insane. Completely insane. And I knew that was exactly what I was dealing with.

Izzy's spirit throbbed and groaned, that energy moving across the ground.

Horror and the hope she'd always had in me.

Silently promised her that this time, I wouldn't let her down.

I took another step along the side of the house, forcing him back another. So close to him being clear. Away from my girl.

He mimicked to the left. My lungs froze when I saw my window. Quick to aim for his shoulder, to incapacitate but not kill, pulling the trigger even faster.

Fear crawled down my spine when I realized he'd seen my intentions in the same second, that he was pulling off a shot.

But I didn't care.

I sprinted his direction.

No thought of the outcome except for the one where Izzy was safe.

Fire blazed up my right side, and my body jolted with the severe, gutting shock. I fumbled, feet wanting to fail, barely able to stand, but somehow, I managed to force myself to keep moving. Sight clouding, I fought to lift my gun again, knowing the only choice I had was to take him out.

Asshole grinned like he'd won as he aimed again.

The grin drained from his face when the butt of a shotgun came down hard on the back of his head.

From out of nowhere.

No warning.

Zachary's eyes went wide before he dropped to his knees and flopped facedown onto the ground.

Mr. Lane rushed to stand over him, a foot on his back and his shotgun at the back of his head as he stood guard. With knowing eyes, he lifted his chin and sent me a look that promised it was finished.

Unable to remain standing, I dropped to my knees.

Relief blistered and blew while pain screamed and tore through my side. Blood soaked my shirt, but I couldn't stop, refused to give up. Groaning, I crawled to Izzy, quivers trembling my hands as I met her eye, whispered a thousand apologies as I untied her bindings.

I managed to free her wrists.

My girl free.

It was the only strength I had left, and I slumped over.

She reached up and jerked the gag out of her mouth. "Oh my God, Maxon. Oh my God. You're hurt. Oh, sweet man."

She fumbled to get to me.

Scrambling to get to her knees, she gathered my head into her lap.

She held my head close to the beat of her heart.

To the sweetness of her soul.

Tender fingers ran through my hair. "I've got you. I've got you. I'm safe. Me and the boys are safe because of you. Now, I'm goin' to make sure you're safe, too. You're safe."

She pressed her lips to my forehead, and I relished in the sensation.

In her touch.

I struggled to draw a breath into my lungs that screamed.

No air.

Blackness closing in.

Movement rustled from the side, and I blinked up and saw the worried face of her mama hovering over me. This woman who'd cared for me so much, and still, in a way that I hadn't understood.

She pressed a towel to my side, and I could see her trembling with fear, but she was smiling. "Just what you need is another scar to make you look even more appealin', Mr. Chambers. My girl here isn't gonna be able to keep her hands off you."

A smile tweaked at the corner of her mouth, and she looked over her shoulder and gusted a sigh of relief when she heard sirens coming up the lane.

Izzy kept whispering her belief into my spirit. "It's okay, my dragon. It's okay. You're gonna be fine. You stay right here with me. Don't close your eyes. Just stay. Stay."

Her mother held pressure on the gunshot wound.

It was almost in the same spot as the wound I'd sustained in the last fight with my father.

When I'd believed my life a sacrifice.

Thinking it noble to turn my back to the light rather than to stand in its warmth.

Through the haze that took me over, I stared up at this girl's beauty. Her voice as a little girl. As the years had passed. As she'd become my all.

At this girl who'd been my savior.

Everything faded as I silently promised to always be hers.

I blinked open my eyes, mind slowed with the drugs I could feel slogging through my veins.

But my sight was clear.

My heart right.

Soul no longer bent.

Izzy was sitting in a chair across the room with Dillon on her lap, quietly reading him a book, while Benjamin was in a chair right next to me, the side of his face rested on the hospital bed as he watched something on a tablet.

Izzy's mom and dad were in the other corner, quietly talking with each other.

Warmth overflowed the room.

Love a slow, sated buzz.

Got the sense they'd been there for a long time.

Settled in.

Waiting.

Standing by my side.

It was Benjamin who noticed I was awake first. His head popped up, and he sent me one of those crooked, beautiful smiles that shattered me all over again.

"Dddddad. You're awake. I was so wwwworried about yyyou."

He fumbled to get closer, and emotion pulsed up my arm when I reached out and touched my fingertips to his cheek. "I'm sorry I scared you. It was the last thing I wanted to do."

His grin widened. "That's oookay. You saaaved us."

"You got that bad guy good, Mack Daddy!" Dillon said, all too eager. "Grand Pop, too. Boom, bam, bang. Sneak attack. Told you that was the best kind, Grand Pop. Seven cop cars came to our house and a helicopter and two ambulances. Did you know that? I didn't get to really see it, but Nana told me you were really brave and you saved our mom and us, and now we get to be a family, right?"

Kid rambled the way he did, and my heart overflowed, throbbed with affection.

It expanded in a stunning way when I met Izzy's gaze.

Soft and sure and right.

Goodness bleeding out.

"Hi," she whispered in her southern drawl as she climbed to standing.

Her mother and father pushed to their feet.

Resolute.

All of them at my side.

Izzy shuffled over, and Dillon leaned down from her arms and kissed my cheek.

"Love you," I told him, my voice hoarse and raw.

"I love you the most!"

Izzy set him onto his feet, and she edged in, pressed her nose to my temple. Just . . . breathed me in the way I'd always done her.

And I finally got it—the fact that this road truly went both ways. That it didn't matter where we came from, as long as we met in the middle.

All of them looked down at me.

This—this was what it meant to be a part of a family.

Izzy softly pressed her mouth to mine, and she whispered, "Endless."

epilogue

MACK

It's funny when you find yourself barreling down a path you never expected. Headed straight for a collision course. No chance of a detour or an exit.

I guessed maybe I should have known I had always been speeding back toward her.

My chest fisted when I looked down at my new wife where I had my arm casually slung around her shoulders. I couldn't do anything but push my nose into the strands of her hair, needing to get closer, never close enough.

Wild jasmine and the sun.

Groaning, I nuzzled deeper into that sweet, soft flesh.

She giggled and pulled back to shoot me one of those

mesmerizing grins.

Around us, herds of excited children screamed and ran, the place so packed we could barely move through the crowds.

"You picked the wrong place for a honeymoon if you're havin' those kinds of thoughts," she whispered, keeping her voice quieted from the rest of our crew.

I tugged her closer. "What do you think that big suite is for?"

"For later," she taunted in her sweet way.

I leaned down and grabbed a kiss, taking it a little deeper than was probably prudent considering the company we were keeping. "I can't wait," I murmured at her lips.

"Ah, man," Dillon said where he was doing circles around my legs. "Is this what it's gonna be like now that you two got hitched? More and more kissin'. Sheesh. And here I thought we'd had enough of that."

"Are you kiddin' me? I get to officially call your mom my wife, and you think I'm gonna stop kissing on her? Not even."

I swept the little guy into my arms, heart overflowing as I peppered a slew of kisses all over his face. "Eww, kisses are gross," he said through his rumble of giggles, kid laughing, loving it every bit as much as me.

"You better get used to it, Lil' Dill. There's a whole lot more of those where that came from."

"Fine, fine, Mack Daddy. If you say so."

Still melted into a damn puddle every time he called me that.

I leaned back so I could take in my son. Dillon had to be the most excited I'd ever seen him, and that was really saying something.

We were celebrating our marriage. *Our family.*

At Disneyworld . . . with the entire crew.

Dillon had contributed his five bucks, wrapping it up like a present for our wedding.

Kid was so damned cute, he could get away with just about anything.

Nothing but a troublemaker.

Instead of matching shirts? Everyone had decided costumes were the way to go.

Guessed we'd gone a little overboard with the festivities.

Mal Pal was Elsa, and Sophie Marie was going as her sister Anna, of course, and their big brother Thomas was wearing a cool rendition of King Arthur. Collin, who was now walking, made a pretty badass Robin Hood.

No duct-taped diaper in sight.

Jace and Faith's kids bobbed along beside their cousins, excited as ever, Bailey Anne going as Belle and her brother, Benton, dressed as The Beast. Their baby sister, Ava, who was curled up in her mother's arms, was dressed as a rose.

Then we had our outlier.

My Lil' Dill.

I grinned down at him, and he twitched his nose that clearly was getting tickled by his fake mustache.

"I don't even know why you think that's a Disney hero costume, Dilly-Dally," Mal Pal told him, all sass and matter of fact where she skipped along at my opposite side. "There aren't even any cops in Disney movies."

Dillon frowned at her.

Two of them were always trying to outdo the other. Best of friends and competing at the same time.

"Um, hello . . . cops are the best heroes there are," he argued right back. "And they're the real kind. I'd rather be a real hero than a fake one, right, Mack Daddy? I look awesome, right? Just like my dad."

His attention jumped between Mallory and me, and I did my best to keep up.

Little dude was dressed in a cop costume, a blue button-up and blue shorts, fake badge intact. Of course, he'd gone and paired it with a sergeant's cap and that mustache and fake aviators.

Yeah.

People were staring.

We didn't care.

"Whose idea was this, anyway?" Ian grumbled under his breath.

Jace laughed where he held an umbrella over Faith and their newborn to block the sun.

Grace swatted at Ian's chest. "Oh, don't be an old grump. This is fun."

"Happiest place ever," he muttered with a sly grin in my direction.

"Yeah, don't be a grump, Uncle Ian. Grumping is only for old people . . . like Grand Pop! Isn't that right, Grand Pop?"

Dillon grinned over my shoulder. I swiveled that way, meeting eyes with Izzy's father who was strolling along with his hand wrapped up in Mrs. Lane's.

My heart damn near overflowed with that, too.

He sent me a smile that was almost imperceptible. Just a twitch of his own mustache.

"What . . . you callin' me grumpy?" he teased.

"You're the grumpiest of the grumps, Grand Pop. Accept it."

Mr. Lane grinned, and my chest was stretching tight. Pressing full with this joy that sometimes I didn't fully know how to process.

"This is it! This is it! This was the one I wanted to go on!" Mallory shouted, racing for the line of the little roller coaster that had about five bumps and dips and probably took about fifteen seconds to go around.

Dillon scrambled out of my arms, right on her tail, Sophie clamoring after them. Bailey Anne and Benton bolted that way, too.

Izzy turned her sweet face to our oldest son, girl's smile so perfect and right when she looked at him.

"Is this one too little for you?" she asked, teasing him a bit since he and Thomas were all about the big kid rides and were clearly itching to ditch their little siblings and cousins.

"Nah. I ddddon't mind."

He sent us one of his crooked grins.

It twisted around me with the force of a thousand suns.

"Thanks for keeping an eye on the little ones, Big Ben." I ruffled my fingers through his hair, wanting to grab him and hold him tight.

Instead, I lifted a chin at him, treating him like the man he was becoming.

Kind and good.

The kid was my definition of a hero.

"Come on, Ben. Let's go," Thomas hollered, walking backward and gesturing for Benjamin to get into line.

He started that way. Slower than the rest of them, his right leg still lagging more than the left.

Bony and thin and angled and the most perfect thing I'd ever seen.

He was wearing a shirt that read 'Princess Protection Patrol' on the back.

We'd left his fore-arm crutches back at the hotel. Just in case. But he didn't need them.

He ran to catch up.

Fucking ran.

Smiling.

Laughter rolled from him when Dillon took his hat and threw it to him like a frisbee. He caught it and put it on his head.

Izzy curled herself to my side.

That energy flashed.

Shivered in this contentment.

"I'm so happy," she whispered.

I kissed the top of her head. "They have it all wrong, Izzy Baby. Happiest place anywhere is with you."

Her hands fisted in my shirt, and she pressed her cheek to my thundering heart.

I glanced around at my family who had gathered by the ride to watch the kids.

I met eyes with Jace and Ian who were both wrapped around their wives, holding on tight and refusing to let go.

Something knowing passed between us.

Each of us had been bred into hardship and poverty.

Our lots cast. No hope for our futures.

Set on a course of crime and wickedness because we didn't know anything else.

But we'd found our strength in these amazing women who'd breathed their belief. Who'd shown us something better. Who'd shown us what it really meant to fight and what we should be fighting for.

Now we stood firm.

Found who we were inside.

Our purpose.

Our reason.

The love for our families the deepest confession of our hearts.

THE END

Thank you for reading *Pieces of Us*!!

I'm so proud of this story and these characters – they are going to live in me forever. Aren't ready to let them go? I have an EXCLUSIVE BONUS scene available for FREE!

READ HERE
https://geni.us/POUBonusScene

Text "aljackson" to 33222 to get your LIVE release mobile alert (US Only)
or
Sign up for my newsletter
https://geni.us/NewsFromALJackson

Did you read Jace and Ian's unforgettable stories? Go back to the beginning!

MORE OF YOU
https://geni.us/MOYAmzn

New to me and want more? I recommend starting with my super-hot, raw rockstar series, Bleeding Stars!
Start with A Stone in the Sea
https://geni.us/ASITSAmzn

More from A.L. Jackson

Redemption Hills

Give Me a Reason

Say It's Forever

Never Look Back

Promise Me Always

The Falling Stars Series

Kiss the Stars

Catch Me When I Fall

Falling into You

Beneath the Stars

Confessions of the Heart

More of You

All of Me

Pieces of Us

Fight for Me

Show Me the Way

Follow Me Back

Lead Me Home

Hold on to Hope

Bleeding Stars

A Stone in the Sea

Drowning to Breathe

Where Lightning Strikes

Wait

Stay

Stand

The Regret Series
Lost to You
Take This Regret
If Forever Comes

The Closer to You Series
Come to Me Quietly
Come to Me Softly
Come to Me Recklessly

Stand-Alone Novels
Pulled
When We Collide

Hollywood Chronicles, a collaboration with USA Today Bestselling Author, Rebecca Shea
One Wild Night
One Wild Ride

ABOUT THE AUTHOR

A.L. Jackson is the New York Times & USA Today Bestselling author of contemporary romance. She writes emotional, sexy, heart-filled stories about boys who usually like to be a little bit bad.

Her bestselling series include THE REGRET SERIES, CLOSER TO YOU, BLEEDING STARS, FIGHT FOR ME, CONFESSIONS OF THE HEART, and FALLING STARS.

If she's not writing, you can find her hanging out by the pool with her family, sipping cocktails with her friends, or of course with her nose buried in a book.

Be sure not to miss new releases and sales from A.L. Jackson - Sign up to receive her newsletter https://geni.us/NewsFromALJackson or text "aljackson" to 33222 to receive short but sweet updates on all the important news.

Connect with A.L. Jackson online:

FB Page **https://geni.us/ALJacksonFB**
Newsletter **https://geni.us/NewsFromALJackson**
Angels **https://geni.us/AmysAngels**
Amazon **https://geni.us/ALJacksonAmzn**
Book Bub **https://geni.us/ALJacksonBookbub**
Text "aljackson" to 33222 to receive short but sweet updates on all the important news.

Made in the USA
Las Vegas, NV
01 September 2023

76945448R00215